DEATH at THE DOOR

Also by Olivia Blacke
A New Lease on Death

RECORD SHOP MYSTERIES

Rhythm and Clues
A Fatal Groove
Vinyl Resting Place

DEATH at THE DOOR

A Ruby and Cordelia Mystery

Olivia Blacke

MINOTAUR
BOOKS
NEW YORK

This is a work of fiction. All of the characters, organizations, and events portrayed in this novel are either products of the author's imagination or are used fictitiously.

First published in the United States by Minotaur Books, an imprint of St. Martin's Publishing Group

EU Representative: Macmillan Publishers Ireland Ltd, 1st Floor, The Liffey Trust Centre, 117–126 Sheriff Street Upper, Dublin 1, DO1 YC43

DEATH AT THE DOOR. Copyright © 2025 by Olivia Blacke. All rights reserved. Printed in the United States of America. For information, address St. Martin's Publishing Group, 120 Broadway, New York, NY 10271.

All emojis designed by OpenMoji—the open-source emoji and icon project. License: CC BY-SA 4.0

www.minotaurbooks.com

Designed by Jen Edwards

Library of Congress Cataloging-in-Publication Data

Names: Blacke, Olivia, author
Title: Death at the door / Olivia Blacke.
Description: First edition. | New York : Minotaur Books, 2025. | Series: Ruby and Cordelia mystery ; 2
Identifiers: LCCN 2025018657 | ISBN 9781250336705 (hardcover) | ISBN 9781250336712 (ebook)
Subjects: LCGFT: Detective and mystery fiction | Paranormal fiction | Novels
Classification: LCC PS3602.L325293 D43 2025 | DDC 813/.6—dc23/eng/20250429
LC record available at https://lccn.loc.gov/2025018657

The publisher of this book does not authorize the use or reproduction of any part of this book in any manner for the purpose of training artificial intelligence technologies or systems. The publisher of this book expressly reserves this book from the Text and Data Mining exception in accordance with Article 4(3) of the European Union Digital Single Market Directive 2019/790.

Our books may be purchased in bulk for specialty retail/wholesale, literacy, corporate/premium, educational, and subscription box use. Please contact MacmillanSpecialMarkets@macmillan.com.

First Edition: 2025

10 9 8 7 6 5 4 3 2 1

For Casey, who made me (and so many others) believe in ghosts

DEATH at THE DOOR

CHAPTER ONE

RUBY

It's hard to keep secrets from my roommate, especially since my roommate's a ghost.

We were at the supermarket picking up ingredients for Sunday night dinner. *My* dinner, that was. I, Ruby Young, needed to eat, preferably a couple meals a day. My aforementioned ghost roommate, being dead, didn't need food anymore, but she was teaching me to cook. Tonight's meal was eggplant parm, which was a little ambitious in my opinion, but Cordelia believed in me and was certain I could manage it.

Even though Cordelia Graves was dead, she always encouraged me. She was a little bossy at times, but I didn't mind, much, since I didn't always know what I was supposed to be doing or how to do it. I had a tenuous grasp on this adulting thing, but luckily my roomie had more life experience. And more death experience, too.

While Cordelia was checking the gazillion tomato sauce options, I snuck back into the front of the store. I passed the produce, with a giant selection of eggplants that looked absolutely *nothing* like the emoji, and wound my way back to what I always thought of as the apology aisle. Which was appropriate, considering I owed Cordelia big time.

Just inside the front doors was a colorful selection of cut flowers and balloons, but that wasn't what I needed. Tucked in behind them were potted plants ranging from a selection of small, colorful cacti—who knew that cacti came in so many shapes and colors?—to several leafy options.

"How to choose? What to choose?" I asked myself, not caring if anyone overheard me. We lived in an era where people were constantly on their phones, with barely visible AirPods in their ears. Strangers didn't pay attention to people talking aloud when seemingly alone, and that came in handy when I was chatting with a ghost.

When she was alive, Cordelia loved plants. No, that wasn't precisely true. She was *obsessed* with them. I learned this when, a short while after her unfortunate death, I moved into her fully furnished apartment in a low-rent building in Boston. Judging from her decorative choices, I'd assumed that the previous tenant was in her eighties with a penchant for afghan blankets, paperback novels, and potted plants. It turned out that she was in her late forties, and all of her furniture came from secondhand stores, which accounted for the old lady smell I hadn't quite managed to rid the apartment of yet.

Her plants—in a variety of lovely, unique pots—turned the otherwise shabby space into a lush green jungle. Despite my best efforts to nurture them, they shriveled and died—all but one. I felt plenty guilty about killing them off *before* finding out that the previous occupant was still hanging around, in the form of a ghost. I couldn't bring Cordelia's plants—or Cordelia herself—back to life, but I could try to replace some of them.

Looking through the selection at the supermarket, there were lovely purple flowers on one of the plants. I read the label. "'Requires lots of light.' That won't do." My apartment, the one I shared with Cordelia, got little natural light.

The next plant had gorgeous white blossoms. It didn't require much light but needed to be watered several times a week. I wanted to think I was up for it, but despite my best intentions, I knew that was more responsibility than I was prepared for.

The third one had no flowers and looked similar to the only plant Cordelia had left, but the leaves had long, irregular holes in them that formed interesting patterns. "'Doesn't require direct sunlight or frequent watering,'" I read. "Nailed it!" That's the perfect amount of maintenance for me. I'd found my Goldilocks plant.

I flipped over the tag. "'Monstera.' Appropriate." I couldn't think of a better plant for someone living in a haunted apartment in Massachusetts, home of the infamous witch trials. Not that I was a witch. I was just your run-of-the-mill twenty-year-old living away from home for the first time, almost on my own. And like any other run-of-the-mill twenty-year-old, I needed to bring this pretty monstera plant home to make the ghost who lived in my apartment happy. I picked it up and hurried back to the canned tomato aisle, hoping to slip the plant into the cart before she noticed.

I could tell by the absence of that weird skin-tingly sensation I sometimes got when Cordelia was around that she hadn't followed me to the plant aisle, because the feeling returned as I approached the cans and jars of tomatoes. I hoped that Cordelia was too busy choosing from the wide selection of low-salt, no-salt, and extra-salt options to realize I'd slipped away for a minute. Unfortunately, she'd also been too distracted to notice that we were no longer the only ones in the aisle.

When two jars of tomato sauce levitated off the shelf seemingly all by themselves, the unsuspecting shopper standing near my cart shrieked. Cordelia dropped the jars. Glass shattered. Tomato sauce splashed everywhere, transforming the aisle into a crimson crime scene that smelled of basil and garlic.

I could barely hold back my laughter as the other shopper, her face ashen and her breaths shallow, turned to me. "Did you . . . Did they . . . You saw that, right?"

"Saw what?" I asked, trying to keep a straight face. Knowing Cordelia, she'd selected the most expensive tomato sauce in the entire store, but I snatched two jars at random off the shelf and tossed them into the cart. I hurried off, the squeaky wheel of my cart chirping louder the faster I walked.

At the end of the aisle, I nearly barreled into a store employee who'd been alerted by the woman's shriek, the sound of breaking glass, or both. "Someone made a mess down there," I told him, pointing over my shoulder. My face was as red as the splattered tomato sauce as I hastily rounded the corner down the next aisle.

"Cordelia," I said under my breath, as a giggle escaped. "You should leave the shopping to me."

I couldn't see her. I couldn't hear her. But I had that someone-standing-over-my-shoulder feeling I got when she was around.

"What's next on the list?" I asked aloud, knowing Cordelia couldn't answer me.

I pulled a crumpled piece of paper out of my pocket and consulted the ingredients. I was the only person in the store with a handwritten grocery list in this, the twenty-first century, instead of keeping one on my phone. That would be Cordelia's doing.

There was something about a ghost in the vicinity that made electronics go wonky. Since she was almost always nearby, I'd adapted by relying on my phone less and less. Sure, it meant occasionally getting on the wrong bus or missing a call from home, but part of me was relieved to not be tethered to a screen like I had been before I moved to Boston.

I stopped in front of a wall of eggs, feeling a little dizzy at the selection. Organic? Heirloom? Local? Free-range? I grabbed a cardboard carton at random and put it in the basket.

The eggs levitated out of the cart and settled back on the refrigerated shelf. A different dozen floated into the front basket of my cart, next to the monstera plant. "Showoff," I told her.

From what I could tell, Cordelia was making up the rules as she went along. Sometimes, when she picked something up, I could see it moving on its own—like some special-effects trick, but in real life. Other times, things just appeared like magic out of nowhere. Sometimes she would walk through a solid wall; other times she would open and close the door like anyone else. There were entire days when she wouldn't leave me alone, and others when she wasn't around at all. It was almost like living with a cat, random glasses getting knocked off the counter and all.

I glanced at the price sticker. "I can't afford these," I argued. "They're three times as expensive as the ones I picked!" I could comfortably afford groceries for the first time since I'd moved out of my family house in Baltimore, but even with a steady paycheck, I didn't throw money around.

In response, my cart started rolling away from the display of eggs.

"Fine," I said, knowing that arguing with a ghost was fruitless. "But you're chipping in on the grocery bills this month."

Cordelia could contribute when she wanted to. She'd left behind an envelope of cash in our apartment, could shoplift when the mood struck her, and once—when money had been particularly tight—had pilfered three hundred dollars out of a rich white lady's wallet after she'd been rude to me.

We took the bus because I didn't have a car, and the last time I'd gotten an Uber, the driver had shown up in an electric car. We didn't get two blocks before every warning light on his dash lit up like a Christmas tree. That was Cordelia's doing, I presumed.

Now that we were home, I had to carry the groceries up the stairs to the fourth floor. Technically, there was an elevator in our building, but it had been out of service as long as I'd lived here. Then again, according to my neighbor Milly, the elevator had been broken ever since *she* moved in, way back in the nineteen hundreds, 1995, to be exact.

Our apartment building was old. The wiring was shoddy. The heat barely worked and water pressure was nonexistent. The neighborhood was questionable. It would never make any of the "Places to Visit in Boston" lists, but it was home.

Also, there had been a murder in the building earlier in the year. Or, two murders, really. When Cordelia was found dead in the bathroom of apartment 4G—now *my* apartment—her death was immediately ruled a suicide. Case closed. She had a long history of substance abuse and bad decisions. No one questioned that her death was anything other than self-inflicted—that is, no one but me.

As I climbed the stairs, I wondered about the wisdom of buying all these ingredients when a microwave meal would have been quicker, and lighter. The longer I carried the groceries, the heavier they got. Even so, I was used to deferring to Cordelia's judgment, even though some of her decisions were questionable, like her actions on the night that ended with her dead in her bathroom.

There were plenty of indications that Cordelia's death wasn't what it seemed. She was found in the bathtub, but she was almost fully dressed. Her front door was ajar, even though she lived in a bad neighborhood and always locked her door. The night she died, a neighbor saw a strange man leave her apartment carrying a laptop bag, even though Cordelia rarely had visitors. And, while she'd fatally overdosed on sleeping pills and booze, there were no pill bottles anywhere in her apartment.

I'd laid all this out for her, but I guess it was a touchy subject. She refused to talk about it. And trust me, if a ghost didn't want to communicate, there wasn't a lot I could do.

I paused on the third-floor landing to catch my breath. "I swear, Cordelia, if I'd known how bad it sucked to live in a fourth-floor walk-up, I would have never signed that lease," I said. "Then again, if I hadn't, I never would have met you."

Despite all those annoying stairs, I loved my apartment, and Boston. Like any city on the East Coast, the obscenely wealthy lived in pretty high-rises overlooking the water. And then there were the rest of us. By American standards, it was an old town with a rich history.

With old relics everywhere I turned, from narrow stone streets to my ancient neighbor Milly, it was a wonder there weren't ghosts on every corner. As far as I could tell, Cordelia was the only one. She had to be lonely, which made me sad. That's why she hung around me so much. We both got a friend out of the arrangement, and as a bonus, she was teaching me how to cook. Or at least, she would, if I ever managed to drag my groceries all the way upstairs to my fourth-floor apartment.

CHAPTER TWO

CORDELIA

"Is it ready yet?" Ruby opened the oven and peeked inside. Cheese threatened to bubble over the casserole dish filled with eggplant parmesan.

From what I could gather, the most elaborate thing she'd ever made before this was Rice Krispies Treats. Her mom apparently didn't have a lot of patience for her and her sisters in the kitchen. As a result, here she was, a nearly grown woman, living on her own, unable to cook anything that didn't involve peanut butter or instant noodles. It ought to be a crime.

I yanked the oven door out of her hand and slammed it shut before the heat could escape.

My roommate meant well, but sometimes she was too eager for her own good. After a rocky start, I'd grown to like the kid. A lot. She had a good heart. Plus, unlike mine, her heart was actually beating, which came in handy sometimes. But if I wanted to keep it beating, I needed to teach her how to take better care of herself.

"Fine. You made your point." She saw that there were still five minutes left on the timer. "How am I supposed to wait when it smells so good?"

"You could start on the salad," I told her, handing her a cucumber. She didn't hear the words, but she'd get my drift.

She stared at the floating cucumber. One of the first tricks I'd learned as a ghost was how to move small objects. I couldn't pick a car up and toss it. I wasn't the Hulk. A cucumber was child's play, but the tricky part was making it invisible while I was touching it. It took a lot of concentration, and I was still hit-or-miss on that one, as evidenced by the spaghetti sauce incident at the grocery store earlier. I'd *thought* it was invisible, but apparently it hadn't been. Oops.

Ruby studied the cucumber as if expecting it to cut itself. "Come on, Cordelia. Are you pulling my leg? I read the recipe. There are no cucumbers in eggplant parm."

"You need to eat more vegetables," I told her. Yes, I knew lecturing someone who couldn't hear me was the very definition of "futile," but that never stopped me. "Preferably organic." I pulled a sharp knife out of the block and set it down on a well-worn cutting board on the counter. I flicked the end and watched it rotate in a lazy circle.

"Fine. You win. I'll cut it."

"That's my girl," I said. Even though she couldn't hear me, it felt like we were having a real conversation.

Being dead had its perks, but it wasn't all sunshine and roses. It was mostly boredom. Hours and days and weeks of soul-crushing boredom. I didn't know what I would have done without Ruby. Getting used to her living in my apartment wasn't easy. She was perkier than any human had any right to be. Even when she was broke and rationing out cheap ramen noodles half a packet at a time, she was an optimist, almost as if she believed that everything would work out in the end.

In her defense, it *did* work out, but I deserved a lot of the credit for that. I'd slipped her a little cash until I could find a job for her that covered her rent and expenses. Which was, for the record, twice as high as what I'd paid when the lease was under *my* name. Our cheating scumbag of a landlord was more than happy to take advantage of poor, naïve Ruby.

As Ruby diced up the cucumbers, I pulled the large wooden salad bowl off the high shelf I knew she couldn't reach and set it down on the counter.

"What's next?" she asked.

"You really are helpless in the kitchen, aren't you?" I opened the refrigerator.

Ghosts and electronics didn't mix. Something about my presence fried their circuits, and caused a feedback loop that was excruciatingly unpleasant on my end. The fridge, however, was ancient and the motor was in the back. I could open the door without affecting the refrigerator much, not counting that poor light bulb. It hadn't stood a chance. If Ruby ever upgraded to one of those fancy models with a video screen in the door, it wouldn't last a day.

I carried the lettuce, carrots, and a vine with juicy red tomatoes on it to the cutting board, not caring that she could see the produce floating. It wasn't as if I was keeping any secrets from her. Well, I was, but not the secret of my presence. I was hiding from other people—they couldn't accept the truth of my existence—but not from Ruby.

"Go ahead and chop these up," I instructed. Yes, I could have done it for her, but that wouldn't have taught her anything useful. The girl needed to learn how to cook.

DEATH AT THE DOOR

Her cuts were sloppy and uneven. Instead of thin slices, her tomatoes were a smushed mess. "What did those poor tomatoes ever do to you?" I asked her as seeds squirted out from beneath her knife.

Even though she took twice as long to chop the salad ingredients as it would have taken me, she was trying to grow up, and I was proud of her. Granted, sloppily diced carrots were just a start, but she'd also snuck a lovely little monstera into the grocery cart while I wasn't looking. She had a long way to make up for all my plants she'd killed when she first moved in, but this was a step in the right direction.

The timer went off, and Ruby hastily scraped all the salad ingredients off the cutting board into the bowl. She left the knife on the counter. I moved it to the sink as she opened the oven. "Smells amazing," she said as the hot air curled around her.

I took a deep whiff. Nothing. "You can do this, Cordy," I told myself.

The sheer amount of concentration I needed to do things that used to come so naturally to me was a pain. I could see in the dark. I had hearing like a bat. So why did I have to work so hard to smell anything? And then the scent hit me. Cheesy, garlicky goodness. I could almost taste the bubbling marinara. Almost.

I'd tried eating some of my favorite foods, but it wasn't the same as when I'd been alive. I couldn't taste anything, and the food went right through me. Literally.

Ruby pulled out the eggplant and the bread and set them on top of the stove to cool.

"Aren't you forgetting something?" I asked her, but she was already walking away. "Come on, Ruby, pay attention." I opened the door to the oven and let it drop with a clang.

"Huh?" Ruby asked. She closed the oven door. I opened it

again. "What am I missing? Ohh." She reached over and turned off the oven. "Thanks for the reminder."

"Good girl," I told her, closing the oven door.

Like the refrigerator, the oven was older than dirt. I could open and close the door all day, but if I got close enough to the circuits to turn it on or off or set the temperature, it could do anything from blowing a fuse to burning down the whole building. Plus, if the oven died, the landlord would probably replace it with an even older model from a vacant apartment or the basement storage, one that hadn't been cleaned in years.

"Smells great. Am I forgetting anything else?"

I grinned. This was the part I was looking forward to. Sure, I wanted Ruby to learn how to cook. Everyone needed to know how to feed themselves. But I had an ulterior motive.

"Timing's everything, Cordy," I told myself as I opened the front door. There were only a few steps between the tiny kitchen and the common hall, so there was no way Ruby would fail to notice the door opening.

"We expecting company?" she asked, going to the door even as I slipped out and rapped on the door across the hall.

The door opened and Tosh stepped out.

Tosh was the newest resident of the building, having moved in earlier this week. The former tenant of his apartment had died under mysterious circumstances shortly after I had. And if it weren't for me and Ruby, his death might have gone unsolved.

At first, I was mainly interested in our new neighbor because of his proximity to us. My newfound protectiveness over Ruby meant that I needed to verify there wasn't some kind of a psycho killer living across the hall. After a few days of intense observation, it turned out that he was a genuinely nice guy. He called his parents often. He had a steady job. He was single. He was cute. He checked all the boxes.

In his mid-twenties, he was too young—not to mention too alive—for me, but he was just the right age for Ruby. He was tall, just a few inches shy of six feet. He was Japanese, with thick, dark hair that always looked mussed like he'd just gotten out of bed, eyebrows that were big without being bushy, and intense eyes.

Ruby didn't have the best luck with men. Her last boyfriend had cheated on her. Heartbroken, she'd moved all the way to Boston from her hometown of Baltimore just to get away from him and anything that reminded her of him. That had been months ago, and she hadn't shown any sign of getting over him anytime soon.

"I know your ex was a dingleberry, but it's time to get back on the horse, Ruby," I told her—not that she could hear me. "And seriously, do you see those cheekbones? They're sharper than the knife you used to mangle the salad."

"Yes?" Tosh asked with a friendly smile, staring through me at Ruby.

What I would do to have a young, handsome man smile at *me* like that.

"Um, hi," Ruby said.

"Seriously?" I asked with a laugh as I turned to face her. Ruby never shut up. Even when the only other person in the room was dead, she was a chatterbox. And now, she could barely string two words together. Her dating skills weren't rusty, they were atrophying right before my eyes. It was a good thing I'd intervened when I did.

"What's up?" he asked.

Ruby's face turned bright red as she realized that she'd been set up. Tosh had no way of knowing that someone neither of them could see or hear was standing in the hallway between them, and assumed that Ruby was the one who'd knocked on his door. The ball was in her court.

"Uh, I'm Ruby," she finally said.

He nodded. His friendly grin grew larger, displaying a sliver of perfect pearly-white teeth. "We've met."

"Oh, yeah."

"Ruby, if I'm not mistaken, you're positively speechless," I said. I wish I'd known sooner that if I wanted to shut her up, all I had to do was toss a handsome guy with intense eyes and messy hair in her path.

"Something smells delicious," he said, looking past our open door as if he could somehow see the source of the odor from out here. "You cooking? If you've come to borrow eggs or something, I'm the wrong person to ask." He gestured over his shoulder toward the pile of boxes filling up the apartment behind him. "I'm still unpacking, and haven't had a chance to go shopping yet."

"Then you're probably hungry. Join me for dinner?" Ruby asked.

"Good girl," I told her. "I knew you'd catch on."

"I'd love to." Tosh stepped across the hall. He paused in the doorway and took in our apartment.

There wasn't a lot to see—six hundred square feet give or take, same as his. Our kitchen was dated, with sagging cabinets, stained countertops, and ancient appliances. The living room was warm and welcoming, with a bookshelf overflowing with my favorite paperbacks. Much of the room was taken up by a comfortable loveseat with a colorful blanket I'd found at a flea market neatly folded over the back and a stack of mismatched throw pillows scattered over the cushions. In the corner stood Eunice, a hearty large-leafed philodendron, and the only plant that Ruby hadn't managed to kill when she moved in. My new monstera sat on the coffee table. There was a small bedroom and bathroom off the living room. That was the grand tour.

I knew from the previous tenant across the hall that our apartments were mirror images. The only real difference apparently was that everything he owned was still in boxes whereas ours was lived in and comfy. After I died, the landlord rented out my apartment fully furnished rather than bothering to clean it out himself. The arrangement worked out because I didn't want him throwing out all my stuff and Ruby hardly had anything to her name.

"Hope you like eggplant parm," she said. "And there's salad."

He followed her into the kitchen where I'd lined up two plates, two sets of silverware, and two paper towels on the raised counter that could be used as a table if we'd had any bar stools.

"Love it," Tosh said. He bent over the stove to inhale the delicious combination of garlic, herbs, and cheese. "Everyone in SoCal acted like cheese is the devil or something."

"Is that where you lived before?" she asked, using a spatula to divvy up healthy servings onto the plates.

I didn't know about Ruby, but I'd been to California exactly once in my life, and that was to pick up my good-for-nothing brother. He'd managed to hitch a ride all the way to the West Coast, but once he got there, he realized that the price of living among the palm trees was too rich for his blood. He called me begging for a ride home. He was only fifteen at the time, or I would have sent him a bus ticket. Instead, I rented a car, drove forty-eight hours to pick him up, turned around, and drove right back. I wasn't even there long enough to get a tan.

"Yup," he said, reaching for the set of tongs sticking up out of the salad. I'd pulled the tongs out of the jumbled utensil drawer when no one was paying attention. Ruby would have scooped her salad out with her fork. "L.A. May I?" He put a serving onto Ruby's plate before getting one for himself. "Dressing?"

"Fridge," she said. "I think."

"You're lucky I'm here," I told her. If it was up to Ruby, the only condiment in the fridge would be the bottle of yellow mustard that had been left over from me. But I'd put a bottle of oil and vinegar dressing in the cart today when she wasn't paying attention.

Tosh pulled the dressing out and placed it on the counter between them. If he thought eating standing up in front of the bar was odd, he was too polite to say anything. He took a bite and his eyes rolled back into his head. "Where'd you learn to cook like this?" he asked, after chewing and swallowing.

"My roomie," she said, without thinking.

"Ruby!" I exclaimed. "What did we agree about talking about me? And to a stranger?"

"Oh, you have a roommate? I didn't realize."

She froze. "Uh, I mean, I used to have a roomie. Before I moved here. I don't anymore."

She'd slipped up at work a time or two and mentioned that she had a roommate, which was particularly dangerous considering everyone she worked with knew me, since I'd had her job before her. Ruby talking about me at work, or with Tosh, wasn't smart. They knew me at TrendCelerate, and more important, they knew that I'd killed myself.

Or, rather, they *thought* I'd killed myself. I didn't blame them for that mistake. I'd actually thought that, too, at first. My death really did look like a suicide. I didn't remember my actual death, or the events leading up to it. I didn't even realize I was dead, not at first. I didn't remember dying at all, like someone had scrubbed those sectors off my hard drive. I supposed it was a blessing in disguise. Who wanted to remember their death? Not me.

But between what little I did remember and what I'd managed to piece together, it wasn't so cut and dried. Too many things didn't add up. Ruby had hinted a couple of times that she wanted to help me figure out what had really happened, but I wasn't willing to put her in harm's way to sate my morbid curiosity.

I didn't know how it would go over at TrendCelerate if they knew the truth. There were already rumors floating around that I was fooling around with one of the company owners—no comment—and that I'd stolen proprietary software code and sold it to a competitor. As if I'd ever do that! Plus, as I looked around the tiny apartment that I still called home even after my death, if I'd been involved in corporate espionage on any level, I could have afforded to move out of this dump.

"Where'd you live before this place?" Tosh asked, snapping me back to the here and now. If I wasn't careful, reminiscing could suck me into a memory. Then I'd miss what was going on around me while I was stuck reliving the worst moments of my past.

The expression on Tosh's face was hard to read, but if I had to guess, it would have been something along the lines of "What's a nice girl like you doing living in a crappy neighborhood like this?" Then again, he lived in the building, too, so he didn't have any room to judge.

"Baltimore. With my mom."

"You and your roommate lived with your mom? Or your mom was your roommate?" he asked.

He was too busy chasing a mangled tomato around his plate to notice her deer-in-the-headlights expression. Ruby wasn't very adept at lying, or hiding the fact that she lived with a ghost. One of these days, she was going to blow it for both of us. "What, you don't call your mom your roommate?"

"Generally, I just call her 'Mom.'" He glanced around. "You live here alone? No boyfriend?"

"Subtle," I said with a laugh. "At least one of you is good at this."

There was no easy way to ask if a person was single, and Tosh's was as effective as any. Then again, it was impossible to tell if he was interested in Ruby or if he wanted to know if she was living alone, and was therefore vulnerable. That thought gave me a chill. It was a good thing I was here to watch her back.

"No boyfriend. You?"

He shook his head. "No boyfriend. No girlfriend, either. I had one, a girlfriend that is, but we weren't serious and we parted ways after I told her I was moving across the country."

"Oh," she said.

"See? You're both single," I pointed out. "I must have missed my calling as a matchmaker."

They dug into their meals in earnest. I felt rather proud of myself. Ruby had done the actual cooking, but I'd picked out the recipe and helped her with the shopping. Sure, I'd made a teensy tiny mess with the sauce at the store, but I'd more than made up for that by helping her select the perfect eggplant, and I hadn't let her forget the garlic toast. It was a team effort.

"That's cute," Tosh said, breaking the silence. He gestured toward the refrigerator. "I haven't seen one of those in ages."

"A refrigerator?" she asked, confused. "They don't have refrigerators in Southern California?"

He laughed as if she'd made the funniest joke in the world, then leaned in to get a closer look. "The poem."

love TASTES *LIKE* MOON LIGHT

Ruby blushed. "One of my friends must have done that," she said.

At least she hadn't credited me this time.

"Do you mind?"

Without waiting for an answer, he set his fork down and walked around the bar to the fridge. He played with the magnets for a minute. When he stepped back, there was a new poem on the door.

> BENEATH *THE* **sunshine** happiness **whispers**
> A **bluebird** SONG of HOPE
> GIGGLES *WITH* surprise

"That's pretty good," she told him.

The magnets were one of the few ways Ruby and I had to communicate. It wasn't a perfect system, but I generally got my point across. Granted, I wasn't quite as poetical as Tosh. I was starting to think he was more than just a pretty face. And more important, Ruby was starting to like him.

When dinner was over, she packed up the leftovers while Tosh insisted on doing the dishes. "Want some to take home with you?" she offered.

I wish I'd thought to pick up dessert while we were out, and a nice wine. Ruby was too young to buy wine, but I could sneak a bottle out of the liquor store. Then again, and as funny as it might be, if my concentration wavered and I failed to make it invisible, like had happened with the tomato sauce jars at the grocery store, a bottle of wine floating down the hallway all by itself would draw unwanted attention.

"Oh, I couldn't," he said. "But thanks for inviting me over. We'll have to do this again soon. How about at my place?"

I liked the direction this was heading. While I doubted any guy would be good enough for her, Tosh was, on the surface at least, close.

"You cook?" Ruby asked.

"Well, no," he admitted with a sheepish grin. "But you could teach me?"

Rather than admitting she didn't actually know how to cook either, she suggested, "Or we could order in?"

"Sounds like a date," he said, walking to my door. "'Night, Ruby."

"'Night, Tosh." He left, and she locked the door behind him. She waited until she heard his door open and close across the hall before turning to address me. "Thanks, Cordelia. You're the best."

CHAPTER THREE

RUBY

Monday morning started off on the wrong foot. My alarm clock hadn't gone off—I blamed that on Cordelia. When I'd finally woken up, the display read 31:27, which I chalked up to living in a house with a ghost. It could have been worse, I suppose. It could have read 6:66.

Once I'd gotten out of bed, half an hour later than usual, I discovered I was out of Pop-Tarts. That was my fault. I'd known I was low, but I forgot to pick up more when we went grocery shopping yesterday. I missed my normal bus and traffic was more snarled than normal. As a result, I was predictably late to work but was determined to not let that set the tone of the day.

TrendCelerate was on the second floor of a multiuse building in a bustling Boston neighborhood. There were three other offices on this floor. One was a tattoo studio that didn't open until noon. Another did advertising. Their hours were erratic. Sometimes I wouldn't see anyone from their office for days, and other times there was a steady stream of traffic in and out, but rarely this early. The last office was unoccupied as far as I knew.

Downstairs was a shoe store, and upstairs were apartments. They were nicer than the apartment I shared with my dead roommate, by a *lot*. More expensive, too. They even came with a small parking structure in the back and a tiny green park out front, but I doubt any of the residents got their own ghost, so I counted myself lucky.

Normally, I was one of the first people in the office, but today that wasn't the case.

"Morning, Ruby," Adam Rees, one of the three founders of TrendCelerate, said as he breezed past my desk. "I don't know if you've had a chance to check your calendar, but we're expecting visitors today. When they get here, get them settled into the conference room. Oh, and order a mid-morning snack from Beantown, will ya?"

Adam was a tall, thin man, but he loved his junk food and made sure there was always some in the office. He was the COO and head software engineer.

He was also friendly. Supersmart without coming off as too nerdy, despite the comic book collection in his office. And, he was smoking hot, to the point of being distracting when he was in the office, which was practically all the time. And the best part was he didn't seem to realize that he was a full-on zaddy.

"Will do," I said, but he was already out of earshot.

The front door opened and Marc Minor, a database administrator, and Seth Riley, a software developer, walked in. Both were dressed slightly better than normal in khakis and company-branded polos rather than their usual jeans and tees.

I didn't own any TrendCelerate polos, and even if I had, no one told me to dress up today. Instead, my T-shirt today was pink and had a cat playing with a ball of yarn under the saying "Are you kitten me right now?" My sister Jordan bought it for me last Christmas. Did she know me or what?

"I've never seen you two here so early on a Monday," I told them.

"Adam warned us what would happen if we were late," Seth said. He pulled a plastic container out of his bag and set it on the edge of my desk. "Homemade chocolate cookies," he said with a wide grin. "For the office."

He headed off to his cubicle, but Marc lingered behind. "Don't eat them," he warned me, shaking his head vehemently before walking away.

Seth was the office clown, who treated every day like April Fools'. I learned my lesson after he'd left a candy bowl filled with colorful candies on my desk. I popped a handful in my mouth only to discover it was a mixture of plain M&M's and Skittles. I'd never look at either candy the same way again.

I knew better than to trust anything Seth brought in, but curiosity got the best of me. I opened up the container to get a peek. The lid snapped shut again.

"Come on, Cordelia," I whispered. "It won't hurt to look."

I took the lid off. They looked like chocolate chip cookies. They smelled like chocolate chip cookies. But on closer inspection, the chocolate chips were, in fact, raisins.

"Gross," I said, and tossed the contents of the container into my waste basket.

Now that I'd saved the office from another one of Seth's pranks, I logged into my computer and pulled up the website for Beantown Deli, a place down the street that had the best takeout in town. "Mid-morning snack," I said to myself, tapping my fingers on the keyboard lightly without actually pressing any keys. I knew what to order from them for lunch. They had the best spuckies—a sub-style sandwich specific to Boston. But I hadn't ordered anything other than spuckies from them before.

TrendCelerate was good about buying lunch for the whole crew. If it wasn't for that perk, I doubted anyone would ever show up to the office, preferring instead to write, test, and market niche computer applications in the comfort of their pajamas at home. Not that coming to the office kept them from wearing pjs—it didn't. But at least the ones they wore here were generally clean. With few exceptions, like Adam who always looked snappy in a suit coat over a button-down shirt without a tie, we'd long ago given up on "business casual" in exchange for just plain "casual," and I was here for it.

"What looks good?" I asked aloud. Even if Cordelia was in the room, I never knew if—or how—she was going to answer. This time, there was no reply. It was a good thing because if Cordelia got too close to a computer, she fried its circuits. Literally. The last thing I wanted was for the VIPs' first impression of the TrendCelerate office to be a blaring smoke alarm and flames shooting out of my workstation.

I pulled down the breakfast menu, wishing Adam had told me how many people to expect. I erred on the side of caution. Fruit. Bagels. Cream cheese. Muffins. It all went in the cart. Had I over-ordered because I skipped breakfast? Nah. My coworkers were ravenous piranhas when it came to free food, and we never had leftovers.

As an afterthought, I added a box of coffee. We had a coffee maker in the break room, but it was one of those single-serving ones that was great when no one in the office could agree on the best kind of coffee to stock, but it was less than ideal for serving a crowd.

"You think that's enough?" I asked, in case Cordelia was hovering over my shoulder.

"Who ya talking to?" a man's voice asked.

I looked up to see Blair Tinsley, one of the software developers, hovering around my desk. I'd worked at TrendCelerate long enough to figure out the email system, but beyond that, I was a little fuzzy on what we actually made here. I especially wasn't sure what exactly—if anything—Blair did to contribute. He seemed to stand around a lot and cause problems, without solving any.

"No one," I replied, realizing too late that I sounded defensive.

"You talk to no one a lot," he said.

"Really? I hadn't noticed." I gave Blair one of my trademark perky smiles, hoping he'd get bored and go away. No such luck.

"It's annoying." He cocked his head to stare at me, but his white-blond hair never moved. It was the middle of May, and he already had the tan of someone who spent the summers on Daddy's boat, likely because he'd just come back from one of several tropical vacations he'd take throughout the year.

No "Good morning." No "How are you, Ruby?" No "Why do you always look like you swallowed something foul when I walk into the room?" from Blair. Would it kill him to show a little humanity once in a while? Sometimes I wondered if Cordelia wasn't the only one around here without a pulse.

"I appreciate your input," I said, my forced grin never wavering.

He hesitated, sensing that he'd somehow been disrespected but unable to put his finger on how. "Yeah well, it's gonna be a busy morning. If anyone calls, put it through to my cell."

"Uh-huh," I agreed, knowing full well that he rarely ever got calls through the main line. If someone wanted to reach him, they'd call him directly.

But I didn't point that out. Despite the fact that I was late this morning—a rarity—I prided myself on what my mom used to call the Three Ps: Professionalism, Promptness, and a Positive attitude. "Ruby, the only way to get ahead in this world are the Three Ps," she'd tell me. What I *really* wanted to say to Blair was neither professional nor positive.

My cell phone rang. When I checked my caller ID, it was Mom. Had she felt me thinking about her?

After the usual greetings, she said, "You've proven your point, baby."

"Mom, I'm at work, and I haven't even had coffee yet!"

"Can't a mother call to say she misses her daughter?"

"I miss you, too, Mom," I admitted.

"You don't have to stay in Boston forever, you know. You set out to prove you could make it on your own, and you have. Don't you think it's time to come home?"

Like the rest of my family, she had no idea that I wasn't actually making it on my own. Minus the Pop-Tarts debacle this morning, Cordelia was pretty good about reminding me to keep food in the pantry, and when I needed some extra help, she chipped in however she could. A little cash here and there. A clean apartment waiting for me when I got home. The occasional set-up dinner with a cute neighbor.

"I like it here," I said. I couldn't tell Mom I was living with a ghost. She wouldn't believe me. At best, she'd drag me back home and force-feed me chicken soup until I gave in and agreed that there was no such thing as ghosts. At worse, she'd send a priest over to cleanse my apartment.

"Did I tell you that Jeffrey is seeing someone?" she continued.

Jeffrey, aka Jerky McJerkface, was my ex, the one I'd fled Baltimore to get away from. So much had happened since he cheated on me that I rarely thought of him anymore. Granted, I wasn't sure that I was ready to risk another broken heart, but after one dinner with Tosh, I was all aboard the dating train again.

"Good for him," I told her. "I wish them all the happiness in the world. Hopefully he doesn't cheat on this one." I doubted it. Jerkface gonna jerk.

My desk phone buzzed. The visitors were here.

"Gotta go. Work calls. I'll call you later," I promised.

I powered off my phone before shoving it back into my purse. I shouldn't have had it on in the first place, distracting me from work and potentially coming into contact with Cordelia and bursting into flames. Plus, if I'd turned off my phone, there was the added bonus of any calls from my mother, eager to spread news of my ex, going straight to voicemail.

Pushing that conversation out of my head as best I could, I clicked the button to unlock the downstairs door. We didn't have many visitors on a normal day, and I was glad that Adam had warned me of their arrival so I could buzz them up without any fanfare.

A few minutes later, I pushed another button that unlocked the frosted glass office door to the TrendCelerate office suite. Four people walked in. Leading the pack were two men, one white and one Black. They both wore somber suits. If I had to guess, they were in their late fifties. There was a short redheaded woman with them, also in a suit, carrying a briefcase.

Behind them was a familiar face. He wore a tie and button-down shirt with jeans and scuffed-up tennis shoes, and had a backpack slung casually over one shoulder.

"Tosh?" I asked. "What are you doing here?"

"Hey, Ruby." My across-the-hall neighbor grinned at me. I'd hoped to see him again after our impromptu dinner last night at my apartment, but I hadn't expected it would be so soon, or at my office. "I didn't know you worked at TrendCelerate."

"Surprise," I said with a grin that, unlike with Blair, I didn't have to fake.

"We're here for the CloudIndus meeting," the Black man said, sounding annoyed that I was addressing Tosh instead of him.

"Welcome," I said, turning my attention to him and ignoring Tosh for the moment. We'd have plenty of time later. "We've been expecting you. Let me show you to the conference room."

"I think we can find it," the older white man said. Behind him, the woman chuckled.

TrendCelerate was set up to feel like a hip, open-concept loft apartment. The glass conference room, with its long metal table surrounded by ergonomic chairs, was hard to miss.

"There's a coffee maker in the break room," I told them. "And food is on the way."

"Thanks, Ruby," Tosh said, following the others.

As they moved into the conference room, another TrendCelerate employee scooted closer to me. "Did I hear mention of food?"

Melissa Branch, one of my favorite coworkers, hovered over my desk. Up until I started working at TrendCelerate, if I'd tried to picture a software developer in my head, I never would have pictured someone who looked like Melissa. She was taller than average, thin, and blond. She wore a lot of pink, always had impeccable hair and makeup, and could drink any of the men in the office under the table.

"I got plenty for everyone."

"It's not wheatgrass, is it?" she asked, making a face.

"Of course not!" I assured her. "Why would it be . . ."

My voice trailed off as Quinn McLauchlan, the TrendCelerate CEO and the person in charge of testing all of our software, stuck her head out of her office. "They're early," she said, looking over at the four VIPs settling into the conference room.

She was about my height—five foot four or so—but she wore designer heels that put her almost a head taller than me. In contrast with the more casual dressers in the office, she wore a sharply tailored suit and expensive jewelry. Her silver-gray hair lay in perfect waves, with bangs framing her heart-shaped face.

I could never pull off bangs. I didn't have the forehead for them. My own dark hair was overdue for a haircut. Right now, it was tied back in a messy ponytail. I could barely afford rent, much less pink teardrop diamond earrings with a matching necklace. Quinn had me beat in the class department. She also had a strict diet, and I was suddenly very glad I'd included fruit in the breakfast order.

"Do you want me to tell them you'll be right in?" I asked.

"No worries," Quinn said. "I just wasn't expecting them so early. I'll take care of it." She patted her hair—even though there wasn't a strand out of place as far as I could tell—straightened her shoulders, and marched into the conference room.

"Don't worry, Adam told me to place the order, not Quinn," I assured Melissa. When Quinn had gone on a raw food kick a while back, that's what she'd ordered for the office at lunch. When she was gluten free, lunch was gluten free. Adam was usually a toss-up between the deli, fried chicken, or pizza.

"Thank goodness," Melissa said.

The door opened and another person I didn't recognize walked in.

"Are you here for the CloudIndus meeting?" I asked pleasantly.

"I didn't get up at the crack of dawn to ride the bus for an hour for my health," he grumbled.

"Don't mind him," Melissa said. "You haven't had the pleasure of meeting Jordie yet, I presume?"

I shook my head. There were several TrendCelerate employees that rarely—if ever—ventured into the office. I recognized Jordie's name from the employee roster, but I'd never talked to him or seen him in person. "I'm Ruby," I told him.

He ignored me, addressing Melissa instead. "What happened to the other chick?"

"You mean Cordelia?" Melissa asked.

My breath caught in my throat. Sometimes I forgot that my roommate, my *dead* roommate, used to be the office manager at TrendCelerate before I started working here. She'd helped me land this job, mostly by pestering me to apply. There wasn't much else a ghost could do to propel my career, but it had been enough.

They didn't talk about Cordelia in the office often. I presume it was because it was too uncomfortable for them, coming to grips with the fact that one of their employees had recently killed herself—or so they thought. I bet they'd be doubly weirded out if they knew that at any given minute, she was still here in the office, silently observing them as they went around their business.

I started to explain my presence, but Melissa interrupted to answer Jordie. "She's not with us anymore. Ruby's the new girl."

That was an understatement, but it was one I'd heard often. Some people didn't like to talk about death, or the deceased. I wondered if that would change if they knew that, at least for some people, death wasn't the end.

Jordie nodded at me. "New girl."

"Ruby," I reminded him.

"Yeah, whatever." He headed to the break room to refresh his coffee.

"Jordie's manners suck, but his code is brilliant," Melissa said at his retreating back.

Jordie paused, turned his head, and said, "I heard that."

Melissa grinned. "I know." She turned her attention back to me. "Don't mind him."

Before I could reply, Adam emerged from his office. He snapped his fingers, looking around the bullpen. "Chop-chop," he said. He headed into the conference room. Melissa, Jordie, Blair, and all the other employees who had been hanging back in their cubicles followed at his heels like he was the Pied Piper of the tech world. Which was, to be fair, an apt description for him. He had one of those magnetic personalities.

A moment later, Franklin Delacorte pushed open the front door. The third TrendCelerate partner, Franklin, who served as the company's chief finance officer and head of marketing, split his time between Boston and New York, and was therefore only rarely in the office. He was a few years younger than Adam and Quinn, yet carried a distinct air of authority with him without coming across harsh like Quinn or as the happy-go-lucky leader of the band like Adam.

"Good morning, Mr. Delacorte. Everyone's already in the conference room," I said. Unlike the other managing partners, he preferred to be referred to by his last name.

"Thank you, Ms. Young," he said, heading straight into the meeting without stopping by his desk first.

I breathed a sigh of relief. Despite my rocky start this morning, I was glad that I wasn't the last person to arrive. It would have sucked, getting to the office *after* the meeting had already begun. Sure, Franklin was late, but he was a one-third owner of the company. I was just the person at the front desk with a ghost over my shoulder.

CHAPTER FOUR

RUBY

The next hour dragged by at work. Normally, I could stave off boredom by chatting with employees, but they were all occupied in the meeting. If Cordelia was around, she wasn't in the mood to communicate. I couldn't even read a paperback novel at my desk because, while no one seemed to care if I did so during an ordinary day, it might send the wrong impression to our visitors in the glass-walled conference room.

The door opened and Quinn appeared. "Ruby!"

"Coming," I said, and hurried over.

"There's a problem with the monitor." She gestured over her shoulder. I couldn't see the display from my desk, but from this angle, I could tell the screen was black. "Please grab a spare HDMI cable so we can swap it out."

"Huh?" I asked. "What's an HDMI cable?"

We didn't have a dedicated IT department at TrendCelerate, since all of the employees were tech savvy—well, everyone but me. I was the least likely person in the whole office to be able to fix a computer problem. Sure, if the copier jammed, I was your girl, but a broken monitor? That was above my pay grade.

"Come with me," Quinn said.

I followed her into her office. As the office manager, my desk was located right by the front door in full view of the office. The majority of the worker bees sat in a central cubicle farm. The three co-owners had actual offices with doors and windows and even a view of the world outside. Quinn's office was a perfect reflection of her—neat, and a little cold. Other than a few framed family photos on her desk, there were few personal touches.

I wondered if her house was like this, too. I imagined it decorated with tastefully curated antiques. Or with a collection of minimalist furniture. Then again, she had a niece who lived with her that she brought to the office on occasion. It was hard to picture Quinn living somewhere littered with toys. It was easier to picture Adam's house. I imagined bookshelves stuffed with comic books and action figures, still in their original packaging.

She opened a drawer and pulled out a cable. "I knew I had one in here." Then she pulled out a bottle of liquor and held it out. I didn't recognize the brand, but it looked expensive. "You like bourbon? You can take it."

I shook my head. "No, thank you. You don't like it?"

Quinn frowned. "I don't drink."

I hadn't realized that Quinn was a teetotaler. It made her feel more relatable.

"We have that in common," I said cheerily. "I don't drink, either." I'd experimented with booze a time or two, and I wasn't a fan. Alcohol didn't agree with me. Being underaged was normally a convenient excuse. I guessed Quinn didn't know how young I was, or she never would have offered it to me.

"Good for you," she said. She pushed the bottle at me. "Drop it off on Adam's desk, will you?" She picked up the cable and hurried back to the conference room.

I stopped at Adam's office. His door was locked, so I took the bourbon to my desk instead. A few minutes later, my phone buzzed. "TrendCelerate," I answered in my perkiest front-desk voice. "This is Ruby. How may I assist you this morning?"

"Yo, Rubes. I'm downstairs. Buzz me in, will ya?"

I recognized the voice as belonging to Marty, one of my favorite delivery people—and not just because he worked at Beantown, one of the best delis in Boston. Marty was funny and never treated me like a lesser being just because all I did was answer the phones when everyone else in the office had an IQ well above "genius." I pushed the button to unlock the door downstairs.

A moment later, there was a bang on the front door and I jumped to open it. "Morning," I told Marty, opening it wide so he could shuffle in. As usual, he was laden down with a huge, insulated tote along with the nondescript black canvas messenger bag he always had with him. In addition, he carried a large paper sack with the Beantown Deli logo printed on it.

Marty was handsome in a boyish way and he always had a grin on his face, like he was thinking of a really funny joke. I didn't know him on a personal level beyond our weekly lunch interaction, but I got the impression that he didn't take his job, or anything in life for that matter, very seriously.

"I was surprised to see you guys on my breakfast run." He put the order down on my desk. Instead of our usual sandwiches and salads, he unloaded an array of pastries and a tray of fruit.

It was funny how any deviation from our normal routine was so notable that even our delivery person mentioned it. "Yeah. Big meeting." I gestured over at the conference room, where almost every chair was taken.

"Want me to take it in?"

"No need, I've got it." Since I had no idea what they were talking about, I figured it would be better if I interrupted the meeting rather than sending in a delivery guy.

"You mind?" He pointed at the bathroom key hanging from a hook behind my desk. "I've *really* got to hit the head."

"Of course. Just don't walk off with it again," I teased him.

It was common for visitors to ask to use our facilities, but the last time Marty borrowed the key, he accidentally pocketed it, locking us out of the bathroom and leaving me to deal with several grumpy employees until he could return after the lunch rush was over.

Quinn stepped out of the conference room.

"Is the cable working?" I asked.

"It's fine. Is that who I think it is?" she asked, gesturing at the front door as it closed behind Marty.

"Yup," I said, hoisting the pastries. "Marty just dropped off our order. One mid-morning snack, coming right up."

"Good," she said, but she didn't sound as happy as most people would have been when faced with a tray of free food. Then again, considering she was one of the owners, I guess it wasn't free for her.

Quinn could be hard to read at times, but she was actually quite nice when I caught her in a rare minute when she wasn't busy. Despite her fashionably gray hair, she was relatively young to be so successful. Any woman under fifty running her own tech company didn't have a lot of time to spare for trivial things like small talk with the receptionist.

Besides, she was only in the office a few times a week. It wasn't that she was disengaged from the business, just the opposite. She worked remotely much of the time, but was always online or available on her phone. In addition to running TrendCelerate, she was on the board of two charities, volunteered at a nonprofit that trained service animals, and fostered a young niece who lived with her. Quinn had a full plate.

My own plate was also full at the moment, literally speaking. It took me a second to figure out how to balance the fruit tray and pastries at the same time. How did Marty make it look so easy? Once I used my elbow to pry open the conference room door, I started laying everything out on the side table.

"Thanks, Ruby," Adam said as I spread out the food. He addressed the assembled audience. "Now that the food's here, let's take a quick break."

As I arranged the snack, the meeting attendees swarmed the table. I swear, if I didn't know better, I'd think some of them had never eaten before. Free food brought out the worst in people, especially highly paid software developers.

"Everyone grab a bite, check emails and whatnot, and meet back here in"—he checked his watch—"five minutes." Adam's voice was made for public speaking, and it carried even above the melee.

I snagged a double chocolate muffin before one of my locust-like coworkers could squirrel it away to eat later. Everyone scattered, grabbing whatever food was within easy reach before heading for their cubicles. It was a novel sight, seeing everyone at their desks. Usually there were three or four people max in the office on any given day. Today, all the desks were full.

Adam disappeared into his office and let the door close before I could get his attention. I picked up the bottle of bourbon and carried it over, but even with his door shut, I could faintly hear him talking on the phone. The TrendCelerate office as a whole was mostly soundproof. I never heard the other offices on the same floor, the apartment dwellers above us, the store below, or the traffic outside. But whatever insulated us from the outside world didn't extend to the inside, where the walls were thin and the doors barely muffled the sound.

"It works better over there." Blair sidled up next to me and pointed to a spot on the wall between a framed photo of the Boston skyline and the TrendCelerate logo.

"Huh?" I asked. "What works better?"

"Eavesdropping," he said with a mischievous grin. "And bonus, from that angle you can see in but he'll never know you're there."

"How do you know this?"

Blair gave me a look like I'd asked an obvious question. "Those flimsy blinds aren't nearly as private as they think they are." He winked at me.

I heard Adam wrapping up his phone call, so I knocked on his door.

"Come in," he said.

I opened the door and popped my head inside. "Quinn wanted me to give you this." I held up the bottle of bourbon.

"Bring that baby over here." He held out his hand.

I crossed the office to his desk. In contrast to Quinn's stark office, Adam's was furnished like a casual corner of someone's house. There were framed comics on the walls and a giant armchair in the corner big enough that I could comfortably curl up and take a catnap on it.

As I handed him the bottle, the overhead lights flickered. We both looked up.

"Call the super and have them take a look at that," he said. One of the light bulbs glowed intensely for a second before popping. "And have them replace that bulb."

"Will do."

On my way out of the office, I almost tripped on nothing. "Cut it out, Cordelia," I said under my breath.

"Excuse me?" Adam asked. His voice was almost as sharp as his hearing. "What did you say?"

I blushed. "Sorry, I just lost my balance."

"No, what did you say? Exactly."

"Uh," I stammered. I knew better than to use Cordelia's name in front of other people, especially people who had known her when she was alive. "Clumsy me?"

"For a minute, it sounded like . . ." His voice trailed off. I stood there, trying to look innocent. "Never mind. I have to get back or the meeting'll start without me." He got up, rounded his desk, and ushered me out of his office.

The other employees were scurrying around, taking advantage of the break before drifting back into the conference room. Once everyone settled back into their meeting, I sent in a trouble ticket to the building about the light bulb. I didn't see much point in getting an electrician out here unless they knew a way to ghost-proof an office, but I requested one as asked.

With that out of the way, I took the opportunity to fix myself a mug of coffee in the break room. I was relieved that no one thought to invite me to the meeting. Not like they wanted the opinion of a humble office manager, but sometimes they asked me to sit in and take notes. I didn't mind writing down everything, but I never understood a word they were saying.

"Agile." "Silos." "Git." "AI/ML." "Holistic design." "APIs." "UX/UI."

I'd worked at TrendCelerate for almost two months and I still had no idea what we did here. It had something to do with data collection, or was it data storage? I remember someone mentioning a data lake once. There was definitely data involved, and a bunch of other moving parts I didn't understand. But the paychecks never bounced, I got free lunch every day, and even Quinn was bearable unless she was on a tear, so I wasn't about to complain.

I wished I could ask Cordelia what they were talking about in there. She'd worked at TrendCelerate for years, and a bunch of other tech companies before that, up until her death. Even though she'd been an office manager like me, I got the impression she understood what the company was doing. According to one of the developers, she'd even beta tested all the software, which, as far as I could tell, meant pointing out mistakes the developers had made.

As much as she had to teach me, it wasn't as if I could ask. I mean, I *could* ask but even when she was in the room, she couldn't always answer. Our communication was rudimentary at best. If I wanted to figure out what "Agile" meant, I'd be better off googling it.

"Hey, Cordelia," I whispered as I headed back to my desk. There was no one else in the bullpen. Everyone who'd normally be working in their cubicle was already in the conference room, but I'd gotten in the habit of whispering. It was bad enough that people were starting to notice me muttering to myself under my breath without them figuring out I was talking to someone who, as far as they knew, wasn't there.

I pulled out the Etch A Sketch and shook it to clear the screen. The previous image, a cartoon armadillo I'd doodled on a particularly slow afternoon last week, faded. Cordelia used the toy as a way to communicate during the workday that didn't make me look like a complete nutcase. "What's going on in there?" I asked. I placed the Etch A Sketch on my desk. Nothing happened.

After waiting a while with no change, I gave up and pushed the Etch A Sketch aside. Cordelia might be ignoring me, or just as likely, she was sitting in on the meeting, unseen in the corner. Or she might be off relaxing on a beach somewhere. Or she could be in that nowhere space she disappeared to when she needed to recharge. I could never tell.

The rest of the morning passed by slowly. Since we'd gotten a delivery from the deli already, I was weighing the benefits of ordering pizza or sushi for lunch when the conference room door opened again and everyone spilled out. Melissa made a beeline to my desk.

"You guys done for the day?" I asked.

"On another break," she replied, hardly looking up from her phone. She held out her hand. After a beat, she tore herself away from the screen and said, "Do you mind? We only have a few minutes before we have to be back."

"Okay?"

Hearing the confusion in my voice, she clarified, "The key? To the bathroom?"

I reached behind me, but the hook was empty. Rats. Marty had forgotten to return it. Again. And I'd been too distracted to realize it, which was my fault. "Just a second."

I grabbed the long metal letter opener from the cup on my desk. I didn't know how to pick a lock and wasn't even sure if the letter opener would do the trick, but I didn't actually need to pick the lock. I had an ace up my sleeve.

The single unisex bathroom was halfway down the hall. We shared it with three other businesses on the second floor. I knocked on the door. No one answered.

"Cordelia," I whispered. "You here?" I crossed my fingers for luck. "A little help?" I jiggled the door handle. As expected, it was locked.

"There's never a friendly neighborhood ghost around when you need her," I said, shaking my head.

Not that Cordelia was contained to the neighborhood. As far as I could tell, she could come and go as she pleased, unrestrained by artificial boundaries. Which meant that, technically, she could live anywhere. She didn't have to share an apartment with me. But according to her point of view, even though I was the one paying the rent, it was *her* apartment and *I* was the uninvited guest.

I inserted the letter opener into the lock and wiggled it around. Nothing happened, which didn't surprise me. I had no idea what I was doing. After a few tries, I gave up and forced it in between the door and the jamb, hoping for better results. There was a click and the door popped open. Then it slammed shut again.

"Sorry, is someone in there?" I asked, louder this time. There was a stall inside the bathroom for privacy, but still, that could have been embarrassing. "Hello?" There was no answer. Had I imagined the door closing on its own? "I'm coming in," I said.

Now that I'd gotten the hang of it, it only took a moment to pop the lock with the letter opener. This time I was ready, and as soon as the door twitched, I shoved it open. The door handle was ripped out of my hand, and the door slammed shut again, but not before I saw the dead body of Marty, the Beantown Deli delivery guy, crumpled on the floor.

CHAPTER FIVE

CORDELIA

"Damn it, Ruby, can't you take a hint?" I said, wrestling the bathroom door closed. I didn't want her seeing the corpse inside, but I was doing a lousy job.

As a relatively new ghost, I'd already learned the basics. I could slip through walls easily. It was the other things I'd believed were impossible when I was alive that I still had a hard time with, like floating up through the ceiling, but I was getting better at that. And yes, technically walking through walls should have been difficult, but I *believed* that ghosts could walk through walls, so I had no trouble with that one.

If I was with someone who couldn't pass through the wall, I had learned how to unlock a door and open it. Holding a door shut wasn't difficult, either, but the smallest lapse in my concentration had been enough for Ruby to force it open against my will.

There was something about Ruby that made me want to take care of her. I wanted to protect her from the big, bad city. For that matter, I wanted to protect her from the world. And I certainly wanted to protect her from finding a dead body. I'd failed.

Which was, unfortunately, very on brand for me. I'd failed at a lot of things. I'd failed at life. I'd failed my brother. And I'd failed my houseplants. Although, the blame for that last one fell squarely on Ruby. She was the one who killed them. I'd forgiven her, mostly. It wasn't her fault that when I'd died, I'd orphaned my entire collection of potted plants. But it *was* her fault that she neglected to water them. If only that was the worst of our problems.

I looked down at the body on the floor. "What were you thinking, Marty?" I asked aloud, as if he could hear me. Although, to be fair, I was kinda surprised he couldn't. He hadn't been dead long, not long enough for his ghost to get up and wander off. He could have already poofed out to whatever—if anything—came next. From what I could tell, not every death spawned a ghost, or Boston would be overrun with us.

"You're a damn idiot, Marty," I told him.

He wasn't, not really. I'd always liked him. He was nice to me. Not everyone was friendly with the lowly office manager, not even my fellow service-industry workers. There was one UPS driver in particular who was rude every time he dropped off a package. I wouldn't have minded it if were him lying dead on the bathroom floor.

"It's cliché, that's what it is," I muttered to myself, looking down at him.

On top of making deliveries for the deli down the street, Marty had a side job providing less-than-legal chemical enhancements for those in need. His death was tragic, but hardly shocking. Marty was a drug dealer. Live by the sword, die of an overdose in a bathroom.

I grimaced at the thought. It hit a little too close to home.

I'd always known that Marty was good for a little pick-me-up, and I'd tried it all at one time or another. You didn't get to be a forty-something, unmarried office manager living out of a hovel without taking a few wrong turns in life. Addiction was a disease like any other, but I never considered myself a drug user. A drunk? Guilty as charged. A druggie? Not hardly. Not that it mattered in the end, as I lay dying in my bathtub with a stomach full of pharmaceuticals and Jack Daniel's.

Marty never dealt in the serious, addictive shit, the hardcore drugs that made the evening news. Even if I'd wanted meth or fentanyl, he would have turned me down. Prescription painkillers, Adderall, and the little blue party pills were about as hard as he carried. I didn't buy from him often. Just on special occasions.

To be fair, Marty rarely carried anything I couldn't have gotten from a legitimate doctor. I had decent insurance, but I didn't have the right equipment to get the Viagra prescription I wanted. The man who I wanted it for would never be so gauche as to get something from the pharmacy that would tip off his wife that he was having an affair. That's where Marty came in.

As I leaned against the cold porcelain sink—at least I imagined it was cold; being dead myself, I couldn't actually feel it—watching time tick by, I grew angrier at Marty. It was futile. I knew that. The more time passed, the less chance there was that he would ghost. If he did, I would take him under my wing. I would show him the ropes. I'd help acclimate him to life as a dead person.

And *then* I'd berate him for sampling his own product.

A heavy fist pounded on the door. "Police! We're coming in!" The order was followed by the scraping sound of a key entering the lock. It must have belonged to one of the other tenants on the floor, or the building manager, because TrendCelerate's bathroom key was on the tile floor next to Marty's dead body.

The door opened, and this time I didn't interfere. I had no reason to. Marty was beyond help. The police and the paramedics were used to sights like this. I didn't have to shield them from the harsh reality of the world. It was only Ruby I wanted to protect. Poor, sweet, obnoxiously perky Ruby.

Now that the authorities had arrived, it was time for me to make myself scarce. Marty wasn't coming back, or he'd have done so already. I guess Marty was one of the unlucky—or was that lucky?—ones who skipped the ghost level and went straight to the end of the game.

I took one last look at Marty. "Rest in peace, friend."

I wish I'd gotten to know him better while we were both alive. Then again, there was a host of things I wished I'd done while I still had the chance, and people I wished I'd treated better. Speaking of which, as I sidestepped the first responders crowding into the tiny bathroom, I noticed an intimately familiar face among the gawkers in the hall.

Adam Rees was, as always, front and center in the crowd. It was one of the things that had first drawn me to him. Yes, he was married. Yes, sleeping with him was wrong on so many levels. But what could I say? We were in love. Or, at least, *I* had been.

Looking at him made my heart ache. As usual for work, he wore a tailored blazer over a crisp button-down shirt, and had one too many buttons unbuttoned to be strictly professional. He looked almost scrawny in his office attire, but I knew underneath it all, he was jacked. It was such a shame that his work clothes covered up defined abs and corded muscles in his back and his perfectly squeezable...

"Nope," I said aloud. "This is not the time to be thinking about squeezing *anything* on Adam." Not like the thought was ever far from my mind. Just a minute ago, I'd been reminiscing about doing a whole lot worse with him, after he'd popped one of Marty's little blue party pills.

These days, Adam was strictly off-limits. Then again, technically, he'd also been off-limits all those years we'd been dating, seeing as he was married and all, but now he was *actually* off-limits. I couldn't touch him even if I wanted to. As I retreated back to the office, I had to flatten myself against the wall to keep from bumping into anyone. When I made contact with a living, it hurt like hell. I avoided it when I could. In this crowded hallway, I didn't stand a chance.

Ironically, if it weren't for this hall being so narrow, I doubt I would have been the first to find Marty. After accidentally shorting out the light in Adam's office, I decided to step out into the hall where I couldn't do any more damage. As I was making my way out of the office, a delivery person was wrestling a stack of boxes on a trolly down the hallway, and to avoid them, I took a shortcut through the floor's only restroom, where I stumbled across Marty's dead body.

Good thing the laws of physics didn't apply to me any longer, so instead of trying to thread my way through the crowd of lookie-loos filling the hall trying to get a glimpse of Marty's body, I slid through a wall and found myself in a deserted office. "That's weird," I said. "I wonder where everyone is."

Yes, I talked to myself. It was a bad habit back when I was alive, and it had only gotten worse since death. Fortunately, I enjoyed my own company and, as my dear old dad used to say when I was just a little kid, I sure did like the sound of my own voice.

I tried to remember who'd occupied this office back when I worked for TrendCelerate. I thought it was a temp agency, one of those farm-'em-out pay-by-the-hour places. I'd done my time as a temp at a place like that back when I was younger. The pay was marginal. The benefits were shit. Job security was nonexistent. But it was a quick way to nab a job when I found myself between opportunities, and it gave me the skills to eventually land a full-time gig.

While I'd never been what could be called a people person, I really did like running the front desk at an office. I didn't have to worry about any life-or-death responsibilities. I got to sit in a comfy chair all day. And when it was slow, I could read a book and no one cared.

Looking around this empty office, I realized that my idea of a slow day was nothing compared to this place. The ability to work from home was transforming the office landscape. At first, people liked remote work because it saved them long, expensive commutes. Then, once people realized that they could finally work from literally anywhere, they moved out of their tiny, cramped apartments in the city into affordable places with actual lawns. This revolution wasn't without its price, though, as offices like this one sat empty.

Although, it wasn't entirely empty. There was a mish-mash of abandoned office furniture piled up in one corner, with a few desks and chairs scattered about. I didn't notice the old army cot until I stepped into it. There was a stained pillow, sans pillowcase, on one end of the cot, and a thick blanket folded up on the other. Had someone been sleeping here?

Curious now, I took a closer look. There was a hot plate, a microwave, and a small cooler. There was a drip coffee maker and a few jugs that had started life as juice bottles but now held water. Someone was living in this otherwise empty office.

Good for them. With rents being what they were in the city, I applauded anyone with the ingenuity to live for free. It wasn't like they were hurting anyone. Plus, the building had heat, running water, electricity. It could be a lot worse.

I remembered one of the places we'd lived at when I was younger. My brother, Ian, hadn't been more than a baby at the time, so I was six-ish years old. Dad was subletting a trailer from a friend of a friend. When we didn't have enough money to keep the heat and the lights on, it got cold in that trailer. Real cold. Dangerously cold. I didn't remember much from that winter except wrapping myself around Ian at night and dreaming of hot cocoa and warm mittens that never materialized.

I shook my head. Sometimes when I wandered down memory lane, I got stuck, losing hours or even days before I popped back into the here and now. Normally, I wouldn't mind taking a mini vacation from reality, even if it was to relive the bad times, but I was worried about Ruby. I *really* wish she hadn't been the one to find Marty like that.

With a tiny bit of effort, not more than I would need to pull a sneaker out of a thick mud puddle, I pushed through the wall separating the not-quite-empty office from TrendCelerate. I noticed that the conference room door was wide open. This morning's meeting had been abandoned as all of the participants crowded into the hall trying to get a peek at the dead body.

Ruby sat alone at her desk, looking paler than normal—and she was deathly pale to begin with. Sure, I was transparent, but I had an excuse. I was dead. Ruby just needed to get out more. There I went, getting all maternal on her for no good reason. She looked and dressed like a child, but I reminded myself that she was a grown woman.

"Cordelia?" she whispered, even though everyone else was out in the hall.

"I'm here," I told her. She couldn't hear or see me. But she seemed to know I was there.

I couldn't get too close to her, since her desk held a shiny new monitor, a high-end computer, and a complicated VoIP phone that would go belly-up if I got too close. But there was a fidget toy on the side of her desk, far away from the sensitive computer equipment, that was made up of a bunch of multicolored magnetic butterflies. I concentrated, and then let my hand reshape the butterflies from a tangled clump into a tall tower.

Depending on how hard I focused, I could slip though solid walls one minute and pick up physical objects the next. Neat, right?

"You're back! Marty, that nice delivery guy, he's dead. Dead in the bathroom." She shuddered. For a moment, she looked like she might throw up. I scooted her trash can a little closer to her, just in case. "Don't worry," she said with a dry laugh. "I'm not going to be sick."

"Come on, Ruby. Tell them you're not feeling well and you need to leave early. They'll close the office for the rest of the day, anyway. We can stop by the market and pick up some of those chocolates you like." Ruby and I didn't have a lot in common, but we both had a sweet tooth and a serious coffee addiction. Friendships have been founded on less.

"Cordelia?" Ruby whispered. "I have a bad feeling about this. We should look into Marty's death."

"No!" I knocked over the fidget toy, scattering butterflies all over her desk. "Not again."

Did I want to know the truth about Marty's death? He wasn't what I would call a close friend. I barely knew him. I mean, sure, I knew him well enough to buy drugs from him on occasion, but I didn't *know him* know him. He seemed like a good guy, other than the whole drug dealing thing. I liked him, but even if I hadn't, his death shouldn't be swept under the rug.

I wish I could honestly say that my interest was purely unselfish, that all I cared about was justice. But it would be a lie. Standing over his corpse laying on a bathroom floor hit just a little too close to home. That could have easily been me. Hell, that *was* me. No one had thought twice about my death. I was just a statistic, not worth a second glance. I was more than a number. *Marty* was more than a number. We both deserved better.

But the last time Ruby and I had gotten involved in a murder investigation, I'd put her life in danger. I'd made that mistake once and vowed to never do it again. Did I want to know the truth about my death? Of course! Was I willing to put my roomie in danger to find out? Hell no.

What's done was done. I wasn't about to let Ruby do something idiotic like sticking her nose into a dangerous murder investigation—not mine, and not Marty's. Not again.

Ruby got her purse out of its designated spot in the bottom drawer and stood up. "I knew you'd agree, Cordelia. Where do you want to start the investigation?"

CHAPTER SIX
CORDELIA

When TrendCelerate closed early, instead of going straight home, Ruby headed to the library, saying she had some research to do. Since I was persona non grata at the local branch—geez, blow up one little workstation and get banned for life. Or is that banned for death?—I decided to swing by the local pawnshop to visit a friend.

Lizard Pawn was near my apartment. The windows were plastered with faded "Sale" signs. A custom neon sign advertising the store was unlit, but for once, it wasn't my fault. That honor rested in the hands of the white man currently perched on the coin-operated pony next to the front door.

"Cordelia! How's it hanging?" he exclaimed when he saw me approach. Despite his enthusiastic greeting, his expression never changed. It rarely did.

Like me, Harp was dead. He was better at the whole ghost thing than I was, but he had forty years of practice. Those years had also erased much of what I still thought of as normal behavior, like smiling for instance. Harp didn't shrug. Or roll his eyes. Or blink. With every passing day, he acted a little less human.

I wondered if I'd eventually go that way, too. In forty years, I might be a shell of my former self. I hoped not. And where would Ruby be in forty years? Hopefully she'd get married and move out to the suburbs and raise a bunch of kids who told all their friends they had a ghost named Cordelia who hung out in their attic. I'd be the life of the party every time someone broke out the Ouija board.

"Hiya, Harp," I said in return, lifting my hand in a friendly wave.

Harp looked to be in his early thirties, but in reality, he was much older than that. He had curly hair with frosted tips, and a gold hoop earring in one ear. He wore vintage Chuck Taylor shoes and a pink polo shirt. The collar was popped. The front of the shirt was riddled with bullet holes and stained with blood.

He was the only other ghost I knew. That was weird, right? People died every day. A city the size of Boston, that had been around for a relatively long time—by American standards at least—should have more ghosts than I could shake a stick at. Not that I would. I mean, who would shake a stick at . . .

"Cordelia?" Harp called my name, cutting my train of thought short. "You cool? You totally spaced out there for a minute."

"Long day," I told him.

"Wanna chat?" he asked.

That was the best thing about Harp. Despite his waning humanity, we could talk normally, about anything, without resorting to magnets or any other ineffective and often misinterpreted means of communication.

I admittedly had sloppy handwriting, and Ruby couldn't read cursive. She couldn't hear or see me except on rare occasions. A few times, I'd touched her and she saw me for a second, but it hurt like hell and drained me for hours after. Her getting drunk worked, too. But then she ended up with a raging hangover and refused to drink again.

Ahh, I remember those days well. How many times had I made the same promise to knock off the booze? More than I could count. But with Ruby, it seemed to stick. Good for her. Bad for me.

One time, completely by accident, we were able to coexist in a tiny sliver of time between sleep and waking. I'd tried every night for a month, but failed to re-create that moment. Which left me with being unheard and unseen to everyone. Everyone except for Harp, that was.

"Today at work—"

He cut me off. "What is your damage?" Since Harp had died in the eighties, he occasionally sounded like an extra from *Valley Girl*. "You spend all day with breathers. At your old office. Like, for free. You need a vacation. Let's go away, just you and me. Someplace bitchin' where everyone's in bikinis drinking beer."

"Now's not the best time," I told him. I couldn't leave Ruby alone, not until I could rid her of the foolish impulse to look into Marty's death.

"I know just the place," Harp said, ignoring me. "Spring Break! Shake a leg."

"Spring break isn't a place," I told him. Back when Harp was alive, in the early days of MTV, "spring break" was very different than it was now. "And besides, we missed it."

"Oh yeah? What day is it?"

"Um . . ." I wasn't sure. It wasn't like the date mattered much to me anymore. Weeks already blurred together, and I'd only been dead a few months. I wondered if I'd be able to keep track at all by the time I was dead as long as Harp had been. "April? May?" It was hard to know for sure without a calendar, and those were all electronic these days and therefore off-limits.

"See? You don't know, either."

"Then you tell me," I said.

"Don't know. Don't care." He leaned forward against the neck of the mechanical pony. "Come with me. It'll be rad."

When I first died, one of the things I struggled with was how to stay solid in an insubstantial world. Strictly speaking, I didn't exist. I shouldn't be simultaneously able to pass through solid matter and also stand here on the sidewalk without slipping through to the center of the earth. Harp shouldn't be able to sit on a coin-operated kiddie ride. I didn't know how it worked. It just did.

"How do you do that?" I asked.

"Do what?"

I gestured at the toy pony. "How can you sit on that and not break it? It's mechanical, right?"

I had to make do without any information other than what I could glean from trial and error. Even after I found a sort of mentor in Harp, I was still playing it by ear most of the time. Then he'd go and do something I didn't think was possible, and I'd learn something new.

"Who says I didn't break it, or that I'd care if I did?" Harp asked. "Got a quarter? We can go for a ride. Hop on." He leaned back and spread his thighs. It figured. The last remaining shred of humanity in Harp was his sex drive.

"Cute. You know I don't have a quarter," I said. All I had were the clothes I was wearing when I died. A ratty tank top. A pair of sweats I'd borrowed from my boyfriend that he was never getting back. There was a plastic clip holding up my hair. If I'd died with a quarter in my pocket, would I have one now? I had no idea. "Hey, you got anything in your pockets?"

"Babe, if you want to get into my pants, all you gotta do is ask."

"Not on your life," I said through gritted teeth. Yes, I knew I didn't have teeth to grit. Nor did I have lungs, a tongue, a mouth, or any of the necessary components to form words. That didn't mean I couldn't grit my nonexistent teeth when Harp needled me.

"What have I told you about using that kind of breather speak? It's... what do the kids call it these days? It's triggering."

"Fine. How about 'Not on your afterlife?'"

"That's better. For the record, you could carry a quarter around if you wanted to, not that you would need one."

"How would that work?" I asked.

"How does any of this work? Matter doesn't matter anymore. Not for us," Harp replied, which, to be fair, was as good an explanation as any. "Now, about that pony ride..." He gave me a lecherous grin, which was somehow even more disturbing than his usual non-expression.

"It's not you, it's me," I told him.

Harp wasn't my type. He wasn't married or otherwise unavailable. Plus, blame it on unresolved daddy issues, but I'd always had a thing for older men. Since he'd stopped aging in the mid-eighties when he died, he looked young, even if he was technically a couple of decades older than me.

"Beggars can't be choosers," he reminded me.

Since Harp was literally the only other ghost I knew, my dating pool was limited. "It's the whole touching thing." I shivered at the thought. I could touch an inanimate object, no problem. Touching a living person hurt. Like being-run-over-by-a-truck hurt. Touching another ghost wasn't quite as bad, more like getting run over by a Kia. At the end of the day, it was still painful.

"You're no fun," Harp said.

"As you love to remind me," I replied. Harp was a pain in the ass sometimes, but he had good intentions. I trusted him with my afterlife. "But something interesting *did* happen at work today."

"I doubt that." Harp rocked back and forth on the mechanical pony while whirling one hand over his head like he was twirling a lasso.

"A man died."

"Oh?" Harp stopped and gave me his full attention. "Who was he?"

"A friend," I said. "Not a close friend, but he delivered to my old office, and we always got along."

"Delivered?" Harp cocked his head, a rare animated gesture from him. "I still can't get over the fact that you can get anything delivered nowadays. People never need to leave the house anymore. What kind of deliveries did your friend do?"

"Sandwiches and drugs," I admitted. "Just prescription pills, only without the prescriptions."

"Shame about your friend. A good dealer's hard to find. Then again, I never did the hard stuff. Just like cocaine and shit."

I snorted and asked, "Cocaine isn't the hard stuff?"

"Duh. It was the eighties," Harp replied. "Your friend, did he ghost?"

I shook my head. "I waited for him as long as I could, but nothing happened."

"Bogus." He didn't sound disappointed so much as bored. Harp hopped off the pony. Instead of answering me, he said, "If that's all, I've got places to be. It's always spring break somewhere." Then he vanished.

"Show-off," I grumbled.

It was just my luck that of the only two people on the planet who knew I existed, one was a breather—as Harp liked to call the living—who happened to share my home address, and the other was a flippant, chauvinistic ghost I had nothing in common with other than we were both dead. It sucked. Ruby was good company, but our communication was in shambles. Harp was a better conversationalist but had the attention span of a horny flea.

"The afterlife sucks," I grumbled.

There had to be other ghosts in Boston. There had to be. I just hadn't found them yet. Had I given up on Marty too quickly? The memories surrounding my own death were fuzzy. When I died, had I ghosted immediately? Had it taken a few hours to materialize? Days? What if Marty was just now coming to, wandering around confused, scared, and alone?

That sealed it. I was going to give him another shot, if not to alleviate my own loneliness, then to help ease him into the transition.

I swung by TrendCelerate first because it was close and I knew my way around. I checked the bathroom. No sign of Marty, physically or metaphysically. The only thing left behind was a prescription pill bottle jammed in behind the toilet that the police had apparently missed. Gotta love their attention to detail.

Next stop was the morgue. I'd lived in Boston my entire life, but I had no idea where the morgue was, and it wasn't like I could google the address. There were times I really missed access to technology. Then again, there were benefits to being dead, especially when it came to commuting.

I closed my eyes and concentrated hard. Since I wasn't sure where Marty's body would have been taken, instead of focusing on an address, I focused on Marty himself. And then just like when Harp decided our conversation was over and went in search of a warm beach filled with bikini-clad women, I vanished from the TrendCelerate bathroom. When I opened my eyes, I was in a morgue surrounded by dead bodies.

Back when I was alive, that would have freaked me out. Although, to be fair, even dead, being in a morgue was still pretty freaky.

I'd always imagined morgues would be someplace dark and

underground, with flickering lights and rows of antiseptic metal tables with sheet-covered bodies on them. In reality, I had no idea if we were underground or not, since there were no windows in the room. There were only two tables, and neither was occupied at the moment. All the bodies were neatly tucked away into what I presumed were refrigerated body drawers along the wall. I couldn't see them, but I could sense them. And yes, the lights did flicker, but that was my fault.

"Marty?" I whispered, feeling foolish. It wasn't like anyone could hear me, not anyone living at least. It just felt disrespectful to talk too loud when surrounded by all this death.

I surveyed the wall of drawers. I found one labeled "Spencer, Martin" and realized that up until now, I had no idea what his last name was. When I'd been alive, I'd seen him at least once a week at TrendCelerate. I had his number programmed into my phone. I'd bought drugs off him for Pete's sake. And I'd never bothered to learn his last name.

A door behind me swung open, and a technician in scrubs walked in. I waited, hoping they would leave so I could open Marty's drawer. Instead, the tech sat down in front of a computer on the far side of the room and started typing.

"Isn't there somewhere else you can do that?" I asked, to no avail.

I briefly considered opening the drawer anyway, but decided against it. If I worked in a morgue and one day, the drawers opened by themselves and dead bodies started sliding out into the room, I'd quit on the spot. Besides, it didn't seem fair to give the poor technician nightmares when they were just doing their job.

That left only one option. I stuck my head into Marty's drawer. It was dark inside, but I didn't need light to see.

"Marty?" I called. The body didn't stir. It just lay there, stiff, silent, and dead. "Marty, you in here?" Still, nothing. If Marty was a ghost, he wasn't hanging around the morgue. Not that I blamed him. It was depressing and made my skin crawl—or it would have, if I still *had* skin.

I withdrew my head from the drawer, and something caught my eye. I studied the tag closer. It listed his name, followed by the cause of death. "'Asphyxiation by choking'?" I shook my head. "Really?" I double-checked. It wasn't "aspiration." It was "asphyxiation."

A few months ago, I wouldn't have known the difference, but Ruby loved her true crime podcasts and listened to them frequently, which meant that now I listened to them, too. True crime had never been my thing. It was too graphic, but now all those details I didn't realize I was picking up came in handy.

"Asphyxiation" covered a range of conditions that could cause someone to stop breathing, from asthma to suffocation. Aspiration, basically suffocating from fluid in the lungs, was a common symptom of overdose, but I'd seen Marty's body on the bathroom floor. There'd been no drool or froth around his mouth, which would be expected in aspiration.

But the tag on the body drawer clearly stated "asphyxiation by choking," which was different. Choking was when a person's airway was blocked. In this case, according to the notes on the tag, his throat and mouth were full of pills.

Marty hadn't died of an accidental overdose. Someone force-fed him enough pills to block his airway. Marty had been murdered.

I couldn't let the killer go free. The police weren't taking Marty's death seriously. They'd already cleared the crime scene without more than a cursory sweep. It was time to take matters into my own hands. Only, being dead, strictly speaking, I didn't *have* hands. Which meant that, despite my desire to protect Ruby, I was going to need to enlist her help. Again.

CHAPTER SEVEN
RUBY

The day after Marty's death, the atmosphere was subdued at Trend-Celerate. It was rarely ever noisy at work, but there was always something going on. Conversations between coworkers. Music leaking out of headphones. Telephone calls. Clacking keyboards. Today, everything felt more muffled than usual, like Marty's death had cast a shadow over the office.

The mood lightened a little when the mail was delivered. Mixed in with the standard flyers and advertisements were the office's copies of *Frolicking Ferrets Monthly*, *Worm Digest*, and *Sailing Yacht Weekly*. The ferret and worm magazines were Seth's idea of a joke. The yacht magazine was Blair's. I didn't know why he had it sent to the office instead of his house, unless it was his way of reminding everyone that he owned a yacht. I set the magazines aside to hand off to them the next time they walked past my desk.

When lunch arrived, I went out instead of eating in the break room. Quinn McLauchlan was the on-site executive today. It was unusual to see her in the office two days in a row and, unfortunately, she was going through a juice cleanse. Which meant that she had me order smoothies for everyone for lunch. I loved a good juice blend as much as the next person, but when I drank too much of it, I had to pee; and frankly, the last place I wanted to visit was the TrendCelerate bathroom the day after Marty died in there.

Instead, I headed down the street to Beantown Deli, where he used to work. It was the lunch rush, and customers were packed into the small space. I'd never been inside Beantown before. I always placed my order online and waited for Marty to deliver.

There were four tables, two on each side of the store and a wide aisle between them leading to the deli counter. All of the action, I presumed, happened in the kitchen behind that, not that I could see over the crowd. But being small had its advantages. I slipped into the pockets between hungry customers and made my way to the counter.

"Take a number," the woman behind the register said, pointing to an old-fashioned ticket dispenser.

"I'm here about Marty," I said.

"Take. A. Number," she repeated, slower this time, punctuating each word.

I took a number.

The deli had mostly cleared out by the time my number was called. Many of the people had been waiting to pick up large office orders, like the kind I normally placed. I had the menu memorized. I ordered a spuckie special for myself, knowing it would fill me up and still leave half to take home as leftovers.

After I placed my order, I told the woman behind the counter that our office normally got deliveries from Marty.

"You and everyone else," she grumbled.

"He's the best," I said.

"He was a bum," she replied with a frown.

Marty had been a great guy, friendly and outgoing. He was never late, and never rude. I liked him, and was surprised by her attitude. "I'm sorry to hear about his passing," I said. I guess, technically, I hadn't heard about it so much as witnessed it firsthand, but there was no reason to bring that up now. Or think about it ever again. "We're going to miss him."

"Why?" She shrugged. "He was a bum when he was alive, and he got what was coming to him."

"He was nice to me," I said.

"He was *nice* to everyone. Doesn't make him any less of a bum. Or any less dead."

I wondered what made him such a "bum" in her opinion, but rather than asking and risking sounding argumentative, I nodded. "My office, TrendCelerate?" If she recognized the name, she didn't react. Then again, judging by the crowd that had been here earlier, I suspected many of the nearby businesses were frequent customers. "We'd like to send our condolences to his family."

"I'll pass that along," she said. I got the impression she had no intention of doing so. She looked over my shoulder. "Next!"

I was nudged out of the way by someone picking up a large order of four heavy-looking bags. The person after that advanced on the counter. "What's a spuckie?" they asked.

"It's a sandwich," the woman behind the register said, looking annoyed. She pointed at the board behind her. It was hand-lettered in chalk, but as far as I could tell, it was the same as the online menu, and that never changed. "Pick one and order. There's a line."

Although, to be fair, the line had dwindled to almost nothing.

While the customer studied the list of sandwiches like there would be a test later, the impatient woman reached behind the counter and grabbed a single wrapped spuckie off the window. "The special?" she asked, gesturing toward me.

"That's me," I confirmed, taking it eagerly. "So, about Marty . . ."

"What about Marty?" she snapped.

"Like I was saying, my company would like to send flowers to the family—"

She interrupted me. "Knock yourself out."

"You think you can give me an address or something?"

"*You think you can give me an address or something?*" she repeated back to me, her tone high-pitched and whiny. For the record, I did *not* sound like that. Much.

"Please," I added.

"Please, she says," she grumbled. She opened a drawer under the counter and retrieved a three-ring binder, faded with age. She flipped through it, found the page she was looking for, and slid it across the counter toward me.

I looked down at the employment application for one Martin Spencer. I didn't recognize the street name, but I committed his address to memory.

"Take a picture, it'll last longer," the woman said with the same sarcastic bite to her words.

"Oh!" I fumbled my phone out of my pocket. Why hadn't that occurred to me before? Living with a ghost who fried electronics if she got too close, I'd reduced my reliance on my phone. I bet my mom wished she'd had a ghost around when I was growing up so she wouldn't have had to yell at me and my sisters all the time to put our phones away at the dinner table. I opened the camera app and took a photo. "Thanks."

She glared at me as she yanked the folder back and slid it into the drawer. "Next!" she called out, even though the confused person in front of her still hadn't ordered.

I cradled my spuckie as I made my hasty exit. As much as I

appreciated her reluctant assistance, I was glad I didn't work with her. TrendCelerate would never give out an employee's personal information that easily, or at least I assumed they wouldn't. If they did, then someone would have noticed by now that my home address was the same as their previous office manager's. The fact that no one had put two and two together yet was baffling, but even if someone did realize that I was living in Cordelia Graves's old apartment, no one would ever guess that I was roomies with a deceased employee's ghost.

It was a nice day, for Boston at least. The high sixties didn't sound like much, but after a long, dreary winter, it was my idea of heaven. I found an empty bench in the tiny sliver of green that passed for a park in this neighborhood, sat, and unwrapped my spuckie. Back home in Baltimore, it would have been a "sub sandwich," but they would crucify me if I called it that here. No matter what it was called, it was delicious.

I could hardly eat half of the enormous sandwich. I rewrapped the remainder and headed back to the office. As nice as it was to eat my lunch outside in the sunshine, a breeze had kicked up and it was getting chilly. Besides, I had phones to answer. I felt guilty taking my break, which was silly. In addition to incentivizing employees to work from the office, a big part of the reason management bought lunch every day was to stealthily encourage everyone to spend more time at their desks. Capitalism. Amiright?

Before I could take two steps into the office, Blair blocked my path. He sniffed the air before zeroing in on my remaining sandwich half. "Is that a Beantown Deli spuckie special?"

I crossed my arms around the sandwich. Gone were the days that I didn't know from where, or if, my next meal was coming. I still had leftover eggplant parm in my fridge at home, but that didn't mean I was willing to give up the other half of my spuckie just because Blair wanted it.

"What if it is?" I jutted my chin out. I'd been planning on stashing my leftovers in the refrigerator in the break room, but now I knew that was a bad idea. Blair had no respect for others, and labeling food in the shared fridge was no deterrent to him. I'd only worked at TrendCelerate for a couple of months, and already he'd cooked fish in the microwave, burned popcorn, and stolen all of Melissa's pudding cups. He was the office menace.

"I had a kale smoothie for lunch. *Kale.* I'd kill for a spuckie right about now."

"They're still open," I said, jerking my head back toward the door. I wasn't going to risk pointing, lest he snatch my sandwich out of my arms and make a run for it.

"I already called. They said they're not doing deliveries today. Can you imagine?" he whined.

"Yeah." I nodded vigorously. "I can imagine. Their delivery person died yesterday, remember? In our bathroom?"

"That was the Beantown Deli dude?" Blair asked, crestfallen. "You sure?"

"Pretty sure," I told him, with a nod. His reaction surprised me. As far as I knew, Blair didn't care about anyone or anything other than himself. I doubted he was actually bothered by the passing of a lowly delivery person, other than how it inconvenienced him. Disgusted by his lack of compassion, I sidestepped him and headed for my desk.

"Twenty dollars," he said, stopping me in my tracks.

I turned around. "Twenty dollars? For what?"

He pointed at my sandwich.

"You'll pay me twenty dollars to go get you a spuckie?"

"I'll give you twenty for that one," he clarified.

I looked down at my hand. I'd already eaten half the sandwich, which had cost me less than what Blair was offering. If I put it in the fridge, he would eat it anyway; if I left it at my desk, it would spoil. But if he was willing to pay me twenty for it... "Twenty-five," I countered.

"Deal. I'll Venmo you." He whipped out his cellphone. I gave him my Venmo name and a second later, my phone beeped. Without checking it, I handed him the spuckie. "Thanks," Blair said, hurrying back to his cubicle.

I checked my phone as soon as I sat down at my desk. Sure enough, I had twenty-five dollars from Blair in my Venmo account.

I wondered if Marty ever got paid that much for a single delivery. When I ordered for the office, I always tipped twenty percent on top of the delivery fee and put it all on the company card. I had no idea how many offices he delivered to, but based on the amount of folks waiting to pick up their orders at the deli, I guessed a lot.

Marty could have cleared twice as much a week on tips alone than I made at TrendCelerate. Not bad.

For a hot second, I considered going back to Beantown Deli to ask if they were hiring. I assumed they were, considering how busy they'd been at lunch and knowing that they were short one delivery person. But my common sense kicked in. Sure, running around on a day like today would be great. But Boston wasn't exactly famous for its temperate weather, and those deliveries got heavy fast. The first time I had to hoof an order a few blocks in subzero temperature I'd be begging to get my desk job back.

And I *did* like it at TrendCelerate. On the whole, people were nice. Sure, Blair was a tool, Quinn was a nightmare when she was on a juice cleanse, and I didn't trust anything Seth offered me. But I could see why Cordelia had stayed here as long as she had. It was a cushy job.

With nothing else to occupy me, I checked the TrendCelerate generic mailbox. As usual, it was mostly spam. Emails from the website all ended up here. If they were actual leads, I would forward them out to the team. Otherwise, I deleted them.

I was in the process of deleting several dozen emails ranging from people telling me I'd won contests I hadn't entered, they could fix problems I didn't have, to they'd tracked down a package I hadn't ordered, when one jumped out at me. It was a perfectly ordinary email, a reminder for a dentist appointment. The email was addressed to Cordelia Graves.

The email box served as a public-facing catch-all. In addition to being the contact email on the website, it was where all emails to resigned, fired, or—apparently—deceased employees ended up.

I stared at it for a moment. I could delete it. I could click on it, and get the dentist's name and number so I could call and explain that Cordelia was no longer a patient. But the longer I thought about it, the more an invasive thought formed. When someone died, it was usually up to the next of kin to cancel credit cards and dentist appointments. Cordelia didn't have a next of kin, at least not that I knew of. Did that mean she still had open accounts in her name?

TrendCelerate had canceled her insurance, but what other reoccurring appointments did she have set up? She hadn't been dead long, just a few months. If she had an annual dental cleaning, there could be other visits I needed to cancel.

"Cordelia?" I whispered. "You here?" I didn't get a response, which wasn't a surprise. I hadn't felt her presence in the office today. I could wait until later, when she was around, but that created its own problems. If she got too close to the computer, hard drives, monitors, and power supplies tended to get wonky and overheat. After the emergency personnel swarming the building yesterday, the last thing I wanted was to trigger the fire alarm and summon the fire department.

"Here goes nothing." I knew the benefits portal address, because for the first time in my adult life, I had my own medical insurance. Cordelia's username was likewise easy to figure out. I typed in "Cordelia.Graves", clicked the button for "Forgot password," and followed the instructions.

As I suspected, her insurance account was suspended, but there was a complete list of doctor's appointments past and future, prescriptions, and balances. Luckily, her balance due was zero. Then I clicked on the HSA button and blinked in surprise. I didn't understand half of my benefits. HDHP, HMO, PPO, HSA, it was all a little confusing. Even my 401(k) didn't make a lot of sense. I'd accepted all the defaults without asking what "vested" meant.

What I *did* understand was the number on the screen in front of me, and it was a lot. Like a lot, a lot. At least for someone like me who'd never had more than a few hundred dollars in their checking account between paychecks, it was a lot. Cordelia's health savings account alone had more money than I'd ever personally seen in one place. It made me wonder what she had in her actual bank account, assuming she still had one.

Out of curiosity, I clicked on the 401(k) link. It prompted me to enter the PIN that had been texted to me. Since I didn't have Cordelia's cell phone, I couldn't log in. For all I knew, the account had already been emptied.

Back on the main page, I scrolled through previous doctor's visits. While she'd been on the TrendCelerate plan for years, she didn't have many medical claims outside of an annual dental appointment and a few spotty checkups here and there. For the record, I wasn't being nosy. Okay, I was being a *little* nosy. Feeling

DEATH AT THE DOOR   69

guilty, I logged out. I made a quick call to the dental office—my original reason for crawling down the insurance rabbit hole in the first place—and tried to put everything else out of my mind. But I couldn't.

Why did Cordelia have so much money stashed away in an HSA? Was she saving for an emergency? Shortly after I'd moved in, she'd shown me an envelope hidden in her silverware drawer stuffed with a thousand bucks in cash. Was this another one of her hiding spots? How many other stashes did she have? And where did all the money come from?

Cordelia's death had been ruled a suicide, but I didn't believe it. People killed themselves for a host of reasons, but Cordelia hadn't checked out over money troubles. If she'd had depression or suicidal ideation, there was no record of it in her medical files. And then there was the sparse prescription list in her history. She got the flu shot every year, but there were no painkillers or sleeping aids. Where had she gotten the pills she overdosed on, if not from a doctor?

"You still here?" I looked up to see Quinn standing over my desk. "It's past five. You can go home. Everyone else left for happy hour ages ago. I'm surprised you didn't go with them."

"Oh?" This was the first I was hearing of an office happy hour. I was a little miffed that they hadn't invited me. But what was Quinn's excuse? "Why didn't you go?" I asked.

"I told you. I don't drink. There's no bigger wet blanket than a sober boss at happy hour." Quinn nodded at me. "It's a good thing you didn't go out with them. You've got a good head on your shoulders, Ruby. You don't have to ruin your life with drugs or alcohol to have fun."

The words "Yes, Mom" *almost* slipped out of me. As far as I knew, she didn't have any children of her own, but in that moment,

Quinn struck me as maternal. I recalled she had a niece who lived with her, the one whose pictures she had in her office.

On rare occasions, she reminded me of my own mother, who'd instilled the "drugs bad, booze bad" message in me and my sisters at an early age. It must have sunk in, because none of us were party kids.

"Yup, that's great advice," I said, turning off my computer and hastily gathering my personal belongings. I was glad she hadn't caught me when I'd been poking around Cordelia's medical history. "I was just leaving. See you tomorrow!" I grabbed my bag and hurried out of the office before she could ask what had kept me so late.

CHAPTER EIGHT
CORDELIA

After my visit to the morgue, I'd paced around our apartment, trying to figure out what I could do with the knowledge that Marty had been murdered. Should I try to find his killer by myself? Fat lot of good that would do anyone. I couldn't capture them alone. I couldn't turn them into the police. And I couldn't testify against them in court.

I could enlist Ruby's help like I did last time we'd stumbled across a death that the authorities hadn't invested any effort into solving, but that meant putting her in danger again. I wasn't so selfish that I was willing to put my roommate, and my only living friend in this world, in harm's way. Been there, done that, learned my lesson.

Even if I had air in my lungs, or had lungs for that matter, I wouldn't hold my breath waiting for the police to do their job. Marty was a low-level drug dealer. The cops weren't going to waste their time looking for his killer. If I had any doubts, finding a pill bottle that hadn't been collected at the scene of a murder was proof enough that the police didn't care.

As I weighed my options, I realized that something was wrong. Ruby should have been home from work by now. So where was she? The only clock in the apartment was on the fritz, but I could tell from the light coming in through the living room curtains that it was later than usual.

All sorts of horrible scenarios flashed through my head. Color me paranoid, but yesterday, Marty had been going about his business and today his body was lying in a drawer in the city morgue. I wasn't about to let the same thing happen to Ruby.

Sure, I could have blinked myself back to her location wherever she was, but that took a lot of energy I didn't want to waste. I wouldn't be much good to Ruby if I found her in trouble, only to get whisked off to that dreamlike state where I was treated to some of the worst memories of my life playing on perpetual reruns, until I recharged. No thank you.

Instead of taking that risk, I hurried out of the apartment, tracing the steps Ruby should have taken to get home. I studied every bus that passed, hoping to catch a glimpse of her in the crush of commuters, fully absorbed in whatever podcast she was listening to with no idea that I was working myself into a panic. Just as I reached the TrendCelerate office, the front door opened, and Ruby stepped out onto the sidewalk.

"There you are," I said. "I've got so much to tell you. Let's go home." I had no idea how I was going to explain what I'd learned at the morgue using only refrigerator magnets, but I was up to the challenge.

Ruby froze. "Cordelia?"

"I'm right here," I replied.

I spotted a dime on the ground. I carefully palmed it so no

passerby would see a coin floating in the air, brought it to Ruby's eye level, and dropped it. The coin bounced on the sidewalk, glinting as it caught the light.

"Hey, there you are," she said, scooping to grab the dime. She tucked it into her pocket. "Thanks. I hope you had a better day than I did," Ruby said, chatting amicably as we headed down the sidewalk together. "It was totally dead all day. Oops! No offense! I meant totally quiet. Then after work, everyone went out for happy hour, and didn't even invite me."

"Sorry. They can be such jerks," I said. I wished she could hear me comforting her. Then I realized that we were heading in the wrong direction. "Uh, Ruby? Bus station is back that way."

She kept walking.

"Seriously, are you turned around or what?"

I couldn't tap her on the shoulder, not unless I wanted to be out of commission for the rest of the day. I settled on tugging on the strap of her bag instead.

Ruby stopped abruptly on the busy sidewalk, causing a man behind her to curse as he dodged around her. "What?" she whispered.

"Who are you talking to?" a woman asked, drawing even with her.

Ruby looked over to see Melissa from work sidle up next to her on the sidewalk. "Oh, hey. I didn't see you there."

"No kidding. You looked spaced." Melissa looked around. Her eyes were glassy. "Who were you talking to just now?" Her steps were unsteady from whatever she'd had at the bar. Even so, she was tall enough that Ruby struggled to keep up with her pace.

"No one," Ruby said. She needed to get better at lying. In the age of Bluetooth, it was easy to pass off conversations with yourself—or your friendly neighborhood ghost—as an ordinary phone call. "You look like you had fun at happy hour."

Melissa dismissed her with a wave. "Both Blair and Seth 'accidentally' left their wallets at home." She made air quotes around "accidentally." Despite having everything handed to him, Blair wasn't a generous person. Seth was big into practical jokes that weren't funny to anyone but him. I came to the same conclusion that Melissa had. They'd forgotten their wallets on purpose. "When they weren't paying attention, I slipped out and stuck them with the tab."

Blair wasn't one of my favorite people. He'd been born with a silver spoon in his mouth and a stick up his ass. He wasn't half as smart or handsome as he thought he was. He was a walking, talking embodiment of a mediocre white man. He was the kind of guy who'd never offer a seat on the bus to a pregnant woman, assuming that he ever stooped so low as to take public transportation.

There were benefits to being a ghost, such as being able to teach entitled jerks like Blair a lesson. One of these days, when he was sitting down, I'd tie his shoelaces together. Then I'd follow him home, scrub his toilet bowl out with his toothbrush, and short out his cellphone charger. But not today. Today, Ruby needed me.

"That was mean," Ruby objected. "How are they supposed to pay?"

I worried that she'd do something stupid, such as go back and try to bail them out, even after they all went out to happy hour without inviting her.

"Not my problem," Melissa said, shrugging. "And really not yours. Don't worry. They'll be fine. They've got their phones."

"True," she agreed, relaxing a little. "If Blair can Venmo me twenty-five dollars for a half-eaten sandwich, he can figure out a way to pay the bartender."

"Good on you," I told her. I'd once offered Blair a hundred dollars to walk into Boston Harbor and never come back. He thought I was kidding. I wasn't. I was proud of her. I'd much rather see her taking advantage of Blair than be taken advantage of by him.

Melissa raised one eyebrow. "That must have been one hell of a sandwich." She looked up and saw a bus pulling in to the stop halfway up the block. "Well, gotta run. See ya at work tomorrow." There was a long line of people already waiting. She got at the back of the line and waved at us. Well, technically, she waved at Ruby, but we both waved back.

After the bus loaded and left, Ruby ducked into the now-empty bus stop to study the map mounted to one wall.

"Where're we going?" I asked. I assumed Ruby had a destination in mind. Even if she'd gotten turned around, she had to know that this wasn't our normal stop.

She pulled out her phone, and I took a step back before I could accidentally fry its circuits. "There," she said, comparing her phone to the map. I couldn't tell if she was talking to herself or to me. She traced her finger along a street, and then double-checked that we were at a bus stop that matched the number on the map.

"Okay, but why?" I asked. Of course, she didn't answer.

Twenty-five minutes later, we found ourselves in a suburban neighborhood with tree-lined streets and older cars parked along the curb. We walked up the steps to a small row house with a blue front door. There was a narrow swath of lawn out front, littered with toys ranging from a toddler's bouncy horse to a purple Hula-Hoop sized for an elementary school–aged kid.

Ruby knocked on the door. Inside, a dog barked, and I could hear a television playing loud cartoons. A harried-looking woman with a young child on her hip opened the door.

"Yes?"

"Hi. My name is Ruby Young. I work for TrendCelerate,

downtown?" She paused. "I got your address from the Beantown Deli."

I glanced over at Ruby. "Beantown Deli? Why were you at . . . ?" Then I understood. This was Marty's house. Now that I knew what I was looking for, I noticed that the woman and child both had the same warm brown curls that Marty had, but not his goofy grin. Then again, they didn't have a lot to smile about at the moment.

"This is a spectacularly bad idea," I grumbled.

The woman deflated. The child she was holding wiggled. She put him down, and he dashed toward the bouncy horse, climbing up with chubby little arms and legs and squealing with delight. The bouncy horse reminded me of the coin-operated one Harp had been sitting on in front of the pawnshop, only smaller and sun-bleached. The little dog we'd heard barking rushed toward the door. Before it could escape, the woman stepped out and let the door slam close behind her.

"Trenderate?" she asked.

"Close enough," Ruby said. "It's TrendCelerate. I'm very sorry for your loss, Mrs. Spencer."

"Miss," she corrected her. She sat on the top step where she could keep one eye on Ruby and one eye on the toddler playing in the yard. "Marty's my brother."

"I'm sorry, I assumed . . ."

"Silly Ruby, don't you see the family resemblance?" I asked her. From what she'd told me, I knew she lived with her mother and younger sister back when she was in Baltimore, before she moved to Boston, so it shouldn't come as a surprise that Marty and his sister lived together, too.

She cut her off. "Happens all the time. I'm Hazel. That's Luca, my son."

"And you lived here with Marty?" Ruby asked.

"Marty and his daughter lived here with us," she said in a biting tone that made me wonder if she'd been entirely happy with that arrangement. I didn't blame her. If my brother crashed at my place for more than a few days, we would drive each other up the wall.

"I liked him."

"He was very likable," Hazel said, with a touch of mirth in her voice. "Everybody's friend, that's our Marty."

"Uh-huh," Ruby agreed, sitting on the step below her. "Awful shame."

Hazel nodded. "Thank you." She looked at Ruby, her body language asking loud and clear, "Is that all?" even though she didn't voice it.

"You're not gonna interrogate his grieving sister, are you?" I asked Ruby. "You shouldn't go sticking your nose where it doesn't belong. Besides, Marty's barely been gone a day. And Hazel looks exhausted."

I didn't know how I would react if something bad—really bad, final bad, not-picked-up-by-the-cops-again bad—happened to my brother. Ian was a pain in my ass. Always had been, always would be. But he was my baby brother. We were all either of us really had in this life, and now he didn't even have that anymore. I wondered for the millionth time how he was doing. Last I'd checked on him, he was in prison in upstate New York.

I'd gone to visit him once after I'd figured out that if I thought hard enough about a person, I could pop to wherever they were. No more TSA or budget airlines with no legroom for *this* ghost. No siree. Who needed to fly when I could teleport anywhere in the world in an instant?

My timing could have been better, though. I popped into my brother's cell when he was, let's just say, otherwise occupied. I would never look at a *Time* magazine the same way again. On the plus side, he did look happy, so I left it at that.

"I was the one who found him," Ruby blurted out.

"You?" Hazel studied her features.

Ruby nodded.

"Tell me. Did he look peaceful?"

Ruby put her hand on Hazel's knee. "He did," she said as kindly as possible. "They say overdoses are quick and painless."

Hazel shook her head. "He didn't overdose. He didn't do that shit."

"Are you sure?" Ruby asked.

I didn't want Ruby getting involved, but if she was hell-bent on investigating, she needed all the facts. As soon as we got a minute alone, I'd figure out how to let her know that Hazel was right.

"Trust me. He learned his lesson. He promised me he'd never use again."

"Where have I heard that before?" I muttered. Addicts rarely changed. How many times had I promised myself I'd never drink again? How many times had I meant it? But my resolve never lasted long.

"How can you be sure?" Ruby asked.

"He's my brother. I'm sure."

I rolled my eyes. "Trust me. You didn't know your brother half as well as you think you did." If their relationship was anything like me and Ian, there was a whole lot about her brother that she didn't know. Ian swore to me that he was done boosting cars, but the district attorney had video evidence to the contrary.

Hazel wanted to believe the best of her brother. I understood that instinct. I wanted to believe the best about my own brother, too, even though I knew for a fact that he wasn't a model citizen.

I knew from my visit to the morgue that Marty hadn't overdosed, but I wasn't convinced his hands were sparkly clean.

"If you say so," Ruby said.

"I do," Hazel said. She sat up straighter, and the dull glaze over her eyes was replaced with anger. "Marty wasn't perfect. You think I don't know that? I know he dealt, but it was strictly pills, and not that street shit, either. Pharmaceuticals only."

Ruby looked confused. "Why would someone who refused to do drugs sell them?" she asked.

Poor, sweet, innocent Ruby. She really did see the best in people, didn't she? Then again, my roomie was a goody two-shoes. She was probably the kind of person who would turn down Ritalin if her classmates passed it around before finals.

"He did what he had to do to get by, and take care of us. Even back when he was using, he never sold the hard stuff. Never." Hazel sounded adamant about that.

I believed her. "I know people bought from him all the time," I said, wishing Ruby could hear me. "But only prescriptions—Viagra, Ozempic—that sort of thing." I wasn't the only person in the office who bought from him. I knew this because I'd helped facilitate drop-offs from time to time. As far as I was concerned, it wasn't any different from signing for other office deliveries.

"Uh-huh," Ruby said. She didn't sound convinced.

"Don't look at me like that," Hazel said, staring down Ruby. "You don't know what it's like. Do you have any idea how hard it is to get a decent job, a job where you can support your family, when you've got a record?"

"Marty had a record? What was he in for?"

"Don't worry, it wasn't anything violent," Hazel assured her.

"Uh-huh," I said. "My little brother was never violent, either, but he sure spent a lot of time behind bars. Doesn't make things easier on the family, does it?"

Hazel continued defending Marty. "He made a mistake and paid his debt to society. But you would have thought he'd killed a gaggle of nuns from the way employers treated him."

"Superfluity," Ruby said.

"What?" Hazel asked.

"What?" I asked.

"Superfluity. It's what you call a group of nuns. A 'gaggle' is geese."

Hazel glared at her. "A superfluity of nuns, then. Look, I love my brother and I know I'm not an unbiased character witness, but Marty never hurt nobody. He was a good man, a single dad who delivered sandwiches for a living for the only place that would hire him after he got out, but that wasn't nearly enough to feed his family. He took care of all of us, his daughter Julia, me, and my son, Luca. He only ever did what he had to."

That was a gut punch. I might as well be looking at my own reflection on that stoop. Luckily my brother Ian didn't have a kid, at least not that I knew about, and I didn't need him taking care of me, but the rest of it? Ouch. It hit home. Hard. I knew what it was like to have a screwup in the family.

"I hate to be the one to break it to ya," I told Hazel. I wish I'd known her back when I was alive. I had a feeling we would have been friends, but I worried that she was overlooking the obvious. "Your brother was a decent guy, but you don't put the weight of the world on one person's shoulders and not expect them to crumble. Everyone makes mistakes."

I turned my attention to Ruby. "I hope you're not getting any ideas." She was on the right track about there being something hinky about Marty's death. Even so, I didn't want her to investigate. It was my job to keep Ruby safe, which meant keeping her far, far away from this.

Just like it was Marty's job to fend for his daughter, sister, and nephew. I knew the pressure of being the adult in the family, and had known it for as long as I could remember. I made dinner for my dad when he forgot to eat and called in sick for him when he was too hungover to work. I taught my baby brother to tie his shoes and helped with his homework. Even after Dad was long gone and Ian was a grown-ass man in his own right, I was still putting money into my brother's commissary account every month.

I wasn't a fan of self-reflection because I rarely liked what I saw. I didn't want to admit that I'd turned out no better than my dad. Or Ian. Or Marty, for that matter. I knew what it was like to need something to take the edge off. I took after my father like that, turning to a bottle. I wouldn't blame Marty one bit if he had occasionally sampled his own merchandise.

"Face it, Ruby," I said. I knew she couldn't hear me. We'd have to have this discussion all over again when we got home. "Marty wasn't perfect. He was into something nasty, and it got him killed. No need for you to get involved."

Not that I planned to take my own advice. I'd already been upset that someone had killed a man I liked and the police weren't doing anything about it. And that was before I knew he had a young kid at home or that he was supporting his sister's family, too.

"Sounds like Marty had a lot to live for," Ruby said.

"He did," Hazel said.

"What about his daughter's mom?"

"Mallory? She's out of the picture. She's doing time in Framingham."

"The women's prison?" I asked, surprised. I knew far more about prisons than anyone who'd never been arrested should know. I blamed Ian for that.

I felt bad for Marty's kid. Her dad was dead and her mom was in the system. At least she had her aunt. I hoped that would be enough.

Hazel continued, "Hit-and-run, a few years back. Mallory was high as a kite. She never saw the lady in the crosswalk."

"I'm sorry to hear that," Ruby said. "Any other romantic partners? Anyone more current?"

"Not that it's any of your business, but no. Marty didn't have time to work two jobs, raise a daughter, *and* date. Everything he did, he did for his family. Now, if you'll excuse me, I need to check on Julia, bathe Luca, and let the dog out." She stood and walked across the lawn to collect her son.

Ruby nodded. "Thanks for talking to me," she said. Then she started retracing her steps back to the bus stop. As soon as we were out of earshot, she whispered, "We've gotta find out who killed Marty."

I sighed. "You're like a dog with a bone, aren't you?" I tapped the air near her forehead, careful not to make physical contact. "How am I going to get through to you?" But I already knew the answer. Ruby was easily as stubborn as I was, and she wasn't going to let this go.

If I couldn't convince her to walk away from this investigation, and I couldn't lock her up in our apartment until Marty's murder was solved, that left only one possibility. "I need your help. So, if you're bound and determined to figure out who killed Marty, I'm going to be with you every step of the way."

CHAPTER NINE

RUBY

It was a long bus ride back to our apartment, made even longer by the fact that I had a dozen questions whirling around my head and no way to bounce ideas off Cordelia in public without looking like a loon.

By the time we got home, I was starving. If I hadn't sold the second half of my sandwich, I could have eaten it while waiting for the bus, but at least I had eggplant parm leftovers waiting for me. While I heated them up in the ancient microwave, I asked Cordelia, "What do we know about Marty?"

PEACE

"Peace? He's at peace? You're telling me he's not a ghost?"

no

"Wait, 'no' that's not what you're telling me, or 'no' as in he's not a ghost?"

KNOT spirit

"Okay, not a ghost," I said. I was glad I had *some* way of communicating with Cordelia, but the magnets had their limitations. We only had so many words to choose from, and sometimes she got creative. The result was a little like texting with my grandma, who thought that the eggplant emoji actually stood for an eggplant.

Speaking of which, the microwave beeped and I retrieved my leftover parm. "Hot, hot, hot," I said, trying to not burn myself or drop the plate. I put it down gingerly and shook my hands to cool them off before grabbing a fork from the drawer.

I glanced over at the magnets, which had moved again.

KNOT OVER **do** S

"Not over do s?" I sounded it out. "Not overdue? Not overdose! Are you trying to tell me that Marty didn't die of an overdose?"

y

I knew from experience that when Cordelia used the "y" magnet, she meant "yes," not "why." I wondered if, when she was alive, she'd punctuated her text messages and spelled out every word. I bet she had.

"You're sure about that?"

y

"Huh. When Hazel said that her brother hadn't overdosed, I assumed she was in denial. But if that's true, then Marty's death wasn't an accident. Which means his killer is out there somewhere. According to his sister, Marty doesn't have a significant other and his baby mama is out of the picture, but I don't think we can count her out just yet. She's a suspect, right?"

The magnets didn't move, so I had to assume Cordelia agreed with me.

"Who's next?"

enemy

"Yeah, I mean that's obvious, right? Marty seemed like a nice guy, a family guy. But everyone's got enemies. A rival? Someone didn't like him, enough to kill him. But why? And why in the TrendCelerate bathroom?"

surprise *you* KNOT know

"Wait a second, do you think that Marty had customers at TrendCelerate? No way." I shook my head. "I find that hard to believe. I'm surrounded all day by literal geniuses. They have to know better."

I worked in a relaxed office, true, but it wasn't *that* relaxed. I was the youngest and least experienced employee. Everyone else had worked there for ages. They had advanced degrees and special certifications and everything. Other than myself, everyone made six-figure salaries. "Every single person, even me, has decent health insurance. If anyone needs a prescription, they're an appointment and a co-pay away from getting it legally."

KNOT *ALWAYS*

I stared at those words, trying to make them make sense. "Just to be clear, you're telling me that some of my coworkers at Trend-Celerate buy drugs from Marty?"

y

I scooted the "y" back into the jumble of magnets. Then I cleared my throat and asked, "Cordelia Graves, did *you* buy drugs from Marty?"

y

"You have got to be kidding me," I said. "I know you're not a saint. But a druggie?" There was a heaviness in the apartment that hadn't been there before. "Sorry. I don't mean to sound judgmental."

I had a gazillion follow-up questions. One of the reasons I was absolutely convinced that Cordelia's death wasn't a suicide was because she overdosed on heavy-duty pain meds, but there were no pill bottles in our apartment and she had no prescription for painkillers. If she'd had some other way to get them, like through Marty, then my theory was—no offense to my ghost roommate whose body had been found in the bathtub—dead in the water.

No wonder Cordelia didn't want to talk about it.

I knew from experience that if I pushed too hard, she'd refuse to answer. She might even disappear for a few days. There's nothing like being ghosted by an actual ghost. And since I needed her help to figure out what had happened to Marty, I knew it was time to change the subject.

"What do you think about his sister?" I asked.

truth

Before I could ask her to elaborate, there was a knock at the door. "Who do you think that is?" I mused, half to Cordelia and half to myself. I went to the door and peeped outside before opening it. "Tosh! What a nice surprise!"

"Hope you don't mind me dropping by unannounced," he said, giving me a shy grin. "You're not getting sick of me yet, are you?"

"Of course not!" I said, trying—and failing—to not sound too eager. Even with work, Cordelia, and Marty's death occupying my attention, in the few minutes I'd had to myself, I'd caught myself thinking about Tosh, and that smile of his, often. As great as it was in my imagination when I replayed Sunday night's dinner over in my head, it was ten times better in person than I'd remembered.

He held up a small bakery box. "How do you feel about cheesecake?"

"Love it," I admitted. I opened the door wider. "Come on in. Unless of course, that's an empty box, in which case you're toying with my heart and we can't be friends."

He chuckled as he stepped past me into the apartment. "Would I do that to you?"

"Let's hope not."

He scanned the room. "You alone? I thought I heard you talking to someone right before I knocked."

"Oh, I, um, I was watching TV," I said, hesitatingly. I was a bad liar, and I knew it. But what other option did I have? I couldn't admit that I was having a conversation with my dead roommate. I hoped he didn't ask me to turn it on because I didn't have a cable box, and last time Cordelia got too close to the TV, sparks came out the back.

"I'm not interrupting, am I?"

"Not at all."

Tosh carried the bakery box to the kitchen and set it on the counter next to my uneaten leftovers. As I pulled out forks and dessert plates, he opened the box and served up two large helpings, one for each of us. I took mine over to the loveseat, and he sat down next to me.

For a moment, I just stared at my plate. It was the perfect cheesecake, with a thick crust and a layer of berries sitting on the thick, creamy center. There was a drizzle of white chocolate topping it all off. "This almost looks too good to eat," I said.

"Live a little," he said, taking a bite of his.

I followed suit, and it was every bit as good as it looked, if not better.

"I don't normally indulge. I think cheesecake might be illegal in L.A. But I saw this as I was walking past a bakery, and I couldn't resist."

"Good thing," I said. "This is delicious." When my slice was gone, I only just managed to keep myself from licking my plate.

"Want another piece?" he asked.

"I shouldn't," I said. He'd already seen me devour an embarrassingly large serving.

"Suit yourself." He took both of our plates into the kitchen and rinsed them in the sink.

"You don't have to do that," I told him.

"I don't mind."

"Seriously, don't worry about the plates. I'll take care of them later."

"If you're sure." He repackaged the cheesecake in the bakery box. "Mind if I leave this here? I haven't unpacked my dishes yet and if I take it back to my place, I'll end up eating it in the middle of the night with my bare hands or something."

"What makes you think I wouldn't do the same?" I asked.

He paused with his hand on the refrigerator door and studied the magnets. "You took down the poem I left you?"

"Uh, I . . ." I stammered. When he'd knocked, Cordelia and I were in mid-conversation. I couldn't remember precisely where we'd left off and was almost too embarrassed to look. What if the magnets were all about murder, drugs, and death?

"But this is cute, too." He opened the fridge and put the leftover cheesecake on the top shelf.

I patted the seat next to me, hoping he'd forget about the refrigerator magnets. "Sit down."

He sat, then stretched his arm over the back of the loveseat. "How was work today?"

"It was a day," I said. I doubted he wanted to hear about my boring day answering phones at TrendCelerate. And how could I explain that after work, I'd visited the sister of a dead deliveryman to ask if she knew anything about her brother's murder? "What about you? You settling into your new job?"

"It's fine."

"It was weird, running into you at my office like that on Monday."

"Right?" he said. "Small world."

When the silence stretched out between us, I changed the subject before he could get bored and leave. "How's the unpacking coming?"

He groaned. "It's never-ending. I didn't know I had so much stuff until it came time to move. Now I'm kinda wishing I'd just tossed it all in the dump and started over once I got here."

"That's why I'm glad I don't have much," I told him.

Tosh looked around the apartment. "Could have fooled me." He pointed at the bookshelf that covered the wall separating the living room from my bedroom. "That's like a dozen boxes all by itself."

"Oh, those aren't mine," I said.

"They're not?"

"I mean, I guess technically they're mine, now." I wondered what Cordelia felt about me living in her apartment, sleeping on her bed, reading her books, and eating cheesecake off her dishes. Was she okay with it? Or did she see me as the annoying houseguest who had overstayed her welcome? "My apartment came fully furnished."

"Lucky," he said.

"Yup. Lucky. Real lucky." I meant it, too. It would have cost me a small fortune that I didn't have to furnish this place myself. If it weren't for Cordelia, I'd be lounging in a camp chair right now, using cardboard boxes for a table. Not that I *had* a table. The apartment was too small.

"I wish I'd known that was an option when I rented my place."

"It was a special circumstance," I told him. "The previous tenant left all this behind."

"Awful nice of them."

"I don't think she had much of a choice," I said. I didn't want to talk about Cordelia, not to a man I'd just met, and especially not in front of Cordelia.

He gestured at across the room to where a flatscreen television was mounted to the wall. "Want to watch something?"

I shrugged and gave him a sheepish grin. "I haven't gotten around to turning on the cable." At first, it was strange, not having the TV on all the time. But now that I'd gotten used to it, I didn't miss it at all.

"Have you tried streaming?" he asked.

"The internet's spotty here."

"Really?" Tosh asked. "My internet is fine across the hall, which is great for the days I work from home."

Yeah, well, he didn't have a ghost living with him, messing up all his signals and blowing up all his light bulbs. Not that I would give up having Cordelia as a roommate for anything, much less little conveniences like internet and cable TV. "That's weird," I said.

"Yeah. Weird." He cocked his head and studied me. "I thought you said you were watching TV earlier when I interrupted."

"No, I was." Oof. He'd caught me in a lie, and the only thing to do now was double down. "I was watching TV on my phone." The words came out in a rush.

"Makes sense." He shrugged. "I hate watching TV on such a small screen. I've got a ton of movies. If you ever want to watch something once I'm settled in, feel free to come over any time."

I could imagine it, us curled up next to each other on his couch, watching romantic comedies while we split a cheesecake. There was nothing wrong with that. "I'd love to."

"Consider it an open invitation," he said. He stood and stretched. "I ought to get going. Got a big meeting in the morning and I haven't figured out which box my work shoes are in." He gestured down at his sneakers. "My boss already yelled at me once for showing up to that meeting at your office on Monday in Nikes."

I got up and walked him to the door. "Thanks for the cheesecake."

"Thanks for splitting it with me," he replied. "'Night, Ruby."

As soon as he shut the door, I made a beeline for my refrigerator. I reached for the door, ready for another helping of cheesecake, but froze when I saw the poem that Cordelia had left, the one that Tosh had called cute.

I *DREAM* of **your** *LIPS*

"Cordelia!" I hissed, even though Tosh was back in his own apartment. "Are you trying to embarrass me to death?" It was probably my imagination, but I swore I heard a giggle.

CHAPTER TEN

CORDELIA

On Wednesday, I followed Ruby to work so I could keep an eye on her, not because I had nothing better to do. Or, at least, that's what I would tell Harp if he asked. Everything seemed normal until Adam popped out of his office with a scowl on his face.

He pointed at Ruby. "My office. Now," he ordered.

She followed him.

"Close the door," he said.

It wasn't fair, I thought, as I studied him. I didn't expect him to mope around mourning my death forever, but at the very least, he could have sprouted some gray hairs, or walked around with bags under his eyes, but instead, he looked exactly the same as he had when I was alive, which was good enough to haunt my dreams. If I still *had* dreams, that was.

I was the first to admit I didn't have the best judgment when it came to men, and I had the scars—physical and emotional—to prove it. I'd made mistakes. A *lot* of mistakes. But Adam wasn't one of them. Sure, he was married to someone else, but no one was perfect.

Ruby closed the door.

"Have a seat."

She sat. She looked uncomfortable. I didn't blame her. I didn't know what was going on, either.

Instead of settling into his high-backed ergonomic executive chair, he perched on the edge of his desk and loomed over her. He slowly, deliberately, took his glasses off and carefully cleaned them. It was a move I recognized as one he used when he was collecting his thoughts.

As usual, Adam was in that in-between mix of business casual and professional. He wore a long-sleeve white shirt, but the sleeves were rolled halfway up his forearms. He had on a blue suit vest a few shades darker than his slacks, but wore no jacket or tie. He looked good enough to eat.

He put his glassed back on, stared down my roomie, and asked, "How did you know Cordelia Graves?"

She gaped at him.

"What's going on?" I asked, inching closer to him. He'd missed a smudge on his glasses. "Why are you asking her about me?"

I suspected Ruby was starting to guess that there had been more going on between me and Adam than a strictly professional relationship, but she looked up to me and I wasn't going to blow that by letting her in on all my dirty little secrets. And, just as equally, I didn't want Ruby talking about me to Adam and giving anything away.

"I didn't," Ruby finally replied.

"You're lying." He leaned in closer. I felt an irrational flash of jealousy. It wasn't fair, that she could get so close to him when I could not. "Try again."

"I swear, I never met her."

Ruby was telling the truth. Kinda. Technically, we'd never met. By the time she moved to Boston, I was already dead.

"I'm going to ask you one more time, and before you answer, let me remind you that I don't employ people who lie to me. How did you know Cordelia?"

God, I loved that man. Even now, with him threatening to fire Ruby for lying to him—which I guess, technically, she had—I wanted to jump Adam and kiss him until I forgot my own name. Hell, I wanted to make *him* forget *his* own name.

"What makes you think I knew her?" Ruby asked.

I heard a tremble in her voice. We'd been so careful to keep the secret that I was here, a ghost of my former self—literally. I wondered how we had tripped up.

"A few times I swear I've heard you say her name. I thought I was imagining things." He picked up a folder off his desk. "Then I came across this."

He flipped open the file. Inside was a list of employees and their contact information. He ran his finger down the list, tapping her name when he came to it. "You put down Cordelia's address as yours. Care to explain?"

I braced myself for what was coming. Ruby couldn't afford to tell anyone that I was haunting her. No one would believe her. They'd medicate her, or lock her away.

She hesitated before saying, "It's a long story."

"Then you better start talking," he growled.

His temper was so close to the surface. I'd never seen this side of him before. I was afraid he would boil over, and I had no idea what he was capable of if that happened. I knew happy Adam. Successful Adam. Drunk Adam. Horny Adam. Giddy Adam. Frustrated Adam. But I'd never met Angry Adam before. I hated to admit that I almost liked seeing him like this, but that didn't give him an excuse to frighten my roomie.

"That's enough, you big bully," I said. "Can't you see you're scaring her?"

I slammed my hands down on his desk, hoping to somehow get his attention and redirect it away from Ruby. He didn't notice the desk shaking until the framed photo fell over.

That damn photo. Adam standing behind Karin with his arms wrapped around her waist. Him, smiling. Her, laughing. His wife, the politician, who always looked so put together when she appeared in public, was relaxed for once. The green, leafy background was artfully out of focus. It could have been taken anywhere. A park. A family picnic. An artist's studio. How many times had I fantasized about throwing it across the room? Incinerating it? Tossing it out the window?

It was one thing to know that the man I loved, the man I'd been in an intimate relationship with for years, was married to another woman. It was quite another to have to look at that photo every time I was at Adam's desk. It was about time I did something about it.

He came around the desk and swept the picture, with its newly cracked glass, into the drawer. I presumed he'd replace the frame later, when he wasn't busy terrorizing my roommate. Wouldn't he be surprised when he came back to it and found the photo torn to shreds? I'd sprinkle the pieces around his bedroom like rose petals. Good luck explaining *that* to Karin, buddy.

"It all started a few months ago when I moved to Boston and was looking for an apartment."

Adam made the "hurry it along" motion with his hands. "Just answer the question. I don't need your life story."

Ruby nodded in that quick, jerky way she did when she was

nervous. "It will all make sense in a minute. I ended up renting a fully furnished apartment on the cheap. The previous tenant had left everything behind and the super cut me a break on the rent if I'd clean it out. Turns out, the former tenant was Cordelia Graves."

Adam's eyes narrowed and he leaned forward. "Tell me more."

Ruby scooted her chair away from him ever so slightly. "You know how sometimes you're thinking about Doritos, *really* craving them, and the next thing you know, you're bombarded with Doritos ads?"

Adam nodded stiffly. I wanted to know where she was going with this. And also, now I really wanted a bag of Doritos. The ranch kind. I could almost taste them. It wasn't fair. I could pick up a chip but I'd never get that flavor dust on my fingers again. I'd never eat them again. I'd never have one break off and stab me in the gums again. In that moment, I missed Doritos *almost* as much as I missed Adam.

"Whatever it is in the algorithm that knows when I'm craving Doritos started sending me help wanted ads from TrendCelerate. This sounds far-fetched, but I think the algorithm confused me with the previous tenant because we shared an address. I didn't know she used to work here when I applied for this job."

Adam bit back a sardonic laugh. "Digital karma."

"Huh?" I asked.

"Huh?" Ruby asked.

"You know what we do here."

Now it was Ruby's turn to look confused. She'd grown up in a world where the internet just worked, without ever questioning how, or why. As a result, she only had a tenuous grasp of the industry-shaping work being done here. "I mean . . . sorta?"

"You have no idea, do you?" Adam shook his head. He leaned

back in his chair, finally relaxing. He'd bought Ruby's explanation, and now he had a chance to talk about one of his favorite subjects in the world—his tech. Me personally? I was just happy listening to him talk about anything.

"We develop software that collects tiny bits of information called metadata from anything connected to the internet and then use that data to predict future actions."

"You're spying on me? On everyone?"

"No, no. It's not spying. It's data collection and aggregation. All perfectly aboveboard. And we don't actually do any collection. We just write the software that makes it possible. Imagine you're on Instagram and you see an ad, but instead of scrolling past it, you pause. Our software flags that and starts sending you similar ads, but not just on Instagram. Now you're getting the ads on Spotify. Hulu. Soon, you're seeing them on digital signs."

"Creepy."

"Not creepy. Effective. What videos you play, what people you follow, and what social platforms you prefer, hell, even what brand of toothpaste you use can be used to predict what kind of car you'll buy, what you'll order online, and even who you'll vote for."

"Yeah, that feels like spying," Ruby said.

"All that matters is that it works. Our software, or something similar, noticed that you were searching for a job from a location associated with a TrendCelerate employee, and started serving up ads it thought would interest you. And it worked."

I clapped my hands in surprise. "Ruby, you sly dog. I had no idea you could lie that convincingly." But the more I thought about it, the more I realized she *wasn't* lying. She had no idea who I was when she moved into my apartment. And she *did* get a help wanted ad from TrendCelerate before I accidentally blew up the computer she was using at the time.

Yes, I had pushed her to apply here, not because of some nefarious agenda of my own, but because she needed a job and this place didn't completely suck. But by the time I got the idea to steer her in this direction, she'd already seen at least one banner advertising an opening at TrendCelerate. It made me question if her getting a job here really was my idea, or if it had been the algorithm all along.

And really, what was creepier? A faceless algorithm following Ruby around, collecting tons of information and then parsing it through a giant supercomputer to figure out how best to influence her decisions, or a pushy ghost who wanted an excuse to spend time with her ex?

"Just to be clear, you're not some kind of corporate spy, planted here to gather intel on TrendCelerate?" Adam asked.

"Huh?" Ruby asked, the blood draining from her face.

"Didn't think so," he said. "Had to ask. You understand."

"Had to ask?" I repeated. "You're kidding, right?"

I knew Adam. I knew how he thought. This wasn't the first time I'd seen him go down a paranoid rabbit hole, but I'd never heard him accuse someone of corporate espionage before. I was glad he dropped it once he was convinced that there was nothing nefarious going on, but I was disappointed he'd gone there in the first place.

He waved his hand at his door. "Go back to work."

Ruby returned to her desk. As I followed her, I thought about my conversation with Harp. He had a point. Was I pathetic for spending my days at work when I could be doing literally anything else?

Too bad I didn't have anything else to do. I made myself at home in Jordie's cubicle, letting his chair slowly swing back and forth when no one was looking. It was the perfect seat for me, almost equidistant between Ruby's reception desk and the co-owners' offices. And it wasn't like Jordie was using it. In all the time I'd worked here, I could count on two hands how many times I'd seen him in the office, and that included the big meeting two days ago.

That meeting was still bothering me. I wish I'd poked my head in to see what the big deal was all about. I might have even been able to do something to prevent Marty's death.

I was a ghost, but I wasn't helpless. I could still protect the people I cared about. Which was the real reason I was cooling my heels at my old office instead of following Harp on his quest to find a spring break destination.

The door to Adam's office opened, and he stepped out. He looked calm and composed, without a hint of his earlier temper. I'd tried to get him to go to a psychic with me, just for fun. I'd booked us on a haunted houses tour one Halloween. Both times, he refused because, in his—may I point out, incorrect—opinion, it was nonsense. He even quoted Arthur C. Clarke to me, about technology being indistinguishable from magic to anyone who didn't understand it. Ruby's explanation made sense to him in a way that the truth never would have, because while he didn't believe in ghosts, he had faith in technology.

Adam paused at the front desk and told Ruby, "I've got things to attend to. I'll be on my cell if anyone needs me."

He was wearing a light jacket. His laptop bag was slung over one shoulder. If he was taking his laptop with him, he didn't intend on coming back today, which wasn't like him. Unlike the other two co-owners and staff, including Jordie, whose cubicle I was currently squatting in, Adam was in the office all day most days. Back when I worked here, we usually had the place to ourselves for hours every day, and we took full advantage of that.

"Where are you going in the middle of the morning, Adam?" I asked, getting up.

Ruby must have seen Jordie's chair move when I stood, because her head swiveled toward it.

Adam looked over his shoulder, trying to see what caught her attention. "You okay?"

"Yup, fine and dandy," Ruby said, laughing nervously. I would have thought someone who lived with a ghost would be less jumpy by now. It was time for my roomie to cut back on the caffeine. "Enjoy the rest of your day. Want me to call a car?"

Rich people like Adam didn't Uber. They had a service. Which was kinda like Uber, but without the sketchy getting-in-a-total-stranger's-Toyota-Corolla factor. Adam had once confided in me that he'd never ridden a city bus in his life. "Nah, it's a nice day. I'll walk."

I regarded Ruby, then Adam. Should I follow him or stay and keep an eye on her? Even alone in the office, Ruby was safe here without me.

My mind made up, I said, "What are you up to, Adam?" I followed him out of the office and down the stairs.

It must have been another warm day, because he shed his jacket as soon as he hit the sidewalk. Despite the mild weather, there were few people out this time of the morning, and I was able to walk next to him, with my hands glued to my sides so we wouldn't accidentally touch. Ironically, this was *more* affectionate than we normally were. He'd been paranoid about getting caught in public with me, and would have never walked this close to me on a city sidewalk back when I was still alive.

After a long walk, we reached his building. We parted ways in the lobby. He lived on the twenty-sixth floor. There was no way he was taking the stairs, and I couldn't take the elevator, not without shorting it out. So he took the elevator. I took the long route.

Under Harp's tutelage, I'd finally mastered the art of floating up through the floors. It was simple once I let go of my antiquated sense of gravity and inertia and all the other science-y terms that I'd never quite mastered in high school and was still stymied by. In my limited experience, much of being a ghost was based on what I believed. If I believed I could pick up a rose, I could. If I believed I could smell it, I could. If I believed my hand would pass right through it, it would. Or, as Harp so eloquently put it, matter didn't matter anymore. Not to us.

Not so long ago, I'd had to concentrate hard to do anything as challenging as levitating, but now that I knew it could be done, it was easier than opening a jar of pickles had been back when I was alive. I could have floated up through the center of the building, but I risked passing through too many electronics that way. Even in bougie high-rises like this one, people still strung overloaded extension cords in inconvenient places, and if I came into contact with them, it was just asking for trouble.

Plus, there was that one time that I was casually passing through a building and I'd literally bumped into a woman with a pacemaker. She'd survived our encounter—barely—but it was something I didn't care to repeat. To avoid such possibilities, I took the much less scenic route up the stairwell, bypassing the stairs themselves and passing straight up through each of the levels until I reached Adam's floor.

Because I'd taken the stairs, more or less, I was at the end of a long hall instead of at the elevator doors that opened up close to his condo. He was already inside.

As I drifted toward his unit, I remembered the first time he'd brought me here. We'd been dating—if I could call it that—for a few months. With his wife out of town on an extended fundraising tour, he had the place to himself for a few days. Which meant no more sneaking around. No more tawdry hotels. No more quickies in his office. Just the two of us for an entire weekend alone.

His bougie condo intimidated me at first. His furniture was brand new. No second- and third-hand thrift-store couches for the Rees family. His pristine dishes and glassware matched. He confided in me that it was because if a plate got so much as a scratch on it, Karin would scrap it all and buy a new set of dishes. And here I was, eating off my chipped plates and drinking coffee out of mugs that were missing their handles, like a Neanderthal.

It was odd, dating a man whose sheets cost more than my first car. As I got used to it, I started seeing my apartment in a new light. My possessions weren't well-loved. They were dingy. Old. Cheap. Things I'd worked hard for lost their shine. For less than he spent on a single coffee table, I could refurnish my entire home and still have money left over.

I wanted to resent him, and all of the one-percenters. How could some people have everything when so many others had nothing? Growing up on the have-not side of the spectrum, it didn't feel fair. Even after I found out that the obscene wealth was technically his wife's, it still felt icky. Adam liked to play the role of an average man, but he was anything but.

He was smart. Attractive. Respected. A rock star in his field. An absolute animal between the sheets. And even if his money actually belonged to Karin, he was richer than some countries. If I didn't love him so goddamn much, I'd hate him.

I braced myself for going back into that condo with the gazillion–thread count sheets and the new-couch smell that never faded since Karin bought new living room furniture every few years when the trends changed. I knew their wedding portrait, blown up to obscene, larger-than-life proportions, hung over their gas fireplace. I knew that her perfume scented the air. I even steadied myself for the slim possibility that Karin herself was home, but that was unlikely in the middle of a workday.

Then the door opened and Adam stepped into the hallway. His laptop bag was gone, replaced by an overnight bag hanging over his shoulder. He had a briefcase in one hand and a garment bag in the other. He looked back over his shoulder, laughing at something someone inside had said.

Karin appeared beside him. I bit the inside of my cheek. I was dead, but I still had feelings. Adam bent over and kissed her. This was no dry, perfunctory kiss. It looked like something out of a romantic movie. I wanted to throw up.

Even in heels, Karin was a foot shorter than him, and so thin a good breeze could knock her over. She was not at all his type. Adam liked women with a little more substance. Women he could put his arms around and squeeze without worrying about breaking them. Women like me.

She took the briefcase first, then draped the garment bag over it. Adam handed her the overnight bag. He gave her that slow grin, the one I thought was just for me, and told her he loved her. He patted her on the rear, and she giggled. He kissed her again, and whispered something in her ear.

With my enhanced hearing, I should have been able to hear what he said, even as far away as I was standing. But I didn't *want* to hear, so it came out as white noise. Too bad I couldn't help but overhear her respond in a normal voice, "Silly, I'll miss my flight."

"What's the big deal? Catch the next one."

"Screw it," she said, dropping her bags. She put her arms around Adam's neck. He dragged her back into the condo, leaving the bags in the middle of the hall.

I felt like I was going to be sick. Adam swore time and time again that his marriage was merely one of convenience. That he was a pretty puppet playing doting husband to prop up her political ambition. That he would divorce her in a heartbeat and marry me instead if it weren't for an ironclad prenup and her buckets and buckets of money. But pretty puppets did not kiss their wives the way Adam kissed Karin.

I wasn't sure what upset me more, that Adam was a bad husband or that he was a good one. Although, to be fair, I knew the answer to that. Adam was a horrible husband. A horrible, cheating, spineless, unfaithful worm of a husband. And he was a horrible, cheating, spineless, unfaithful worm of a boyfriend. So why did I miss him so badly?

Not able to stand the thought of them together any longer, I turned and fled.

CHAPTER ELEVEN
CORDELIA

I got as far as the TrendCelerate office before I realized where I was headed. Here I was, dead, and when things got rough, the first place I headed was to work. Harp was right. I was pathetic. Then again, as I floated up through the stairwell, I realized that I hadn't been thinking about my old job at all. I was thinking about Ruby.

Once I reached the second floor, I noticed that the door to the supposed-to-be-empty office next to TrendCelerate was open just a crack. Unlike our frosted glass front door, this one was solid wood. I passed through it.

At first glance, it appeared that nothing had changed. Still the same army surplus cot. Still the same jumble of office furniture shoved into the corner. Still the same hot plate. But there was a crumpled-up sandwich wrapper next to the hot plate that hadn't been there before, and several of the jugs of water had been moved.

Last time I was here was the day that Marty died. I was having a hard time keeping track of time. Even now, the creaky old cot looked inviting and if I could sleep, I'd be tempted to curl up and take a nap. Unfortunately, I had no control over when—or if—I'd wake up again, and I didn't want to leave Ruby alone for too long.

Whoever was living here was nowhere in sight. If they were squatting, they wouldn't want to be caught coming and going by anyone. The tenants routinely held the downstairs door for someone dressed in business attire or a delivery person, but they wouldn't let a person who didn't look like they belonged follow them into the building. Did they have a key? If so, how had they gotten one?

A noise caught my attention. The door to the office creaked open. A man slipped inside before easing the door closed behind him. He was a medium-height, medium-build sixty-something white man with shaggy brown hair and eyes hidden behind cheap sunglasses.

"Who *are* you?" I asked.

He, of course, did not answer.

Careful to not make enough noise to alert anyone in one of the adjoining offices of his presence, he extricated one of the abandoned chairs from the jumble of furniture leftover from when the last tenant moved out and set it up near the window. He needn't have bothered. Between the soundproofing and the majority of employees choosing to telework, no one would have heard him.

Offices were standing empty more and more lately, as employers found that they could save money on real estate by going to a purely remote work model. It worked for employees, too, who no longer had to commute or waste money on dry cleaning and buying lunches out every day. Instead of crowding into a city, they could literally work from anywhere.

What would happen to spaces like this as the world continued to move away from traditional office settings? Would the business district in cities like Boston become obsolete? What about delis like

Beantown? Would it go out of business when downtown became a ghost town? Sure, they could convert buildings like this into apartments, but who wanted to live in a cramped apartment in the city center with ridiculously high rents when they could live in a cabin by a lake or a sprawling house in the suburbs?

One good thing about this office, and all the offices in this building, was that it was practically soundproof. The last time the building had an overhaul, it was reconfigured to host retail space on the first floor, offices on the second, and apartments on the third. No one wanted to live above a loud office, and an office didn't want to set up shop above a noisy storefront, so the renovations added in industrial sound barriers. As long as the squatter didn't blast death metal at top volume, no one—except me—would ever know he was here.

I wondered how long the squatter had been living down the hall from TrendCelerate. Days? Months? Years?

He dragged a lamp out of the pile of forgotten office furniture and plugged it into the wall next to his chair. It was still midday outside, but instead of risking opening the window shade, he turned on the light. Its warm glow illuminated his corner of the abandoned office.

He was lucky that the office still had electricity. It hadn't been occupied in a while. How long would it take for the building owners to realize that someone was using their power, their space, and their running water for free? If he was careful, it would barely make a blip on the bill. A lamp here. A hot plate there. The bathroom down the hall wasn't metered. The door was locked and keys were only issued to companies that had offices on this floor, but locks didn't slow some people down. My brother, Ian, was living proof of this.

He must have done laundry earlier, in the break room sink or in the shared bathroom down the hall, because he'd draped wet clothes over some of the abandoned office furniture to dry. They dripped on the bland, industrial carpet. If he stayed here too much longer, the building owners would have a serious mold problem on their hands.

Then all thought of creeping black mold and dripping clothes flew out the window as the man pulled a nondescript black canvas messenger bag out from under his pile of belongings. I recognized the bag.

"That's Marty's bag," I said, pointing at it. "How did you get Marty's bag?"

I'd never seen Marty without his bag. It wasn't the insulated tote he carried his Beantown Deli deliveries in. He carried his *other* deliveries, the less-than-legal ones, in that black canvas satchel. Apparently, the squatter knew it, too.

He opened the flap, unzipped it, and rooted around. Not finding what he was looking for, he upended the bag on the carpet. Pill bottles spilled onto the floor. He squinted at the labels on the prescription bottles before finding what he was looking for.

"Bingo," he said to himself.

His hands trembled as he fumbled with the child safety lid. He shook a few pills out into his palm. They were white and oblong, slightly wider in the center than they were on the edges. I didn't need to see the imprint on them to recognize them as sleeping pills—the good kind.

I'd never been much for sleeping pills. I preferred drinking myself into a coma every night. It was barely a step up from repeatedly hitting myself in the head with a hammer, but it worked. More or less.

I only recognized the pills because Adam enjoyed a little chemical assistance on occasion. Ambien to sleep. Xanax and Valium to chill. Viagra when we had a whole weekend to ourselves and we wanted to spend it in bed. Adderall when he had to get up and meet with important investors Monday morning after staying up all weekend fooling around.

He had access to oodles of money and excellent health insurance. He could have easily gotten prescriptions from legitimate doctors, even if he had to exaggerate his need for them, but Karin would never have allowed that. How would it make her look if a story leaked that her husband was popping ED pills or taking mood stabilizers? Prescriptions were supposed to be private, and mental healthcare was nothing to be ashamed about, but all's fair in politics.

Adam, like everyone else at TrendCelerate, got his supply from Marty. He used to be too embarrassed to use his services, and sent me to do his dirty work instead. It was only a short step from that to becoming the go-between for the whole office. Marty would drop off pills with me at the same time as he delivered sandwiches, and my coworkers would find excuses to stop by my desk throughout the day to pick up their orders.

Had Adam recruited someone else to get his drugs from Marty after I died? Had he stopped using them? Or did he get over his hang-ups and go directly to the source? Had he told Karin to stop being so worried about what people thought of her and finally got a legit prescription?

The squatter now was in possession of his own private pharmacy. But when, and how, had he come by Marty's bag? Marty never let that bag out of his sight. It was filled with illicit drugs worth who knows how much money. That bag was his life.

Did the squatter take the bag before Marty died? After? He was in possession of a small fortune of drugs that Marty never would have given him without a fight. The squatter was scrawny, but if he felt threatened, he might have been able to hold down Marty long enough to shove enough pills down his throat to kill him.

"You son of a bitch. Where'd you get this?" I asked. He didn't answer, because of course he didn't hear me. I'd just have to find the information another way.

As soon as he turned back toward the window, I snatched up the bag. Making the bag disappear while I was holding it took effort, but it was worth it when I didn't want someone to witness something like a messenger bag floating through the air on its own. I concentrated on the bag and *poof* it vanished, at least from the squatter's point of view. I could still see its ethereal outline.

Now came the hard part. I'd just recently figured out how to walk through a wall while carrying a solid object. "You can do this, Cordelia," I said. Hyping myself up was more than building my confidence. It reminded me that if I could believe it, I could do it.

I believed I could pick up tangible items, even though I was no longer tangible myself. I believed I could make objects invisible when I was holding them. I believed I could walk through walls. And lastly, I believed I could carry something solid with me through that wall.

"I've got this," I muttered, and stepped through the wall separating the squatter's office from TrendCelerate.

I heard familiar voices talking and realized that they were heading in my direction. I couldn't concentrate on staying out of their way and keeping the bag transparent at the same time, so I lunged toward Ruby's seat. I dropped the bag. It materialized and hit the ground with a soft thud. Fortunately, no one noticed its sudden appearance, not even Ruby, who was laughing at something Marc had said as they headed for the door together.

"Ruby! Wait!" I called out, but she was oblivious. "Fine. I'll come with you."

I reached for Marty's bag again, but my hand passed right through it.

"Oh no. Not now," I said, trying again, and failing. I'd overspent myself tracking Adam around the city. I'd let myself get too emotional when he'd rendezvoused with his wife. And then, the nail in the coffin, I'd wasted what little energy I had left retrieving the messenger bag. I tried one last time, but instead of grabbing the bag's strap, I tumbled into darkness.

CHAPTER TWELVE
RUBY

After Adam left the office, I finished the book I had in my desk. I spent the rest of the afternoon aimlessly surfing the internet until it was time to lock up and go home. I had no idea where Cordelia was. I hadn't seen any sign of her since that guy Jordie's chair had done a one-eighty by itself. Had she followed Adam on whatever errand he'd gone on? All I knew was that she wasn't around.

At the end of the day, I followed Marc out of the office. During the bus ride home, I kept all my senses peeled for signs of Cordelia, but there was nothing. It wasn't until I got home that I got that familiar feeling that someone was in the room with me.

"I'm home," I called out. Cordelia could see and hear me, but I couldn't see or hear her. It wasn't fair, almost as unfair as spending the whole day at work doing nothing while there was still a piece of cheesecake calling my name at home. I went straight for the fridge and opened it, but the cheesecake was gone. "What? Who finished off my cheesecake?" I asked, not expecting anyone to answer.

"I did," a man's disembodied voice said.

I screamed and twisted around, colliding with the open refrigerator door.

"Whoa," the man said. I could barely make out a shape on my loveseat. He reached over and clicked on the reading lamp next to him. For a split second, I thought he was a ghost, but I could see him. I could hear him. And he cast a shadow.

"Who are you?" he asked.

"Who am I? Who are *you*?" I asked, my voice trembling as I kept the open refrigerator door between us. It was dark in my apartment. The curtains were closed and the light bulb was out in the kitchen, as it nearly always was. That was Cordelia's fault. The super had stopped responding to my requests to replace the bulb and flat out refused to call an electrician. The bulbs in the lamps blew out often, too, but they were within reach so I could easily replace them. The kitchen one was too far over my head.

"Dude, relax," he said.

"Relax? You want *me* to relax?" I shouted back. "Get the hell out of my apartment!"

In a perfect world, I would have done something cool. Grabbed a knife out of the block and chased him out of my apartment. Or whipped out a baseball bat. But I didn't have a baseball bat and I couldn't reach the knife block, so I did the next best thing. I grabbed the yellow mustard out of the refrigerator door and hurled it at him.

"Ow!" he exclaimed as it smacked him on the side of the head. He scrambled off the loveseat, his back to the bookshelf.

I grabbed a bottle of salad dressing and threw it at him. He ducked. The bottle of dressing sailed over his head and bounced off the wall behind him.

"I said get out!" I yelled. I should have called the cops before resorting to throwing condiments at the intruder, but the cops didn't have the best response time in this neighborhood, if they bothered to show up at all.

He held up his hands in surrender. "Before you throw anything else, you should know I'm allergic to ketchup."

I froze, fumbling around the door for anything else to throw. "You are?" I knew there were more important things I should be worrying about right now. Who was this man? How did he get in my apartment? How could I get him to leave? But I'd never heard of anyone being allergic to ketchup before and that made me pause.

"Not really." He kept his hands up. "That was a lie. It's just that ketchup is terribly messy and I really don't want to get stuck on KP."

"KP?"

"Cleanup duty," he clarified.

"Who cares?" I yelled, coming back to my senses. "Get out of my apartment!"

"Hey, I'm sorry if I scared you." He took a step closer.

Condiments obviously weren't working, so I yanked open the silverware drawer, grabbed a handful of forks, and hurled them in his direction. The silverware clattered noisily to the floor.

"Okay! I'm going! I'm going!"

He rounded the loveseat. For a split second, I was sure he was going to take a run at me, but instead, he headed toward the door. "Look, this was just a big misunderstanding. I didn't know Cordy had a roommate. If she'd return my calls once in a while instead of ghosting me, I might know what was going on in her life."

"What?" I paused, my hand still fumbling in the silverware drawer, hoping to find something more dangerous than a butter knife. Had he said "Cordy?" Did he mean Cordelia? "Who?"

"You know, Cordelia Graves? She lives here? She gave me the key."

"She doesn't live here," I said, dumbfounded. I didn't know what was going on. This man claimed he knew Cordelia well enough to have a key to my apartment, but he didn't know that she died last December? "Not anymore."

"Let me guess. She moved in with one of her loser boyfriends." He paused near the door and looked around. "Her furniture's still here. You're what, a sublet? One of those Airbnbers? You know what, just do me a favor and text her. She's been dodging my calls."

"She's not dodging you," I said. Now that my pulse was returning to normal, I could *almost* think straight again. There was still a strange man in my apartment, but if he'd wanted to hurt me, he would have done so long before I threw salad dressing at him.

"Yeah, well, could have fooled me. I haven't heard from her in ages."

"Uh, you might want to sit," I told him.

He gave me a boyish grin. "A second ago, you're screaming at me to get out, and now you want me to make myself at home?"

"You made yourself at home when you let yourself into my apartment and finished off my cheesecake," I snapped. Then I reminded myself that the cheesecake was the least of my concerns. "Never mind. I don't know how to break it to you, but the reason Cordelia's not answering her phone is because she passed away."

"She . . . what?"

"She died," I said, as gently as possible. "A few months ago. Around Christmas."

I watched as his face went from annoyed to confused, and then melted into absolute grief as he slid down the wall. He hugged his knees to his chest as he dissolved into tears, his breath heaving.

He was blocking the door, the exit to my apartment, but he didn't seem like a threat anymore. I nudged the refrigerator closed, leaving the kitchen in semidarkness. There was a floor lamp between me and the loveseat. I clicked it on and approached the stranger cautiously.

"I'm sorry to be the one to tell you. I assumed everyone knew by now."

He hiccupped. "What happened?" he asked, rubbing his face with his hands.

That was the real question, wasn't it? I had no idea who this man was or why he had a key, but they couldn't have been that close if he didn't even know she was dead. He didn't need to know that Cordelia had, in all likelihood, been murdered. He didn't need to know that while she *was* dead, she was still hanging around as a ghost. I decided to stick to the official story.

"She committed suicide."

"Shit," he said. He rocked forward. "This is all my fault."

"I'm sorry for your loss," I said, not knowing what else to say. I crouched down on the floor next to him.

He gathered himself back into a sitting position. When he turned to me, I got my first clear look at him. He was an extremely pale white man with short, auburn hair. He was all spindly arms and sharp angles. Despite the black tattoos peeking out from underneath the sleeves of his T-shirt that should have made him look tough, he looked very young and very lost.

"I'm really sorry," I said, patting his back. "You and Cordelia must have been very close."

He looked up at me. His baby-blue eyes were filled with tears. "You could say that. I'm Ian." At my blank expression, he clarified. "Ian Graves? Cordelia's my big sister."

CHAPTER THIRTEEN
CORDELIA

Dad was on a bender.

We were living in a tiny one-bedroom apartment. Ian was still in elementary school, so fourth or fifth grade. He'd been summoned to the principal's office for being a dumb nine-year-old with too much energy and too little attention. What had it been that time? Fighting, probably. It was almost always for fighting.

Ian wasn't a bad kid. He just wasn't capable of taking shit from anyone. Never had been. Other kids picked on him for being skinny for his age. I blamed that on a steady diet of boxed generic mac and cheese or cheap frozen fish sticks for dinner—when we were lucky. For never having the right answer when the teacher called on him. For being poor. They'd tease him, and the next thing they knew they had a broken nose and Ian was in trouble. Again.

"Yes sir, I understand," I said dutifully, standing in front of a principal whose name I couldn't remember. We moved too often to keep track of them.

I was dressed in a pair of too-short shorts and a loose T-shirt with my current school mascot on it. When the school came to find me because Dad wasn't picking up the phone, I'd been at volleyball practice. I didn't particularly like volleyball, but I was tall and made a good blocker. Every time we transferred to a new school I went out for the team, knowing it was the quickest way to make friends.

"This is the second time this week," the principal said, glaring at me. He ignored my baby brother, who sat on a bench on the other side of the open door, looking tiny and innocent. Looking innocent was his favorite trick, and he was very, very good at it.

I nodded gravely. "Dad'll speak to him."

"And where exactly is your father?"

I didn't know. We hadn't seen him for a few days, which wasn't out of the ordinary. Could be he met a girl at a bar and he was shacking up with her until her husband came home. He was just as likely in an alley, in a flophouse in a drunken stupor, or couch surfing with his buddies. Or, he was dead in a ditch somewhere.

"He sends his apologies, but he's working a double." That was a lie. I'd gotten good at lying. Dad hadn't worked in months. But the principal didn't know that. "Otherwise, he'd be here, of course." Adding "of course" was overkill, but the principal didn't notice.

He puffed up his chest. "I can't release Ian to you. You're what, thirteen? Fourteen?"

"Seventeen." Another lie, but men took me more seriously when I said I was seventeen. I'd been seventeen for years. I wasn't sure what that said about men that they couldn't tell the difference. Then again, I'd often been told that I was old for my age, mostly by men who didn't care that I was only fourteen.

"Well then," he chewed on his lip, considering his options.

I knew those options well. He could wait with us until Dad miraculously materialized, which he knew could be hours. He could call the Department of Children and Families, but that meant paperwork and more waiting. Or, he could take the path of least resistance.

"Our neighbor brought me," I lied again, jerking a thumb at the door as if he could see an imaginary kindly neighbor in an imaginary station wagon idling patiently at the curb outside. In my fantasy, she drove a Subaru and rescued greyhounds, and sometimes she gave me hand-me-downs or took me to the mall to teach me how to put on makeup. "She didn't come inside because she couldn't leave her dogs in the car, but she'll drive us home."

It was the final nudge that he needed. There were hundreds of kids in the school. No need to waste his afternoon on a little brat like Ian. He'd seen his transcript and knew we'd transfer out of his district by the end of the school year or the beginning of the next, tops. Then we'd be someone else's problem. Not his.

"Just see to it that it doesn't happen again. And I'll want to speak to your father at the next PTA meeting."

I nodded, solemnly. Dad couldn't even *spell* PTA. He'd never been to a parent-teacher night in my life. I'd been signing my own report cards since kindergarten. Even when Dad was home, I signed Ian's report cards and permission slips. I showed up when he got in trouble or was sent to the nurse's office with a black eye. "He told me he's looking forward to it."

The principal had to have known I was lying, about everything. About Ian not getting in trouble again. About my age. About my dad ever stepping foot in the school. About the imaginary neighbor waiting in her imaginary Subaru to take us home. But it was easier to accept the lie than to pick up the phone and call DCF, something I counted on. The laziness of men like him had saved my ass more than once.

Sometimes I lay awake in my bed, or my cot, or the back seat of whatever car we were living out of temporarily, and wondered what it would be like if the principals of the world ever did call DCF. Would we get three hot meals a day? Shoes without holes in them? I could finally get braces. But they'd separate me from Ian and, as much as that kid was a serious pain in my ass, he was my baby brother. He was my responsibility.

As I left the principal's office, Ian saw me coming and flipped me the bird.

"You're welcome," I said, returning the gesture. That's what passed as affection with us. It was our little inside joke. Some people, so-called normal people with their summer vacations to Disney and piles of presents under the tree at Christmas, might think it was rude or even weird that I'd give my nine-year-old brother the finger as a sign of endearment. Those people could go suck an egg.

"Come on, Booger. Let's get out of here,"

He shuffled behind me. I missed the days when he used to hold my hand.

We got outside. It was sunny, but about twenty degrees too cold to be walking around in my volleyball uniform. I wrapped my arms around myself to keep warm. "How many times do I have to tell you? Don't draw attention to yourself," I said.

"But, Cordy, Johnny called us trash."

"We *are* trash," I told him. I sighed. "Sometimes I think you *want* to get in trouble."

To absolutely no one's surprise, Ian didn't miraculously wake up one morning and decide to walk the straight and narrow. I'd hit the nail on the head that day, walking him home from yet another visit to the principal's office. He enjoyed being in trouble. He certainly excelled at it.

I snapped back into the present. One drawback to being dead was the annoying highlight reel of my greatest failures that ran through my head whenever I let myself drift off. It was like sitting through so many trailers that you forget what movie you'd gone to see. I didn't sleep, and I didn't dream, but at the most inconvenient times, I found myself reliving memories that I'd rather forget.

Ian had a starring role in enough of my memories that I was used to seeing him in my flashbacks. What I hadn't expected, when I popped back to the present, was to see him in my apartment, in the flesh.

"What the actual hell?" I asked.

Ian was sitting on the carpet just inside the door. His eyes were red from crying. His hair was shorter than it had been the last time I'd seen him, and he had a few new janky tattoos sticking out of the sleeves of a ratty shirt that was two sizes too big for him, but there was no mistaking him.

"Ruby, what's my brother doing here?" I asked, looking over at my roommate. She crouched in front of him, looking almost as lost as Ian was. She handed him a cup of coffee. That was so like Ruby. A stranger could barge into her apartment, and she'd comfort him and ask if she could get him something to drink. "And why'd you let him inside?"

Ruby wasn't fragile, but she was just so damn young and naïve. Add in her petite frame and her big eyes, and it triggered a long-buried maternal instinct in me that had previously been reserved for my baby brother and my beloved houseplants. Not that my little brother wasn't beloved. He was just a screwup. And, my houseplants never disappointed me or wrote bad checks out of my bank account.

She got up and moved closer to the kitchen. "He didn't know," she whispered so softly only I could hear. She was glancing around as if hoping to catch a glimpse of me. I couldn't tell if she somehow sensed that I was in the room, or if she talked to me even when I wasn't there.

"Damn. I should have found a way to tell him sooner," I admitted aloud.

When I'd died, I hadn't left any way for anyone to contact my brother. He had no way of knowing. I could have remedied that once Ruby moved in and we learned to communicate, but I hadn't asked for her help for the same reason I'd never listed Ian as an emergency contact. I didn't want to admit to anyone, not even Ruby, that my brother was in jail.

He wasn't due to get out for months, and usually ended up getting in trouble and having time added to his sentence, so I thought I'd have a while before I had to figure out how to break the news to my brother. Then again, I had no idea how long I'd been away, trapped in the flashback. Time passed differently ever since I died. I could blink and a week could have passed. I didn't think it had been that long, but I had no idea what else I'd missed. On the plus side, I felt refreshed and ready to take on the world.

"I'm so sorry you had to find out this way," I told him, kneeling beside my brother. He wasn't crying anymore. Instead, he rocked back and forth, his bloodshot eyes focused on nothing as he clutched the coffee, hands wrapped around the mug. "Really, it's not so bad, Booger." He couldn't see me. He couldn't hear me. He had no idea I was there. But *I* knew. I let out a dry laugh as I realized I wasn't comforting Ian. I was comforting myself. "See? Being dead isn't much different than being alive. You never did listen to me."

Now that I was no longer around to coddle him, maybe Ian would finally grow up. He'd get a job. A mortgage. He'd meet a nice girl and settle down, and they'd give me some nieces and nephews. He might even name his first daughter Cordelia. He could clean up his credit and finally go straight. And monkeys might fly out of my butt.

"It's almost like she's still right here," Ian said, taking a sip of his coffee.

I wondered if it would be more sugar and milk than coffee. He spent half his adult life behind bars, but when he was out in the world, he drank coffee like I used to fix it for him long before he was old enough that he should have been drinking coffee.

He shook his head. "Like any moment, she might come walking through the door."

"About that," Ruby said, then hesitated.

"No. No no no no no no no. Don't you *dare*," I said. "Don't even *think* about it."

I was dead. As much as I tried to convince myself otherwise, it sucked for everyone involved, me most of all. My brother would get over being abandoned. He would move on. He had plenty of practice at that. But if he knew the truth? That I was still right here? That might break him. No way. He wasn't a kid with a skinned knee anymore. He was a grown-ass adult who had to face the world on his own two feet, for the first time ever.

"This is a wicked bad idea, Ruby," I said. I needed to get through to her. The refrigerator magnet trick was out of the question. He could notice. I could grab her arm and try to talk to her directly. I'd done it before. It hurt. It was worse for me than it was for her, but she might jerk, or cry out. And what if despite all that she still couldn't hear me? I couldn't take the risk.

"There's something I need to tell you," Ruby said.

"Ruby, think about this. Be smart." I was out of time. Another few seconds and she was going to blurt it out. And good luck getting rid of my completely helpless man-child of a brother then. Not gonna happen. I loved my brother with my whole heart, I did, but

I wouldn't wish him latching onto another soul—living or dead—like a parasite.

I had to do something, fast. The buzzer! My attention flitted to the ancient intercom on the wall. When Ruby had first moved in, so damn alive and perky it made my teeth ache, I wasn't exactly happy about having her around. I tormented her, trying everything in my inconsiderable power to get her to leave. Not my proudest moment.

She forgave me because of course she did. Ruby was a nice person. The nicest. Too nice, actually. Ian would take advantage of that niceness until there was nothing left. I felt a surge of fierce protectiveness toward her.

"Hold that thought," I told her. "I'll be right back. Don't. Say. A word."

I blinked, and when I opened my eyes, I was standing outside my apartment building. *Our* apartment building, I reminded myself. I leaned on the buzzer marked 4G.

A second later, Ruby's voice came through the static. "Hello?"

I let up on the buzzer. Then I punched it again. Short bursts, annoyingly loud, would come through on her end.

If the buzzer had been a modern CCTV system, me being this close would have fried its circuits. But the last time this building had gotten any upgrades, we hadn't landed on the moon yet. The simplicity of the intercom, coupled with the low-voltage battery powering the whole thing, meant it wasn't as sensitive to electrical interference as modern appliances were, or so I assumed. I wasn't an electrician. All I really knew for sure was if I got too close to a cell phone, it bought the farm. But I could play with the buzzer all day and all I got was a tingly, not altogether unpleasant, sensation in my toenails.

"Hello?" Ruby's voice dropped so low I could hardly hear it through the static. "Cordelia?" she whispered.

I hit the buzzer twice in rapid succession. One knock for "no," two knocks for "yes," right? Or was it the other way around? It didn't matter. As far as Ruby knew, I was the only ghost on the block. She had to assume it was me, which meant two buzzes for yes.

"I have company right now," she said, in a normal voice. Was Ian standing over her shoulder? Or was he still on the floor, nursing his beverage and feeling sorry for himself, oblivious to the world?

Two quick buzzes. "Yeah, I know you have company, silly."

"Would you like to talk to them?" she asked.

One long, loud buzz. "No."

"Are you sure?"

Two short buzzes. "Yeah, I'm sure."

"I can tell them to—"

I interrupted her with a long buzz.

"I was going to say I could ask them to leave." Ruby sounded irritated. I didn't blame her. The buzzer *was* annoying. Which is why I'd used it to torture her in the first place. Not that I would do that now. I mean, yes, sure, I was using it now, but not to be mean. This was an emergency.

Two buzzes.

"You really want them to leave?" she asked, sounding perplexed.

How to explain a lifetime of sibling dynamics using only "yes" and "no"? If I could talk to her, I would start with, "Ian is about my favorite person on the planet but also, he's a leech. He's not dangerous, but he's not harmless, either. I wish I could say that my brother was a sweet kid who grew up to become a well-adjusted contributing member of society, but he was a shit kid then and he's a shit adult now. I hope you have eyes on your wallet because I can guarantee that he does."

But the best I could do was two short buzzes.

"Yeah, okay then."

I concentrated on the inside of my apartment, blinked, and . . . nothing happened.

Nothing was fair in life, but less than nothing was fair in the afterlife. A second ago, I was able to transport myself to the front stoop of the building without even trying. I wanted to be outside and *poof*, I was outside. The reverse should work just as effortlessly, especially considering I'd just recharged. But whatever cosmic joke I was stuck in had other ideas.

"Whatever," I grumbled to myself. In the back of my head, I knew that if I really wanted to, I could have popped back into the apartment because the only thing keeping me from defying the laws of the universe was, well, me. Which meant that in my heart of hearts, I didn't want to be back in my apartment.

After a lifetime of trying, and failing, to protect him, I didn't want to see my brother's face when Ruby kicked him to the curb. If it felt like I was choosing her over him, it was because I was. I'd never chosen anyone over my brother before, not even myself. And look how that had turned out. It was too late for me to fix everything that was broken, but I had to start somewhere.

I slipped through the closed front door of the apartment building. Next came the long trek up to the fourth floor. These stairs had been the bane of my existence when I was alive. Now, they were merely an annoyance, especially when I'd rather teleport. But despite holding myself back from taking the quick way back into the apartment, I knew I needed to hurry. It wasn't a good idea to leave Ian alone with Ruby.

He wouldn't hurt her, not physically at least. Ian didn't have a mean bone in his entire body. When he got into a fight, which was often, it was because he felt like he had no other choice. It was his go-to defense mechanism. He'd no sooner hit a woman than he'd . . . well, I wasn't sure what. But he would never hit a woman, at least not one who hadn't hit him first.

But he could hurt her in other ways, even if he didn't intend to. He could memorize her credit card numbers and order up a dozen televisions to turn around and sell on the black market. He could swipe her phone and scam someone into sending him a small fortune in gift cards. He could apply for loans with her social security number with zero intention of ever paying them back. Or worst of all, he could promise her that he'd put his nonsense behind him and he was going to be there for her from now on out, only to get pinched boosting a car a few hours later.

It was never a surprise when Ian let me down. Everyone did, eventually.

He'd pulled all those scams, and more, on me. Ruby was naïve, but when it came to my brother, I was *always* the biggest sucker in the room. At that thought, I scrambled up the rest of the stairs and hurried down the hall. I'd never been able to protect myself from Ian's sticky fingers, but I could still keep an eye on him as long as he was in our apartment.

CHAPTER FOURTEEN

RUBY

After Ian left, I locked all the locks, even the chain at the top. If Ian did come back, he wasn't getting inside without making an awful lot of noise.

Then, I turned to Cordelia. Or, rather, I turned toward where I assumed she was. Sometimes I could feel it when she was in the room with me—although that might have been wishful thinking—but I could never pinpoint her precise location. I picked something to focus on, usually the refrigerator because that's where the poetry magnets were, and hoped for the best.

"Why were you so eager for me to get rid of him?" I waited a beat for an answer that never came. "He's your *brother*, Cordelia. I'd think you'd be happy to see him. If one of my sisters dropped by unannounced, I'd be ecstatic."

Well, not unannounced. As much as I loved my sisters, and missed them, it was nice to have my own place for the first time in my life, even if everyone in my family was four hundred miles away. Even if I shared it with a ghost. In any event, I would hope that they would at least text me before heading out—giving me eight hours to straighten up first.

There was a drop in temperature in the apartment. During the winter, that usually meant that the heater was on the fritz. Again. But now that the weather was warm, sudden cold spots usually meant that Cordelia was mad. Or sad. Or cranky. It was the ghostly equivalent of a very aggressive eyeroll and was completely open to interpretation.

"Got nothing to say now?" That was a rhetorical question. Cordelia never had anything to say. Or if she did, I couldn't hear her. "That buzzer trick was . . ."

My voice trailed off. I knew she hadn't meant anything by it, but when I first moved in, Cordelia was so desperate to communicate that she'd rung the door buzzer more or less constantly, day and night, trying to get my attention. If I ever heard that high-pitched buzz again, it would be too soon.

Of course I couldn't tell *her* that. I wouldn't want to hurt her feelings, especially when she'd been nothing but kind to me.

". . . cute." I finished my thought, but the word fell flat. "Although, I'd really appreciate it if you didn't use the buzzer at all, if that's okay with you."

I *really* hoped that Cordelia couldn't read my thoughts. She'd be terribly upset if she knew how much the sound of that door buzzer drove me up the wall. Seriously, I'd almost moved out because of that constant noise, twenty-four seven. It had been that bad. Then, Cordelia and I found another, better way to communicate, and the buzzing finally stopped.

"Ian was devastated when I told him," I said. I perched on the arm of the loveseat so I could continue to face the refrigerator. "I'm not sure how much you heard. How is it that he didn't know you were dead?"

DEATH AT THE DOOR   131

There was no answer, not that I was expecting one.

"He freaked out. Can't say I blame him. If one of my sisters, well, you know . . ." My voice trailed off. There were some things I didn't want to ever think about, much less say out loud. Anything bad happening to my sisters was at the top of that list. "If he knew you were a ghost, he might feel better."

no

nothing

KNOT ever

NONE

"Yeah, I got that," I told her, although I didn't understand. Why was she so adamant? I knew better than to go around blabbing that I had a ghost. They'd lock me up faster than I could say, "Just kidding!"

I hadn't told my mom or my sisters, and I wasn't in the habit of keeping secrets from them. Not big ones, at least. Likewise, I'd kept my mouth shut around my friends back home and everyone at work. But this was different. This was her *brother*.

"Come on, Cordelia, if you'd let me talk to him, explain everything, he could find some solace."

I stared at the refrigerator, willing the magnets to move. Nothing happened. "You are the most stubborn ghost I've ever met," I told her. Sure, she was the *only* ghost I'd ever met, but she knew what I meant.

Even though I could still feel a heaviness in the atmosphere that I'd come to associate with Cordelia being nearby, there was no response, not even so much as another fluctuation in the temperature.

"Fine. Have it your way." I got up and moved toward the refrigerator. The apartment was small enough that the kitchen was only separated from the living room by a few steps, but I didn't mind. It was plenty big enough for just me. Well, me and Cordelia, but she didn't take up much space.

I cleared the magnets, letting them mix in with the other words that could be used to form endless combinations. Then I opened the door and looked inside. I needed to go grocery shopping again soon. After hurling the mustard at Ian when I thought he was an intruder, instead of putting it back on the shelf, I'd thrown it in the trash. I wasn't in the habit of tossing out perfectly good food—my mother had raised me better than that—but I had no idea how old it was, since like all of the furniture, it had come with the apartment. I rarely ever used mustard. I wouldn't miss it. I was, however, upset that the last of the cheesecake was gone.

If he was telling the truth and Cordelia had given her brother a key, why hadn't she warned me? Who else had a key to my apartment? I needed to get the locks changed, ASAP. Cordelia's brother or not, I didn't like the idea of strange men having keys to come and go as they pleased.

I thought of the TrendCelerate bathroom key that Marty had borrowed and not brought back. Having a locked door hadn't helped him any. He still ended up dead on the tile floor. The more I thought about it, the more his death and Cordelia's had in common.

When I moved into the apartment, it was exactly like Cordelia had left it, from the clothes in the closet to the rancid trash in the garbage cans that hadn't been emptied in weeks. There were liquor bottles, both empty and full, but there were no pills laying around. From my previous snooping—I mean considerate review of Cordelia's medical files to helpfully alert her doctor and dentist to remove any upcoming appointments—I knew that she didn't have any medications prescribed to her.

Cordelia had been a drunk, and there was evidence of that everywhere I looked. But I hadn't found a single pill stronger than Advil. If she'd had an empty pill container of whatever she'd taken next to her when she died, the paramedics might have taken it as evidence when they wheeled her body out. But there should be pill bottles around the apartment, not just Jack Daniel's bottles. There'd been no evidence that she took drugs regularly, but maybe I'd overlooked the obvious since, by her own admission, she'd bought from Marty in the past.

Marty's sister swore he didn't use hard drugs. According to her, he didn't sell anything you couldn't otherwise get with a prescription. He wasn't a drug dealer, in her mind, just a delivery guy. Which tracked, because Marty really *was* a delivery guy. He just happened to deliver unprescribed drugs along with spuckies.

"Marty's sister, Hazel, has to know more than she told us," I said aloud. If Cordelia was confused by the sudden change in topic, she didn't give me any sign. "She swore Marty was a good guy trying to support her and the kids. The pay at Beantown Deli wasn't bad, not if he got to keep the tips plus some kind of hourly wage, or a cut of the delivery fee. But he had an awful lot of mouths to feed. So who had anything to gain from his death?"

MOON y

Cordelia had learned to be creative with the magnetic poetry. When the word she needed wasn't available, she'd make one. I'd gotten better at figuring out what she meant, but this one was easy because she'd used it before.

"Money, exactly. Follow the money," I agreed. "Hazel seemed sincerely distraught over her brother's death. Even if he left a little insurance, considering how hard he worked, he's worth more to her alive. Hazel would have to be completely heartless to kill her own brother and orphan his child for a payout—no matter how large."

Growing up, I'd threatened to kill my sisters a time or two, and they'd said the same about me. We never really meant it, though. It was always some silly little squabble easily forgotten. There wasn't enough money in the world to tempt me to actually hurt either of them. But then again, I might have been broke, but I wasn't desperate and I didn't have anyone relying on me.

"I doubt Marty had insurance, at least not a lot of it." I thought back to my first day at TrendCelerate. The benefits package had a life insurance option. I selected the default because it was no cost to me. But Marty had a kid, and a sister and nephew he supported. He would have selected a higher amount. But all of that was assuming that Beantown offered benefits to their delivery guy and that he could afford the premiums.

For all I knew, they treated Marty like an independent contractor so they didn't have to put him on the payroll. If so, they deserved to have their name dragged through the mud if anyone found out that Marty used his delivery job as a cover for dealing drugs. Or they already knew and killed him to get rid of him.

"That's silly. If they wanted him gone so badly, they would have fired him," I said to myself.

?

The single question mark appearing on the refrigerator reminded me that Cordelia was just as invested as I was in finding Marty's killer, but we weren't always on the same wavelength.

"Sorry. Never mind. Not important," I said, beginning to pace as the wheels in my head turned. "Do we know where Marty got the drugs he was selling? I've got a friend who sold drugs for a hot minute back before a month in juvie scared him straight. The guys he ran with were downright ruthless. If Marty's supplier had something to do with his death, I'm not sure we should get involved."

you THINK?

I had to laugh. "That might be the most coherent sentence you've ever made," I told Cordelia.

As charming as the magnetic poetry trick was, there were some times it wasn't sufficient. I headed for the bookshelf. I had to stand on my tippy-toes to reach the book I wanted, which was on the top shelf. I managed to wiggle my fingers under it, and several books moved at once. A stack of four hardcover books slid off the shelf and I caught them. They were classics. Dickens. Austen. Christie. Shelley. They were nothing like the other books in Cordelia's collection, which were mostly contemporary paperbacks.

Another thing set them apart from the other books. The four books had been cleverly glued together and then hollowed out, making the perfect hiding space, camouflaged among the rest of Cordelia's extensive home library.

I'd found it purely by accident one day. When I tried to open one, I discovered their secret. Nestled inside the hollowed-out books were four tiny airplane-size bottles of Jack Daniel's. I assumed that this was her emergency stash. And considering that this *was* an emergency, I felt no shame in dipping into her supply, especially since I wasn't old enough to walk down to the liquor store and legally buy my own bottles.

I took three of the bottles and lined them up on a lower shelf before shimmying the hollowed-out books back into place. "Bottoms up," I said to myself. I unscrewed one of the lids and tried to down the bottle. Instead, I sputtered as it burned my throat. I forced myself to swallow as much as I could. "This had better be worth it." I pinched my nose and finished the tiny bottle.

"One down." I removed the lid of the next bottle and braced myself. I closed my eyes and chugged. When I opened my eyes, where a second ago there had only been an empty apartment, there was now a woman standing in front of me.

I knew from reading her obituary that Cordelia was in her forties, but those must have been a hard forty years because this woman looked older. She had no makeup on and obviously hadn't moisturized enough when she was alive.

She was tall, taller than me, but most people were. She had red hair worn in a messy bun. She was pale, but not so much so that she would stick out in Boston where everyone was pale after the long winter.

"Cordelia Graves," I said. I felt a drop of liquid on the corner of my mouth and caught it with my thumb. I sucked at the drop of Jack. It didn't taste so bad this time. My taste buds were numb from the alcohol. "Nice to see you."

She grinned at me, and her face lit up. "Hiya, Ruby Young. Nice to be seen."

CHAPTER FIFTEEN

CORDELIA

"I thought you swore off the booze," I teased Ruby. "'Never again.' Those were your exact words."

When I first discovered that I could hold actual, bidirectional conversations with the living as long as they were drunk enough, I'd tricked Ruby into shotgunning a bottle of vodka. We had the best time. It was like the perfect girls' night out, minus the hair braiding. She could see me and hear me, but she couldn't touch me. Which was a real shame, because I seriously needed to brush my hair.

Then she woke up the next morning with the hangover from hell and zero recollection of our time together. Understandable. I'd had a few mornings like that, myself. And like Ruby, I'd sworn off alcohol more times than I could count. It never lasted. Ruby, on the other hand, had been serious.

"You're a bad influence on me, Cordelia Graves," she said, trying—and failing—to keep a straight face before dissolving into giggles. That's my Ruby. She's a lightweight.

I almost told her to call me Cordy. Practically everyone close to me did. But there was something about the way she said my name, pronouncing each of the four syllables—"Cor-DEAL-ee-uh"—instead of the more common "Cor-deal-yah" that made me smile.

"You wanted to talk, Ruby Young?" If she could use my full name, I could use hers.

"Ian," she said.

"Ian," I repeated.

"What on earth? Why didn't you tell me about your brother?" Her words were slightly slurred.

"I was embarrassed," I admitted. "He was in prison."

"What?" Ruby asked. "But he's innocent, right? They got the wrong man? The corrupt injustice system had it out for him?"

I had to laugh. "Hell no. Ian's guilty of everything they've ever charged him with, and a whole bunch of other things they couldn't pin on him, to boot."

"Maybe he got caught up in the wrong crowd," Ruby suggested.

"Please. Ian *was* the wrong crowd. But it's not his fault. He's had it hard."

"Don't make excuses for him." She had a hard time getting the word "excuses" out, pronouncing it with an "s" instead of an "x." "If he's guilty, he deserved to go to jail. Is that why you were so eager to get him out of here? Because you're ashamed of him?" Ruby asked.

I handed her the third tiny bottle. "It's complicated."

"I don't think this is necessary," she said, adding extra syllables to "nec-ess-ess-sary."

She was right. Two bottles in and she could see and hear me just fine. To be completely honest, the third bottle wasn't for her. It was for me. After months of forced sobriety, I could only get drunk vicariously through my tiny, endlessly cheery roomie. "Drink up."

She did.

"Ruby, you gotta promise me you won't tell Ian about me."

"Like I ever would," she said.

"Promise," I insisted.

"I won't tell him about you! Even if I wanted to go around waving my hands and telling the world that I'm off my rocker, and I don't, I have no way of getting ahold of him."

"You're not off your rocker," I assured her.

"I'm sitting in an empty apartment getting drunk with my dead roommate," she pointed out.

"That's beside the point."

"That's exactly the point." After just three teensy tiny bottles, she was already belligerent. It was adorable. "Is the ghost in the room with you, Ruby?" she asked in a falsetto voice. "What's the ghost doing now, Ruby?" she continued in a deep baritone. "Funny-farm city. No, thank you."

"Good," I said. I couldn't imagine what Ian would do if he knew about me. He'd never been able to keep a secret, which was why he kept getting caught.

"Good?" she repeated. "Ghosts are real! They exist! *You* exist! That's the coolest thing ever, and no one would ever believe me."

I sighed. "Ian would definitely not believe you. He didn't even believe in the monster under his bed. One time, I caught him watching a *Night of the Living Dead* marathon. Those movies used to give me nightmares. I slept with the light on for a week after watching my first zombie movie. But Ian? My little Booger? He was eight years old, and thought they were the funniest things he'd ever seen. Ian would watch them at two a.m., then sleep like a baby."

"And you wonder why he ended up in prison," Ruby muttered. "He's damaged."

"No," I snapped. "He's not. He's a good kid. He is." Then I

came back down to earth. Ian had never been a good kid, and I knew it. I didn't have to defend him anymore, so why was I doing it?

"Then you're telling me he's trustworthy?"

"Not even a little," I said. "Don't leave him alone with your purse, your wallet, or with anything he could trade, pawn, or sell."

"Yeah, sounds like a real winner," she mumbled.

I raised an eyebrow. "A kid can have a big heart and sticky fingers at the same time."

"He's not a kid, Cordelia," Ruby said. "He's almost twice my age."

"No way. He's . . ." I had to think about it. He was five years younger than me. Since I wasn't getting any older, in a few years, we'd be the same age. Eventually, assuming he didn't do anything stupid, he'd be older than me. That was hard to wrap my head around. "Doesn't matter. You're more mature than he is."

"Let me get this straight. I can trust him, but I shouldn't. He's older than I am, but also younger."

"That's about it," I agreed.

Ruby giggled.

"What's so funny?"

"Nothing. Everything. Should I tell her about the insurance?"

"Her?" I asked. "Who's 'her'? Me? And what about the insurance?"

"Did I say that aloud?" Ruby slurred. "Or did you read my mind?"

"What insurance?" I repeated, wondering what she'd found.

I'd had some life insurance. It wasn't much, but it was more than nothing. Ian was my beneficiary, obviously. However, when I died, TrendCelerate and my insurance company had no way to get ahold of him since no one knew he was in prison except for me.

Now that he was back in town, it was only a matter of time before he found out about the policy. Maybe it would soften the blow of my death. Then again, he'd probably waste it. He'd never been good with money.

"Has the room always been this spinny?" Ruby plopped down on the loveseat.

"We were talking about insurance," I prompted her.

"I don't wanna. You'll get mad." She burst into a fit of giggles.

I rolled my eyes. I'd never gotten this drunk off three itty-bitty shots. I shouldn't have encouraged her to drink the third one. "I won't be mad. I trust you to do the right thing, Ruby."

"I like you," Ruby said.

"And I like you," I admitted. Ruby was a lightweight, but at least she was a happy drunk.

"Duh."

"Do kids even say 'duh' anymore?" I asked.

Ruby poked a finger at her chest. "Not a kid. Neither is Ian."

"Fine. You're right," I agreed.

"Duh," she repeated. She closed her eyes.

I waited. When she didn't immediately open them again, I called her name. "Ruby! Ruby! Wake up."

"Not asleep," she mumbled without opening her eyes. "Just spinny." Talking to drunk Ruby was like holding a conversation with a two-year-old.

"I need to talk to you about Marty," I said.

"Marty! It's so sad."

I squatted in front of her. "Ruby, this is important. I need you to remember this." When she didn't respond, I snapped my fingers in front of her face. She opened her eyes. "Remember how I told you with the magnets that Marty didn't OD?"

She pushed herself more upright. "Are you sure?"

"I went to the morgue. I saw his body. The cause of death was choking, not overdose."

"Whoa."

"Yes, whoa," I agreed. "Someone forced a bunch of pills down his throat. Marty was murdered."

Ruby shook her head. "Poor Marty."

"Someone killed him," I repeated. I hoped I was getting through to her. Even if she forgot the rest of this conversation in the morning, I needed her to understand. "Someone was physically in the bathroom with him, in our building."

She blinked at me, letting that sink in. Then, she said, "Cordelia?"

"Yes, Ruby?"

"I'm gonna be sick." She got up and ran toward the bathroom.

"We should do this more often," I said before she could slam the door.

"Never again. And this time I mean it!" she yelled back.

When she finally returned, she was pale and shivering. "Cordelia?" she asked, looking around the room.

"Right here," I told her, but she didn't look at me.

"Cordelia?" she asked again. "You left me."

"I didn't go anywhere," I assured her, even though she could no longer hear me. "I'm not going anywhere."

She grabbed the blanket from the back of the loveseat and wrapped it around her shoulders before shuffling off to bed. I had a bad feeling she wouldn't remember any of this tomorrow. I followed her to the bedroom to make sure she remembered to take her shoes off before crawling under the covers.

She hadn't, so I pried them off—careful to not come into physical contact with her skin—and tossed them into the corner.

"Thanks, Cordelia," she muttered as she rolled over.

"Anytime, Ruby."

"Love you," she murmured.

"Love you, too, kiddo," I replied with a grin. That wasn't something I said—or heard—often, and I was surprised to realize I meant it.

I backed out of the room. Normally, once Ruby was asleep, I would wander the city alone. I loved nights when I had the whole city to myself. Sometimes, I'd hang out with Harp instead. If I told him everything that was going on, we could go out looking for Marty one last time, together, just in case he was a ghost and I'd missed him. It's true what they say about four eyes being better than two, especially when Harp had so much more experience than I did.

There were plenty of other things I could do tonight. I wanted to check in on Hazel. Marty's sister had come across as almost as naïve as Ruby. She mentioned that Marty had a hard time getting a job because he'd been in and out of jail a few times. I could relate to that. Ian had the same problem. What I didn't understand was how she could still be so doe-eyed innocent and convinced that her brother could do no wrong. Was she delusional, or was she hiding something?

But in the end, I didn't go out searching for Marty's ghost again. I didn't surveil Hazel. Instead, I stayed home and kept an eye on Ruby.

I told myself that I needed to be here in case she got sick again, or if she woke up looking for me. I told myself that the reason I was sitting in the darkened living room staring at the front door was because I was bored, not because I was waiting for the soft scratching sounds of my brother picking the lock in the middle of the night.

I hated lying to myself.

CHAPTER SIXTEEN
RUBY

Thursday morning, everything hurt. I didn't want to get out of bed. I didn't want to take a shower. I didn't want to get dressed. I didn't want to take the bus. But I did all those things, with a determined smile plastered on my face, because I was a responsible grown-up and could handle responsible grown-up things.

I'd moved to Boston to get a fresh start after breaking up with Jerkface, but despite how it looked, I wasn't running *away* from someone. I was running *toward* something. Independence. Responsibility. Adultness.

And so far, I was killing it. I had an apartment. I had a job. Every day I proved to myself that I could make it on my own, and today would be no exception. After all, if I could make up words like "adultness," I could get through a day when I was so hungover my hair hurt.

I got to the office on time, barely. If ever there was an excuse to be late, it was after staying up all night getting drunk with my dead roommate discussing a murder, but I'd already been late once this week and look what happened. Not that I thought Marty was killed because I was late to the office, but if I'd been a little earlier, I could have done ... what? Prevented his death?

It was silly. I was blaming myself for something I'd had no part in and falling into a trap of wishful what-ifing, despite knowing that never went well. What if I'd never dated Jerky McJerkface? I would have never gotten my heart shredded, but I also would have never moved to Boston and met Cordelia. Or what if Cordelia hadn't died under suspicious circumstances? I would never have met her. I wouldn't be living in her apartment or sitting at her desk at TrendCelerate, doing her job. What if Ian had been notified about his sister's death while he was in prison? He wouldn't have let himself into my apartment, and I wouldn't have ended up getting drunk with Cordelia.

Hazel had told me that Marty hadn't overdosed. Cordelia's magnets had told me that Marty hadn't overdosed. But it wasn't until I had a real, face-to-face conversation with her that I got the full picture. Cordelia had gone to the morgue, without me, and had learned the real cause of Marty's death. It wasn't that there were too many drugs in his bloodstream, but rather that he'd choked on the pills.

Someone had killed Marty, on purpose. And they'd done it in the TrendCelerate bathroom, right down the hall from me. The killer had been in this very building. With the big meeting, there were a lot more people in our office on Monday than usual. There were three other offices on the floor, the building manager had a key, and anyone could have piggybacked through the open door; but ordinarily, only a few people had access to this floor. Had they walked past me that day? Had I talked to them? Did I know them? Did I work with them?

Adam finally showed up at work, which gave me an excuse to

think of something else. He was late, which was odd. Most days, he was at the office long before I was. "Any messages?" he asked in lieu of greeting.

"Good morning," I told him with a smile. "No calls, but I routed a couple of emails to your mailbox."

"Yeah, I already took care of those." His brows were furrowed. "No calls for me? Are you sure?"

"Yes, sir," I said. "Are you expecting someone? If so, I'll put them straight through if they call."

"No worries," he said. Without an explanation, he went to his office and let the door slam closed behind him. My pounding head did not appreciate that.

To get my mind off my hangover, I tried to figure out what was eating Adam. I couldn't just come out and ask him, any more than I could ask him if he picked Beantown Deli for lunch every week so Marty could drop off other illicit deliveries. Did Adam really like spuckies? Or was he was ordering something else that wasn't on the menu?

Why would a man who was loaded and had good insurance buy prescription drugs from Marty instead of going through legitimate channels? There was a perfectly good pharmacy just a few blocks from the office. Adam probably passed a dozen more on his way home. And if he was too busy to stop, he could always get his prescription delivered right to his doorstep.

I shook my head. I couldn't imagine a single reason why he'd use Marty's services.

"What's his deal?" Melissa asked, approaching my desk. Even Melissa noticed that Adam was off his game today.

"I'm sure it's nothing," I said.

"Hey, you got any plans this weekend?"

I went over the to-do list in my head. Repot the monstera plant

I'd bought for Cordelia. Check my phone two thousand times to see if Tosh texted me. Facetime my mother. Fold laundry. Solve a murder.

"Nothing much," I said.

"It's my birthday on Saturday, and a couple of friends are taking me to that axe-throwing place and then out for beers after."

I had a hard time picturing Melissa, with her love of fitted pastel outfits, throwing an axe. I would have expected her to hold her birthday party at a tea shop. A hip bar where women drank for free. A Sephora. Not someplace where the floor was covered in sawdust and flannel was the predominant fashion choice.

"You should come," she continued. "And bring your roommate. They're welcome, too."

A pencil lying next to my keyboard rolled off the desk under its own power and bounced off the floor. Melissa didn't appear to pay any attention to it, so I ignored it, too. Cordelia was annoyed that I'd accidentally slipped up at work and mentioned that I had a roommate, but if she kept moving things around the office, someone was bound to notice her presence eventually.

Despite their petty squabbles and often juvenile appearance, my coworkers at TrendCelerate were smart. Not just smart, genius smart. Even Adam with his comic book collection, Quinn with her constant fad diets, and Franklin, the third partner who was rarely in the office, were certifiably brilliant. We both needed to be more careful if we didn't want to get caught.

I wondered what would happen if there was alcohol at this axe-throwing birthday party. Would anyone get drunk enough to see Cordelia? From what I could tell, it took more than a buzz for someone to see ghosts. Heavy drinking while throwing sharp axes didn't seem like the best combination. "Let me see what I can do," I told her.

Melissa nodded. "Cool."

"Hey, can I ask you something personal?"

She spread her hands out wide. "I'm an open book."

I didn't like interrogating my coworkers, but someone, possibly someone who worked for TrendCelerate, had murdered Marty, and I was determined to get to the bottom of it. "That delivery guy who died? I heard rumors about him."

"What kind of rumors?"

"I heard he sold drugs."

She flapped a hand at me in a dismissive gesture. "Whoever said that doesn't know what they're talking about."

"Oh really?" Cordelia said he was a drug dealer. His own sister admitted he was a drug dealer. What did Melissa know that no one else did? "Did you know him well?"

"Not really, no, but he wasn't a dealer. I mean, not really. He was just the kind of guy that could get things, you know?"

"Why would anyone with a six-figure salary and health insurance buy who-knows-what from a deli delivery person instead of a pharmacy?" I asked, still shaken by the idea that my coworkers were his customers.

"Things happen. Like there was this one time when I misplaced a brand-new packet of birth control. My usual pharmacy wouldn't give me a refill, and my doctor's office was giving me the runaround, but Marty hooked me up, you know."

"Hooked you up?"

"He took care of it. He said he had an in with someone, and the next thing you know, I had my prescription. He was a good guy. I'll miss him." Melissa shrugged. "I've got to get back to work, but I'll text you the axe-throwing details."

"I'm not sure if I'll be able to make it or not," I warned her.

"Your call. And don't take this the wrong way, but you look like hell. Can I get you some water or something?"

"Thanks, but I'm good," I assured her.

Once Melissa was in her cubicle, I headed for the break room. She was right. After all that booze last night, I needed to hydrate, but somehow, I accidentally ended up at the coffee maker instead. What could I say? The heart wanted what the heart wanted.

While I waited for the coffee to brew, Marc joined me in the break room. He stood beside me, clutching his empty coffee cup and staring at the coffee maker without paying me any attention.

"I'll be done in a second," I told him.

"Huh?" he asked. Then he glanced over at me. "Sorry, I didn't see you there."

I bet that was how Cordelia felt when no one noticed her. Then again, she was invisible. I wasn't. "Been here all along," I said, turning to study him.

A Hispanic man in his thirties, Marc was a database administrator, I thought. I could never keep their job titles straight. The other employees were closer to my age. Even the company owners were surprisingly young. As far as I could tell, despite Quinn's silky gray hair, Adam Rees was actually the oldest, and he was just shy of fifty. I wondered if all tech companies skewed young, or just this one.

Today, Marc looked like he had a decade on Adam. He had dark, heavy bags under his eyes, his facial hair was patchy, and his shirt was misbuttoned.

"You look exhausted," I said. "Everything okay?"

The coffee maker beeped, and he reached for my cup before realizing that his mug was still in his hand. "Oh, shoot. Sorry." He handed me my coffee and set up the machine to make his serving.

"I don't think I've slept more than two hours a night since the twins were born."

I couldn't function at all without sleep. I wondered if that was why Cordelia liked plants so much. They didn't keep her up at night.

Marc chuckled. I guess I was staring off into space, because he said, "You're more out of it than I am."

"Yeah, got a lot on my mind," I said. I was worried that someone might find out I was harboring a ghost. I was nervous that whoever killed Marty might come back, or worse, was already here. And people at work were starting to notice that something was off with me, so it was time to change the subject. "How old are the twins now?"

"Eight months. I'd hoped they'd be sleeping through the night by now, but I swear they've made a pact with each other to never sleep at the same time. If one so much as yawns, the other wakes up." Mentioning yawning triggered a yawn of his own.

"Is this a new development?" I asked. I hadn't been around enough babies to know if that was normal or not.

"I wish." He let out another jaw-cracking yawn. "It's just worse lately. I had a, uh, prescription that helped me stay alert at work, but it's run out and I don't know if I can get a refill."

The way he hesitated before calling it a prescription rang a bell. "I bet Marty could have hooked you up," I blurted out. If I hadn't had such a pounding headache or if I'd taken even a sip of my coffee first, I would have been more discreet, but I wasn't exactly operating at a hundred percent right now. Who was I kidding? I was barely operating at seventy-five percent.

If Marc noticed my faux pas, he didn't point it out. Then again, he wasn't exactly firing on all cylinders, either. "Yeah well, Marty had to go and shoot up in our bathroom, and now where am I supposed to get my meds?"

I almost corrected him, but then realized I had an advantage. I'd assumed, like everyone else, that Marty the drug dealer had overdosed in the bathroom. Now, thanks to Cordelia, I knew the truth. The cops knew what really happened, and I assumed they'd told his sister, but no one else knew the real cause of death, except for the killer.

Marc thought Marty OD'd, therefore I could cross Marc off the list of suspects.

He misinterpreted my sigh of relief for a sigh of frustration, because he said, "I know. It sucks. I didn't realize you bought from Marty, too," Marc said.

I blinked at him. It was one thing to suspect that Marc had gone to Marty for his pick-me-up pills, but I wasn't expecting him to outright admit it. His lack of sleep was affecting him more than I'd realized. Since he was feeling chatty, I said, "Well, sure. Didn't everyone?"

"Everyone I know did. Melissa. Seth used to. Even Blair."

Despite what Cordelia had told me, I was having a hard time wrapping my head around the idea that everyone at TrendCelerate bought illicit drugs from Marty. Melissa admitted that she'd gone to him for birth control, and Marc was getting something to function on no sleep. Both sounded like worthy causes to me. But the others?

It was a good thing I ordered from the deli at least once a week, which gave Marty an excuse to deal to my coworkers. Then I realized that wasn't quite right. I was the one who placed the order, but it was Adam who always suggested it. Who else in the office was buying from Marty? What about Sally in HR? Quinn, the CEO?

Jordie, the software engineer who almost always worked from home but had been in the office on Monday?

"Wait a second, what do you mean Seth used to buy from him? Why did he stop?"

"Marty cut him off," Marc said with a chuckle. "He pushed him too far."

"Marty pushed Seth too far?" I asked.

Marc shook his head. "*Seth* pushed *Marty* too far, so Marty cut him loose."

I thought about that for a moment. What could Seth have done that caused Marty to turn down a paying customer? Did that make Seth angry, angry enough to seek his revenge? I had a hard time imagining that the practical joker of the office would hurt anyone, but before this week, I never would have imagined anyone at TrendCelerate getting involved in drugs.

The coffee maker beeped. Marc pulled his mug out and took a deep whiff. "Oh yeah, that's the stuff." He turned and walked out of the break room.

It surprised me to learn that Marc was one of Marty's regulars. He seemed like someone who had his life together. He had a lovely wife and two infants. He had a well-paying, in-demand job. And apparently, he relied on prescription uppers to get through the day. Which meant he relied on *Marty* as well.

As his supplier, Marty was worth more to Marc alive than dead, and he'd mistakenly thought—like I had—that Marty overdosed. Taken together, it pretty much proved he was innocent. However, he gave me a handful of new suspects, all of whom had been at TrendCelerate the day Marty was killed.

CHAPTER SEVENTEEN
RUBY

The frosted-glass front door to TrendCelerate opened and a girl who couldn't have been much more than five years old burst into the office. "Hello!" she called out in a singsong voice.

"Hi," I said back.

The girl turned to study me. She had big, blue eyes. Her shiny hair was pulled up in two perfect pigtails. She folded her arms across her chest. "I'm not supposed to talk to strangers."

I heard Quinn's voice in the hall call out, "Regina, slow down."

"You're Regina, aren't you?" I asked.

"Stranger danger!" the girl yelled.

"We've already met," I told the little girl. She'd come to the office a few times before, but I didn't know that we'd ever been introduced. "Don't you remember?"

She studied me. "No."

Quinn came through the front door, slightly out of breath. "Regina, I told you to wait for me."

I was surprised to see her. No, scratch that. "Surprise" was when Quinn was in the office more than once a week. Today's visit made three times this week, which in my tenure at least, was unprecedented. "Good morning, Quinn. She's quite a firecracker, isn't she?"

"Mind keeping an eye on my niece? It won't be but a minute." Before I could respond, she turned to the child. "Regina, behave for Ruby. I'll be right back." Quinn disappeared into her office and locked the door behind her.

"'Ruby' is a kind of gem," Regina said, unfolding her arms as she approached my desk.

My baby sister had gone through a phase when she was about Regina's age where she spouted out random facts she thought were appropriate. I was a little sad when she grew out of it. Jordan was only a year and a half younger than me, but it had seemed like a huge age gap at the time.

"And 'Regina' means 'queen'," I told her.

"I know that," she said smugly. "Although I'm not a queen."

"You're not?" I asked, playing along.

"I'm a princess."

I nodded. "I should have guessed."

Regina leaned across my desk to grab my fidget toy. "Pretty," she said as she pulled the magnetic butterflies apart and laid them out in a row. She giggled when the magnets caused the butterflies to snap together or slide apart.

"Uh, I'm not sure you should be playing with that." I wasn't sure how old Regina was, but when my little sister was young, she'd put anything in her mouth. I remembered hearing about the danger of kids swallowing magnets. "Maybe there's something in your aunt's office you'd rather play with?" I suggested, even though the last time I'd been in Quinn's office, it had been starkly furnished.

"What's in here?" Regina asked, diving into a messenger bag that was propped up against the wall behind my desk.

"I have no idea," I admitted. The bag wasn't mine. I'd never seen it before. Or had I? It looked familiar. But why was it behind my desk? Who'd put it there?

"What's this?" Regina asked, pulling a black USB drive out of the bag.

"That doesn't belong to you," I said, plucking it out of her hand. Then it struck me where I'd seen that messenger bag before. Every time he'd done deliveries to TrendCelerate, Marty had that bag slung over his shoulder. He didn't use it for food orders—he had a Beantown-branded tote for that. So what did he carry in it? And what was on the drive?

"Mine!" she said, reaching for the memory stick.

I had a bad feeling it wasn't something a kid should be playing with. To keep it out of her reach, I dropped it in my top drawer.

Had one of my coworkers found Marty's bag and dropped it off at my desk for me to deal with? That tracked. Everyone expected me to do the odd jobs around the office. But it was more likely that someone else, someone whose name rhymed with Bordelia, had left it for me to find. Which meant it was a possible clue.

To distract Regina, I pulled out the Etch A Sketch and handed it to her. "Do you need me to show how it works?" I asked.

She narrowed her eyes at me. "I'm not a *baby*," she said.

After five minutes of twiddling with the dials, she brought it up to my desk. "Show me how to use this," she demanded.

I gave her a quick demonstration, and then went back to work as she happily sat on the floor behind me and doodled, all the while peppering me with questions.

"How old are you, Ruby?"

"Twenty."

"That's old. What's your favorite color?"

"Purple."

Between the Etch A Sketch and the question-and-answer session, Regina was sufficiently distracted, so I eased the top drawer of my desk open and retrieved the USB drive she'd found in Marty's messenger bag.

"Mine's pink. What's your favorite dinosaur?"

"I don't know, Regina, I'd have to think about that," I said, only half paying attention as I popped the top off and lined the memory stick up with one of the USB slots on the front of my computer. It didn't fit, so I flipped it over. This time, it went in.

"Mine's triceratops. It's got three horns and a fancy neck."

"Yeah, that's a good one," I agreed.

A message flashed up on my screen. "Unknown device detected! Security scan could not be completed!" I hadn't anticipated triggering a security scan, and was afraid it had sent some kind of alert to my bosses. I moved my mouse down to the icon to eject the USB drive.

"What do you want to be when you grow up?"

I laughed. "I wish I knew," I said even though technically, I *was* a grown-up. I liked my job. I loved my haunted apartment. But I had no idea what I was doing, in life or, apparently, on my computer.

"I want to be an eagle, or a race car."

"I don't know that little girls grow up to be birds or cars," I said. Instead of ejecting the drive, I must have accidentally opened it, because a new folder popped up on my screen. It was filled with files with nonsense names. I knew I should pull the memory stick out before I got caught, but my curiosity overwhelmed my sensibility.

"Little girls can be anything they want to be," she informed me gravely.

"I stand corrected," I replied. I held my breath and clicked on one of the files. It opened, displaying line after line of gibberish. Just my luck. Cordelia had already scrambled the poor drive's circuits.

"No, you're sitting down."

I had a newfound respect for my mom. I couldn't imagine putting up with three little Reginas at the same time, while holding down a job and running a house. Quinn's door opened.

"Sorry, that took longer than expected. Thanks for keeping an eye on her. Hope she wasn't too much trouble," Quinn said, heading in my direction.

"No trouble at all," I said. I gave up on trying to eject the USB stick gracefully and yanked it out of the port before Quinn could notice it sticking out of my computer. I let it drop into my lap.

"Come on, Regina, let's go."

Regina stood up, her arms wrapped tightly around my Etch A Sketch, and headed to the exit.

"Excuse me? I need my Etch A Sketch back," I said, holding out my hand even as I felt the memory stick shift in my lap.

"Mine," Regina said. Tears glistened in her eyes.

"No, it's mine," I insisted, reaching for it.

Regina jumped back, out of my reach, and wailed.

Quinn gave me an annoyed look. "Just let her have it."

I shook my head, hoping that while I was arguing over the toy, the USB drive didn't fall off my lap, land on the floor, and get noticed by Quinn. I should have let it go, but that Etch A Sketch was one of the few reliable methods I could use to communicate with Cordelia. "I'd really rather not."

"I'll buy you a new one," Quinn said, looking as exasperated as I felt.

"I'm not sure they make them anymore," I told her. I wasn't sure if that was true or not. I had an iPad growing up, not an Etch

A Sketch. I was already panicking over the memory stick, and now the thought of not being able to talk to Cordelia at work if she couldn't find a replacement made it worse. "This one has sentimental value."

"Fine. Whatever." Quinn plucked the toy away from Regina and dropped it on my desk. She turned to the girl, who was now in full-on tantrum mode. "Come on, Reggie. We'll order one from Amazon on the way home." She gave me a dirty look as she left with the kid in tow.

"Wow, that was cold," Melissa said, popping up over her cubicle wall.

"It has sentimental value," I repeated. The USB drive slid onto the floor. I hastily moved my foot to cover it up.

"Uh-huh," she said sarcastically, oblivious to my furtive motions. "It's been in the lost-and-found drawer for over a year."

"And I'm very sentimental about that fact," I told her. I scooped up the Etch A Sketch and slid it back into the drawer.

"Good on you for sticking to your guns. The last time Quinn dumped her with me, that little brat made off with my favorite stress ball."

"Did you ever get it back?" I asked.

She shook her head, then returned to work. As soon as she did, I reached down and grabbed Marty's memory stick and shoved it into my pocket.

Up until she threw a fit when it was time to leave, having Regina in the office hadn't been the worst thing. At least she made the morning fly by. Before I knew it, it was lunchtime.

Some days the phone rang off the hook, or I'd get tasked with fixing a printer or entering a bunch of numbers into a spreadsheet. This was not one of those days. Since I'd finished the book at my desk and hadn't brought in a new one yet, I played with the magnetic fidget toy on my desk. I doodled on the message note pad that I hardly ever used because it was just more convenient to IM people, especially when few people were ever in the office. I even opened the deep catch-all drawer where I kept various lost-and-found items like the Etch A Sketch, and twiddled with the dials, making lopsided circles on the screen.

Bored almost to tears, I leaned back in my chair and stared at the ceiling. It was an industrial drop ceiling with huge off-white panels. On slow days like this, I often found myself looking for shapes in the old water stains. Today I was lucky. I found a duck.

Then, my luck ran out. I'd been studiously avoiding drinking more than a few sips of coffee, but by two o'clock, I knew if I didn't give in and use the restroom, I'd end up embarrassing myself. I was thirty minutes away from my apartment by bus. I didn't think I could hold it that much longer. Would the nice folks at Beantown Deli or one of the many restaurants or retailers on the street let me use their bathroom? Unlikely.

Businesses never let strangers into their restrooms. TrendCelerate was no exception. That's why we had a key to our unisex bathroom and only handed it out on an as-needed basis. I hadn't thought twice about giving Marty the key when he'd asked, because I knew him. Unlike today, I'd been so busy that morning that I'd forgotten he even had the key until Melissa pointed out it was missing, and when I went to check on him, I found him dead.

That was *not* the train of thought I needed while I was trying to psych myself up to go back into the restroom. With a force of will, I pushed those memories down to the deepest recesses of my brain, grabbed the key, and headed off at a hurried pace.

Once the necessities were out of the way, I washed my hands. Still feeling squeamish about being in the same place where I'd so recently found Marty, I tried to not look around, but my gaze kept going back to where his body had lain. I turned my head quickly, and noticed a movement out of the corner of my eye as an amber-colored pill bottle rolled out from under the open stall door.

"Cordelia? Is that you?" I asked, and then immediately felt foolish. Who else would be in a locked bathroom with me, rolling pill bottles across the floor?

I bent over and grabbed the generic pharmacy bottle with its bright white cap and diamond-shape blue pills inside. The label seemed standard: a pharmacy, a barcode, a physician. I didn't recognize the doctor or the pharmacy, but I blushed when I read the prescription: "Viagra, 50 milligrams."

I knew I should be adult about such things, but I cringed as I checked for the name of the patient. There were a few other offices on this floor. We shared the hallway bathroom, and they each had their own key. Anyone could have dropped anything at any time. It could have belonged to anyone.

"Please don't let it be someone I know," I said, steeling myself.

I read the label. The bottle of Viagra belonged to Marty Spencer.

CHAPTER EIGHTEEN
CORDELIA

"I found a clue!" Ruby exclaimed, holding up the pill bottle like it was a trophy.

"You found a bottle of Viagra prescribed to Marty," I corrected her. "Not exactly a smoking gun. We already knew he was dealing. You're missing the important part. And seriously? *You* found a clue? Give me a *little* credit. And if it *was* a clue? Good job getting your fingerprints all over it."

It bothered me that the bottle had gone unnoticed for so long. The police hadn't even pretended to look for evidence or they would have seen it. The fact that they missed something so obvious was proof that we were on our own. And the cleaning crew was doing a bang-up job, too. Tucked in behind the toilet bowl, it wasn't exactly in plain sight, but I hadn't missed it. How had they?

As frustrated as I was with the police and our cleaners, I did think it was cute how Ruby had blushed when she read the prescription name. "There's nothing wrong with Viagra. It treats a legit medical condition. You wouldn't get embarrassed if you found aspirin or eyedrops, would you? And stop and think about it a minute before you claim that *you* found anything."

Normally I avoided bathrooms as much as possible, for the creep factor alone, but I was glad that I'd decided to tag along. Without me, Ruby never would have noticed the prescription bottle. The bathroom in our apartment was strictly off-limits—my rule, not hers. I'd spent an entire week trapped in that bathroom after my death, before I figured out how to get out. I hadn't realized I was a ghost at the time, so I hadn't figured out that I could have walked through the door anytime I liked. Instead, I wasted days focusing on prying the very physical door open with my completely immaterial hands.

The bathroom at work, on the other hand, had no such unpleasant memories. In fact, there was that one time that Adam and I . . .

"No," I told myself. "No more of that." I'd wasted more than enough time pining over Adam, and frankly, I wasn't sure how much more I could take. I didn't know how much more I *wanted* to take. Seeing him make out with his wife in the doorway of their condo was more than I had bargained for. It was one thing to be alive and corporeal and know that while the man of my dreams would never actually be mine, at least I could touch him. Losing that, too? Pure, unadulterated torture.

Unadulterated. Ha. Good one, Cordy.

I could feel the edges of a memory of our time together tugging at me, threatening to pull me under. I shook it off. We had more important things to do. I could recharge and revisit my biggest mistakes later.

"The pill bottle is more important than the pills," I said. I nudged it just enough that the little blue pills rattled around inside of it, just like I'd nudged it so it would roll out from its hiding spot and catch her attention after everyone else had missed it. Sure, I could have picked it up and handed it to her, but where was the fun in that?

People, as a whole, weren't very observant. Something about evolution and being on the top of the food chain had made us lazy. Add onto that a couple billion people crammed onto a planet that was constantly screaming advertisements at us twenty-four hours a day, and was it any wonder that our senses were dulled? *Not* noticing every detail around us had become a modern-day survival strategy. Which was great for people who spent too much time nose-down in social media, but not helpful for someone trying to solve a murder.

The cops didn't care. What was one more dead drug dealer to them? They probably saw it as a win. But Marty was more than a drug dealer. He was a brother. A father. An uncle. A friend.

And, for what it was worth, it wasn't like he was selling meth or fentanyl on a playground. He was providing a service to the community. Was that service in a gray area? Yeah. But he got ordinary prescriptions for people who couldn't, or wouldn't, get them through normal channels. And now that *I* had found this pill bottle and got Ruby to pick it up, we knew what drugstore he was getting them from.

"How do you feel about swinging by the pharmacy after work?" I asked Ruby.

Since she couldn't hear me, she headed for the hall, but I held the door closed, much like I had done on Monday. But instead of keeping Ruby from getting inside and being traumatized by finding Marty, now I wanted her to *stay* inside the restroom just a little longer.

Because as much as I wanted to keep Ruby safe and far away from this investigation, I needed her help if I was going to find out who killed Marty.

"What are you trying to tell me?" Ruby asked.

In response, I turned on the hot water and let it run into the sink. Unlike our apartment, the hot water at the office actually ran hot, and only took a moment to warm up. Within a few minutes, the bathroom was thick with steam. As soon as the mirror fogged over, I wrote "Pharmacy?" in carefully printed letters.

She studied the letters hard as they dripped with condensation.

"Oh come on, my handwriting isn't *that* bad," I grumbled.

"Pharmacy?" Ruby reached over and turned off the faucet. The letters on the mirror faded. "Of course we're going to the pharmacy, as soon as I get off work."

"Glad to see we're on the same page," I said, opening the door and holding it as Ruby walked through. It felt like we were finally moving in the right direction.

We were the last people out of the office. Ruby checked that all the lights were set to auto, turned off the coffee maker and the big photocopier that hardly anyone ever used but took forever to warm up, and rattled the doors of the executive and HR offices to verify they were all locked. Then she set the alarm and locked the office behind us.

Ruby had no trouble finding the pharmacy, which was conveniently located only a few blocks beyond Beantown Deli. For all I knew, Marty made pickups there during his normal lunch delivery route and no one was ever the wiser.

Like the bigger chain pharmacies, the store was devoted to a mix of things to help people live healthier, like vitamins, and the less-than-healthy options, like high-fructose snacks. There was no line at the pharmacy counter, so Ruby walked right up to the window. "Can you tell me which one of your pharmacists filled this?" she asked, setting the bottle of Viagra in the pass-through.

The pharmacist ran the bottle under the scanner. It beeped. I took a step back lest I interfere with the computer. She scowled and ran the bottle again. It beeped again.

She shook her head and placed the pill bottle back on the counter. "Didn't come from here."

"Are you certain?" Ruby asked. "It's got your label on it."

"Don't know what to tell you. That barcode doesn't exist. It wasn't filled here."

"Can you run it again?"

"That might be my fault," I told Ruby as if she could hear me. "We could get me a heavy-duty X-ray gown or one of those hazmat suits people wear that work with radiation. It might cut down on the tech-splosions." Then again, that would be the least of our problems after people saw an empty hazmat suit walking down the street under its own power.

I'd already learned that anything electronic that was more intricate than the old intercom system at my building was subject to random acts of kablooey when I got too close, and the computers at the pharmacy were a lot more sensitive than the average light bulb.

The pharmacist looked annoyed. "I already ran it twice."

"Can you try it on a different computer?" Ruby asked.

The pharmacist crossed over to the counter that separated the shelves of medicine from the checkout window. She ran the pill bottle through the second scanner. It beeped. She shrugged and returned empty-handed. "It's not in our system."

"Thanks for trying," Ruby said. "Can I have my pills back, please?"

The pharmacist shook her head. "Sorry. No can do. I can't let those pills leave with our label on them until I verify the content and the prescription. Don't worry. Once I confirm they're not counterfeit, we'll call the person they were prescribed to and have them come pick them up. Have a nice day."

"Uh, yeah, sure," Ruby said, and hurried away from the counter.

"Bad news," I muttered.

I knew Marty's prescription racket wasn't completely aboveboard, but I hadn't stopped to consider that he might be selling counterfeit pills, not even when I was buying from him. And now a real pharmacist at a real pharmacy had the bottle with his real name on it and the potentially counterfeit pills inside. This was *not* the way I wanted to involve the cops, not when Ruby's face was on every security camera in this store.

Except, I realized, it didn't have to be. After Ruby left, I looked around. There were two cameras over the pharmacy counter, one pointed out at the customers and one pointed at the pharmacists. The first one threw off sparks as I waved my hand through it, but no one noticed. A sharp pain ran down my arm as I fried its innards, but it was worth it. Then I repeated the process until all of the cameras in the store had been disabled.

I'd always disliked surveillance cameras. Sure, they provided a layer of security, but at what cost? Didn't people have the right to go about their business without being filmed all the damn time? Taking out the cameras in the pharmacy was fun. That could be my new thing. After all, everyone—even a ghost—needed a hobby.

Since I was already futzing with the cameras, I decided to erase all evidence of our visit by walking through both computers the pharmacist had used to scan the bottle.

"What's going on?" the confused pharmacist yelled as smoke poured out of the computers. "Call IT! Call nine-one-one!"

While she wrestled the fire extinguisher off its brackets, I scooped up the Viagra bottle. Might as well be thorough, right?

Finally, I slid through a door marked "Employees only" and found the video controller. One little poke of my finger, and all evidence of our visit was erased.

As I stepped away from the computer station, my foot slid straight through the floor.

CHAPTER NINETEEN
RUBY

For the second time this week, there was a man in my apartment when I got home, but since I was pretty sure he wouldn't hurt me, and he was studiously making dinner in the kitchen, I didn't kick him out, at least not right away.

"Excuse me," I said, clearing my throat loudly.

Ian Graves turned around. He had a carrot in one hand and a peeler in the other. There was a blue and white kitchen towel slung over his shoulder and a savory aroma emanating from my oven. I didn't own a carrot peeler or dish towels. While the rest of the apartment was comfortably furnished, thanks to Cordelia, the kitchen was more of an afterthought with plenty of coffee mugs and not much more.

The few towels that had been there when I moved in went in the trash, along with the sheets. Living in an apartment with a dead woman? No problem. Sleeping on a dead woman's sheets? Eww. No thank you. I'd since bought a bath towel, a few washcloths, and a sheet set, but I hadn't gotten around to cloth napkins or dish towels.

"You're late," he stated.

"How can I be late? I didn't invite you over," I countered.

"I don't need an invitation. I'm not a vampire," he said.

"There's no such thing as vampires," I replied. At least, I didn't think there was. What did I know? A few months ago, I wasn't sure that ghosts existed. Then I met Cordelia.

"Good to know." He turned back to the counter and finished peeling the carrot before slicing it up on a chopping board. "We got off on the wrong foot. I wanted to apologize for my reaction the other day, but I didn't have your number. I thought I could make you dinner, you know, as a peace offering, but since you weren't home, I let myself in."

"You let yourself in," I repeated. "So Cordelia *did* give you a key?"

Ian finished one carrot and reached for the bowl. "Hand me that, will ya?"

I hung my bag up next to the door and came around to the kitchen. I picked up the bowl, but instead of passing it to Ian, I wrapped my arms around it. "You didn't answer my question."

He took a step closer and plucked the bowl out of my arms. He put it on the counter and then started scraping a pile of carrot slices from the chopping board into the bowl. "Cordy let me stay over here a lot."

"Even if that's true, Cordelia doesn't live here anymore," I said, my arms still crossed.

I got the impression that Cordelia didn't invite people over often, and there was no sign that anyone else lived here. There was only one bedroom. The loveseat was barely adequate for me to take catnaps on, and I was a good foot shorter than Ian, at least. I hadn't found an inflatable mattress, extra pillows, spare toothbrushes, or any men's clothing or toiletries when I moved in. If Ian stayed here regularly, he would have smelled like strawberries and baby powder after using her shampoo and deodorant.

I wondered if Cordelia was in the room with us now. I hadn't felt her presence since fleeing the pharmacy, but that didn't necessarily mean anything. She could be standing over my shoulder for all I knew, but if she was, she wasn't giving me any sign of whether Ian was lying or not.

"I realize that," he said. His voice had a sharp edge to it. He turned his attention to a pot boiling on the stove, adding a dash of salt and paper. "Do you have any siblings?"

"Two of them. Sisters. One older and one younger." And suddenly, I wanted more than anything in the whole world to see my sisters. To hug them. To tell them how much I loved them. Baltimore had never felt so far away as it did right at that moment. "I don't know what I would do if I lost one of them."

"And I hope you never find out." Ian's voice was rough. Then he abruptly changed the subject. "Hand me the heavy cream."

"I don't have any heavy cream," I told him.

"Check the top shelf."

I opened up my refrigerator and stared at the contents. It was fully stocked. There was chocolate milk. Diet Coke. Three types of cheese, including the stuff that came in a spray can that I wasn't entirely sure qualified as cheese. In the door was a new bottle of yellow mustard and a plastic container of lime juice. On the shelf was a carton of eggs, a bundle of celery, and a package of pudding cups. And of course, a small carton of heavy cream.

"You went shopping," I said, handing him the heavy cream. Then I helped myself to a Diet Coke. I didn't often splurge on soda, much less name-brand soda, but it was in my refrigerator, so I was going to drink it.

Ian poured heavy cream into the bowl, along with some

melted butter and a ton of brown sugar. He handed me the bowl, along with a long wooden spoon that I didn't recognize as belonging to me. "Stir this," he told me. "Someone had to go shopping. Your fridge was bare. Also, I watered your plants and moved the little one onto the windowsill. What happened to the other ones?"

"The other plants?"

"No, the other windowsills," Ian said sarcastically. "My sister loved her plants more than she loved me. Everything else of hers is still here, but most of the plants are gone. Was there some kind of plant apocalypse? Or do you just hate the color green?"

"I don't hate the color green," I told him. "I'm just not real good with plants."

There *had* been some kind of apocalypse, and that apocalypse was me. I didn't know how to take care of plants, and all but one had died under my neglectful watch. But in my defense, Cordelia *did* know how to tend to plants and could pick up a watering can as easily as I could, so she bore at least some of the responsibility.

"Good, because there's mint chip ice cream in the freezer. I wasn't sure what you like, so I took a guess."

"I like mint chip," I told him. "Is that what's for dessert?"

He dried his hands off on the towel. "I don't think mint chip ice cream would go very well with pie, but there's some vanilla in the freezer, too." He slid the casserole dish Cordelia and I had used to make eggplant parm earlier in the week toward me. "Pour the carrots in here and I'll pop that in the oven."

"What are you making?" I asked, as I carefully poured the mixture into the dish.

"Baked macaroni and cheese with mashed potatoes and roasted carrots." He put the carrots in the oven and checked on the macaroni.

I didn't recognize the pan it was in. Where had all these dishes come from? Knowing he probably wouldn't give me a straight answer if I questioned him about the unfamiliar dishes, I asked, "That's an awful lot of carbs for one meal, don't you think?"

"Comfort food. It's my mom's specialty."

"Really? I thought your mom wasn't in the picture," I said.

Ian froze. Behind him a giant pot of potatoes boiled nosily. "Who told you that?"

I blinked at him. How was I supposed to explain it?

Before I could think of a plausible explanation that didn't break my promise to Cordelia, he asked, "Have you been going through my sister's stuff?"

I latched onto that. "She left a lot of junk."

"That's not *junk*," he said, raising his voice. "That's Cordy's *life* you're talking about." His voice hitched, and he spun away from me, directing his attention back to the stove. He turned off the burner and picked up the pot. "Coming through." I stepped out of his way and he dumped the potatoes into a colander in the sink. Steam rose up from them.

The funny thing was I didn't *have* a colander or a big pot. Cordelia's kitchen had been bare bones. Despite her new crusade to teach me to cook, I didn't think she did much cooking herself.

"I'm sorry," I said. "When I moved in, the super said that there was no next of kin and rented the apartment to me as is. I kept the furniture, and the books and things, but I got rid of everything I couldn't use."

"Got rid of," he repeated, his voice strained.

"I gave it away to charity. Like her clothes and stuff," I explained. I hadn't thought anything of it at the time, but I had no use for clothes that didn't fit me and a shoebox of documents and old photos a dead woman had in her closet. Now that I knew Cordelia was still around, at least on some level, and her brother was right here in my kitchen, I felt guilty about tossing anything, but there was nothing I could do about that now. "She has a locker in the basement that I haven't gotten around to cleaning out yet," I told him. "You're welcome to anything down there."

"Thanks," he said tersely. "I appreciate that."

He chopped the steaming potatoes before returning them to the pot on the stove. He emptied the rest of the heavy cream into the pot, and then tossed the empty container into the trash. From what little I remembered about my drunken conversation with Cordelia, her brother was essentially a man-child incapable of taking care of himself, but he seemed to know what he was doing in the kitchen.

Maybe Cordelia didn't know her brother as well as she thought she did. What if Ian *wasn't* a chronic screwup?

There was a knock on the door.

"Get that, will ya?" Ian said.

"Uh, my apartment, remember?" I reminded him. I opened the door. Tosh was standing in the hall, holding a frozen store-bought pie.

"Am I early?" he asked.

"Right on time, buddy!" Ian yelled from the kitchen.

"Hey, Ruby," Tosh said, handing me the pie. "Thanks for the invite."

I stepped back and he followed me inside. "Yeah, sure," I agreed. "Have a seat. Be right with you." He headed for the loveseat. I headed for the kitchen. "What the hell do you think you're doing? You're grocery shopping? Making dinner? Inviting my neighbor over? What's next, you're gonna move in?"

"If you insist," Ian said with a grin. "Fair warning, though, I'm a blanket hog." He saw the shocked expression on my face and backpedaled. "Just kidding. Great place you got here, but your kitchen is woefully understocked. Makes sense. My dad didn't cook, so it was always Cordelia's job growing up. Once she was out on her own, she couldn't be bothered."

"Oh really?" I asked. I didn't know how much I could admit that I already knew without arousing Ian's suspicions. I'd almost blown it with the comment about his absent mother. I'd guessed that Cordelia didn't cook much based on the state of her kitchen, but I hadn't known why until now.

"Anyway, Tosh here was more than happy to lend a bit of cookware for the promise of a hot meal. Isn't that right?"

"Yup," Tosh said from the loveseat.

"How did you two meet?" I asked.

Before Tosh could say anything, Ian answered, "I had my arms full with the groceries, and my man Tosh here gave me a hand."

"Is that so?" I asked, studying Ian. I set the pie down on the counter. "Can I get you something to drink?" I asked Tosh.

"I'm good."

"Go entertain our guest, Ruby," Ian said, shooing me out of the kitchen. "Dinner should be ready in a few."

I didn't like the idea of Ian making himself at home in my kitchen, or him inviting people over to my apartment. But I *did* love the smells coming out of my kitchen, and I wanted to spend more time with Tosh. Throwing them both out at this point seemed needless and, frankly, rude. So instead of making a scene with Ian, I settled onto the loveseat next to Tosh.

"Your roomie's a hoot," Tosh said.

"Oh, he's not my roomie."

"He's not? Then who is he?"

"He's my dead roommate's brother" was what almost came out of my mouth, but I stopped myself just in time. "He's just Ian," I said with a shrug instead. "How are you settling in?" I asked to change the subject.

"It's a lot colder than I'm used to in SoCal," he replied.

I barked out a laugh, which Ian echoed from the kitchen.

"What? What's so funny?" Tosh asked.

"I don't know how to break this to you, but this is warm. Just wait until winter," I cautioned him.

"Oh, I'm looking forward to it!" He leaned toward me. "I've never seen snow in real life. Can you imagine? Do you think it might snow this winter?"

"Count on it," Ian said.

Tosh looked pleased. "I know it sounds silly, but I can't wait for my first snowball fight."

"I can't remember the last time I got into a snowball fight," I admitted. "It's been ages."

"My sister and I used to have wicked snowball fights," Ian said.

I had a hard time imagining Cordelia getting into a snowball fight, but then again, I hadn't known her when she was alive, much less when she was a kid. There was something about the word "ghost" that made me think of old Victorian ladies in high-necked dresses, not tank tops and sweatpants. Before I met Cordelia, I imagined ghosts with enormous bouffant hairdos, not messy buns. And for some odd reason, whenever I pictured a ghost in my head, they were always in black and white.

"What's so funny?" Ian asked.

I realized that while I was grinning at the thought of how many ways Cordelia did *not* fit the ghost stereotype, he'd come over with two plates heaped with food. "Nothing. That smells delicious."

"Hopefully it tastes as good as it smells then," Ian said, handing one plate to me and the other to Tosh. He went back to the kitchen to serve himself.

When I settled my plate on my lap, I shifted in my seat and the USB drive in my pocket dug into my thigh. I'd very nearly forgotten all about it in my excitement over finding Marty's pill bottle. "Question for you," I said, turning to face Tosh.

"I'm an open book," he assured me.

"You work with computers. If you found a USB drive, but when you opened it up, it was gibberish, is there a way to recover it?" I asked.

"Well, first off, if I found a USB drive, the absolute last thing I'd do is put it in my computer."

"Really?" I asked. The lump in my pocket felt like a secret begging to be cracked, but now I was starting to worry because I'd done exactly that. I'd stuck it in my work computer without a second thought. "Why not?"

"Those things can be riddled with viruses. You might as well write your password down on a Post-it note."

I blushed. I'd done that before. I knew my generation had a reputation for being tech savvy, but in my house, we didn't have a lot of money for high-end electronics, so sometimes I was behind the curve. "What if you opened it anyway, and all the files were random letters?" I asked.

"Two possibilities. The data's corrupt, or the drive's encrypted."

"Corrupt" sounded about right, given Cordelia's track record with electronics.

"My money's on encrypted," Ian said, returning with his own plate.

"If it's not damaged, how would you unencrypt it?" I asked, scootching over to make room for Tosh next to me. I couldn't rule out the possibility that Cordelia hadn't scrambled its innards like an egg, but if the drive was encrypted, at least I stood a chance at recovering the data.

"You can't. That's the whole point of encryption," Tosh said with a shrug. "Why do you ask?"

"A ghost gave me a dead drug dealer's memory stick, which might be a clue to their murder, but I can't open it," I said aloud, without thinking.

CHAPTER TWENTY
RUBY

"Excuse me?" Tosh asked.

Why had I said that? I knew better than to mention Cordelia in front of her brother. And to claim to get a clue to solve a murder involving drugs from a ghost? What was I thinking?

"Ha ha." I forced myself to laugh. "Just kidding. Obviously."

My life had become so ridiculous that I didn't even realize what I was saying sounded unhinged until it was already out of my mouth. Plus, dinner was delicious and I was sandwiched between two cute guys I barely knew. I wasn't thinking straight. Call it the macaroni and cheese defense.

"Someone's been reading too many mysteries," Ian said, gesturing at the bookshelf with his fork, even though the shelves were mostly lined with romances, not mysteries.

"Or sci-fi," Tosh added.

"You two don't have any sense of humor." People wouldn't believe me that I was living with a mystery-solving ghost even if I told them, but it was downright reckless of me to let anything slip. "But seriously, my mom, she, uh, found a USB drive in my sister's room. It was, um, hidden. Mom got curious and tried to see what was on it, but she can't read the files. Now she's more determined than ever to find out what's on it, and since I work at a tech company, I told her I'd ask one of my smart friends."

I glanced over at Tosh first, then at Ian. They both looked skeptical.

"Your mom needs to be having this conversation with your sister instead of you," Tosh suggested.

"Or she could put it back and pretend she never found it," Ian offered.

"But if she *really* wanted to see what's on the drive?" I asked.

Tosh sighed. "She can try opening it on your sister's laptop. But even if the software to decrypt the files is installed there, she'll need a PIN."

"Sounds good," I said. "I'll let her know." I dug into my macaroni and cheese with gusto, making a show of how good it was, hoping Ian and Tosh would forget about my odd outburst and focus on dinner instead. "This is delicious."

"It is," Tosh agreed. "I don't think I've ever had macaroni and cheese this good before. Where'd you learn to cook like this?"

"Prison," Ian said.

I blinked at him. On one hand, I was grateful that he'd brought up the subject, because Tosh would forget about my USB drive questions entirely, but on the other hand, I was surprised Ian was so casual about revealing his checkered past at dinner.

Tosh almost choked on his bite of macaroni. "Is that, um, what you do, then?" he asked. "You're a chef at a prison?"

"Oh no, nothing like that," Ian said, scooping up a forkful of the roasted carrots—which were amazing by the way. The dish was mostly dairy and sugar, but there were carrots, too, so technically it counted as a vegetable dish. "While I was incarcerated, I bribed a guard to get me on kitchen duty. It beat sweating my ass off in the laundry and, obviously, they wouldn't let me anywhere near the motor pool."

"Obviously," Tosh said, his eyes growing to the size of quarters. Even though I was sitting between them, he wiggled closer to the armrest, putting more distance between Ian and himself.

"It makes no sense, right? I mean, I know more about cars than half the so-called mechanics, but they wouldn't let me work in the garage. And yet, when they lose the keys to the transport bus, who do they call to hot-wire it?" He pointed at himself with one thumb. "This guy."

"Well, I for one am glad you spent your time learning to cook instead of changing oil," I said, trying to sound like Ian's criminal history was no big deal. "Because this is really good. I would have never thought to use heavy cream in the mashed potatoes instead of milk."

"The secret to good mashed potatoes is first, you buy a box of the instant potato flakes. Then you throw that in the trash and use actual potatoes instead."

Ian laughed at his own joke. I laughed along. Tosh looked like he was thinking of a way to escape. I didn't blame him. I was still trying to come to terms with the fact that Ian had a criminal record, too.

"So Tosh, what do you do for work?" Ian asked, changing the subject.

Tosh chewed and forced himself to swallow. "I'm a data analyst."

"You work at CloudIndus, right?" I asked. I hadn't asked him what he actually did for a living the last time he'd come over. I was too busy being awkward.

"Yup. And you work at TrendCelerate. You're our biggest competition," Tosh said.

"So why were our two companies meeting this week?"

I'd stuck my foot in my mouth about the USB drive, Ian had narrowly avoided a land mine with his prison revelation, and now it was Tosh's turn in the hot seat. "You should ask your boss at TrendCelerate," he stammered.

"Come on, dude, don't be like that," Ian said. "Just answer the lady."

"I can't. I signed an NDA," Tosh said, as his ears turned bright red.

"That's okay," I jumped in to take the pressure off of Tosh. "I'm sure I can find out at work tomorrow. What's with the name CloudIndus anyway? Sounds like a Pokémon. Your boss must be a huge Pokémon fan."

Tosh looked confused. "Not that I know of."

"I loved the cards when I was a kid," Ian said.

"My sisters and I used to play in our old neighborhood in Baltimore," I told them.

"Do you still have your cards?" Ian asked.

I shook my head. "We only ever played on our phones."

"You can play Pokémon on your phone?" Ian asked.

How long, exactly, had he been in prison? Cordelia had made it sound like it had been a short stint, but then again, I'd been drinking at the time and our conversation was a little fuzzy. I couldn't have been much more than thirteen or fourteen when the Pokémon game came out. That made me realize two things very clearly. Ian had been in and out of jail since I was in eighth grade, and he was older than I'd originally thought.

Ian let out a barking laugh, breaking the awkward silence. "Of course I know what the Pokémon phone game is. I'm just pulling your leg." He stood, and suddenly it felt like there was too much room on the loveseat. "Anyone else want seconds?"

I looked down at my plate. I'd devoured my meal, even the carrot dish. My mother would be so proud. She had to force me to eat my veggies. I guess she should have tried drowning them in butter and brown sugar. "I'm good. I couldn't eat another bite."

"Me too," Tosh said. "In fact, I should get going."

"Nonsense," Ian said, collecting our empty plates. "The pie should be almost ready. You can't leave without having a slice of the pie you brought." He took our plates back to the kitchen.

As soon as Ian turned on the sink to rinse them, Tosh leaned his head toward mine and lowered his voice. "He was kidding, right? About prison? Like you were joking about the USB drive belonging to a dead guy?"

I shook my head. "I don't think so." It was getting hard to remember who had told me what, or what I'd told them. It would be easier to keep my stories straight if I didn't have to lie all the time, but also, I couldn't go around telling everyone I had a ghost, either, not even if they thought it was some sort of a weird joke.

"There's always room for pie," Ian said as he returned with three small plates, each with an enormous slice of pie with a scoop of rapidly melting ice cream on top.

"What'd you do, cut the pie into fourths?" I asked him. Not that I was complaining. I was full, but the pie smelled delicious. I was hoping that he'd left enough that I could have the rest for breakfast in the morning.

"Eat up," Ian said, instead of answering me. I noticed that about him. He was very good at avoiding answering questions.

"Seriously, thanks for dinner, but I'm full." Tosh put his plate on the coffee table and stood up. "Walk me to the door?" he asked me.

"Of course." I put my pie down, too. "Don't you dare touch mine," I warned Ian playfully. Like Tosh, I was full, but not so full that I wanted Ian to eat my share.

"Thanks for coming over tonight, and for loaning us your dishware," I told Tosh as we walked toward the door. "I'll wash it all and return them tomorrow."

"Perfect." He stepped out into the hall and held out his hand.

I took it awkwardly, and he pulled me into the hall, closing the door behind me.

"Are you okay being alone with him?" he asked.

"Who, Ian? Yeah, he's fine." Cordelia had called him harmless, and I trusted her. She hadn't led me astray yet.

Although, I wasn't certain Cordelia was around. I hadn't felt her presence all through dinner. Normally, there was something. A tingle in the air like a thunderstorm was approaching. Lights flickering. Shadows moving. I knew it was irrational and a symptom of growing up in a big household and now living on my own for the first time in my life, but I missed her when she wasn't around.

"If you need anything, anything at all, I'm right across the hall," he told me.

I smiled. I'd been in Boston for almost four months without making a single friend, but now, Melissa invited me to her birthday party and Tosh had come over for his second dinner in my apartment this week. My social life was looking up.

"I appreciate that. And we'll do this again sometime?"

"Definitely." He squeezed my hand. "Just you and me next time?"

"Sounds like a date," I told him.

I turned to let myself back in my apartment, but when Tosh pulled the door closed, he'd inadvertently activated the automatic lock. My key was inside. I was locked out of my own apartment.

If Cordelia had been with me, getting locked out of my apartment would have been no big deal. She could easily pass through doors and open them from the inside for me, but she was off who-knows-where doing who-knows-what. Instead of relying on Cordelia, I had to knock. On my own door.

Ian opened it. "Hello? Do you have an appointment?"

I rolled my eyes at him before turning to Tosh. "See ya later."

He nodded. "You can count on it."

"He seems nice," Ian said as I followed him back to the loveseat to reclaim my spot, and my pie.

"You sound like my mom whenever I'd bring a boy home," I said. "*He seems nice*," I added in a falsetto that sounded absolutely *nothing* like Mom.

"And what would she think of me?" he asked.

"A convicted felon almost twice my age that just lets himself into my apartment anytime he wants? Oh, she'd love you."

"Moms always do," Ian said with a boyish grin.

I should have kicked Ian out when Tosh left, but this was an opportunity to pry. Cordelia was tight-lipped about her past, literally and figuratively. If I couldn't get my roomie to open up, Ian could fill in the blanks. "What about *your* mom? The one with the great macaroni and cheese recipe? What was she like?"

Ian shrugged. "No clue. She left when I was still in diapers. My sister raised me."

"And your dad?"

"Nah, he was already raised."

"That's not what I meant," I said. The way Ian evaded every question was annoying but his banter was *almost* fun enough to overlook that.

"Didn't see much of him growing up. He worked erratic hours at a bunch of odd jobs that may or may not have been completely legit. When he wasn't working, he'd rather be out with his friends shooting pool or fishing then hanging out with his snot-nosed brats."

There was something about the way he said "snot-nosed brats" that made me think those were his father's words, not his.

"And when he wasn't shooting pool or fishing, he was passed out drunk. A real prince among men. Made me what I am today."

"Sounds challenging. You still close?" I asked. Cordelia never talked about her parents. Prying the life story out of a reluctant ghost was next to impossible.

"He died when I was little. After that, it was just me and Cordy."

"I'm sorry."

He glanced over at me, his pie-laden fork halfway to his mouth. "Don't be. We did okay. Besides, that was a long time ago."

He finished both his serving of pie and ice cream and Tosh's untouched portion. I couldn't understand where he put it all. He was as skinny as the proverbial rail. Ian sucked at the last bits that clung to his fork. Then he set his fork down on top of his empty plate, nudging the fork to make it spin.

I recognized that as something Cordelia sometimes did to get my attention or to let me know she was in the room. He saw me staring and chuckled.

"Old habit," he said. "When I was . . . dunno . . . young. First grade? Dad got a job working at a diner."

"I thought you said your dad didn't cook?" I asked.

"He couldn't. But he could scrub the hell out of a sink of dishes. If someone was paying him to do it. At home, that was my job. Cordelia cooked. I cleaned. After school, we'd sit in a back booth of whatever greasy spoon Dad was working at that month. Sometimes, if we behaved, one of the servers would take pity on us and bring us a plate of fries or a soda. After Cordy finished her homework, we'd see who could build the highest stack of creamers or who could make the silverware spin the longest." Ian gave a tight grin. "She always won. Then again, she cheated."

"How did she cheat?"

"I didn't say I could *prove* she cheated. She was just always better at it than I was, and I spent hours practicing. Although, come to think of it, that's a pretty good way to keep a kid busy for hours." He shook his head. "She always did have a trick up her sleeve." He flicked the fork again. As it slowly spun to a stop, he asked, "Do you think Cordy would have been disappointed in me?"

I hesitated. "I'm sure your sister would have been proud of you." That was a lie. I knew she was ashamed of him. But knowing that wouldn't make him feel better.

"Ha!" Ian stood and gathered our plates. "Just goes to prove that you don't know Cordelia." He paused. "That's a shame. She would have liked you."

I smiled. I wasn't so sure of that. If Cordelia and I had ever crossed paths in life, we wouldn't have had anything in common. We were so different, I doubted we would have clicked. But it didn't matter, because our paths *did* eventually cross, and we *had* learned how to get along. I was wrong earlier, when I'd thought I hadn't made any friends before today in Boston. I had Cordelia, and that was all that mattered.

CHAPTER TWENTY-ONE

CORDELIA

It was dark and cold, but I woke up sweating. It took a moment to orient myself in the unfamiliar room. I was in a motel, out by the highway. Neon lights shone in through the thin curtains. Outside, I could hear the constant stream of traffic.

At first, I couldn't figure out what had woken me. I was a heavy sleeper, by necessity. Both my father and brother snored loud enough that even when I was lucky enough to get my own room, I could hear them through the walls. More often than not, we lived above pool halls or bowling alleys, or in crappy boardinghouses where no one with any other options would voluntarily choose to stay. I could sleep through anything.

Anything, except the loud pounding of fists on the door, followed by a cry of "Police! Open up!"

For someone who'd never done anything wrong in her life—not counting shoplifting for necessities and occasionally borrowing Dad's car without permission or a license—those words drove fear into my heart. It was a lesson that had been drilled into me from a young age.

The police are not your friend. Do not talk to the police. Do not cooperate with the police. The police will take you away. The police will split up your family.

I rolled over and rubbed sleep out of my eyes, trying to focus on the clock on the bedside stand. It was three o'clock in the morning. Nothing good ever happened at three o'clock in the morning.

"Cordy?"

My brother was awake now. He was long overdue for a haircut, and his stair stood up in every direction, making him look even younger than he was. He wasn't wearing a shirt and even in the dark, I could count every one of his ribs.

"Shh." I put a finger to my lips. "Go hide in the closet, Booger. I'll take care of this. Don't come out until . . ."

"I *know*," he said, in that singsong voice of sleepy children everywhere. If he'd been more awake, he would have flipped me the bird, which was as affectionate as he ever got. "Don't come out until you come get me."

"Hurry," I told him.

I didn't wait to make sure Ian would follow my orders. He was fifty/fifty on a good day, arguing until he was blue in the face or just blatantly ignoring me, but this was different. This time it was serious, and he knew the rules.

When I opened the door, I made a big show of rubbing my fists over my eyes and yawning. "You've got the wrong room," I told the officer. I doubted it, but playing innocent went a long way, especially when I had no idea what we'd done.

Had Dad used a stolen credit card to rent the room? Was he in the drunk tank? Please tell me he hadn't urinated on an ATM again.

"Graves?" the officer asked.

Crap. Right room. "Yes?" I was wide awake now.

"I need you to come with us, Miss," he said.

"Why?"

"We can talk down at the station."

"Talk about what?" I asked.

"Let's go."

"Gimme a sec to get my shoes." I closed the door. As I dressed, I whispered, "Ian, stay in the closet until we're gone. I'll be back for you, but it might be a few hours. Do *not* leave this room, not for any reason. Do you hear me?"

A tiny voice, too tiny to belong to an eleven-year-old who should be asleep and dreaming of superheroes instead of hiding in the closet of a cheap motel, floated out to me. "Okay, Cordy."

"Stay put. I'll be back as soon as I can." I put on my shoes, grabbed the key off the TV stand, and went outside.

The officer let me ride in the front on the way back to the station. I'd never ridden in the *front* seat of a cop car before.

"What's this about?" I asked.

"We'll talk at the station," he told me. We stopped at a red light. "Aw shit." He looked at me, then corrected himself. "I mean shoot."

I was sixteen and tall for my age. With makeup and heels, I could pass for old enough to buy smokes and beer for Dad without getting carded. I'd never been mistaken for someone younger before, and wasn't accustomed to grown-ups apologizing for cursing around me. It was something about my eyes. An old soul, they called me. I wasn't used to being treated like a child.

"There was supposed to be a boy with you."

It felt like someone had hit me with a cattle prod. What was going on? What did he know? I forced myself to remain calm. I could hear my dad's voice in my head. "Do not talk to the police. Do not cooperate with the police. Do you hear me, Cordelia?"

Yeah, Dad. I heard ya.

"Oh, you mean Ian? He's with Mom." The lie rolled off my tongue with the familiarity of years of practice.

"You want to talk to Mom? Shucks. You just missed her, but she'll be right back. I'll let her know you dropped by," I would tell the nosy neighbor who wanted to complain about the little boy running around the parking lot unattended, kicking rocks at cars.

"Gee, Dad's sleeping. Just got off a double at the hospital." I'd blink doe-eyed at the bill collector knocking on the door. The hospital line almost always worked. It made him sound like a valuable member of society. "I could go wake him if you want me to. No? It's not important? Why don't you try back later?"

"Hey, Mom, someone's at the door! Okay, I'll tell them. Sorry, she's in the shower. Is there something I can help you with?"

"I should be talking with her, then," the officer said.

"Sure. I'll give you her number." When we got to the station, I rattled off an old number we had before it got disconnected for nonpayment. I got lucky. The number hadn't been reassigned yet. The officer asked if I was sure I had the number right. I repeated the number back to him again. "She's probably late with her phone bill again. What can I do for you?"

That's how I found out that my father had fallen asleep at the wheel, drifted across the center line, and taken out a minivan. He was drunk, as usual. The minivan was carrying a family returning to their home in Bangor after a vacation in Myrtle Beach. There were no survivors in either car. Dad was gone.

When the officer stepped away to grab a soda, I slipped out of the station and hitched a ride back to the motel to collect my brother. We drifted around for the next two years, flying under the radar until I turned eighteen and petitioned the court for guardianship. Six months after that, Ian was in juvie for the first time. He was barely thirteen.

I blinked, trying to orient myself in the unfamiliar room. It was dark. There were no windows. A few bare bulbs were mounted at intervals along the wooden ceiling, but they were switched off. It didn't matter. I didn't need light to see anymore.

There were stacks of boxes along the wall and exposed pipes running overhead. One had a slow leak. It dripped rhythmically on the concrete floor. I was underground. I could feel the earth pushing against the walls on all sides of me. A basement?

The last thing I remembered, before getting sucked into a flashback, was destroying the surveillance system in a pharmacy. I must have expended too much energy and slipped through the floor while I was unconscious. There was a time when I would have been trapped down here, but I'd been working on this with Harp. I concentrated like he'd taught me and let myself drift upward like a feather until I was standing in the middle of the closed pharmacy.

"See, Cordelia?" I said to myself. I dusted myself off as if somehow, I'd gotten dirty as I passed through the floor. "Easy as cake."

The overhead fluorescent lights flickered. When we'd come in to check on the Viagra prescription I'd found in the bathroom, it was just after five. Judging by the early morning sunlight streaming in through the windows, I'd missed the whole night, at least. Who knew how much time I'd lost? Hours? Days? Weeks? And who was keeping an eye on Ruby while I was off in la-la land?

I assumed Ruby had made it home safe without me. She was a big girl and could take care of herself, more or less. It just made me feel more comfortable when I could watch over her. Our apartment wasn't in the nicest neighborhood, and people around me were dying at an alarming rate too high to be a coincidence.

First me. Then Jake, my neighbor across the hall. Now Marty. Nope. "Coincidence" had gotten off the bus several stops ago. Refreshed and recharged, I bypassed the long walk home and popped right into my apartment instead.

Ruby wasn't home. Something felt off, but I couldn't put my finger on it, not that I could put my finger on much of anything these days, at least not without putting my mind to it. I wandered around looking for anything out of place.

The bedroom was as it always was, with an unmade bed and an overflowing dirty laundry hamper. The living room, likewise, was as expected. I didn't check the bathroom. I made a habit out of not going in there. The door was open and the room was empty, so I didn't feel the need to investigate further. It was only after I got to the kitchen that things got weird.

There was a large, clean baking dish I didn't recognize drying upside down on a blue-and-white towel that I didn't own. In the freezer, where yesterday there had just been an accumulation of frost so thick a yeti could have moved in and made themselves at home, there were three different kinds of ice cream: plain vanilla, mint chip, and butter pecan. As far as I knew, Ian was the only person in the world who actually liked butter pecan ice cream. What was his favorite ice cream doing in Ruby's freezer?

I opened the fridge, and it looked like a ten-year-old-boy's grocery fantasy. Soda. Pudding. Chocolate milk. Spray cheese. There wasn't a fruit or vegetable in sight, not counting a quarter of a berry pie sitting uncovered, still in a disposable tin, on the middle shelf.

"Who's been doing your grocery shopping, Ruby? A teenage boy?"

I had a feeling I knew the answer to that question, and I didn't like it. One thing was certain. Ruby wasn't home right now. And if Ian had been here, he was long gone.

Ruby was probably at work. I was tempted to pop over there, but I needed time to clear my head. I was imagining Ian all over my kitchen. Lots of people drank chocolate milk. And just because I didn't personally know anyone else who ate butter pecan ice cream, companies still made it and grocery stores still stocked it, so obviously someone other than my brother liked it. Otherwise, the entire supply chain would have dried up while he was in prison.

As I took the stairs down to the street and headed in the direction of TrendCelerate, my path took me past Lizard Pawn, where Harp spent his time. Today, he was sitting in front of a chessboard set up in front of the corner store, zooming the pieces around the board with no regards for whether anyone living might be watching. Too bad there was no one but me around to witness this.

"Hey, Harp," I said. "Whatcha doing?"

"Playing chess," he said.

"I can see that. But those aren't any rules I've ever seen before," I said as one of his pawns leapt forward three spots and knocked over a queen.

"Rules are for suckers," he replied. He kicked out the seat across the table from him in a half-assed attempt to be a gentleman. "Take a load off."

I sat. As long as I didn't wonder why I didn't fall through the chair, it was fine. But the moment I questioned it, I'd drop through it and land on the sidewalk below. If I thought too hard about it, I'd fall through the sidewalk, and just keep falling. I didn't want to find out what happened after that.

"Remember the other day, how I told you someone died at my office?"

"Did you?" he asked. "Radical."

"Not radical," I corrected him. "He was a friend."

"Friends come and go," Harp said. I couldn't tell if he was being a wisecracker or was just plain wise. "What can you do? People die. That's life." He grew bored of playing his made-up version of chess and started balancing the pieces on top of each other to form an unstable pyramid.

"But he didn't ghost. Why didn't he ghost?"

It wasn't like I'd been around a lot of dead bodies in my life, or my afterlife. When my across-the-hall neighbor died, the one who lived in the apartment now occupied by Tosh, he ghosted. But he didn't last long, a few minutes at most. Nevertheless, he was one of us for that brief time. So why hadn't Marty become a ghost?

"Was his death intentional? Violent?" Harp asked.

"Yup. Someone choked him to death. Does intention matter?"

"Of course it matters," Harp said. "Not everyone who dies comes back as a ghost. The majority don't."

That much I'd already figured out. There were simply too many people and too few ghosts to be otherwise. If everyone who died became a ghost, we would outnumber the living a billion to one. Harp was the only ghost I knew.

"It takes a nice violent death, you know?" he continued, gesturing at his own bullet-riddled shirt. "Ghosts aren't created by accidents, only from intentional deaths. A jaywalker that gets creamed by a bus does not a ghost make. And honestly, aren't you glad? The last thing I want to do is meet a walking, talking smear stain. Talk about problematic."

I shuddered. I didn't want to think that hard about death, especially not my own. I hadn't actually faced what had happened to me yet. It was more like stepping on a rusty nail and then waiting a few days to see if I *really* needed to visit the doctor or if it would heal on its own. Only instead of healing, my body was rotting in the ground somewhere. Which was exactly what I was trying to avoid dwelling on.

"Marty's death was intentional," I confirmed. It was easier talking about Marty's death than my own. "But he didn't ghost."

"What about unresolved conflicts?"

"I'm gonna go out on a limb here and guess that he had a tragic backstory. He was a single dad willing to do anything to make ends meet," I said.

"And you and I wouldn't know *anything* about tragic backstories, would we?" Harp said with a dour laugh.

And there it was again, that old rusty nail just digging deeper and deeper. "Speak for yourself."

"Oh please. We're both cuckoo bananas, and you know it." He made a spiral with his finger beside his temple. "If we hadn't died, eventually someone would have stuck us in a padded cell, loaded us up on crazy pills, and fed us crayons."

"Seriously dude, that's not how civilized adults talk about mental health anymore," I corrected him.

"Who said I'm civilized?" Harp replied. "Or an adult? Point 'em out so I can give them a wedgie."

It was time to get the subject back on track. "We've established that Marty had a violent, intentional death, and some unresolved issues. But he still didn't ghost."

"Guess luck wasn't on his side," Harp said.

"Good luck or bad luck?" I asked.

"Exactly," he replied. Which wasn't an answer, at least not the one I was looking for.

I'd been so wrapped up in our conversation, I didn't notice when two middle-aged white women, neighborhood regulars, approached until one of them plopped down in the chair I was already occupying.

"Son of a bitch!" I exclaimed as a gazillion-volt shock zapped me. I flung myself out of the chair, directly through the table. Harp's tower of chess pieces collapsed, sending plastic rooks and knights and pawns flying in every direction. Since my death, I'd gotten better at the whole mind-over-matter side of being a ghost, but I had yet to come into contact with another being—living or dead—without being in immense pain.

The woman who'd sat on me clutched the edge of the table. "My word! Clarice, did you see that?"

"Did I see you knock over them chess pieces?" The other woman, Clarice I presumed, bent over to start collecting them. "You always were a klutz."

"I didn't lay a finger on them!" the first woman protested.

I tuned out their conversation as I tried to shake off the agonizing effects of coming into direct contact with a living human. "That freaking *hurts*," I said, balling up my fists and flexing the muscles in my arms. Yes, I knew I didn't have fists. Or arms. Or muscles. But that didn't make the pain any less real.

"It only hurts because you think it hurts," Harp said.

"Bite me," I snapped.

"It's not a pleasant sensation, sure, but it's only pain if you let your mind interpret it as pain." Harp tapped his temple. "It's all in your head. Literally."

I hadn't thought of it like that before. Not that I wanted to go around testing his theory until I'd had a chance to convince myself that touching someone wouldn't feel like getting hit with a cattle prod. Harp had a point. I only existed because I believed I did, so I could bend reality by thinking it so. Unless, of course, he was playing a cruel prank on me. I wouldn't put it past him. Harp got bored easily, and grabbed any excuse to entertain himself, not caring whose expense it was at.

"Let me get this straight. Touching someone doesn't have to hurt?" I asked. Harp nodded. I wasn't sure I believed him. "But it still drains you, right?"

"Yup," Harp agreed. "Then you gotta go recharge, whether you want to or not."

"What is it for you?" I asked. "For me, it's always something I regret. Like a one-night stand with a guy who never called me back, or a fight with my boyfriend."

"Lucky you," Harp said. "I'm always stuck at a Boy George concert."

"That doesn't sound bad."

"Spoken like someone who's not been caught in a loop at the same Boy George concert for the last forty years," he replied. "And the worst part is, I never liked Boy George. Now run along. Don't forget to say hi to your little *friend* Ruby for me," he said as he made scissoring motions with his fingers.

"Knock it off," I told him. He might not understand my odd friendship with Ruby, but he was right that I didn't like leaving Ruby alone for too long, especially when there was a killer running around Boston. I closed my eyes and concentrated on Ruby. When I opened them, I was in the hallway outside of TrendCelerate.

CHAPTER TWENTY-TWO

RUBY

Friday, the office was more crowded than normal. I was used to Melissa, Marc, Blair, and Seth coming and going through the week, but rarely were they all at their desks at the same time. Even Jordie wandered in around ten. He mumbled his hellos before slinking into his cubicle. All three co-owners were on site, with their doors wide open.

Sally from HR emerged from her office. The only Black woman in the office, normally she was the best-dressed person at Trend-Celerate. Today was no exception, but she was a little less dressed up than normal, with gray slacks in place of her usual skirts and a sweater set instead of a tailored blouse.

The only time I'd seen Sally look more relaxed was when she had forgotten her headphones at her desk and swung by the office before heading out on what she called a "leisurely" ten-mile run. I'd known that Sally was a long-distance runner in training for the Boston Marathon. But that did not prepare me for her appearance dressed in skintight short-shorts, a fluorescent crop top with coordinating sweat bands, expensive sneakers, and a bladder of water strapped to her back.

"Is that everyone?" she asked me.

"Everyone, who?" I asked. "Who all are we expecting?"

She glanced around the bullpen area, taking a head count. "Anyone hear from Andy?"

Andy was the only employee I hadn't met yet. According to TrendCelerate gossip, he'd only made an appearance once, on his first day of employment. He'd stayed long enough to collect his laptop and leave. But his work was steady, and apparently he was brilliant when it came to whatever it was he did, so everyone was willing to overlook his physical absence.

Without answering my question, Sally turned and stuck her head in Adam's office. "We're all here."

Adam came out, dressed-down more than usual, in dark jeans and a purple polo shirt. I supposed it was casual Friday, but I hadn't gotten the memo. Then again, every day was casual Friday at TrendCelerate.

"Okay, folks, you might be asking why I told everyone to work from the office today," he said.

I hadn't gotten that notification, either. However, since I was expected to be in the office every day, I suppose they didn't feel the need to include me on the team email. Or they had forgotten me.

"You said it was *mandatory*," Jordie piped up. He gestured at Andy's empty cube. "If I'd known it was optional, I would have stayed home."

"Andy's not your concern," Adam told him. Then he addressed the group. "It's been a stressful week for all of us. Between the unfortunate death in the building and this CloudIndus announcement..."

"What CloudIndus announcement?" I asked. I might be just

the office manager, but I was feeling left out. First, I'd been excluded from meetings, then memos, and now this big mysterious announcement that everyone except me seemed to know about.

Adam looked startled that I would interrupt him. "I'll fill you in later."

I nodded. "Thank you."

"As I was saying, we could all stand to blow off some steam."

"Does this mean we get to knock off early?" Seth asked. He stood and unplugged his laptop. "Sweet!"

"No, it does not." Adam glared at him. "Sit back down."

Sally placed a hand on Adam's arm and took over. "What Adam's trying to say is that today, we're going to do a team-building exercise."

Everyone groaned.

"I came in for this?" Jordie complained.

Ignoring him, Sally continued, "There's a van waiting for us downstairs."

"Where are we going?" Melissa asked.

"It's a surprise," Adam said. "Leave your laptops here. Let's go."

As we filed out the door, Franklin and Quinn emerged from their offices and joined the queue. Like Adam, Franklin was wearing jeans, but he'd paired his with a short-sleeved button-down shirt. Quinn was in slacks instead of her normal suit and wore flats that put her at almost my height. But whereas I was wearing a T-shirt that featured a cartoon capybara with the caption "Don't worry, be capy," Quinn had on a silk blouse and a pearl necklace. I guess we all had our own idea of what "dressing down" meant.

While I sat between Seth and Melissa in the back row, it occurred to me that everyone in the van—with the exception of the driver—had been in the office on Monday morning when Marty died. Along with the other scarcely used offices on the second floor and our CloudIndus guests, which included Tosh, we were the *only* people who had access to the bathroom where Marty had been killed. Which meant his killer could very well be one of us.

A chill ran down my spine at that thought. I could be in a van with a murderer, going who-knows-where. I had the faint sensation that Cordelia was nearby, but I couldn't get a read on her. She would never let anything bad happen to me, but I was still curious where they were taking us. "Where are we going?" I asked.

"A strip club?" Seth suggested.

"Last time we did a team-building event, it was a ropes course," Melissa said.

Marc, who was sitting in front of us, turned around. "I hope it's not that again. We had to go all the way to New Hampshire, and didn't get back until almost midnight. I promised my wife I'd be home by three today. The twins have a playdate."

"It's not a ropes course," Adam called back from the first row that he shared with Franklin and Quinn.

"Thank goodness for that," Melissa said, blissfully unaware that she might be sharing a ride with a killer. "They stuck me on a team with *Blair*."

"You're welcome," Blair replied, without turning around. He was seated between Marc and Jordie. I couldn't see where we were going because his spiky hair blocked my view.

"He used every obstacle as an excuse to grab my ass," Melissa said, glaring daggers at the back of his head.

Blair twisted around in his seat. "I told you. It was for *balance*." He sniffed. "Like your ass is so great anyway."

From the front passenger seat, Sally called back, "Blair, we talked about this."

"Yeah, yeah, I'm not supposed to talk about asses at work. Which is hard when I'm surrounded by them," Blair responded.

"I don't think this was such a great idea," Sally told Adam.

"They'll behave," he assured her. "Won't you?" he called over his shoulder.

A chorus of half-hearted mumbles came from the back rows of the van.

"See? I told you. It'll be fine," Adam said.

"As long as there's not another white water rafting incident," Seth said, waggling his eyebrows.

"What white water rafting incident?" I asked, feeling more left out than ever. It was one thing to hear snippets of office gossip from holiday parties past, but I was starting to realize that everyone except me had worked, and played, together for a long time, and they had all of these shared experiences I would never have with them.

"You swore you'd never talk about that again," Blair said, turning all the way around in his seat to glare at Seth.

Melissa nudged me with her elbow. "I'll tell you all about it later."

"Like hell you will," Blair said through clenched teeth.

"Blair!" Quinn barked. "You turn around this very instant. You are wearing a seat belt, aren't you?"

Blair turned back. There was a click as his seat belt snapped together. "Yes, ma'am."

"I thought so." Quinn turned her head to survey everyone else. "And that goes for the rest of you, too."

There was a minute of fumbling as we all found our seat belts tucked back into the seat cushions, sorted out whose was whose, and put them on. Despite not having any biological children of her own, Quinn had Big Mom Energy. It made everyone sit up a little straighter. I had no doubt she had that freaky mom strength, too. I just wished she was as strict with little Regina as she was with the rest of us, instead of spoiling her rotten.

The rest of the ride was as quiet as if she'd told us all to sit on our hands and look out our own window, like my mother used to do when my sisters and I argued in the car. After ten more minutes, we pulled into a parking lot. Since I was in the back of the van, I was one of the last people to climb out. Once I did, I realized that we were standing outside of a pirate-themed miniature golf course.

"Here's the deal," Quinn announced. We were a decent-size group standing outside in a noisy parking lot, but we didn't have any trouble hearing her. Quinn's voice carried. "Three teams of three. Franklin, Adam, and myself are team captains. Any questions?"

There were three owners, plus Melissa, Blair, Seth, Marc, Jordie, Sally, and me. If there were three people per team, then someone was going to be left out in the cold. I had a sinking feeling I was going to be the odd person out. "But there's ten of us," I said.

"I'm just here to keep things fair," Sally said.

"How come she doesn't have to participate?" Jordie grumbled.

"Can we play with our own balls?" Blair asked.

"One more comment like that out of you and you'll spend the rest of the day in the van," Adam told him.

"Promise?" Blair asked.

"And if you're lucky, we'll leave the window cracked for you," Adam added.

Considering what had occurred to me in the van about Marty's killer possibly being on the field trip with us, I thought this could be an opportunity to get to know everyone a little better. "Instead of small teams, how about we rotate?" I suggested. "Isn't that the point of team building? Everyone participates?"

"Don't worry, Ruby," Sally assured me. "Everyone's a winner."

I was assigned to Franklin's team with Seth. Up until now, I'd only ever exchanged a few words with Franklin. This would be a good time to remedy that.

Franklin took the first whack at his ball. It bounced along the green artificial grass, careened off a treasure chest, and landed in the open mouth of a plastic alligator. The alligator slowly rotated and spit the ball out into the cup. "Hole in one," he announced.

"Wow. Have you done this course before, Mr. Delacorte?" I asked.

Franklin looked taken aback. "It's simple math," he said. "And you should probably call me Franklin, while we're out here."

"Watch this, Frankie," Seth said. He lined up his ball and whacked it as hard as he could. It hit the low retaining wall hard enough to pop out of play. It rolled across the footpath and splashed into a retaining pond with water a color of blue not found in nature.

"*You* can call me Mr. Delacorte," Franklin told Seth with a frown. "And that counts as two strokes." He headed off to study the second hole.

"Doesn't this feel weird?" I asked Seth as he teed up his ball for his second try.

"What? Playing a game designed for kids in the middle of the workday with a bunch of stuffed shirts? When I started at Trend-Celerate, my first team-building exercise was going out to the arcade by the harbor. I kicked Adam's ass at Donkey Kong, and he threatened to fire me."

He hit his ball again, softer this time. It rolled a few feet, hit a bump, and rolled back to him.

"No, I mean, a man died, and we're out here, playing minigolf."

"People die all the time," he told me. He took two more swats at the ball before getting it in the hole. "That's par," he said, writing a three down on his scorecard.

"You shot a five," I corrected him.

"How about this, if you can beat me on this hole, I'll take a ten. If you can't, the three stands."

"Fine," I said.

I hadn't played minigolf in ages. I didn't have Seth's completely unwarranted confidence. I didn't have Franklin's grasp of angles and force and whatever else went into his calculations. But I had an ace up my sleeve.

I tapped the ball, and it careened up the green. It wove drunkenly around the obstacles. At one point, it seemed to hover over the artificial grass. It slowly rolled toward the hole, coming to rest at the very edge of the cup. Then, it toppled over into the hole.

"Hole in one," I said, grinning at Seth.

"How'd you do that?" he sputtered.

I shrugged. With Cordelia on my side, I could do anything, even minigolf. "It's like Franklin said. Math."

We walked to the next hole. Franklin was nowhere in sight, having already played the hole and moved on. So much for team building. "Did you know him very well?" I asked Seth.

"Who?" he asked. This time, he took his time lining up his shot. He got it around the sunken ship, and it looked like it was on track when it suddenly careened to one side, hit the barrier wall, and reversed course. It rolled to a stop at his feet. "You've got to be kidding me," he muttered, whacking at it again. His putter connected solidly with the ball, but it barely moved. He swung a third time. It rolled a few feet and then came to an abrupt stop.

I pressed my lips together, trying not to laugh at Cordelia's antics as Seth tried again. The ball took a crazy bounce, ricocheted back, and rolled all the way past the start line, back onto the path.

"Unbelievable," he grumbled, turning red.

"Marty," I said. I made sure that Franklin hadn't come back to check on us, and then lowered my voice. "I heard he wouldn't sell to you?"

Seth miscalculated his swing and instead of hitting his ball, slammed the head of his club into the artificial grass, leaving a dent. He spun to face me. "Where'd you hear that?"

My mouth was suddenly dry. "I, um, I don't remember."

"Uh-huh." He kicked his ball hard, straight into the cup. "Your turn." He picked up his ball and headed to the next hole.

I hit my ball. Without Cordelia showing off, it took me three strokes.

I hurried to catch up with Seth, but I needn't have rushed because when I caught up to him on the next hole, his ball ping-ponged between two mermaid tails before popping up and striking him on the thigh. "Ow!"

I giggled. Now I knew why Cordelia hadn't stuck around to help me. What I couldn't be sure of was if she was torturing him on purpose or if she was just slowing him down so I could question him.

"It's not funny," he growled. "That stung."

"Sorry. Now, about Marty," I started again.

"What's your obsession with this dude?" Seth asked. He hit his ball. It popped straight up into the air and came down to land back where he'd started. "Shit. I hate this course."

I was getting nowhere fast, so I tried a different tactic. "I'm new in town. I don't know who to go to now that Marty's gone. I thought maybe you'd understand since he'd already cut you off."

"Why didn't you just say so?" He tried to hit his ball, but right before he connected, the ball rolled away. He hit the head of his club against the ground in frustration. "What exactly are you looking for? Adderall? Ozempic? Ritalin? Molly? X? I could use some Valium right about now."

"X? I thought Marty only carried prescriptions," I said.

"That's true. I kept bugging him to hook me up with the fun shit. Eventually he cut me off completely. His loss."

"I'd be livid if Marty had stopped selling to me. I mean, it was so convenient." I was fishing, hoping that Seth would admit that he'd gotten upset. Was it worth killing over? Maybe it was, depending on how badly Seth wanted those pills.

"Right?" Seth agreed. "Marty was an idiot. Can you imagine getting Molly delivered with lunch? Paradise." He chuckled to himself. "Although, there would be chaos in the break room if there was an assortment of goodies alongside the sandwiches."

He brought up an interesting point. When we got a delivery, my coworkers descended on it like a horde of starving locusts, grabbing food more or less at random without even checking the contents. So how did Marty manage to pass out prescriptions to individuals without someone accidentally picking up the wrong pills?

"I always wondered how everyone got the right order in all that mayhem," I said. I was taking a risk by admitting I didn't know how the system worked, but Seth didn't seem to notice.

"That was supposed to be *your* job," he said. "I mean not you, specifically, but you get the picture."

Actually, I didn't, but then it hit me. "Cordelia."

Seth's ball rolled over and hit me in the foot hard enough to sting. I didn't think Cordelia was comfortable with the turn the conversation had taken. I didn't blame her.

"Things were simpler when she was around. Too bad she had to go and off herself. After she was gone, it was all cloak-and-dagger distractions so Marty could pass out the goods. I'm surprised he didn't ask you to take over her role, since you were a customer. Guess he didn't trust you yet."

"Guess not," I agreed.

"Well? You never answered my question. What are you looking for?"

Shoot. I couldn't remember the list he'd spouted off earlier, so I blurted out the first thing that came to mind. "Uh, Viagra?" Then I blushed. When I'd found the bottle of Viagra in the bathroom, I'd been embarrassed at the idea that someone in my office was taking it, and now I'd just told Seth that I wanted some. I couldn't look him in the eye.

Seth grinned and nodded his head slowly. "I judged you all wrong, Ruby. I had no idea you were down for a freaky good time." He scrolled through his phone contacts. "I know just the person. I'll text the contact info to you. Just tell her I sent you."

"But she's not as good as Marty, right?" I pressed. I hadn't gotten a reaction out of him earlier, but I wasn't ready to give up yet. "Aren't you just steaming mad that he refused to sell to you?"

"No biggie. Plenty of fish in the sea, you know what I mean?" Seth hacked at his ball. It bounced around like a pinball before coming to a rest at his feet again.

He bent over and scooped up his ball. Then he tore his scorecard in half and tossed it to the ground. "I'm done. If anyone's looking for me, I'll be at the bar." As he stomped away, he tossed his club and ball into the nearest trash can.

Despite all of his jokes, Seth had a temper, that much was clear. He claimed that he wasn't upset that Marty had cut him off, and I believed him. But he also started whacking his golf club indiscriminately the minute things didn't go his way on the course, and this was just a game. Whoever killed Marty had enough rage to shove an entire bottle of pills down his throat. From the glimpses I'd seen just now, Seth had a lot of pent-up anger, but did he have enough to kill?

CHAPTER TWENTY-THREE
CORDELIA

Adam, followed closely by Melissa and Jordie, walked up to the hole Ruby was standing on. "Where's the rest of your team?" he asked.

"Franklin, I mean Mr. Delacorte, played on ahead. I think Seth just quit," she said.

Adam bent over and picked up the pieces of the scorecard. "Ten on the first hole, seven on the second? No wonder he gave up."

He put the scorecard in his pocket rather than litter. It wasn't fair. A man as hot as Adam needed *some* flaws. But no, Adam recycled. He donated to charity. He stopped at crosswalks. Then again, he wasn't absolutely perfect. He did cheat on his wife.

"I guess you're on our team now," Adam told Ruby. "You're up first."

She shot her ball between the mermaids. It began rolling up the ramp, but was losing speed. I kicked it—careful to not make it disappear when I touched it—and it shot up into the giant clam. I gave it a nudge, and it looped for a moment, fell into the trap, and shot out the other side, dropping in the cup with a satisfying thud.

"Damn, girl!" Melissa squealed.

"Good job," Adam said.

"Huh," Jordie grunted. He dropped his ball and tried to replicate Ruby's shot. Without my help, his ball rolled back down the ramp and he had to go the long way around instead of taking the giant clam shortcut.

Melissa bypassed the clam and finished the hole in three strokes, compared to Jordie's four. "Suck on that," she told him.

"Guys, keep it civil," Adam said. "We're supposed to be team building, remember?" He overshot the clam. His ball rolled to a halt in a blind curve. I kicked it toward the cup so he was able to finish the hole in two strokes.

As he retrieved his ball, he glanced over at Ruby's scorecard. "Two holes in one already?" He draped his arm over her shoulders.

"Whoa, hands off the girl," I warned him.

His arm didn't move as he told her, "If I'd known you were some kind of minigolf savant, I would have invited you to join my team sooner."

Melissa grabbed Ruby's arm and tugged her away from him. "You two play on ahead. We're going to grab a snack. We'll catch up in a minute."

I trailed behind them down the path toward a lemonade stand. Melissa bought two drinks. She handed one to Ruby, then pulled a flask out of her purse. "Want some?"

Ruby shook her head. "No, thanks."

It was just my luck that out of all the possible roommates in the world, I'd end up with the straight-edge one.

"Suit yourself." Melissa upended the flask into her lemonade and took a big sip. "Now *that* hits the spot."

"How can you play minigolf drunk?" Ruby asked her.

"How can you play minigolf sober?" she countered. "Can I say something? As a friend? Without hurting your feelings?"

I blinked at her. When had Melissa and Ruby become friends? I felt a spark of jealousy, but I pushed it aside. It was a good thing that Ruby was making friends at work. I had nothing to feel jealous about.

"Yeah. Sure."

"You need to dial it down around Adam."

"Dial it down?" Ruby asked, confused.

"I don't want anyone to get the wrong impression."

Ruby shook her head. "I'm not interested in Adam."

"Yeah, she's not interested in Adam," I echoed.

"I'm sure you're not. It's just that sometimes, well, you're awful friendly and all, and people talk."

"What do you mean?" I asked, irritated that Melissa would suggest such a thing. "I don't know what minigolf game you were watching, but from where I was standing, Adam put his arm around her without any provocation."

"I'm not that friendly," Ruby argued. "Wait a sec. Is that why everyone assumes that the former office manager had a thing for him?"

"Excuse me? Who have you been talking to, Ruby?" I asked. "No one at work knew about me and Adam."

Melissa laughed and took another big sip from her spiked lemonade. "Not hardly. They were totally screwing. They weren't even trying to be discreet."

"You take that back," I told her. How could everyone in the office know about us? I thought we were being so cautious. Was there nothing sacred anymore? I hated being fodder for gossip. "We were totally discreet."

Melissa continued, unaware that she'd just yanked the rug out from under me. "Just be careful. I don't want everyone to jump to the same conclusion about you, too, if you start to get too chummy."

Ruby pursed her lips. "I have no intention of getting chummy with Adam, or any of the guys at work."

"I know you don't," Melissa said. "Just keep your distance, okay?"

"Okay," she promised.

I trailed behind them as they headed back. Only, before they caught up with the others, they ran into Sally. "Why aren't you two with your group?" she asked.

Melissa held up her lemonade. "Refreshments. Don't worry, we're headed back now."

"Have either of you seen Seth?" Sally asked.

"Seth stormed off earlier," Ruby told her. "In his defense, he was having a run of bad luck."

Run of bad luck? That was one way to put it. Like everyone at TrendCelerate, I'd been the victim of Seth's practical jokes more times than I could count over the years, like that time he replaced the cream in the Oreos in the break room with toothpaste. And now, I had a chance to pay him back. I'd had the time of my afterlife messing with his golf ball. Who knew he'd get so sore when he was the butt of the joke for once?

Once Sally was out of earshot, Ruby suggested, "Maybe you should get rid of that drink before anyone catches you with booze."

"Good idea," Melissa said. She downed the spiked lemonade. "Sorry I'm in such a bitchy mood today. Two of my roommates got into it last night, and I tried to play mediator. Now *both* of them are moving out, which means rent shares go up, and everyone else in the house blames me."

"Sounds like a mess."

"It totally is. You're living in Cordelia Graves's old apartment, right?"

"What?" I asked. "How'd you know that? Is nothing a secret anymore?"

"Where'd you hear that?" Ruby asked, looking as dumfounded as I felt.

Melissa let out a derisive snort. "Blair accidentally overheard you telling Adam that you rented Cordelia's old apartment before you started working here. Hell of a fluke, if you ask me."

Blair *accidentally* overheard it? Eavesdropped is more like it. I should have known. I wondered what else he'd overheard.

"Yeah, funny coincidence, right?" Ruby said.

She was playing it cool but I was freaking out. What would happen if everyone at TrendCelerate figured out there was an ongoing connection between Ruby and me?

"Anyway, I know you've got one roomie already, but is there any chance you've got space for another? It would just be for a little while, until I found something on my own."

Ruby had let it slip one day that she had a roommate, and Melissa would not let it go. Not that I thought any of my old coworkers would ever figure out that I was still here, but it was a chance we couldn't afford to take.

Ruby shook her head. "Oh gosh, I'd love to help, but my place is tiny."

"That doesn't bother me. I can't afford my own place right now, but I'd pay my fair share," she pleaded.

"Sorry, but my roomie would never go for it," Ruby said.

"Damn right I wouldn't," I replied.

Ruby continued, "Can't you stick it out where you're at now while you look for a new place?"

Melissa sighed. "Yeah, I guess a few more weeks won't kill me."

She looked over at Adam and Jordie, who were waving them over. "But those two just might. Come on, Ruby, let's get this over with."

The rest of the round, if Adam got too close, Ruby found an excuse to move as far away from him as possible. Jordie kept mumbling to himself. Melissa's swings got more and more erratic until I was afraid she might actually hit one of them, or herself, with her club.

With the four of them on the same team, it wasn't long before the last group caught up and demanded to be allowed to play through. Marc looked miserable. Blair and Quinn were chatting about yachts and some hot new destination spot. Blair's dad and Quinn were old friends. It was how Blair got, and kept, his job.

Everyone finally made it to the finish line, where Franklin and Sally were waiting. After turning in their scorecards, Blair was declared the winner, despite Ruby's "miraculous" holes in one. Apparently, skipping the fourth hole with Melissa disqualified her.

I wasn't disappointed that after all my hard work, Ruby had lost the tournament, but I *was* disappointed that she lost to Blair. Predictably, he was insufferable on the ride home. Seth had already grabbed an Uber, so there was more room in the van on the way back. I was able to sit in the back row between Melissa and Ruby instead of clinging to the roof like I'd done on the drive down. Harp had a lot more know-how than I did when it came to ghostly matters, and if he said touching someone didn't have to hurt, he was probably right. But since that ran counter to everything I'd personally experienced so far, I wasn't taking any chances.

CHAPTER TWENTY-FOUR
RUBY

The minute I got home, I turned on my phone. Almost immediately, it rang. I checked the caller ID and accepted the call. My mom's face filled the screen.

"Ah, there's my baby!" Mom said.

I rolled my eyes. The middle child of three, I'd only been the baby of the family for all of eighteen months, and that was twenty years ago. "I'm not a . . ."

"Don't roll your eyes at me," Mom said. Even if we hadn't been on a video call, she would have known. She had superpowers. "Are you getting enough sleep? Drinking enough water? You've got bags under your eyes they could see from space. What's wrong?"

Whoever invented video calls should be ashamed of themselves. It was probably a tech company similar to TrendCelerate that had no idea of—or didn't care about—the consequences of their software.

"Nothing's wrong, Ma. Nothing to worry about."

"Nonsense. I don't mind worrying about you. Are you eating enough? Do you need money? I can send money."

I appreciated the sentiment, but I knew she couldn't afford it. We'd lived in the Baltimore row house for as long as I could remember, and the rent went up every year. The price of heating had skyrocketed last winter. I knew she was behind on her bills. Fortunately, I didn't need anything right now. I had a steady paycheck, and in an emergency, I had a ghost who had sticky fingers and a small fortune socked away in a health savings account.

"Thanks, but I'm good." Since I started at TrendCelerate, I'd made a point to transfer a little every pay period to her bank account. She'd protested at first, but I knew she needed it more than I did. Me moving out of the house meant slightly lower expenses, but without my income, there was less coming into the household, too. I made a mental note to cut back on all the organic produce Cordelia kept pushing on me so I could send a bit extra this month.

"How's Luce?"

Last time I'd talked to my older sister, Lucy, she'd been knee-deep in wedding preparations. She and her longtime boyfriend—now fiancé—were tying the knot next fall and she was freaking out trying to pick the perfect font for her invitations. I loved my sister with my whole heart, and while part of me was sad that I was missing out on the endless wedding gown try-ons, mostly I was happy to live far enough away to be out of the direct line of fire.

"Oh, you know Lucy," Mom said, with a shrug.

"I do," I agreed.

Lucy had always been a handful, and it came as no surprise that she was a difficult bride-to-be. She'd done a few commercials as a baby, and I guess it had gotten in her blood. Growing up, she'd been in drama club and debate club and any kind of club where she could hog the spotlight. Frankly, I loved that for her. As long as everyone was paying attention to her, I could coast under the radar with my B average and a complete lack of any extracurricular activities.

"Which is why Jordan is staying with you this summer."

"Wait, what?" Jordan was my baby sister. I knew I wasn't supposed to have a favorite sibling, but Jordan had that role nailed down from the moment Mom brought her home from the hospital. I'd shared a room with her for almost eighteen years of my life, because of course Lucy got her own bedroom. This was my first time living alone, and I wasn't ready to give that up—not for Melissa at work, no matter how badly she needed out of her current housing situation, and not for my baby sister.

Not that I lived alone, not really. Cordelia didn't take up any space, per se, but she was always around. Even if I wanted to share my apartment with someone else—and I did not—how was I supposed to explain the ghost?

"No, there's no way Jordan can spend the summer here, not in my tiny apartment."

"Why on earth not?"

"It's just a bad time. I'm still settling in, and what would she do while I'm at work all day?"

"I'm sure she'll think of something. She's a smart kid. Only one of all my children to go to college."

"Yes, she's the smart one," I agreed, as if I hadn't heard that more times than I could count. "And what about her school?"

"She's not taking summer classes. Too expensive."

"What about Lucy? Doesn't she need someone to help her with all the prep?"

Mom lowered her voice. "Jordan's over the whole wedding prep. I'm not spending the entire summer running interference between those two. Last time she was home for the weekend, she called your sister a bridezilla. Can you imagine?"

I nodded. "Yeah, Mom, I can." Whoever invented the word "bridezilla" had my older sister in mind. Not that Lucy was all that bad, but the family dynamic in our house was simple. Lucy and Jordan were too much alike to get along without me there to play referee.

"Speaking of which, when are you coming home for a visit? I'm not asking much. A weekend. I miss you."

"Miss you, too, Ma, but it's an eight-hour train ride in each direction. That's a lot for a weekend trip."

"Fine, then I guess you'll have to make it a full week." She let out a long-suffering, well-timed sigh.

I'd walked right into that one. I'd wanted to come home for the long Memorial Day weekend that was just around the corner, but with everything else that had happened with Marty, I wasn't sure I could swing it. "I'll see if I can get some time off around July Fourth," I promised.

"That's so long from now," Mom said, pouting.

There was a knock at the door.

"Don't worry, I'll be home before you know it," I promised her. "I gotta go. Someone's at the door. Love ya!" I disconnected before she could pile on any more guilt.

I dashed off a text to my youngest sister: "no matter what mom sez ur *NOT* coming 2 boston this summer!!!" The three exclamation points might have been excessive, but I wanted to make sure she got the point.

There was another knock at the door. I pressed my eye against the peephole. An immaculately dressed Black woman stood in the hall. I recognized Penny Fisher, a reporter for the *Herald* I'd met a few months ago after my neighbor Jake was murdered. I opened the door. "Hello."

"Hello to you, too," she said, brushing past me without waiting for an invitation, which was normal behavior for her. Penny wasn't overly pushy, for a reporter. She did, however, have a nose for a story and didn't let anyone stand in her way.

"Make yourself at home," I said, wryly. I was getting a lot of unexpected visitors lately. At least she'd knocked, unlike Ian. But they both made themselves at home without waiting for an invitation.

Penny headed straight for my kitchen. "Coffee?"

"I just got home from work, but I can make some," I told her.

"Don't mind me. I'll take care of it," she said as she busied herself with making a fresh pot.

As close as I could tell, Penny Fisher was in her thirties. While she always had a warm smile, lurking under her friendly attitude was a sharp mind and an even sharper pencil, always ready to break the next story.

When I first met her, she'd come sniffing around because she thought it was suspicious that the previous tenant—and unbeknownst to her, current ghost—of my apartment supposedly committed suicide, and then the witness who claimed to have seen a man leaving Cordelia's apartment the night she died was murdered outside our building. I had to admit, it was a hell of a coincidence. But Cordelia and I had uncovered our neighbor's killer, and they were behind bars now.

Penny sensed that something was fishy. She didn't know my apartment was haunted—or at least, I didn't think she did—but she wasn't going to stop coming around until she got to the bottom of everything. It was inconvenient, but I admired her tenacity.

"How was your week?" While the coffee brewed, Penny turned her attention to my cabinets, where she zeroed in on a bag of store-brand chocolate chip cookies.

She ripped open the package and popped one in her mouth. "Oh, that's good." She held the package out to me. It would have been thoughtful, if they weren't *my* cookies she was offering me. "No? Suit yourself." She ate another cookie before closing the bag and putting it back on the shelf. "Don't mind me. Claire's on a diet, which means I'm on a diet. The most unhealthy thing in our apartment right now is oatcakes that are apparently flavored with toenail clippings and abandoned dreams."

"Claire sounds like a riot," I said.

"Well, she puts up with my hours, so I put up with her oatcakes." Penny watched the coffee drip into the pot with painful slowness. "The things we do for love, right?"

Despite her barging in and opening the cookies I'd been saving for a special occasion, I actually liked Penny. She had a way of putting everyone around her at ease, which I guess was a talent that came in handy for an investigative reporter.

"Spill the beans," Penny said.

"I'd rather you didn't," I said. She'd left the bag of coffee grinds open on the counter. I moved past her, folded the lid over, and tucked the bag back into its place behind the coffee maker. I knew I should store them in a container with a good seal, but a bag never lasted long enough in my apartment to go stale. I drank coffee the way I should drink water. Although, if I thought about it, coffee was mostly water so I was ahead of the curve.

"That's not what I meant, and you know it."

"What are you talking about?" I asked, trying—and failing—to sound innocent.

Penny raised one eyebrow and stared me down. I didn't know if she had kids, but if she did, I'd bet they didn't get away with anything. I recognized that look because my mom used it on me and my sisters when we were up to no good. It was a look that could get me to confess to anything, even if I'd done nothing wrong.

"Martin Spencer?" Penny asked. "You think a man can die under suspicious circumstances at your place of employment and I wouldn't have questions?"

I knew better than to ask how she'd heard about Marty's death.

If anything, I was surprised it had taken her this long to pick up on the story. "What about him?"

"You tell me," she said.

Tired of waiting for the coffee to finish brewing, she took the half-filled pot and poured herself a mug, even as coffee continued to drip and sizzle on the hot plate. She put the pot back and pulled a carton of milk out of the fridge. "Whole milk. Bless you." She upended the carton into her coffee, but nothing came out.

For the record, since moving to Boston, I really had gotten a lot better at adulting. I did my own laundry, on a semi-regular basis. I even set my CharlieCard up on autopay so I'd always have enough funds on my card to take the bus. Thanks to Cordelia, I was learning to cook. But some habits die hard, and I'd slipped up and put the empty carton back in the refrigerator.

Penny gave me a disappointed look as she walked the empty milk carton over to the trash can and heaved a loud sigh as she tossed it inside.

"I think there's still chocolate milk," I said. Ian hadn't returned since he'd stocked up my refrigerator with all of his favorite junk foods.

"I'm fine." She pulled her phone out of her pocket, laid it on the counter, and pulled up an app. "Hope you don't mind if I record this." I knew her phone wouldn't record a word we said, not while Cordelia was in the room, scrambling the delicate electronics. "What can you tell me about Martin Spencer?"

"Marty used to deliver sandwiches from Beantown Deli. TrendCelerate orders from them a lot."

She nodded. "I know the place. Their Italian spuckie is a delicious heart attack waiting to happen. Claire would murder me if she caught me eating one. I wonder if they're still open?"

I shook my head. "They close after lunch. That's one heck of a diet Claire has you on if you're craving a spuckie this late at night. And why do they call it a spuckie, anyway?"

Penny rested her coffee mug down next to her phone. "Why does anyone do anything?" She tapped the screen to her phone. "I don't know what it is about this place but my phone goes haywire the second I open up the voice recorder in your apartment." The same thing had happened the last time she tried to interview me. Cordelia sure did enjoy messing with her equipment.

"Old wiring," I said quickly. Too quickly, like I had something to hide.

"That must be it. Marty Spencer," she repeated. "Give me the deets, and be specific. What do you know?"

"He died in the TrendCelerate bathroom last Monday, mid-morning."

Penny was normally perfectly composed at all times, but when I said that, I swear she flinched. "And this Marty guy, you knew him pretty well?"

"Not really. He seemed like a good guy. It's a shame he died, and at my place of employment. Plus, I was the one who found him."

"Oh no! Are you okay?" Penny looked genuinely concerned, but I couldn't be certain this wasn't part of her carefully crafted plan to get me to spill my guts. If Penny pricked her finger, newspaper ink would come out instead of blood. I'd do well to remember that.

"I've been better."

Penny poured me a mug of coffee and brought it over. She'd make the perfect hostess—if we were in her home instead of mine. "I'm sorry. That must be awful. I know what that's like."

"You do?" I asked. I found that hard to believe. It sounded like a trick to get me to open up and tell her more. "You've found someone dead in a bathroom?"

"Yes. Yes, I have." Her eyes darted to my bathroom, where Cordelia had died. We both shivered.

I didn't think I was going to get over the trauma of finding Marty's body quickly enough to be comfortable in any bathroom for any length of time. Last night, I'd even skipped brushing my teeth. This morning, I'd taken a lightning-fast shower without washing my hair. Drinking coffee this late in the evening wasn't a great idea. I set the mug down on the nearby coffee table.

"I'm sorry to hear that."

"Thank you," she said. "You too."

"Can I ask you a favor?"

She nodded.

"Do you have access to police files?"

"I can get access," Penny confirmed. "What do you need?"

"Can you get a copy of Marty's autopsy? While you're at it, can you dig into his background? I know he's been arrested before, and he's done time. I tried to look it up, but I hit a wall."

"No problem," she said. "It might take a while, but a lot of that stuff is public record if you know where to look."

"And you know where to look?" I asked.

"I do. Why are you so interested in this? You said you barely knew him."

"Yeah, but I can't stop thinking about his death. If I knew what the autopsy says, I could get closure." Then I turned it around on her. "Why are *you* so interested? This isn't the kind of story you're normally interested in."

"Cordelia Graves? The woman who used to live here? Before she killed herself, I was working on a story that involved Trend-Celerate. She was one of my sources."

I blinked at her. This was news to me. "What kind of source?"

"The confidential kind."

Conversations with Penny were a lot like conversations with Cordelia, now that I thought about it. They were never a two-way street. Penny took information, and gave back little in return. Cordelia's dialogue was limited to magnetic poetry and Etch A Sketches. Penny had no such excuse.

"Fine. Don't tell me. But at least tell me what the story was about."

Penny shook her head. "No can do. Doesn't matter anyway. It didn't go anywhere. But it's weird, right?" She leaned forward. "First Cordelia Graves dies in this very apartment. Then, last spring, your neighbor Jake Macintyre is killed on the front steps of your building. And now, Martin Spencer dies at your office. I can't help but feel it's all connected."

CHAPTER TWENTY-FIVE
CORDELIA

Penny Fisher wasn't my favorite person. Sure, she was all nice and helpful on the outside. She was friendly. Smart. Sweet. Tenacious. Everything a reporter should be. She was good at her job. Too good.

I liked my privacy. I liked my secrets. Penny wasn't someone who respected either of those things. She'd do anything it took and bust down every door in her way to uncover any dirt that someone was hiding to get her story. Grudgingly, I had to admit that those were all good qualities for a reporter. I just didn't appreciate it when it was *my* dirt she was digging up.

I didn't love Penny telling Ruby I was her source. Against my better judgment, I'd let her pester me into to talking to her. She set up a meeting. When I didn't answer the door, she let herself into my apartment. If Penny was the kind of person who let a little thing like a closed door stop her, it might have been ages before anyone checked on me and found my dead body in the bathtub.

The TrendCelerate offices closed for two weeks over the winter holidays. It was easier than trying to maintain a skeleton crew when everyone requested leave at the same time. So in lieu of an end-of-the-year bonus, TrendCelerate threw a decadent holiday bash the weekend before Christmas and gave everyone leave until the Monday after New Year's. Adam was the only person who might have noticed my absence during those two weeks. But we'd broken up. No one would have missed me.

Would TrendCelerate have assumed I'd quit if I didn't show up for work after the office reopened? People quit jobs without notice all the time. Adam would've thought I'd left to avoid him. And my apartment? My bank account was healthy and my bills were on autopay. It could have been months before a payment bounced, and even then, my automatic overdraft coverage would have kicked in.

It sucked to admit it, but there wasn't anyone in my life who would have come looking for me when I disappeared. My neighbors would have figured it out, eventually, when my mail piled up and my apartment began to smell. But, since it was the dead of winter and the heat in this building hardly worked, I could have remained a Cordeliacicle until spring thaw.

Poor Penny. Finding my body had been traumatic for her. Speaking as the one who had been found, I know it was traumatic for me.

After Penny finished her coffee and left, Ruby crossed the room and pulled down my fake-book hiding spot from the top of the bookshelf. She had to stand on her tippy-toes to reach it.

"Whatever happened to little Miss Never Again?" I teased her.

I was a bad influence. Before she met me, Ruby didn't drink at all and now she was reaching for the booze just because it made it easier for us to talk to each other.

"Seriously, you should just put that away," I said, reaching for the books.

Before I got close, Ruby hugged the books to her chest. "Back off for a sec, Cordelia."

"You're getting better at sensing me," I said, proud of her. I took a step back. One of these days I'd get up the nerve to test Harp's theory that I could touch someone without pain if I believed it, but not today.

She opened the fake books, and next to the remaining mini bottle of Jack Daniel's was a black USB drive. I took another step away, not wanting to scramble the circuits of the tiny flash drive by getting too close. "Whatcha got there?"

"This is your doing, I suppose?" Ruby asked.

"Huh?" I was used to Ruby not understanding me. It came with the territory. But usually, I understood her. That wasn't the case now. "What do you mean, my doing?"

"I found it in Marty's messenger bag, but you already knew that," she said.

That explained a lot. I'd gotten sucked into a flashback after dropping the bag off at Ruby's desk, and hadn't been able to stick around long enough for her to discover it. I was surprised that the drive hadn't fallen out when the squatter dumped the rest of the contents out on the floor, but it must have been in a different pocket than the pill bottles.

"Good. You finally noticed the bag. A squatter had it. I think he had something to do with Marty's death." Shoot. Now would be a good time for Ruby to take a sip out of that last liquor bottle.

I moved over to the refrigerator and stared at the magnets, trying to figure out how to explain everything to Ruby. I know she struggled with reading my handwriting, but I'd give my right arm for a notepad and pen right now, if I still had a right arm, that was.

man live INSIDE door

"You've got to be kidding me," Ruby said, letting out a frustrated puff of air. "What's that supposed to mean? How does someone live inside a door?"

I arranged the magnets again.

from DRESS

"Front desk?" Ruby asked.

Good. She recognized that bastardized phrase from the last time I'd used it. The magnetic poetry might not be easy, but nothing worth doing ever was. I moved another magnet into place. This one I'd picked up from work ages ago. It had the TrendCelerate logo on it.

"TrendCelerate front desk," Ruby said. "There's a man living inside TrendCelerate?"

"So close!" I scanned the magnets until I found the one I was looking for, and pushed it into place between the existing words. "There's a man sneaking around, living next door to TrendCelerate. That's where I found Marty's bag. He's involved somehow. We need to go interrogate him."

KNOT INSIDE

"Not inside?" Ruby said, pursing her lips together as she stared at the words. "Oh, I get it!"

"Finally." I sagged with relief that somehow, she'd managed to understand my cryptic message.

"Let's go," Ruby said.

I followed her out of the apartment and to the bus stop. It was getting late. The buses weren't running as frequently as they did during rush hour, but we got lucky and one pulled up soon after

DEATH AT THE DOOR 229

we arrived. Ruby boarded the bus, swiped her card, and took a seat immediately behind the driver. When we got to TrendCelerate, Ruby didn't move, and we rolled right on past our stop.

"Ruby, TrendCelerate's back there," I said. Good thing I was there with her. I stretched out, careful to not touch anyone, and pressed the tape to request a stop. I got a mild electronic tingle from it, but luckily it still worked.

Ruby reached up, then noticed a stop had already been requested and let her hand drop. She got off the bus, but instead of walking the block or so back to the office building, she stayed at the bus stop.

"What are you waiting for?" I asked her. It was after-hours, but since she was often the first person to arrive and the last one to leave, she had a key to the office and the code for the alarm.

Another bus rolled up and she boarded it.

"Where are we going?" I asked.

Ruby didn't answer.

Twenty minutes later, she requested a stop and got off the bus. I recognized Hazel's neighborhood. We'd been there before, when we'd gone to talk to Marty's sister.

"This is what you got out of 'not inside the office?'" I asked. "Do my magnetic messages mean nothing to you?"

Ruby marched along the sidewalk, oblivious.

Hazel's house was dark. Even with my enhanced hearing, there was no sound coming from inside. "I don't think anyone's home," I said.

Undeterred, Ruby rang the doorbell. Somewhere from inside the house, a dog barked frantically, but no one came to the door. She knocked. The barking intensified.

"No one's home," Ruby said, echoing my earlier statement.

"Can we go back to TrendCelerate now?" I asked.

"Cordelia?" Ruby whispered.

"No need to whisper," I told her.

"Why don't you go inside and have a look around? If Hazel's not there, can you unlock the door?"

"'Not inside' was *not* supposed to mean 'breaking and entering,'" I said.

"Please?" Ruby asked when nothing happened.

I had no idea what Ruby had in mind, but we'd come this far already. I asked a lot of her, and she never hesitated to come through for me. It was my turn now.

"Fine. Stay here. I'll be right back," I told her, as I passed through the front door.

It was dark inside, not that it mattered to me. I could see just fine even if it was pitch black. The dog's frantic barks were now accompanied by a scratching sound. I turned to the right and saw a wire dog crate in one corner of the living room. Inside was a little tan puggle trying desperately to escape.

"Sorry, little buddy," I told it. It looked right at me and redoubled its barking while pawing at the bottom of its crate, trying to dig through the plastic. I was tempted to let it out before it could hurt itself. Puggles were usually friendly, but I couldn't predict what it would do when I let Ruby inside. Would it try to lick her to death, or would it bark so much it passed out?

Trying not to worry about the dog, I quickly searched the rest of the house. As I'd suspected, it was empty. Good thing I didn't need a key. My brother never let little things like locks stand in the way of what he wanted, and now that I was dead, neither did I.

As I unlocked the door, I wondered how I could explain to Ruby that as much as I loved Ian, I would never give him a key to my apartment. I opened the door. Ruby hesitated a moment before stepping into Hazel's house. She flipped the nearest light switch. The light bulb directly over my head exploded in a shower of sparks and glass.

"Cordelia," she admonished me.

"It's not like I can control it!" I replied.

Ruby pulled her cell phone out of her pocket and turned on the flashlight app. She shone it around the small entryway, flinching every time the dog let out a volley of barks.

"Don't worry, it's locked up," I told her, feeling more and more sorry for the dog. I wondered if that was how Ian had felt when he was behind bars. Then again, after all the time he spent in prison, it was his home away from home.

Ruby crept down the hall. The first bedroom had a long, narrow bed on one side and a smaller kid's bed on the other. The floor between the two beds was covered with stuffed unicorns and plastic dolls with shiny hair.

"Marty and his daughter's room?" I guessed.

"I bet this was where Marty stayed," Ruby said.

The next room was smaller and neater than the first. Giant plastic bins filled with toys were stacked against the wall. Ruby shone her light on the toddler bed, making sure it was empty before backing out of the room and closing the door like she'd found it.

The final bedroom was obviously Hazel's. There was a dresser, a bed with a black and red comforter, a makeup vanity, and a small desk. Ruby stepped inside.

"What are you looking for?" I asked her.

She opened the laptop that sat in the middle of the desk. It sprung to life. The home screen popped up without prompting for a password. Ruby pulled the drive out and inserted it into one of the USB ports. When it came up, it was nothing but folders with random numbers and letters. She clicked on one of the folders and opened a file, but it was more of the same.

"Rats," she said, ejecting the drive. "Maybe it *is* corrupted."

Ruby retraced her steps to Marty's room. "See a computer in here?" she asked me. There could have been a whole data center under the pile of plushies covering the room, and we never would have noticed it.

Refusing to get discouraged, Ruby approached the floor lamp. "Take a few steps back, Cordelia," she warned me, before switching it on. Light flooded the room. After another minute of searching, she found a laptop buried under a collection of plastic ponies. "Score."

She opened the laptop. Unlike Hazel's, it went to a lock screen. "Figures," Ruby muttered. "Hey, what was his kid's name again? Julie? Jules?"

There was a small pink box under the bed. I pulled it out, and when I opened it, a ballerina popped up and started to spin to the notes of *Swan Lake*. Inside was a beaded necklace. I tossed it to Ruby.

"'Julia'!" Ruby exclaimed. "Thanks. How'd you know that would be in there?"

"What little girl doesn't love jewelry with her name on it?" I replied. "And what proud papa doesn't use his baby girl's name as a password?"

"I'm in," she said. Ruby plugged the memory stick into the USB port. A window popped up, asking for a code.

"Hold on. I saw a calendar in the kitchen." I took off down the hall. The puggle had finally calmed down, but it caught a glimpse of me and started barking all over again. I wondered what I looked like to the dog. Was I a shadow or a full person to them? "Poor pupper," I said, which just made it bark harder.

Hazel's refrigerator, like mine, was covered in magnets. That's where the similarities ended. Her magnets were photos of the kids' faces and held up crayon drawings. Out of curiosity, I took a peek inside her fridge. It was filled with healthy food, like carrot sticks, tofu, and low-fat cottage cheese.

But I wasn't here to compare food choices. A calendar hung on the wall next to the refrigerator. I took it, not bothering to make it invisible. Ruby was the only person in the house, and she was used to seeing things float through the air by now. If someone else came home and saw it, well, that would be the least of our problems.

"Try this," I said, flipping through the pages of the calendar.

"Cordelia?" Ruby looked startled. I guess I was wrong. I guess she still got spooked by little things like objects appearing out of nowhere and moving on their own. Then again, we *were* breaking and entering, so maybe she was already on edge.

I found what I was looking for and dropped the calendar on top of the keyboard.

"November?" she asked. "What's so special about November?" Then she spotted it, the date circled with "Julia's Birthday!" written in pink marker. "I've only got one guess left," she said.

I looked over her shoulder at the screen, and sure enough, there was a warning that if she didn't enter the correct PIN, she couldn't try again for twenty-four hours.

"What have you been doing while I was in the kitchen?" I asked. "Trying random numbers, just hoping you'll get lucky?"

"Here goes nothing," she said, and punched in "1106." The program opened, revealing the drive's now unencrypted contents.

"What do we got here?" I murmured, leaning closer. There were a dozen or more folders, each with the name of a local business. One was marked "TrendCelerate." "Click on that one!" I exclaimed, pointing at the screen.

The laptop screen flared. Sparks shot out of the keyboard. Ruby jumped back, almost colliding with me. I got out of the way just in the nick of time to prevent her from passing right through me, but not quick enough to save the USB drive. Its plastic case melted and warped even as the aptly named Blue Screen of Death popped up.

The laptop let out a squeal that sounded like an excited elephant seal and went dark.

"Cordelia!" Ruby yelled at me. She grabbed the laptop, yanking it away from the cord, which was still plugged into the wall outlet. "Ow, ow, ow," she said as she carried it into the bathroom, holding it away from her body. A smoke detector wailed to life as she tossed the laptop into the shower and turned on the water.

A cloud of steam and the acrid smell of fried electronics filled the bathroom.

"Happy?" Ruby asked.

"Do I look happy?" I replied, not that she could see or hear me.

I should have known better. I *did* know better. I'd just gotten caught up in the moment and forgot that ghosts and laptops didn't mix.

"You saw that, right?" I asked.

"We need to get out of here before we get caught," Ruby said. She hurried back toward the front door, pausing to consider the dog. "Should we let them out?" she asked. The fire was out, but the smoke detector continued to wail.

"Leave it to me," I said. I picked up the crate and carried it to the front door. "A little help?"

Ruby saw the crate hovering in the air next to the door, and got the drift. She opened the front door. Just because I could carry something material through a solid object didn't mean I was willing to do so with a dog. Even if they came out the other side physically intact, who knew what kind of mental strain it would cause? I placed the crate in the front yard, where the puggle wouldn't have to listen to the smoke detector wail and wouldn't be underfoot if the fire department showed up.

"Sorry buddy," I told the dog. "Come on, Ruby, let's get out of here before anyone sees you."

CHAPTER TWENTY-SIX
CORDELIA

Ruby was still sound asleep, recovering from our adventures last night, when someone knocked on the front door Saturday morning. When had my apartment become Logan International? Back when I was alive, no one ever visited, and that was fine with me.

She rubbed the sleep out of her eyes and checked the peephole. I'd already stuck my head out and knew it was Tosh. When she saw who it was, she flung the door open, apparently not caring that she was still in pjs and her hair looked—and smelled—like she'd spent the night in a smoky wind tunnel.

I came from a generation of women who put on makeup before leaving the house. Ruby, on the other hand, had been raised by the IDGAF norms. Honestly, I didn't know which one of us got the short end of that stick. I was guessing it was me. Either way, hanging around Ruby made me feel positively old-fashioned.

"Good morning! What a nice surprise. Want coffee?" she asked.

I groaned. I missed coffee. If I'd known that cup of coffee

would be the last one I'd ever have, I would have savored it more. Then again, there were a lot of lasts I would have appreciated more if I'd known the end was near.

"I was wondering if I could treat you to a cup. Have you been to Mazzy's? I hear it's amazing."

Ruby shook her head. "Mazzy's is overrated. And crowded."

She was right. The hipsters loved it, but it was overpriced for mediocre fare. I was proud of her. Ruby would be a true Bostonian in no time.

"Trust me, it's not worth it. But I do know a local place that's a hundred times better," she said.

"My treat?" he offered.

"If you insist. Just let me throw on some clothes first."

I got to the bedroom before she did and laid out an outfit for her. She grabbed the clothes and hurried off to the bathroom, because she was ridiculously shy about changing in front of me.

When she came out, she looked more presentable. As she left the apartment, I tossed a sweater over her shoulder. I swear that girl would walk around barefoot in the winter if I wasn't around to remind her to wear shoes.

"Thanks," she whispered.

Tosh was waiting in the hall. She followed him down the stairs and outside onto the sidewalk, where it must have been chilly because she immediately put on the sweater. Tosh wore a heavy, mid-length brown plaid coat. It looked like something someone would wear to go duck hunting in Merry Olde England or to drive too fast in a classic sports car with the top down.

"Aren't you dying in that?" she asked, touching his elbow though the sleeve of his coat.

"I *am* a little chilly," he admitted. "I should have worn something warmer."

Ruby laughed. "I forgot. You're from California. Don't worry, by the time winter gets here, you'll have thicker blood."

"Count your blessings," I told him. "You're lucky you can feel anything at all."

"I don't know about that," he said, adjusting the collar. "I get a chill when someone turns on the AC. I don't know if I'll ever acclimate."

"You'll adjust," I assured him. It felt good to be a part of the conversation, even if no one else could hear me.

Ruby smiled at him. "You'll like it here. Nice people. Lots to do. Plus, we're right on the water."

"I was right on the water in L.A. You may have heard of our famous beaches?" He sighed. "They're the best."

"If you love L.A. so much, why did you move?"

"Work," he said. "How long have you worked for TrendCelerate?"

"Not long."

"Tell me about it."

"Why are you so interested in TrendCelerate?" I asked, suspiciously. I liked Tosh, but I couldn't quite get over the coincidence that he worked for our biggest competitor. First, he moved in across the hall from us. Then, he shows up at the office for the meeting last Monday. Now, he's asking questions? What gives?

"I'm just making conversation. You like it there?"

"It's a good job. Great people."

"Ha!" I couldn't help myself. "Half of your coworkers buy illicit drugs. And whoever killed Marty had access to the floor that the TrendCelerate office is on. They're not *saints*, they're *suspects*."

They stopped in front of a favorite local coffee spot. Tosh looked up at the sign. "When you said you knew a place, I wasn't expecting Dunkin' Donuts."

"Around here, we just call it Dunkin'." Ruby opened the door and gestured to him. "After you."

It was crowded inside, like it always was in Dunkin' at any time, day or night, but even more than usual because it was a Saturday morning.

"Hey, I see a booth. I'm gonna grab it. Iced Americano and a Boston Kreme?"

"Coming right up," Tosh agreed.

I slid into the booth, and Ruby sat next to me to wait as Tosh got into line.

He got their order and sat down across from her. When Ruby added sugar to her drink, he stared at her like she'd grown a second head.

"What, no one in L.A. uses sugar?" Ruby asked.

"No one *I've* ever met," he answered.

"In that case"—she paused to add another packet of sugar—"welcome to Boston."

When Ruby first moved into my apartment, she could barely afford coffee, much less sugar and cream. It was nice that she didn't have to worry about the basics anymore.

Tosh hid his grin behind a sip of his coffee. "But you're not really *from* here, are you?"

"Not originally, no. I just moved here a few months ago."

"What brought you to Boston?"

"It's personal," she replied, pursing her lips together and leaning back.

"Sorry, I didn't mean to pry."

"No, I didn't mean it like that," she said quickly. Ruby put her coffee down and toyed with the cup for a moment. "I mean I moved here for personal reasons. I'd just gotten out of a bad relationship, and thought it would be easier to start over someplace new."

"Don't waste your time thinking about that guy," I told her. "You're so much better off without that cheating tool."

"So, you're single now?" he asked.

She nodded. "I am." Ruby took a bite of her Boston Kreme donut. A dollop of chocolate icing slid off and landed on her chin.

Tosh reached over and dabbed it away. Then he wiped his finger off on a napkin. "I don't know how you eat those things," he said. "They're so messy."

"You just gotta embrace the mess," she replied.

I envied the easy way she enjoyed the delicious donut and wished I could taste it.

She chewed and swallowed. "That's kinda my new life philosophy, come to think of it. I should put it on a bumper sticker."

"That's one way to put it," I said. Ruby *was* truly chaotic. First, she moved four hundred miles to get away from an ex-boyfriend, then she moved into the apartment I haunted. Somehow, we ended up becoming friends and landed in the center of not one, but now two murder investigations. If that wasn't messy, I didn't know what was.

Tosh draped one arm casually over the back of the booth. "Could have fooled me. Seems like you have your life together."

Ruby laughed so hard I was afraid Boston Kreme filling would come out of her nose.

"Me? I'm about as together as an . . . uh . . ." She pointed at a giant glob of cream on the table in front of us. "I'm about as together as this donut."

"You've still got me beat." Tosh swirled the coffee in his cup before taking a sip. "Speaking of messy, did you ever figure out what was on that drive?"

"Huh?" Ruby asked.

"You didn't go telling Tosh about the USB drive we found, did you?" I asked her. I accepted that Ruby was a little too trusting at times, but this was ridiculous.

My hand was poised above her coffee, ready if needed to spill the whole cup into her lap to keep her from saying any more. Sure, that was mean but at least it was *iced* coffee. It wouldn't hurt her.

It was bad enough that she'd apparently told Tosh—who was practically a stranger, and one who worked for a rival company to top it off—that *she'd* found the memory stick I'd practically gift wrapped for her. Sure, I didn't know when I retrieved Marty's messenger bag from the squatter in the office next to TrendCelerate that the USB drive was inside, but if it wasn't for me, she wouldn't have had the bag in the first place.

I flexed my nonexistent fingers. "Don't, Ruby. Don't tell him more." She wasn't naïve enough to confess about our B&E, was she? Who was I kidding? Of course she was.

"The, um, drive?" Ruby asked. She was trying to look innocent, but I realized the signs. She was nervous. Twitchy. Guilty.

"Yeah. The other night? When your friend Ian made dinner?"

"Wait a sec," I said. "Ian made dinner? When?" It must have been when I was stuck in the pharmacy basement in a memory loop after erasing the security cameras. "When did Ian learn to cook?"

Obviously unaware of my presence, or my confusion, Tosh continued, "You mentioned that your mom found a USB drive in your sister's room, and she was trying to figure out how to unlock it?"

"Oh, that," Ruby said.

I withdrew my hand. I should have had more faith in my roommate. She'd made up a story already to cover our tracks. She could be a little simple at times, but she wasn't foolish.

If anything, I was the foolish one. After going to all the trouble to break into Hazel's house and crack the password so we could open the USB drive, now it was toast, and it was all my fault. I'd gotten excited, and for a moment, I forgot I was dead.

The last thing I'd seen on the screen before the laptop melted down was a folder labeled TrendCelerate. What was in that folder? Our deli orders or our trade secrets? Marty wouldn't need to encrypt a history of what we ate at lunch. He didn't have to know, or care, what was in the Beantown delivery bags to drop them off.

I liked and trusted Marty. So did Ruby. He came in and out of the office regularly. No one paid much attention to him. As soon as he dropped off a delivery, the entire office swarmed the break room, leaving Marty alone, able to wander unsupervised around TrendCelerate. He could have plugged that USB drive into any computer on-site and made off with a copy of everything we were working on while the coders squabbled over sandwiches.

"Did she get it open? What was on it?"

"Uh, I don't know," Ruby said. "Mom never got back to me."

"Come on, text her now. I'm dying to see how it turns out," Tosh encouraged her.

Ruby shrugged. "I'm sure it's nothing. I don't even have my phone on me."

Tosh looked more surprised than when Ruby had loaded her coffee up with sugar. "You left the house without your phone?"

"That's my fault," I said. "Ever since I showed up in her life, Ruby's used her phone less so I don't accidentally zap it." I touched the tabletop with my finger and imitated the sound of a bug flying into a mosquito zapper on a warm summer night.

CHAPTER TWENTY-SEVEN
RUBY

"It's not like I need a phone to enjoy a cup of coffee with a friend," I said.

Tosh had a point. I used to feel positively naked without a phone in my hand. When I first moved to Boston, even when all I could afford was a pay-as-you-go plan and was always running out of minutes, I still carried my phone for emergencies. Now, I had Cordelia instead.

"That's nice," Tosh said. "You know, when work moved me to the other side of the country where I know nothing and no one, I wasn't sure I would meet anyone."

"You met me," I pointed out, gesturing with the last bite of my donut.

"And I'm grateful. You might be my only friend on the entire East Coast. I thought once I got here, I'd at least meet people at work, but everyone works from home."

"So why aren't you telecommuting from California?" I asked.

Most of the TrendCelerate employees were hit or miss about coming to the office. Some of them, like Jordie, I rarely ever saw. And I still hadn't met Andy. If someone worked out of state, they'd have the perfect excuse to never commute again. They'd miss out on the free lunches and team-building exercises, but they'd get to work out of the comfort of their own home.

"Because my boss is a thousand years old and still believes in face-to-face meetings."

"Sounds like my job. No one except me, one of the owners, and a few coders who get no peace at home are ever in the office more than a few hours a week," I said.

"Your company owners seem cool," he said.

"They are," I agreed.

"Tell me more about them."

"Well, there's three founders that seem to be more or less equal partners. Quinn's the CEO and quality control lead. She's hyperfocused All. The. Time." That was me being nice. In reality, she was so uptight that I was uncomfortable around her. "She's got this niece who's totally spoiled that she brought to work the other day."

"At my old office, hardly anyone brought their kids in, but a bunch of people brought their dogs to work."

"Fun! No one brings their dog to TrendCelerate," I said.

"What about the other owners?" Tosh prompted. "They cool?"

"Franklin, the CFO, is supersmart. His partner works on Wall Street, so he splits his time between Boston and New York. He's our marketing guru." Even after the supposed team-building event, I hardly knew him.

"And then, there's Adam." He'd probably been a huge nerd when he was a kid, but I thought he was cool. "He's the COO and apparently also writes code. He's married to some senator." I shrugged. "He doesn't act like the other owners. He's down-to-earth. Nice. If I met him on the street, I'd never know he was a rich dude."

"Must be nice. I've never met our company owner," Tosh said. "I mean, she holds these quarterly meetings and throws a big Christmas party every year where she does a big speech, but she doesn't exactly chitchat with us worker bees."

All three company owners at TrendCelerate never hesitated to roll up their sleeves and work right alongside the rest of the employees. I couldn't imagine working for someone I'd never even met.

"But you like it? Your job?"

"Love it." He leaned forward, coffee forgotten as he talked animatedly. "Last month I was working on this big project and someone on the UX team found a flaw in the interface that caused it to . . ." He glanced at me. As much as I'd tried to pay attention, I must have looked like I was checked out because his voice trailed off. "Sorry. I'm boring you."

"No, not at all! It's fun seeing you get excited. Besides, I work at a tech company but I don't understand what my coworkers are talking about half the time, so I'm used to it."

"What exactly do they do there?"

"Like I said, I don't really know. You know more about it than I do. We do something about data aggravation."

"Data aggregation?" he suggested.

"Yeah, that sounds about right."

"How about I swing by your office sometime next week and take you out to lunch?" he asked.

"That would be nice." I grinned. Four meals in the course of two weeks? There'd been two dinners, now breakfast, and soon, lunch. We were doing things a little out of order, but I liked where this was headed.

He gathered up the trash from the table. While we'd chatted, half a dozen people had shot dirty glances at us for continuing to take up a booth after we finished our donuts. "Thanks for joining me for coffee, but I've got to get back to unpacking."

"Want some extra hands?" I offered.

Tosh's face lit up. "Yeah, that would be great."

"Then it's settled." As soon as we stood up and took our trash to the bins at the front door, two groups swooped in and argued over the booth we'd vacated.

Back in Tosh's apartment, after unpacking several boxes, I asked Tosh, "You planning to stay in Boston a while?"

I broke down an empty box and set it to the side. We would take the boxes down to the recycle bin later, but if this was anything like my old neighborhood in Baltimore, the odds were good that someone would claim them before the garbage trucks came through. It was the same with furniture. Someone could put an ugly, old couch out by the curb and it would disappear, only to reappear days or weeks later and get claimed again before the city could pick it up.

He cut his eyes toward me. "This project could last a few years." Surrounded by rapidly emptying boxes, piles of packing stuffing, and all the jumbled trinkets people collected over the course of their lives, Tosh looked defeated.

We both could use a break, but we were making progress, so I focused on finding places in his kitchen for the dishware while he alphabetized his enormous DVD collection. "You know, there are these things called streaming services nowadays," I teased him as he opened his third box of movies.

"I'm old school," he explained. "I spend all day with my head buried in next-gen tech. It's nice to come home and pop in a DVD and relax without having to think about servers and internet speeds and data mining. Besides, DVDs don't have commercials.

"The thing about predictive analytics," he continued, opening yet another box of DVDs, "is that it's only as good as the data it collects. Almost everything I own is secondhand. For example, my movies came from friends who didn't want them anymore, so there's no record of me buying them. Although, I often end up with multiple copies. At one point, I had three *Clueless* DVDs."

"I love that movie," I told him. "I used to watch it with my sisters. I didn't realize until years later that my mom had been sneakily introducing us to Jane Austen from an early age. Plus, Paul Rudd is super cute."

"I prefer Paul Rudd in *Ant-Man*," Tosh said.

"I haven't seen that one yet," I told him.

"Got it right here." He handed me a DVD.

I set it aside. "I don't actually own a DVD player. I had one, but I pawned it for peanut butter money." It had been Cordelia's DVD player, not mine. But I was hungry and broke, and didn't yet realize that while my apartment's former tenant wasn't technically *living* there anymore, she hadn't moved out, either.

Thinking of Cordelia, I glanced around, almost expecting to see her. I could feel her nearby. I wondered if she was bored out of her mind or if she enjoyed Tosh's company as much as I did.

Tosh continued, "I get a lot of stuff from pawnshops. They don't collect as much data as the big box stores. The algorithm can't learn what I like if I refuse to feed it any information."

"You're going to starve the poor algorithm," I said.

When Adam had cornered me and demanded that I explain how I'd ended up living in Cordelia's old apartment and working at TrendCelerate, I thought I was done for. Then the mysterious algorithm popped into my head. I still wasn't sure how it worked, or even exactly what it was, but he'd bought it completely, because apparently it was plausible.

"Don't worry, the algorithm will survive. It always does." Tosh stepped back to survey his apartment. "I need more shelves. Where'd you get those great bookshelves in your living room?"

I grabbed another box to drag to the kitchen.

"Here, let me help." He picked up the heavy box effortlessly and placed it on the counter.

I looked around for the box cutter. I didn't see it, so I peeled off the packing tape instead. It was almost as satisfying as popping bubble wrap. "My apartment was fully furnished when I moved in, remember? I got lucky because I don't have nearly as much stuff as you do."

"I didn't realize I *had* this much stuff until it was time to pack up and move. Your way is easier. I didn't know that getting a furnished apartment in this building was an option."

"It was a one-time thing," I explained. "The previous tenant died. No one claimed her stuff and the super didn't want to pay someone to haul it away. I needed a place cheap and didn't have so much as a mattress, so it worked out."

And lucky for me, Cordelia came with the apartment, I thought to myself.

"Eww." He shuddered. "I know that with apartments there's lots of turnover and people die all the time, but that's just weird to think about, you know?"

"You get used to it," I told him. I wondered if this was a bad time to break the news that he only got this apartment because the last guy that lived here, Jake Macintyre, had been murdered outside on the front steps of the building. I decided that what he didn't know couldn't hurt him.

"Need a hand?" He took the waffle iron from me, reached over my head, and slid it into place on the top shelf.

"What I need is a step stool," I admitted. "It's the curse of being short. I never bump my head, but the top shelves—and sometimes even the next-to-top shelves—at the grocery store are out of reach. There could be gold bars stashed in the top cabinets back in my apartment and I'd never be the wiser."

"Why would there be gold bars stashed in your apartment?" Tosh asked.

Considering how I was still discovering all of Cordelia's little hiding spots, I wouldn't be surprised if there were still a few I'd yet to find. But actual gold? I doubted it. "Heh, that's just an example, of course," I said.

"I've actually got a step stool. Somewhere. It's in one of these boxes. Once I find it, you can borrow it anytime you want."

"Next time you move, you should label what's in the boxes," I told him.

While the stack of unopened boxes had dwindled to a manageable level, there were still plenty more to go through. I wondered if there was enough room in the tiny apartment to fit everything.

"I'll keep that in mind. Hopefully I won't be moving again for a while."

I grinned. I liked the sound of that. Tosh was a good neighbor.

"You'll love the neighborhood once you have a chance to explore," I said.

"What's it like?" he asked.

"The bus stop is real close. The library's just down the street. And the bar on the corner? O'Grady's? It's okay, I guess, but I'm banned from there."

"Aren't you a little young to be hanging out in bars?"

Instead of waiting for a step stool to materialize, I climbed up on the counter. "Pass me those," I said, pointing to a stack of gadgets still in the original boxes.

There was a panini grill. A mini donut maker. A tortilla press. Even if he thrifted everything, he'd spent a lot on appliances. Tosh thought he'd circumvented the algorithm, but some ad exec somewhere had his number.

"And I don't hang out in bars," I clarified. "The bartender there just doesn't like me, is all."

"Sounds like he doesn't have very good taste, then. But I didn't mean the neighborhood, even though I haven't had much time to explore. What's it like to live in an apartment where you know that the former tenant died? And you're surrounded by all their furniture and stuff. Isn't it weird?"

"Not really. Before I moved here, I lived at home, and half of our furniture were hand-me-downs from aunts and uncles and grandparents. Even our dishes came from my great-grandma, and she's dead."

"Yeah, but those are family heirlooms. Not a stranger's old junk."

"It's no different than getting DVDs from friends that they were going to throw out. And shopping at secondhand stores? You can almost guarantee that some of your stuff came from dead people."

"Touché," he said. He looked around the apartment. Despite everything we'd gotten done, there was still a stack of boxes. "I'm done for the day. I can't even look at another box."

I finished putting away the last of his dishes. "Oh! I almost forgot. I still have some of your dishes over at my place. Let me run over and grab them. Don't worry, I washed them."

"I'm not worried," he said.

He picked up his keys and followed me to the door. What a

gentleman. He was going to walk me home, even though home was only a few feet away.

As we stepped into the hall, I heard a door open and turned to see Milly in 4F appear. "What's all the racket?" she asked. Today, she had on an orange velour tracksuit, and her red hair dye had faded to pink. She looked like a tiny, wrinkled sunset. "Who's that?"

"Hiya, Milly," I said. My neighbor was grumpy more often than not, and nosy all of the time. "You've met Tosh. He just moved in next to you."

She pursed her lips together. "You can never be too careful."

I nodded. "I was helping Tosh unpack, but thanks for looking out. We didn't mean to disturb you."

"Almost done then?"

"Almost," Tosh said.

Milly nodded and retreated back into her apartment.

"Is she always like that?" Tosh asked.

"She grows on you," I told him. "She's actually very sweet once you get to know her."

Then again, considering I'd once briefly suspected that she murdered the previous tenant of Tosh's apartment for being too loud, it wouldn't hurt to keep it down.

"Thanks for walking me home," I told Tosh.

"No worries. Thanks for helping me unpack."

I unlocked my door and flicked on the light switch. Nothing happened. I flicked it back off and on again. Still nothing. That, unfortunately, was to be expected.

I knew Cordelia didn't do it on purpose. Electronics just went haywire when she was around, like when she'd blown out the light in Adam's office. The last time I'd tried to turn on the TV, I was met with a shower of sparks. That I could forgive, but if she blew up the coffee maker, I'd be forced to call an exorcist.

"Something wrong?" he asked.

"Shoddy wiring," I said with a shrug. "You know how it is."

It was a good excuse, but eventually he'd start to wonder why the lights in his apartment were fine but mine burned out at an alarming rate.

The casserole dish, colander, and giant pot Ian had borrowed from him were stacked neatly on the blue and white towel in my kitchen. The towel matched all the other towels in Tosh's kitchen. It was a good sign when a man owned matching towels. I'd never had matching, or even coordinating, towels.

I handed them all over to him. "Thanks for letting me borrow these."

"And thanks for inviting me over for dinner, both times. Well, I ought to get going. I'm gonna pop in one of those DVDs and veg out in front of the TV for a while."

"Just don't turn up the volume too loud, or Milly might get mad," I said, before closing the door behind him. Alone at last, I looked around my apartment. "Cordelia? You still here?" In response, the heavy living room curtains snapped open.

My stomach growled loudly. If anyone other than Cordelia had been around to hear it, I would have been embarrassed.

The refrigerator door opened and Cordelia started pulling out various items. She lined them up neatly on the counter.

"What are we making?" I asked. I spent the next ten minutes assembling ingredients, then popped it in the oven. I didn't expect I'd ever become a chef, but with Cordelia's help, at least I'd learn how to feed myself, and that was a start.

CHAPTER TWENTY-EIGHT
RUBY

Sunday afternoon I was heading off to the supermarket, reusable canvas totes in one hand and a shopping list in the other. Cordelia had shown me a few new recipes in her cookbook, and I picked one that seemed simple enough. I opened my front door, and standing on the other side of it was a woman I didn't recognize, her hand raised to knock.

"Hello?" I asked, startled. I hadn't been expecting company. Then again, people kept showing up, whether I was expecting it or not.

"Ruby, I presume?" She was huffing and puffing after the walk up the stairs. She was white. Tall. In her thirties or forties. Her blondish hair was pulled back and she had a pair of reading glasses dangling from a beaded chain around her neck. "I don't know how you manage those stairs every day."

"It gets easier," I said. It hadn't yet, not in the months since I'd moved in, but it had to get easier, eventually, or so I told myself. "Who are you?"

"A friend."

"Funny, I don't remember you, *friend*," I said.

"I said I was *a* friend, not necessarily yours. Not yet." She gestured at me to step back. "Let's go inside and chat."

"I'm good here," I replied. I was tired of having strangers in my apartment, and after Mom threatening to send Jordan to stay with me this summer, I was feeling overprotective of my personal space. I was starting to figure out why Cordelia never had any visitors.

"Suit yourself. I guess you don't want to know about Marty." She turned and started walking back down the long hall toward the stairs.

I really *did* want to hear what she'd come all the way here to tell me, starting with who she was and what she knew about Marty.

"Wait."

The word was out of my mouth before I realized I was going to say it.

The woman paused, but didn't turn around.

"Would you like to come in and get a glass of water or something?"

"Coffee would be great," she said, turning and grinning at me as she approached for the second time. She held out her hand. "Call me Chelle."

I couldn't put my finger on it, but there was something about her that unnerved me. Even the way she introduced herself put me on edge. "Call me Chelle" wasn't exactly the same as "My name is Chelle." It made me wonder what she was hiding.

"Have a seat." I gestured to the loveseat as I set up the coffee maker. While it brewed, I studied my guest.

She didn't seem bothered by the silence, or my scrutiny. I was the opposite. I wasn't comfortable unless someone was talking. The first few weeks in this apartment—long before I even suspected

Cordelia's presence—I'd talk to myself all day long, just to break the long stretches of quiet. Now that I knew that I'd had a ghost watching me, I felt kind of foolish. She must have thought I was a terrible chatterbox.

One of us had to speak first. To absolutely no one's surprise, it was me. "How do you know Marty, Chelle?"

"He worked for me."

I felt myself relax. "Oh, you must manage Beantown Deli. Great place. I order from there at least once a week." It was odd, someone from Beantown Deli showing up at my doorstep. How did she get my home address? I guess she could have called or emailed TrendCelerate, but I would have known because I would have been the one to answer that call or email. But, considering that I'd convinced the person at the cash register to give me Marty's home address the other day, it was only fair that they knew mine.

"Not *that* employer," Chelle said. She stared at me with a completely blank expression. There wasn't so much as a hint of a smile or the shadow of a frown. Her face was neutral, not even betrayed by her eyes.

"Not that employer? Then who?" I asked, confused. Then it hit me. Marty wasn't just a deli delivery person. He was also a drug dealer, which meant he had a drug supplier.

I studied Chelle with renewed interest. She didn't look like what I pictured when I thought of a drug kingpin. She was too young, for one thing. I didn't know what I was expecting. An expensive suit. Tattoos. Lots of jewelry. A flashing neon sign above her head that declared her a Bad Boss Bitch.

She had none of those things, but then again, a flashing neon sign was a sure way to attract the wrong kind of attention, the kind that came with handcuffs and warrants for your arrest.

I had lots of questions floating around my head. How exactly did one become a drug supplier? Was there some kind of certificate you went to school for? But instead of asking any of those questions, I busied myself pouring coffee into two mugs. "Sugar? Cream?" I offered.

"Black is fine," she said.

I brought both mugs over and handed one to Chelle. "My condolences for your loss," I told her.

She laughed. Without that carefully blank expression that made her look more like a wax figure at Ripley's than a real person, she had a kind face, a face that belonged on a PTA mom, not a drug boss.

"Thanks. Marty was a good kid." She took a sip of her coffee.

I was on the fence about that. Yes, he took care of his sister and her son. And he was a single dad. He worked two jobs to support his family, but one of them was dealing illicit drugs. And he had a criminal record. In my opinion, a good kid got passing—if not spectacular—grades in school and sent money home whenever she could afford it, like I did. Good kids didn't do prison time.

"He seemed nice."

I should have been more nervous. There was a drug boss in my living room. A year ago, that would have freaked me out. But now I was living with a ghost, and her recently-released-from-prison brother apparently had a key to my apartment. In the short time I'd lived in Boston, I'd stumbled into not one but two murder investigations. I would have noticed Chelle if she'd been at the TrendCelerate office on Monday, so while she was the furthest thing from a law-abiding citizen, she wasn't Marty's killer.

She set her drink down on the coffee table in front of the loveseat and focused her attention on me. "With Marty gone, I've got an opening in my organization. Know anyone who needs a job?

Someone who won't sample the merch? Someone who won't hide things from me? You, maybe?"

Her mug tipped over with a crash, spilling hot coffee all over my coffee table and dripping down to splash on the carpet. I jumped up to grab a towel from my bathroom and started mopping up the mess. Part of my agreeing to take this apartment as-is, furnished, was that the building manager hadn't made me pay a security deposit, which was a good thing. I doubted I could ever get that coffee stain out of the carpet.

Although, the carpet had seen better days long before I moved in. The same could be said for the coffee table. There were water stains on the wood, along with a host of scratches in the varnish. Considering how meticulously clean Cordelia kept her apartment, I had to assume that the coffee table had been secondhand. Was she thrifty, or was she paranoid like Tosh?

I swiped at the spilled coffee, trying to get it all up, but I ended up pushing coffee deeper into the scratches. The coffee table might be old, but I didn't want to go buy a new one, and if I knew myself, I'd end up living with a stain before I'd spend an afternoon learning how to refinish it.

"Sorry about that," Chelle said. She righted her mug and held it under the lip of the table, using her hand to gingerly push the hot liquid back into the mug. It was a nice idea, but she just ended up getting even more coffee on the carpet. I could get a rug and pretend the stains didn't exist.

"Not your fault," I assured her. "Everything in this apartment is . . ." I paused, looking for the right word. Possessed? Haunted? "Well, nothing is level."

"Still, it's completely my fault."

Not hardly. It was Cordelia's fault. I'd bet money on it. Not that I blamed her, not really. If my roomie was being recruited to deal drugs, I'd do everything in my power to interrupt the conversation, too.

"What did you mean by not sampling the merch?" I asked.

"Let's say that hypothetically, I sold candy. Easy access to that many sweets?" She shrugged. "It's a temptation. It's also the cost of doing business. But just once I'd love to recruit reliable help that didn't dip their hand in the cookie jar."

"And Marty was dipping his hand in your cookie jar?" I asked, then blushed. I hadn't meant it to sound quite so dirty. Chelle was a drug supplier. Marty was a drug dealer. I could only assume that the "candy" in Chelle's scenario was drugs. Marty's sister said he didn't partake, but his supplier seemed to believe otherwise.

"He's dead, isn't he?" She was so matter-of-fact in her response, like she saw this every day. Then again, for all I knew, she *did* see this every day. The pills Marty peddled weren't completely illegal, but they were regulated for a reason. "How about that job? You interested?"

I took the towel, now sopping wet, and Chelle's coffee mug into the kitchen and left them both in the sink. It gave me a minute to craft my response. "No offense, but—"

Chelle interrupted me with a wave of her hand. "Now, before you say no—"

"No," I said.

Chelle laughed. Her laugh was genuine and cheery. If she'd been anyone else, any*thing* else, we might have become friends. But I didn't think I'd ever get over the whole drug dealer thing.

"Hey, no, I get it. You're young. Smart. Quick on your feet. Don't take this the wrong way, but this building is a shithole." She gestured at the newly stained coffee table. "Where'd you get your furniture? The dumpster?"

I bristled. Cordelia's furniture wasn't museum quality, but it was literally all that was left of her in the world. And despite keeping cash hidden in the apartment and stashed away who-knows-where, like her bloated health savings account, she'd led a frugal life. I was frugal out of necessity. Who cared what my coffee table looked like, anyway?

"You could be doing better." She shrugged. "A lot better."

"Let's say I could," I said. The temperature in my apartment dropped ten degrees, as if someone had just opened a window on a blustery day, or perhaps, upset a ghostly roomie. I wish there was some way of reassuring Cordelia that I had absolutely zero intention of agreeing to Chelle's employment offer. But how was I going to learn more about Marty's death unless I played along?

"Oh, you so could."

"How does it all work?" I asked. "What would I do? Walk around all day with a purse filled with bottles until someone comes up to me and asks if I have an extra Vicodin for sale?"

Chelle pointed at my nose. "Good question. Now this is all just in theory, mind you. Marty was real popular, if you know what I mean, but hypothetically, it wouldn't take but a few days for his customers to start coming to you to satisfy their sweet tooth once they realize there's a new candyman in town. If one of these hypothetical customers wanted to place an order, they'd text me, and Venmo me the amount. All you have to do is drop it off, like Grubhub."

I blinked at her. Drug dealers took Venmo?

"I let you know who you're meeting and what to give them, and once the deal is done, I transfer you your cut. Before you know it, you'll be rolling in so much cash you won't know where to put it all."

She said that, but I happened to know that the silverware drawer was a great place to keep cash. After all, Cordelia had done just that. I wondered, not for the first time, *why* Cordelia had felt the need to hide money in the silverware drawer, and where she'd gotten all that cash in the first place. I could ask her, but I doubted she'd give me a straight answer.

"Sounds great, except for the part about me going to jail if I get caught," I said. Since I wasn't seriously considering Chelle's offer, I wasn't worried about going to jail. I wasn't going to end up with a record like Marty or Ian.

Chelle continued. "That's the beauty of it. Hypothetically, you're not holding anything illegal. Even if you got stopped and searched, all you've got on you is a prescription with your name on it. That's why you can't get into trouble for working for me."

"Yeah, but then a bunch of people would be walking around with pills in bottles with my name on it," I pointed out.

Chelle let out another one of her laughs. "Silly girl, you keep the bottle. The customer keeps the candy."

"And if they get caught . . . ?" I let my voice trail off.

"Not my problem. Or yours. Now, with Marty, it was easy for him to move around and not get noticed, with his delivery job. Your day job is more static. I assume you don't want customers coming to you?"

"Hell no," I said.

"Figured. I mean, except for your coworkers. I assume that's not a problem."

I'd confirmed that Melissa, Seth, and Marc were all buying from Marty. How much further did it go? "Like who?" I asked.

She patted my knee. "We're getting ahead of ourselves. Do you run errands at lunch? Pick up food for the office? Fetch supplies?"

I shook my head. "Everything is delivered."

"Not a problem. We can work with that. A couple of innocent mix-ups and they'll be begging you to go out instead. We'll use that as a cover for you to do drop-offs. What do you say?"

"But isn't it dangerous? I don't want to be running around with pockets full of cash."

"You won't be. We're cashless. Venmo, remember?"

Well, there went one of my theories. If Marty didn't carry cash, then he wasn't killed for any money he might have had on him.

"And you're only carrying a tiny bit at a time." She looked me over. "You're such a little thing. No one would ever suspect you. You'll be a perfect addition to my team."

"Gosh, I don't know," I said. There was a loud noise coming from the kitchen as Cordelia tried to get my attention. I ignored her, but Chelle's head swiveled toward the sound. "Did Marty make any enemies? Dissatisfied customers? Rivals?"

She returned her attention to me. "Don't you worry yourself about that. My customers are always satisfied. And as for rivals, they're more worried about me than my team members. Trust me, you'll do fine."

Chelle had systematically shredded several of my theories about Marty's death, but I couldn't categorically rule out his drug-dealing hustle as being the reason he ended up dead on the bathroom floor.

I shook my head. "Gee, thanks for thinking of me and all, but I'm really not interested." Then it hit me that she apparently knew everything about me, from where I worked to where I lived, but I didn't even know her last name. "How did you even find me?"

"Hazel," she said.

"Hazel? Marty's sister Hazel?"

"She said you came sniffing around right after Marty's death. Said you were supposedly there to offer your condolences, but you were asking a lot of questions, she assumed you were looking to replace him. You *do* ask a lot of questions."

I shook my head. How had Hazel gotten that out of our conversation? Then again, I guess it *was* odd that a total stranger came around right after her brother died, not to mention coming home to find her dog on the front lawn, her door unlocked, and the smoldering remains of her brother's laptop in her shower. "She misunderstood. I'm not looking for a new job."

"Suit yourself." Chelle stood. "When you change your mind, let me know."

I wouldn't. Even knowing that Marty only dealt in prescriptions, my mom hadn't raised a drug dealer. But I might have more questions later that only Chelle could answer. "I don't know how to reach you."

"Don't worry," she said with a smile. "If you ask around, you'll find plenty of people who can get a message to me." She paused at my door. "Marty didn't give you anything before he died, did he?"

"Like what?" I asked. "He dropped off pastries and a fruit platter. Is that what you mean?"

"Never mind. Talk to you real soon," she said, and let herself out.

It didn't occur to me until after she was gone that even if Hazel had told her that I might be open to working for Chelle, Hazel had no idea where I lived. Chelle would have had to get my address from someone at TrendCelerate. It wouldn't have been hard, since now they all knew I was living in Cordelia's old apartment.

I'd already confirmed that some of my coworkers bought from Marty, but how would any of them know Chelle? With Marty out of the way, there was an opening for a courier job that probably paid a lot more than I was making now. It probably even paid more than what anyone I worked with earned, which could be good incentive for someone looking to move up in the world. If Chelle was telling the truth, it was easy money. Was Marty's job worth killing for?

CHAPTER TWENTY-NINE

CORDELIA

There were lots of things I would have asked Chelle if I'd been alive and sitting on the loveseat with her instead of hovering over the coffee table, watching her try to tempt my roomie into a life of crime. And what was her obsession with my furniture, anyway? Sure, mine had seen better days, but accusing me of dumpster diving? Who did she think she was?

So what if I didn't spend a fortune on my furniture? Did she have any idea how expensive quality furniture was? I had a stable job when I was alive, but there had been plenty of times in my life where I'd been forced to pick up and move in the middle of the night, and every time that happened, we could only take what we could carry. What was the point of investing in an expensive coffee table knowing that any minute we could get evicted, or Dad might stub his toe on something while stumbling around drunk off his ass and make Ian or me haul it to the curb?

Besides, I never invited people over. Who was I trying to impress? No one, that's who. Ruby would let half the neighborhood make themselves comfy in *my* living room, but the only person I ever had visit was Ian. And trust me—the broker Ian thought I was, the better. If he thought my coffee table was worth more than a few bucks, it would disappear, only to reappear in the closest pawnshop.

It wasn't that Ian wanted to hurt me. He didn't. He just had the mindset that what he needed in the moment was the most important thing in the world. If I could afford to buy a nice table, I could afford to replace it. I didn't think he even considered it stealing. The way Ian saw it, the world—and that included me—owed him. And his lifelong streak of bad luck had *nothing* to do with his bad decisions, of course.

I sighed. Here I was, dead, and still making excuses for my no-good baby brother. A brother who never thought twice before stealing from me. And now that he was out of jail, I couldn't help but wonder why he'd broken in the other day. I loved my brother, but I'd never been stupid enough to give him a key to my apartment.

He was looking for a handout. A couch to crash on. A few dollars to help him get back on his feet. An easy score. It was the same story every time. Only now, I had Ruby to worry about.

I had a nagging feeling in the back of my head that she hadn't seen the last of him. Ian was an opportunist. Ruby was young, cute, naïve. Ian could be boyishly charming when he wanted to.

I'd let my guard down for men half as charming, and I had the scars—physical and emotional—to show for it. I couldn't fault Ruby for her lack of judgment. God knew I'd tripped and fallen into bed with my share of charming jerks.

Working backward, there was that guy at last year's TrendCelerate holiday party. What was his name again? Frankie? Freddie? No, it was Eddie. Eddie wasn't so much charming as he was simply in the right place at the right time. After Adam left the party early with his wife instead of me, I'd sat around feeling sorry for myself. What had started as drinking to dull the pain evolved into drinking myself into oblivion. I would have gone home with anyone that night. Eddie just happened to be that anyone.

He seemed nice, what I remembered of him. He was in town from . . . where? If he'd told me, I couldn't recall. I'm pretty sure he was in Boston on business, but what kind of business? He could have been a paper salesman for all I knew, or cared. I was lonely and he was there. That was all that mattered at the time.

Before him, of course, was Adam. How many years had that gone on? Too many. I had a fuzzy memory of Adam introducing me to Marty's side hustle in the first place. He suggested we experiment with a bit of chemical assistance. Marty dropped off a few blue pills that afternoon with our lunch order. Easy as pie. From there, I'd somehow found myself acting as intermediary for half the office.

I'd done it as a favor to Marty, and hadn't thought much about it. He was supplying a needed service, and I was helping a friend. Until he'd turned up dead in the TrendCelerate bathroom, I'd never considered the consequences. And now his supplier was stopping by my apartment uninvited, trying to recruit sweet, innocent Ruby.

I was doing a pretty shitty job of protecting her. First, I exposed her to Ian and now a drug kingpin?

When Chelle left our apartment, I followed her. Turnabout was fair play. She knew too much about Ruby, and I knew practically nothing about her. She had a car double-parked at the curb. It was a new car, but not a particularly high-end one. It wasn't the kind of car anyone would look twice at. The same could be said for everything about Chelle.

Her clothes were brand names that could be found at any mall in America. Nothing couture. Nothing tailored. But I'd bet she didn't wait until they were on sale to buy them. Her shoes, too, weren't expensive, but she hadn't bought them at Payless. Even her jewelry was subdued quality without being overly flashy.

As I relaxed in the leather back seat of her car, I tried to remember what soft leather seats felt like. I couldn't. It was another drawback of being dead. I couldn't feel anything.

Chelle stayed with traffic, never going more than five miles over the speed limit. She drove past the condo where Adam and his wife lived. Past the fancy hotels where celebrities stayed. Then, she pulled into the underground parking lot of a building overlooking the water.

I couldn't risk taking the elevator, but I didn't want to lose her. After Chelle parked in her reserved spot, I gave her a few minutes' head start, then popped straight to her location and found myself in a spectacular living room. For all that Chelle tried to cultivate a nondescript, outward appearance that no one would look twice at, her condo was first-rate.

There was a wall of windows and a large outside deck. I gave her fancy, high-end appliances a wide berth, keeping in mind that if she bothered Ruby again, it wouldn't take much effort for me to turn them into scrap metal. Her floors were hardwood and her layout was open concept. The price tag was easily over a million, and I'd never missed Zillow more, if for no other reason than to gloat over what had to be a sky-high tax bill.

Chelle kicked off her shoes before pressing a few buttons on an espresso machine that was smarter than I was. She carried her drink to a table out on the balcony and sipped it while watching the water far below us. Her phone went off half a dozen times. Each time, she glanced at the screen without responding. I guess even drug dealers could take a Sunday off if they wanted to.

As she relaxed, drinking her espresso, the front door opened and in walked a tall blond man with a jaw like a marble statue. He reminded me of someone, one of Adam's comic book heroes. Adam and I bonded for the first time at a late-night superhero movie. I'd gone to the theater because I was bored and lonely. He'd stood in line for an hour because he was a die-hard fan. This guy looked like the big blond superhero, the one with the hammer. His name escaped me at the moment but I'd always thought he was hot.

He bypassed the kitchen, making a beeline to the outside deck. He took a seat next to Chelle. "How'd it go?" He had a deep, rumbly voice like thunder.

Thor! That's who he reminded me of, only with short blond hair.

"Dumb bitch doesn't know anything," she said. She ran a finger around the lip of her espresso cup.

"Dumb bitch?" I asked. "Who are you calling 'dumb bitch'? I knew it. You weren't trying to recruit naïve Ruby. You're checking up on her. I've got half a mind to blow up your fancy espresso machine to teach you a lesson." Not that I wanted to punish an innocent espresso maker for Chelle's nefarious activities, but I didn't have to admit that aloud, even knowing she couldn't hear me.

"How can you be sure she's not working for Rocco?" the big blond man asked.

He leaned back and propped his bare feet up on the table. Chelle cleared her throat, and Thor dropped his feet back to the ground. "Sorry," he said sheepishly, as he wiped any traces of his feet off the table.

"You shoulda seen her place," Chelle continued. "If I had her apartment and another on skid row, I'd live on skid row and sublet her apartment. It was a total dump."

"One more remark like that out of you and the espresso machine, innocent or not, gets it," I warned her.

"Rocco pays his runners shit," Thor said.

"I know this. I offered her a job, to see if she'd nibble."

"And?"

"Nothing," Chelle said. "Like I said, she doesn't know squat. She's clean."

"Then how come she was at Marty's house the day after he died? And a few days after that, went sniffing around at the pharmacy? And where's your missing stuff?"

"Sniffing around at the pharmacy?" I repeated. "Were you watching us?" No, that didn't make sense. Any electronic surveillance would have been rendered useless when I went on my security footage rampage. That meant someone *at* the pharmacy had told Chelle or her henchman that we were there. Who? The pharmacist? One of the other employees?

They had to have an insider at the pharmacy, someone who could print the labels and fill the drug orders. Ruby asking about one of Marty's prescriptions would have set off alarm bells. As much as I wanted to protect my roomie, I'd made a mistake that had put her in Chelle's crosshairs.

Chelle shrugged. "No clue. She acted all innocent, but no one's that nice. Plus, you've never heard someone ask so many questions. Keep an eye on her."

"Sure thing," Thor agreed. "But in the meantime, I can think of a better way to pass the time." He plucked the coffee cup out of her hand and set it down on the table. Then he held his empty hand out to her and grinned.

She stood. Thor scooped her up and carried her inside.

I followed. A ghost had to get entertainment however she could. It's not like I had Netflix anymore. I had a shelf full of books at home, and while turning a single page wasn't difficult, by the time I got through three hundred pages, I was exhausted. My only other option these days was to follow Adam around and watch him make out with his wife. No thank you.

The mere thought of Adam and Karin together had the same effect as dunking my head in a bucket of cold water.

I no longer had any interest in what Chelle and Thor did in private. But before I left, I decided to give them a little taste of their own medicine, literally. Chelle's visit to my apartment had a dual purpose. She could get a measure of Ruby, while also making a subtle threat that she knew where we lived. And now *I* knew where *she* lived, and I knew just how to rattle her.

I'd swiped the Viagra bottle prescribed to Marty to erase all evidence of our visit to the drugstore. Chelle had a connection at the pharmacy. She knew that we'd been asking questions, so she would know that we had one of Marty's bottles.

When I'd first become a ghost, it had taken me all my concentration just to pick something up without my hand going straight through it. I thought back to the conversation I'd had with Harp the other day, about how I could easily carry a quarter around if I wanted to. I must have taken that lesson to heart because I reached into my pocket, and sure enough, there was the bottle of Viagra prescribed to Marty.

It was time to return it to its rightful owner. I carefully placed the bottle of blue pills in the middle of her otherwise empty kitchen table, where she'd be sure to notice it. I was half-tempted to stick around to see her reaction, but from the sounds coming from the bedroom, it might be a while.

That taken care of, I let myself slip downward, pausing at each floor to take a brief look around. People should be sitting down to dinner, eating Kobe steaks and drinking gimlets or whatever froufrou cocktail rich people drank on their ridiculously huge balconies overlooking the water. Instead, the condos I saw were empty save for expensive furniture. These weren't the kind of people who had coffee-stained tables.

Then again, even furnished, the units I passed through had the undeniably empty feeling of unoccupied homes, like the owners only visited Boston in the summer, or corporations kept a condo for out-of-town bigwigs. It seemed a waste, paying millions for a home no one lived in. If I'd known places like this existed back when I was alive, I would have found a way to sneak into the overpriced building and have a long hot bath in the deep soaking tubs, which were the exact opposite of the dinky tub I'd died in that I couldn't even stretch out in. I bet they had unlimited hot water in this building.

As I continued to drift through the floors, I wondered if I could convince Ruby to take a weekend vacation here. B&E or B&B, what's the difference? I stopped myself with the sobering thought that I was starting to think like my brother. Just because someone had more than I did didn't mean I was morally justified in helping myself to their excess.

I found myself on the street in a neighborhood I barely recognized. I knew almost every inch of Boston, or so I'd thought, but this section was too tony for a ghost like me. What had been a short car ride here would be a long walk home, but it was a nice day and I had relatively few pleasures left to me. Walking the streets of Boston was one of them. I enjoyed a long walk. It cleared my head.

Night was falling. Streetlights flickered as I walked under them. Cars and pedestrians passed without noticing me. People were too wrapped up in their own lives to notice much of anything around them, much less an invisible, silent ghost. A man taking his tiny doodle mix for a walk was startled when his dog suddenly lunged at me. I laughed, and stuck my tongue out at the dog.

I didn't know how dogs knew I was there. Some, like Hazel's puggle, barked. The doodle I'd just passed tried to bite me. Others tried to make friends. Some street dogs followed me for miles, growling or whining to get my attention while others ignored me altogether.

Cats couldn't be bothered. They'd watch me, following me with their eyes, but wouldn't hiss or scurry out of my way, even when I had to step over them. On the whole, I preferred the cats. But then again, I'd always been more of a cat person.

The neighborhoods got progressively worse—not that I minded, not anymore—and the streets got narrower until I finally reached my building. As I floated up the stairwell, one of the emergency exit signs popped and went dark when I didn't give it a wide enough berth.

It was relatively quiet on the fourth floor except for the television blaring from Milly's apartment. As I entered my apartment, I heard Ruby chatting up a storm as she carefully repotted the monstera plant she'd bought from the supermarket. At first, I thought she had company, but a quick look around told me she was alone.

"Are you talking to me?" I asked.

Ruby continued her diatribe, uninterrupted, "... and that's why Baltimore crab cakes are objectively better than Boston crab cakes, don't you think?"

"Please, like Baltimore crabs can hold a candle to Boston's," I told her. But instead of trying to figure out a way to convey that when she was clearly wrong, I drew a smiley face in some of the dirt that had spilled on the coffee table while she was transferring the plant.

"I'll take that as a win," she said. She watered the plant and cleaned up the excess soil. "What do you think?"

"I think I'm a good influence on you," I replied.

CHAPTER THIRTY

RUBY

When I got to the office on Monday morning, Adam Rees was already there, passed out in my chair.

"Adam?" I said gently.

He didn't budge. He was leaned all the way back. His mouth was open and he was snoring in great, ragged breaths. His glasses were askew on his face and his hair was mussed.

"Um, Mr. Rees?" I tried again. He still didn't stir.

Should I shake him? Should I let him sleep? If I had fallen asleep at my desk, I would want someone to wake me and save me from the embarrassment of the boss catching me sawing logs, but Adam was one of the owners. He *was* the boss. Who would say anything?

I stepped closer. "Adam, wake up," I said in my loudest voice.

He stirred, but did not wake.

If I could roll my chair, with him in it, into his office, I could park it just inside the door so he could finish his nap in peace. When I leaned over to grab the back of my chair, the smell hit me.

Either Adam had been drinking last night, or he'd soaked in a barrel of bourbon.

He'd been acting erratic recently. Leaving early. Coming in late. Losing his temper when he found out I was living in Cordelia's old apartment. Asking repeatedly if he'd missed any calls. And now, he was drunk at work. On a Monday. Before nine a.m.

What was going on with him? Did it have anything to do with the big meeting with CloudIndus last week? Or was it something personal?

"Adam, get up!" This time I shook his shoulder. Just a little at first, and then harder.

"Huh?" His head jerked up and he struggled to focus on me. "What?" He straightened his glasses, and his bloodshot eyes uncrossed.

"You're asleep. At my desk. At TrendCelerate," I added, in case he didn't know where he was. Frankly I wouldn't be surprised if he didn't know his own name in his current state.

"Ruby," he said. He had to clear his throat. "What are you doing here so early?"

"I'm always early," I said, feeling defensive. I'd worked for TrendCelerate for a few months, and the only time I'd been late happened to be the morning that set off a chain of events that ended with Marty dying in our bathroom. Trust me, I wasn't going to be late again.

I knew Adam wasn't a teetotaler like Quinn, but I hadn't clocked him as a lush like Melissa, either. I'd never pictured him as someone who would drink enough to pass out at the office. And what was he doing at my desk instead of his own?

"What time is it?" he asked.

"It's morning." I took a step back from him, to get away from the sour smell of last night's bender. "Monday morning," I added, in case he was really out of it.

I wondered if I smelled like that, the morning after drinking. Not that I made a habit of it. I'd only ever gotten drunk three times in my life, and twice it was Cordelia's fault. Both times it was so we could have conversations I barely remembered the next morning.

Did Adam get drunk so he could talk to Cordelia, too? No way. He didn't know she was a ghost, did he?

"Did you see her last night?" I asked.

"See who?"

I felt the blood race to my cheeks. Of course he didn't know about Cordelia. I was just being silly. Silly, and... jealous? Was I jealous of the possibility of Cordelia talking to someone besides me? I knew she and Adam were close, but that didn't threaten our unique relationship.

"See who?" he repeated, sounding agitated.

I shook my head. "No one."

He stared at me, studying my face as if what I was hiding was written across my forehead. Then again, with as hard as I was blushing, maybe it was.

"Who are you talking about?" he asked again, sternly this time.

"Are you okay?" I asked, trying desperately to steer the subject away from Cordelia.

"Do I look like I'm okay?"

No, he did not. "Want to talk about it?"

"It's this nonsense with CloudIndus."

"You promised you'd get me caught up, but I still don't know what's going on," I reminded him.

"We had a killer tool that was going to blow the lid off the market. A real game changer. Then, right as we're putting the final touches on it, CloudIndus launches their own version. I don't know how they got their hands on it, but it's nearly identical to ours in every way that matters. They're threatening to sue us into oblivion if we release our version. Our very existence is at stake."

Adam's head dropped. "I don't know what we're gonna do."

"It can't be that bad," I said, trying to console him.

"Trust me, Ruby. It's that bad." He looked up at me. "Real bad."

I swallowed the lump in my throat. I'd finally found a job, a job I liked, a job I was good at. And now it looked like the whole company was teetering on the edge. For Adam, Quinn, and Franklin, it would be a blow to their egos if a company they founded folded, but they'd all still be filthy rich. The software developers would get another job somewhere else, like CloudIndus, in a heartbeat. They'd all land on their feet.

Then there was me. I only had a few months of experience doing a job that was being phased out as more companies transitioned to fully remote work. Who needed someone covering the front desk when the front desk was virtual? There were still companies mired in the traditional office model, but reception jobs were getting scarce and I didn't have the chops to compete. I'd have to go back to letting my ghost pick rich women's pockets to pay the rent.

"I'm sorry. I shouldn't have . . ." Adam waved his hand as if to indicate the entire office. "Don't tell anyone, okay? Just for a few days, until we figure out the next steps."

"Yeah, sure," I said. Even if I'd wanted to, I didn't understand what was going on well enough to gossip about it. "In the meantime, it's getting late. People will be coming in soon. You might want to get cleaned up."

"Cleaned up?" He sniffed his shirt, blinked, and looked away as if offended. "Shit. Yeah. You're right. Sorry." As he stood, I heard something hit the floor.

"Let me get that for you." I knew that the few times I'd had a hangover, just breathing had been painful and nauseating. I couldn't imagine trying to bend over without throwing up. I reached down and saw my Etch A Sketch, the one Cordelia and I used to communicate, on the carpet under my desk.

I picked it up. The best I could normally manage were shaky letters or wonky figures made of thin black lines. Getting the lines to go where I wanted was a pain. I had to twist and turn the dials just right and, as often as not, I twisted too hard or in the wrong direction. Since there was no way to fix mistakes other than to erase the whole thing and start all over, anything I managed to draw was a mess.

Despite her sloppy handwriting, Cordelia's efforts were much better than mine, but then again, she'd played with an Etch A Sketch as a kid. I hadn't. It was deeply funny to me that a ghost had a better grip on the Etch A Sketch than I did, but her blocky messages were literal child's play compared to the image now on the screen.

It was a detailed portrait of a woman. It was only a line drawing—Etch A Sketch wasn't capable of color or shading. Still, the portrait was striking. The woman had a half smile on her face and her eyes were heavily lidded like she was waking up from sleep. Every feature was meticulously captured and was a labor of love if I'd ever seen one.

I'd never met Adam's wife, but I'd seen Senator Karin Rees on the news. Everyone who lived in Boston had. And I'd seen her framed photo in Adam's office, before it fell over and broke. The woman on the Etch A Sketch was *not* Karin Rees.

"Who is this?" I asked, but I already knew the answer. I'd only seen her in person—more or less—a few times, but I recognized my roommate. "Is this Cordelia Graves? It is, isn't it?" Looking at the drawing, I could see a strong resemblance to Ian as well.

I considered the rumors about Adam and Cordelia messing

around. But the portrait on the Etch A Sketch was not something a man just having a fling would have drawn. "You cared about her, didn't you?" I asked.

"I don't know what you're talking about." Adam snatched the Etch A Sketch away from me. I could hear the inner workings of the Etch A Sketch shift with his rough handling of the toy, and I knew pieces of the gorgeous portrait were being wiped away.

"Careful! You'll ruin it."

Adam glanced down at the drawing, then back at me. Holding my gaze, he deliberately turned the Etch A Sketch on its side and shook it vigorously. When he handed it back to me, only a faint impression of the portrait still remained. "It was just a doodle," he said. Then he ran his hand through his hair, which made it more of a mess than it was before.

"Were you in love with her?" I asked.

He frowned. Instead of answering me, he said, "You know what? I might be coming down with something. I'm going to head home, take a few cold pills, and try to get some rest."

"Yeah, whatever." I knew better. Adam didn't have a cold. He had a hangover. And he wasn't going to answer my question.

The pieces started to click into place, and they formed a picture that wasn't nearly as pretty or as elegant as the drawing on the Etch A Sketch. Cordelia bought pills from Marty in the past. Cordelia overdosed on pills that she didn't have a prescription for. Had those pills come from Marty?

Adam was the one who always asked me to order from Beantown Deli, which gave Marty an excuse to drop off the office's illicit orders. If he knew that Marty sold pills—and it seemed that everyone did—he could have easily made the connection between Cordelia's death and Marty's wares. The woman he loved was dead, and Marty was to blame.

Adam never bought breakfast for the office before, but on the day that Marty died, he'd asked me to place an order with Beantown, ensuring that Marty would visit TrendCelerate. As Chief Operating Officer, it fell to Adam to organize the meeting with CloudIndus, like he'd organized the minigolf outing. It guaranteed there would be more people in the office on Monday than usual. The chaos was convenient for anyone looking to cover their tracks.

And the method of death? Someone had to be strong to hold Marty down and force-feed him his own pills, leaving him to die on a bathroom floor. Was it a coincidence that it was so similar to Cordelia's death? Was it cold-blooded revenge?

"Ruby?" Adam asked, breaking my train of thought.

"Yes, sir?" I asked. My voice trembled. I was alone in the office with a possible killer.

"Call a car for me, please." He rubbed his hand over his face. "Tell them I'll be right down." He grabbed the bathroom key off the hook behind my desk and left.

Five minutes passed, then ten, as I waited on the edge of my seat for Adam to return with the bathroom key. My desk phone rang. "Hello?"

"I've been waiting out here forever. You want a car or what?" came a stranger's voice.

"Yeah, of course," I told the driver. "Hold on one more sec and I'll send him down."

The driver would get paid for their time, so waiting a little longer wouldn't hurt, but still, I hurried down the hall. I paused at the bathroom door, fist raised to knock. Then I hesitated. The last time I'd knocked on that door, I'd found a dead body.

I *should* knock though. I should check on Adam. Make sure he hadn't passed out again. Or got dizzy and hit his head. Bathrooms were full of hard surfaces and sharp edges. But try as I might, I couldn't do it. I couldn't knock. I couldn't call out his name.

The door popped open. Adam stopped short when he saw me standing in the doorway, hand raised but unable to knock. "You okay?" he asked. "You look like you've seen a ghost."

I stared at him. He had no idea how dangerously close he was to the truth.

"Oh right, the key." He dug it out of his pocket and tossed it to me. "See ya tomorrow. And Ruby?"

"Yes?"

"Don't repeat what I said. Not to anyone."

"I won't," I replied. "I promise." I didn't want to know any more of Adam's secrets. I didn't need for him to see me as a threat. I took a step back so he could pass. The bathroom door swung shut behind him. "Your car's downstairs."

"Thanks," he said, waving over his shoulder instead of turning around. He'd had an unhealthy green tinge to his skin when he'd gone into the bathroom, and while the green hue was gone, he still looked pale and sweaty. I probably looked the same.

Once Adam was gone, I headed back toward the office. Halfway there, I heard a clanging noise, followed by a loud bang.

As far as I knew, I was the only person on the floor. Adam had gone home, and I hadn't seen anyone else come into TrendCelerate. Neither the tattoo studio nor the advertising agency was open yet. The fourth office should have been empty, but the door was open a crack and the sounds were coming from inside.

"It's none of your business, Ruby," I told myself even as I inched closer. I was certain it was nothing. The landlord, doing minor repairs in preparation for a new tenant. A business getting an early-morning tour of some available downtown office space. A cold-blooded murderer, hanging around just a few feet away from where Marty had been killed a week ago. Something completely innocent like that.

I pushed the door open wider, trying to not make any unnecessary noise. Not that anyone would have noticed over the melee. A stapler flew at my head and I ducked. It smashed into the wall behind me.

There was a heavy thump as a fire extinguisher came off its brackets, slammed to the ground, then rolled across the floor at breakneck speed. It hit the corner of a wall before spinning, then abruptly changed direction and rolled back toward me. It thudded across the floor like a heavy bowling ball careening down a warped lane, until it banged into an office chair and went whirling in the opposite direction.

Something landed on my back. I clawed at it, and came away with a dripping wet sock. Where had that come from? Another sock landed on the dull gray carpet next to me with a squelching splat. I looked up, and what I saw was so bizarre it took me a moment to make sense of it. There were several pieces of clothing clinging to the ceiling. As I watched, a pair of men's tighty-whities dropped to the floor. I dodged out of the way.

"What's going on here?" I asked, my voice going high and squeaky like it did when I was scared or nervous.

I heard a noise and whirled just in time to see a hot plate fly through the air toward my face. I was so surprised that, instead of ducking, I shrieked. The hot plate stopped midair, just a hair's distance from my nose. I felt a familiar presence. It felt like the first step out of an air-conditioned room into the sunlight. Like the smell of warm bread fresh from the oven. Like a hug at the airport from someone you hadn't seen in ages.

"Thanks, Cordelia," I said. At least, I assumed it was Cordelia. It *felt* like Cordelia.

She'd told me that she was the only ghost she knew, but while something—or someone—was holding the hot plate, an office chair on the other side of the room rose up out of a pile of discarded furniture to smash itself against the floor. Wood splintered and flew in several directions.

"What's going on?" I asked. "Who else is here?"

"Please, please, no, stop!" a man pleaded. "Leave me alone!"

"Who's there?" I asked.

The muffled voice came again. "Go away! I swear it wasn't my fault!"

"What wasn't your fault?" I asked. Emboldened by the knowledge—or, at least, the presumption—that Cordelia was by my side, I made my way toward the voice, dodging flying debris the entire way.

I found an older white man huddled under a folding table near the back wall. He'd built a makeshift fort under a table, with an old army-style cot on one side of him and a large multi-function printer on the other. He'd stacked cardboard boxes in front of the table, but when I squatted down, I could see him clearly through the space where several boxes had fallen over. A heavy boot flew through the air and collided with another cardboard box, knocking it aside.

I could hardly think over the racket, not to mention my fear that at any moment I'd get decapitated by flying rubble. Cordelia would never let anything bad happen to me, but I had a funny feeling she wasn't the only ghost in the room.

"Knock it off for a sec!" I yelled. To my surprise, it worked. Taking advantage of the momentary calm, I looked the man in his eyes. "I'm Ruby. What's your name?"

"I don't gotta tell you that," he growled at me. "I don't gotta tell you nothing." He looked past me, into the apparently empty room. "You hear that? I ain't gonna talk. I'm no rat!"

"I'm sure you're not," I said. Tired of squatting down, I shifted until I was sitting cross-legged in front of him. "Let's try this again. I'm Ruby, and you're . . . ?"

"Jaz," he said.

"That your first name or your last?" I asked. "Is it short for something?"

"Just Jaz."

"Okay then, Just Jaz, that's a start." I thought about the wet laundry that had been clinging to the ceiling. Not exactly standard office decor. "You live here, Just Jaz?"

He glared at me. "What's it to you?"

I shrugged and tried to look harmless, which wasn't hard considering I was five foot four and looked like I could lose a wrestling match to a decorative throw pillow. "We're neighbors. I work at the office next door. Didn't know anyone was living here, though."

"Didn't say I was."

"Yeah, okay." I nodded. "How long you been here?"

His shoulders sagged. "Depends. What day is it?"

"Monday."

"No, I mean what *day* is it?"

That stumped me. "May twentieth. Or the twenty-first?" I'd never been great with keeping track of the days of the month. Even when I started working at TrendCelerate, where I managed the team calendar, I never needed to know the date because the computer did that for me.

"Two months, give or take."

"Two months?" I was flabbergasted. A man been living in the formerly unoccupied office next to TrendCelerate for two months without anyone noticing? I felt sorry for anyone living like this. It had to be uncomfortable. My apartment was small, but it was cozy.

I had a fully stocked kitchen, nice neighbors, and a soft bed. I had a loveseat and working plumbing.

"What about it?" he asked.

"Just getting to know you, that's all."

"Uh-huh." Jaz didn't sound convinced.

I didn't blame him for not trusting me. He didn't know me from, well, from Adam. Speaking of which, if Adam had heard the ruckus instead of me, how would he have reacted? He would have called the police. What Jaz was doing was trespassing and was technically illegal, but he didn't deserve to be arrested for it.

Then again, just because a man was down on his luck didn't mean he was innocent.

"Hey, Jaz, you wouldn't happen to know anything about a man dying in the restroom across the hall a few days ago, would you?"

"I told you, I ain't no rat," he said, spitting on the ugly gray carpet to punctuate his point.

"No siree, I can see that," I said, holding my hands up. "But between you and me, if you *did* know something, it would be awful good of you to share it with me."

CHAPTER THIRTY-ONE

CORDELIA

It had been Harp's idea to scare the ever-loving shit out of the squatter. I'd gone to him for advice on how to get the squatter to talk to me, and he said he knew a surefire way to get him to confess. I knew that Harp was more experienced than me, but watching him work was awe-inspiring. That ghost was a beast. Tossing that fire extinguisher around was an absolutely brilliant move.

However, I'd made a critical miscalculation. I had no good way of communicating with him. Screaming "Tell us what we want to hear and we'll leave you alone" didn't have the desired effect when the man I was screaming at couldn't hear me. Then along came Ruby to save the day.

But before she could help, Harp almost crushed my roomie's face with a flying hot plate. Luckily, I caught it in time. "Harp! Knock it off! We're just supposed to scare him, not murder my best friend!"

Harp let out a maniacal laugh. I didn't think he'd had this much fun in decades. "What? Like watching someone's melon splatter all over the wall wouldn't scare him?"

"Leave Ruby out of this," I warned him. "She's off-limits."

"Whatever."

Harp hurled a boot at where the man huddled under a table, nearly hitting Ruby.

"That's enough," I said, placing myself between Ruby and Harp. "No more." Harp could toss anything he wanted and it would go right through me unless I made a conscious effort to stop it, but it was the best I could do under the circumstances. "We softened him up. Let's see what she can get out of him."

Within a minute, Ruby had the guy talking. She already got his name, which was more than we'd accomplished in an hour. Then again, he never would have opened up to her if he wasn't already scared half to death. It was like when one person loosened the lid on a pickle jar, and the next person came along and popped it open with minimal effort. Harp and I loosened it. Now Ruby could get the pickles.

"... if you *did* know something, it would be awful good of you to share it with me," Ruby was saying. She was so sweet and sincere, the ultimate good cop to my smash-and-bash approach. Then again, I didn't have as many tools at my disposal as Ruby did. I couldn't gently win his trust, not in my current condition.

"Maybe I saw something," Jaz said. He poked his head out from his makeshift fort and glanced around.

"It's okay. You can come out," Ruby assured him, offering him her hand. "It's safe."

He crawled partway out. "What's happening?"

"Don't worry, it's over now," she said. "You were about to tell me what you saw?"

He pursed his lips, considering his options. Behind me, there was a crash. I turned to see Harp shrug as an older monitor lay at his feet, the screen shattered. "Oops," he said. "My bad."

"It was a few days ago. Normally I hole up in here when the offices are open so as no one sees me coming and going, but I musta overslept. I needed to use the bathroom something fierce. When I couldn't hold it no more, I stuck my head out but someone was already going in there."

"Did you recognize them?"

"Yeah, it was the dude from the deli. I remember thinking he was a little old to be delivering sandwiches."

"*You* try getting a decent job when you've got a record," I scolded him. "Ask him how he ended up with Marty's messenger bag," I told Ruby. Solving a mystery with my living roommate was frustrating, like trying to put together a puzzle when someone else had half the pieces, and the pieces I *did* have were blank.

"You knew Marty?" Ruby asked Jaz.

"I knew who he was. Can't say I ever talked to him," Jaz clarified. "I see most everything that goes on around here, but no one ever sees me."

"Tell me about it," I grumbled. I turned to Harp. "It would be so much easier if Marty had stuck around as a ghost, then we could simply ask him who'd killed him. Do you remember anything about the day you were killed?"

He looked down at himself, at his bullet-riddled pink polo shirt. "It was a gnarly stickup. Two-man crew, one tall, one short. They wore ski masks. The neighborhood didn't use to be so great, you know."

I snorted. "You don't say." The neighborhood wasn't great now. How much worse had it been in Harp's day?

He continued as if I hadn't spoken. "It was our second or third stickup of the month. I knew the drill. Give them a couple of bucks from the register and they go away. But these dudes must not have gotten the memo." He gestured at his shirt.

"What did it feel like?" I asked. "Getting shot?"

"No idea." Harp shook his head.

"But you remember everything else?" I asked. It didn't seem fair. I couldn't remember anything about the day leading up to my death. It was frustrating, because I had nothing but questions. Who had come to visit me that night? Did they take my laptop? And why did they kill me and make it look like a suicide?

"Caught the whole thing on camera," he replied. "I musta watched that tape a dozen times, at the pawnshop, at the police station, and at the trial. Got to be where I couldn't tell if I remembered the event or remembered the video." He shrugged, his shoulders tense. "Not that it matters. Outcome's the same either way."

"That sucks," I said. That was an understatement. I felt incredibly sorry for him. I could barely face the fact that I might have been murdered, and here was Harp, reliving his death over and over again.

"It totally does," he agreed.

"Then what happened?" Ruby was asking.

While Harp and I had been chatting away about a forty-year-old shooting, an actual witness to a current unsolved crime was busy spilling his guts to my roommate. I hoped we hadn't missed anything important.

"I was keeping my eyes peeled, waiting for my turn, when someone followed him in," Jaz said.

"Oh, really?" Ruby asked. "What office did they come out of?"

She'd worked in the building long enough to know the layout. There were four separate offices on the floor that shared the single unisex bathroom in the hall. The door was kept locked, so visitors and employees had to check out a key from one of the offices. When someone had to use the restroom, they were supposed to knock first before unlocking the door. There was a stall inside for privacy.

But Marty hadn't died in the stall. He'd died on the floor by the sink. It hurt me to think about it. The thought of him in pain, scared, and alone was almost too much to bear, and not just because our deaths had so much in common. We both spent a lot of time at TrendCelerate, and we both ended up dead, full of pills, in bathrooms. At least I'd died in the privacy of my own home.

Jaz shrugged. "I didn't pay attention where they came from."

"Can you describe him?" Ruby asked. "The person who followed Marty into the bathroom?"

"Not him. Her," Jaz replied.

"Her?" I asked. "No way." All this time, I'd assumed that a man had killed Marty. That would teach me to make assumptions.

"Her?" Ruby echoed. "It was a woman? Are you absolutely sure?"

Jaz nodded.

Ruby looked relieved.

I didn't understand why she was so happy to hear that a woman was responsible. I thought back to the women we'd talked to in relation to Marty's death. There was his sister, Hazel. If anything, she had the most to lose with her brother's death, and she seemed genuinely distraught. She was innocent. I would stake my unlife on it. She'd told us that Marty wasn't seeing anyone and that his daughter's mom was out of the picture, but could she have been mistaken? I suffered no illusions that my brother was a saint, but even so I never knew exactly how low he'd sunk until he got caught.

There was Chelle, his dealer. As much as I wanted her to be guilty, if she had a reason to kill Marty, I couldn't figure out what it was. She implied he'd been "dipping his hand in the cookie jar," but from what I could tell, he was a loyal employee who made her a lot of money. Now, not only had she lost the drugs he had on him when he'd been killed, but she was out one of her best distributors.

Plus, there was the small problem of her not being at TrendCelerate the morning of Marty's death. Whoever killed him had been physically present in our building.

There was that rude woman behind the register at Beantown Deli when we were trying to get Marty's address. She didn't give me the warm fuzzies, but just because someone was bad at customer service didn't make them a killer. On the contrary, anyone who *liked* interacting with the public was suspect in my book. I was sure more women worked at Beantown than just her, but like Chelle, they had no reason to be on our floor.

Ruby continued to press Jaz for details. "What happened next?"

"As soon as I saw someone in the hall, I ducked back into my office and partially shut the door before anyone might notice me. I didn't get a good look at the person who followed him into the bathroom," he insisted. "I had to wait for the paramedics to leave before I could finally use the facilities. That's when I found his bag."

"His bag?" Ruby asked. "Marty's messenger bag? I wondered where that had come from."

"Good girl," I told her. When I took the bag from Jaz and put it someplace I knew Ruby would find it, I had no idea that there was a USB drive inside or that the drive would contain a file on TrendCelerate. Ruby had inadvertently uncovered how the bag ended up in Jaz's possession, but since I'd accidentally melted the drive, we had no way of knowing what that file contained.

"Yeah, it's right over here," Jaz said. He crawled the rest of the way out of his hidey-hole. He rummaged through a pile of his belongings and came up empty-handed. "It was here earlier."

Ruby glanced around the room, and when she did, I noticed for the first time how much damage Harp and I had caused. We'd tossed everything that wasn't nailed down, and a few things that were, in an effort to scare the living daylights out of Jaz. The office was trashed.

Oops.

"Don't worry about the bag," Ruby said. She knew as well as I did that Marty's bag was back in our office where I'd left it. "I'm sure it will turn up. In the meantime, is there *anything* else you can tell me about this woman you saw following Marty into the bathroom?"

"Wait a second," I said. "What if he's talking about Ruby?"

"What do you mean?" Harp asked.

"Ruby went into the bathroom after him. That's when she discovered Marty's body," I told him. "If Jaz saw a woman go into the bathroom . . ." I let my voice trail off. We needed clarification from Jaz, but how?

The refrigerator magnets were back in the apartment. The Etch A Sketch was in Ruby's desk drawer next door. I'd had some success drawing letters in fogged-up mirrors, but it was a mild day in a climate-controlled office building.

"Duh," I said to myself. I picked up a box of pens the former tenant had left behind. I tipped it over and slid one of the pens into my free hand. I dropped the box and popped the cap off the pen.

The movement caught Jaz's attention. "Not again," he said, scrambling back into his hiding spot.

"It's okay," Ruby tried to assure him. "It's safe. I promise you."

"Harp, grab me a piece of paper, will ya?"

He plucked a cardboard box out of the mess we'd made and handed it to me. "Will this work?"

"Perfect." I scratched off a message, then held it up for Ruby to see.

She tilted her head, concentrating.

"Give me a break. My handwriting isn't *that* bad," I said.

Harp leaned forward so he could see the box. "Yeah, it, like, totally is. What's that supposed to say? 'Ark abut yon'? Who's Yon?"

"'Ask about you'?" Ruby said. Then her eyes lit up. "Oh!" She leaned forward. "Was it me? Was I the woman you saw go into the bathroom?"

"Not you." Jaz's voice was muffled slightly from inside his cave. "She was tall, and had light hair."

"Are you sure she followed him inside?"

"They were both in there having a hell of an argument," Jaz said. "I could hear them from here."

"Is there anything else you can tell me about her?"

"She's real pretty. Loud, though. She works next door."

"Next door? At TrendCelerate?" Ruby asked.

"Is that the office with all the nerds?"

Ruby nodded. "Yeah. And you've seen that woman come out of TrendCelerate before?"

"Yup."

I turned to Harp. "You know what this means," I said.

"That you worked with a bunch of nerds?" he asked.

"That someone at TrendCelerate followed Marty into the bathroom and killed him."

Harp gave me the same blank expression I'd grown accustomed to. It would have been less disconcerting if he smiled on occasion. Or frowned. Or blinked. "Does that mean we're done tossing this place?"

"Yeah, we've got what we need. No reason to scare Jaz any worse than we already did," I told him.

"In that case . . ." Without bothering to complete his sentence, Harp vanished.

CHAPTER THIRTY-TWO

RUBY

The killer worked at TrendCelerate, or at the very least was in our office on the Monday that Marty had died. Whoever killed Marty had been on our floor, in our bathroom with him, and was a woman. Which meant that Adam was no longer a suspect. He was off the hook, along with every other man in the office.

There weren't a lot of women who worked at TrendCelerate, a fact I'd noticed from day one. There were plenty of women in tech jobs, doing everything from running cables to designing complex software solutions. TrendCelerate just wasn't doing enough to attract them and, frankly, fostered a tech-bro environment that let mediocre white men like Blair thrive while the lone woman on the software development team, Melissa, had to work twice as hard to get half the recognition. And she had to be twice as loud as any of the men in the office to get anyone to listen to her.

Personally, I wished Quinn would do more to hire more women, but now that I thought about it, that was holding her to a double standard just because she was a woman herself. Adam and

Franklin, as the other co-owners, had just as much responsibility to foster diversity and inclusion.

Not that Melissa was the only woman at TrendCelerate, but she was the only one who fit the description that Jaz gave. Sally in HR was taller than me even when she wasn't in heels, but she was Black and had dark hair. I couldn't imagine her spoiling her marathon training with prescription pills, so she had no reason to have a beef with Marty. There was Quinn, but she was petite and had gray hair. Since she didn't drink, there was no way she was buying drugs from Marty, either.

There'd been a woman with the CloudIndus delegation, but she was a redhead and I was looking for someone with light hair. I could rule myself out, of course. That only left Melissa. Pretty, blond, tall, loud Melissa.

She'd admitted that she'd bought from Marty before. Plus, she was having problems with her living arrangements and needed money to get her own place. Marty's supplier had strongly implied that someone at TrendCelerate had a way to get in contact with her. If Melissa had already talked to Chelle about taking over Marty's job, she'd know her phone number. And once she started working for her, she'd make enough money to never need a roommate again.

"Please don't let it be Melissa," I said aloud. I liked her. She was fun. She was nice. She was smart. I *really* didn't want to find out that she was a killer. But she was the only person in the office who matched Jaz's description. "No way. I don't believe it."

Melissa was the first living person in Boston who'd been genuinely nice to me. Not like everyone else at TrendCelerate was overtly mean or anything, but she invited me to her birthday party. She showed me the ropes around the office. She warned me about Adam. She seemed like a good person. We were on our way to becoming friends.

"You're mistaken," I told Jaz. He had to be.

He shrugged. "If you say so."

An alarm buzzed on my phone. I looked down at the screen. "Shoot. Now I'm late for work. I'll come by later to check on you, okay? I'll bring you something. Do you like gyros? I was going to order gyros for lunch for the office."

"Why are you being nice to me?" he asked.

I shrugged. "Everyone should be a little nicer to each other, don't you think?"

I let myself out of what I now thought of as Jaz's office and walked the few steps back to TrendCelerate. On the way, I glanced over my shoulder at the door to the shared bathroom. From his office door, Jaz couldn't have seen much. He wasn't the greatest eyewitness and didn't have a clear view, but if he said he saw a woman entering the restroom after Marty and having an argument with him, I had no reason to doubt him. I just hoped he was wrong about that person being someone who worked at TrendCelerate.

Thinking back on that morning, I remembered it being especially hectic. There was the big meeting, with several people I didn't know. There were the CloudIndus visitors, with Tosh in tow. All three co-owners and most of the employees—even Jordie—had also been in attendance, a rare occurrence.

Had Melissa been at work that day? Melissa was one of the few people who liked to work from the office. She said it was because she didn't have any privacy at home with all her roommates running around, plus she'd confided in me that it was an excuse to get dressed up and leave the house. I spoke to her almost every day, so I wouldn't have necessarily noticed if she was there or not the day of the big meeting.

I settled behind my desk. Even running late because of my encounter with Jaz, I was the only person in the office now that Adam had gone home to sleep it off. I didn't love knowing that one of my favorite coworkers might be a killer, especially since it wasn't unusual to be alone with any of them at any given time. But was I alone? Was I really? Cordelia was never very far away, and I knew she'd watch my back.

The front door opened and I started. Quinn breezed in. I let out a sigh of relief.

"You're jumpy today. Might want to cut down on the caffeine, Ruby," she told me.

I nodded. "Good idea," I agreed, even though I'd only had one cup this morning. "I hope you're not upset about the other day with Regina. I didn't mean to set her off."

"Don't worry about that. She'd forgotten about the Etch A Sketch by the time we got home. How about you order up some donuts for the break room?" she suggested.

"What about your juice cleanse?" I asked. Not that I was complaining. Quinn was much easier to deal with when she had some carbs in her, and she was in a better mood than normal today. Maybe she'd figured a way out of the CloudIndus mess Adam had confided in me about.

"Cheat day," she said with a grin. She glanced over at Adam's closed door. "He in?"

I shook my head. "He said he was coming down with something."

"Yeah, he's got a case of his wife's out of town. I wouldn't be surprised if he had a girl over."

I blinked at her.

"Oh, come on Ruby, don't pretend to be shocked. Adam's not exactly subtle. Surely you've noticed by now that he's a player?"

Melissa had straight out said that everyone knew he was screwing around with Cordelia, but judging by the Etch A Sketch portrait I'd found, they'd been in a serious relationship. He had been coming in later and leaving earlier than normal. I thought back to our conversation on Friday morning when he kept asking if anyone had called for him. I'd thought it was odd at the time, but it wasn't like I could come right out and ask any of the big bosses what was eating them. And now I find him passed out drunk at work.

Quinn was right. Adam was anything but subtle.

"Sorry, I don't know what you're talking about," I fibbed. After his behavior this morning, I was worried about him, but that was his business. Not mine.

Quinn let out a sigh of frustration. "In any event, I really do need to talk to him. In person would be best. See if you can get ahold of him, and if he can squeeze me into his busy schedule, have him meet me around ten o'clock."

"Will do," I agreed.

Quinn went to her office and closed the door behind her. I checked the team calendar. Not counting Adam and Quinn, Melissa, Blair, and myself were the only ones scheduled to work from the office today. I ordered a dozen donuts. That ought to be enough to go around, with one or two left over to share with Jaz.

Then I texted Adam. He took longer than normal to respond, but he agreed to a ten o'clock meeting with Quinn.

With the important business taken care of, I called Penny. When she answered, I said, "Hi, it's Ruby."

"I know," she said. "I have caller ID."

"I called from the office phone. It could have been anyone."

"It's always you, Ruby. No one else at TrendCelerate would talk to me."

"Why's that?"

She laughed. "Remember how I told you I was researching a

story on you guys a while back? Tightlipped office you got there. Couldn't get a single quote, so my editor killed the story."

"Oh." I was curious what kind of story she was doing, but last time I'd asked, she'd refused to tell me and I doubted she'd changed her mind. "Hey, I'm following up on Marty Spencer. Did you learn anything more about his death?"

"You know this isn't a TV show, right? It takes more than a couple of days to get lab results back." Penny sounded annoyed, which was out of character. She was usually so charming and easy-going. It was part of what made her so easy to talk to, and what made me afraid I'd slip up and say the wrong thing in front of her.

"I know that," I told her. I'd listened to enough true crime podcasts to know that lab results took weeks, sometimes even months. "But they should know something by now."

In the background, I heard a keyboard clicking. "Martin Spencer, age thirty-three. Died from asphyxiation. Someone stuffed a whole bunch of pills in his mouth and he choked to death."

"That's horrible," I said. This wasn't news to me, but it was reassuring to hear Cordelia's information officially confirmed. "Do the police have any leads?" I didn't know what I was hoping for, exactly, but anything to prove Melissa's innocence would be a good start. "What kind of pills were they?"

"Viagra."

I'd found a bottle of Viagra in the bathroom. I guess it was true what everyone said. Marty only dealt in prescription meds. Not that it made a difference in the end. He was still dead, killed by his own merchandise.

"Yup. And I pulled that arrest record like you asked. Not sure how much good it will do you, though. Want me to drop it off later?"

Penny was a great person, but she made me nervous. Every time I talked to her, I had to watch what I said and did lest she glean too much from it. I had too many secrets, some that weren't mine to spill. What if I inadvertently mentioned that the ghost of Cordelia Graves was still floating around? Or that I was convinced that her death wasn't a suicide like everyone else assumed?

"Can you email it?" I asked. I gave her my TrendCelerate email address.

As we wrapped up the call, Melissa walked into the office and leaned against my desk. I forced myself to smile. I didn't want her to suspect anything. Could she have shoved enough pills down Marty's throat to choke him? Was she desperate enough, or strong enough, to pull that off?

Was Melissa a cold-blooded killer? She didn't look like one. She didn't act like one. But how well did I really know her? If I was keeping secrets from her, and everyone else, it made sense that she'd keep secrets from me, too.

As soon as I hung up the phone, she said, "You missed my party."

"Oh shoot." Here I was, suspecting Melissa of killing Marty *and* flaking out on her axe-throwing birthday party. I hadn't lied, exactly, when I told her my roomie would never let her move in, but she needed a place to stay and I hadn't stepped up. Some friend I was turning out to be. "That was this weekend, wasn't it?"

"Yup." Her reply wasn't cold, exactly, but she wasn't her normal chatty self, either.

Or I was looking at her in a different light today. Now that she was a—if not the best and only—suspect in Marty's murder, I was glad I hadn't accepted her invitation. I wasn't sure going axe-throwing with a potential killer, much less letting her move into my haunted apartment, was a great idea.

"I'm so sorry! It was a very strange weekend. I had a lot going on, and it completely slipped my mind."

Melissa flapped her hand in my direction in a dismissive gesture. "No worries. We'll do something some other weekend."

"We'll see," I said. In the back of my head, I was thinking that if Jaz was right about her, she might be spending her weekends, and weekdays, in a tiny jail cell for a long, long time, but I didn't say that aloud.

"Cool." The door opened, and Blair walked into the office. Seeing him, Melissa scurried off to her own cubicle.

I'd never been so happy to see Blair before. Although, if I had my choice between Blair and an axe-wielding, possibly murderous Melissa, I wasn't completely sure which one was worse. At least Melissa wasn't rude or entitled. "Hey, Blair?"

"Yeah?" He paused in front of my desk.

"You knew Marty the delivery guy, right?"

He glanced around. "What have you heard?"

I blinked at him. Yeah, that wasn't suspicious at all. "I heard that he was the guy to go to. You know, for, um, things."

"Sounds about right." Blair set a disposable to-go cup of coffee on the lip of my desk. TrendCelerate had a policy against single-use containers, but the rules didn't seem to apply to Blair.

"With him gone, is there a new go-to guy?"

Blair gave a tight shrug. "Why would I know?"

"I heard you two were acquainted." That was a fib. Blair's name *had* come up, but I didn't have any specifics. Then again, considering the guilty expression on his face, I'd hit a nerve.

"Who told you that?" he asked, leaning forward.

"So, you two weren't tight?"

"I don't know what you heard or who you heard it from, but I barely knew what's-his-name. Last year, Seth spread a rumor that he found Adderall in my desk, but it wasn't mine. If you ask me, it was his." Blair sniffed. "We all know Seth is twitchy. If anyone's taking Adderall in this office, it's him."

"Uh-huh," I said, noncommittally. What was that saying about every accusation being a confession? Even though Seth had all but admitted to buying prescriptions from Marty, between the two of them, I would still take Seth's word over Blair's any day of the week, unless chocolate chip cookies were involved.

My computer dinged and the new email notification flashed up on my screen. I glanced at the monitor. It was the email Penny had promised. It could wait.

Blair wouldn't tell me anything I didn't already know, but it didn't hurt to ask. Considering how he normally dismissed me without much thought, I might never have a chance to grill him again. "I don't know anything about that. That was before my time. Did the pills come from Marty?"

"Who knows? We proved they weren't mine."

"Proved how?" I asked. I was pretty sure he was blowing smoke. People who pounded their chest and hollered about how everyone knew they were innocent without any proof to back it up were usually guilty as sin.

"Don't worry about that. Like you said, it was before your time." Blair took a step away, hesitated, and returned to my desk. "Why do you ask?"

Instead of answering him, I asked, "Who introduced you to Marty in the first place?"

"This chick, Cordelia." He swung his arm in a gesture that encompassed my entire desk. "She had your job before you."

I nodded, tight-lipped. I doubted Cordelia appreciated being referred to as "this chick." But if she was around, and was offended, she could fight her own battles. I wouldn't be surprised if Blair had a string of bad luck befall him over the next couple of days. "Yeah. I've heard of her. But who *introduced* you?" I made air quotes around the word "introduced."

"You mean who told me that Marty was the guy who could get things?" He nodded. "Yeah, that would still be Cordelia."

As much as it hurt to take Blair's word on anything, that only reinforced what I'd already learned. It made me sad. Cordelia was friendly. Helpful. She cared about people. She cared about Ian. She cared about Marty. She cared about me. No one's perfect, but I wanted to think that Cordelia had been as good of a person when she was alive as she was now that she was dead. I was still having a hard time reconciling the Cordelia I knew with someone who would pass out illegal drugs to her coworkers or have a torrid affair with a married man.

"Tell me about her."

"Her, who?" he asked.

It wasn't just that the only person Blair cared about was himself, it was that the only person Blair even *thought* about was himself. Classic narcissist. I shook my head.

"Cordelia," I said, trying to sound patient. "What was she like?"

He shrugged. "I don't know. I guess she would have been pretty, if she lost some weight and put some effort into herself. I still don't understand what the big man saw in her." He jerked his thumb in the direction of Adam's office. "Have you *seen* Adam's wife? Stone-cold hottie. And rich, too. If she plays her cards right, that broad might get herself elected president someday. You don't cheat on a nine with a six."

"Classy," I said, unable to help myself. Men who assigned numerical values to women depending on how much they wanted to sleep with them deserved to have a hole in the toe of their sock every day for all of eternity.

Fortunately, Blair being Blair, he assumed I was insulting Adam. "Right? What did he see in her? Pathetic and sad."

Personally, I thought if anyone was pathetic, it was Blair, but I kept my mouth shut. "Sad, as in depressed?"

Cordelia had always seemed upbeat to me. Her insurance records didn't include visits to a therapist or a prescription for antidepression medication. But everyone who knew her back when she was alive readily accepted that she might kill herself, which wasn't a good sign. Could Cordelia have been clinically depressed and I just missed it?

"Sad as in a joke. She sold us out, you know."

"How so?" I asked, leaning forward.

Blair glanced around, checking to make sure no one was close enough to overhear. He didn't know that Cordelia could be right over his shoulder. I didn't know where she was exactly, but I had that weird skin-tingly feeling that indicated she was nearby.

"She sold TrendCelerate secrets to CloudIndus."

"Seriously? The company that was in here last Monday for that big meeting?"

"The same," he agreed.

I didn't want to believe it, but the coincidences were piling up. I'd seen Cordelia's LinkedIn profile. CloudIndus was her previous employer before coming to TrendCelerate. She probably still knew people there. Then again, Tosh, my friendly across-the-hall neighbor, worked there now.

As I pondered the implications of the connections, Blair continued, "I mean, I can't prove it of course. But her laptop goes missing." He put "missing" in air quotes, copying my earlier gesture. "CloudIndus gets the jump on our biggest project. And then Cordelia, overcome with guilt, offs herself."

Did Cordelia really steal company secrets from TrendCelerate and sell them to CloudIndus, her former employer? Why would she do that? Was that why she had so much cash sitting around her apartment? Did it have anything to do with her death?

"Oof," I said.

Now I understood what Adam was talking about when he said that CloudIndus was going to run TrendCelerate out of business. I didn't correct Blair's assumption. Until we proved otherwise, it was just as well that everyone continued to believe that Cordelia committed suicide. But the time was coming when I could clear her name—I would prove that she hadn't killed herself and she hadn't stolen company secrets—with or without her help.

Although, I was still kicking myself for letting one of the pieces of evidence that could have exonerated her get destroyed. If I still had Marty's USB drive, I could give it to Adam and let him see the TrendCelerate folder for himself. I had no idea what had been in that folder, and now I never would. Was it the stolen code?

"'Oof' is right. Now if you don't mind, I got stuff to do." Without waiting to see whether or not I did, in fact, mind, Blair strode off toward his desk, leaving a dozen questions hanging in the air.

I didn't think this new information was going to help me find Marty's murderer, but I never knew where a lead would take me. Like who did Jaz see follow Marty into the bathroom? Was it Melissa? If so, why would she kill Marty? If she'd killed once and gotten away with it, would she kill again to keep her secret safe? And if it wasn't Melissa, who could it have been?

Before I could drive myself batty worrying about the implications, the downstairs door chimed. I picked up the phone and was pleasantly surprised to hear Tosh's voice. I buzzed him in, and a few moments later opened the frosted glass door to the office for my neighbor to step inside.

CHAPTER THIRTY-THREE
CORDELIA

I did not have Tosh showing up at TrendCelerate again on my bingo card. I was happy that Ruby was starting to come out of her self-imposed dry spell. In my opinion, she still spent far too much time thinking about her loser ex-boyfriend. Her interest in Tosh was healthy. It was just that his timing absolutely sucked, showing up right as we made a breakthrough about Marty's murder.

Tosh wore a fitted T-shirt under a trim-cut suit jacket, with jeans and shiny black ankle boots. He had a leather satchel slung over one shoulder and sunglasses hooked over the neck of his shirt.

He grinned as he approached Ruby's desk. "Hello, Miss Ruby," he said.

"Hello back," Ruby said. She checked out his outfit. I was appreciating the fit of his jeans and hoped my roommate was noticing as well. It would do us both some good to keep this one around for a while. "I see you found your shoes."

"Right?" He looked down at his feet. "They were in the second-to-last box. Can you believe my luck?"

Ruby perked up. "Does that mean you've finished unpacking?"

He nodded. "I did. And since I had to be in the office this morning, I thought I'd swing by here and take you out for a celebratory cup of Dunkin' and some of those messy donuts you like. My treat."

"I can't get away right now, but as luck would have it, we have donuts in the break room." She pointed, even though its location was obvious in the wide-open office. "Come on, I'll show you."

"You're busy," Tosh said. "How about I grab a cup of coffee and a donut for you instead, and I'll take a rain check for some other time?"

"That's very thoughtful," she said.

"Smart play," I told Tosh, following him to the break room. "Guys make the mistake of coming on too strong and expecting women to adjust their schedules around them, not the other way around. You might be good for our Ruby."

While her coffee brewed, Tosh leaned on the doorway and looked out over the bullpen.

The rapt attention he paid to the cubicles made me uncomfortable. "What exactly *are* you doing here, Tosh?" I asked, mimicking his position on the other side of the doorway.

It seemed perfectly innocent, him popping into Ruby's work to say hi. But how many times could Marty have taken advantage of his deliveries to TrendCelerate to download proprietary information onto his USB drive? I wasn't going to make the mistake of taking my eyes off a rival CloudIndus employee while he wandered around the office unescorted.

From where we stood, we could see into the backs of a dozen cubicles lined up in rows facing reception. The bland cubicle walls were covered in posters and photos thumbtacked in place. Toys and action figures were everywhere. A few cubes had plants. Seth's had a fake fishbowl, or to be accurate, a real fishbowl with fake water and fake fish. Even Jordie, who was hardly ever in the office, had personalized his area with colorful rubber duckies.

Each cubicle was outfitted with anywhere from one to three monitors, with a docking station, a wireless mouse and keyboard, and an ergonomic chair. Every monitor had a privacy screen mounted to it so only the person using that station could actually see what was on the screen. Even so, I worried about Tosh seeing proprietary information he had no right to.

After the coffee maker beeped, he took the coffee and a donut, wrapped in a paper napkin, back to Ruby's desk.

"Quiet around here," he noted.

"Mondays usually are," she agreed.

I glanced around at the occupied cubicles. Melissa was at her desk. She worked out of the office because she had too many roommates hogging her home internet connection. Marc wasn't in this morning, which was unusual because he usually alternated office shifts with his wife so they could take turns watching the twins. Both of them liked to work from the office because it afforded them the peace and quiet they couldn't get at home.

"Last Monday wasn't," Tosh pointed out.

Ruby frowned, no doubt thinking about Marty. "That wasn't a normal Monday."

I had to agree with her.

Blair stood and headed for the break room. I suspected he only came in to show his face and prove to management that he was working, when he was really goofing off. He rarely bothered to lift a finger, much less contribute one iota of work to whatever project he was assigned to. Blair was that person who never contributed to a group project but still got the same grade as those who did all the work.

I didn't like how he treated Ruby, but at least he noticed that she was alive. When I'd been in her chair, Blair never gave me the time of day unless he wanted something. But then again, I was a woman over forty. Even when I was corporeal, I was invisible to trust-fund bros like Blair.

Seth wasn't in today. I had no idea why he ever worked from the office, especially when he lived out in the suburbs and had a long commute. Plus, unlike everyone else at TrendCelerate, Marty refused to deliver drugs to him, which was one of the advantages of working from the office that his coworkers took frequent advantage of. He was an extrovert, though. He needed to be around people.

"My office is the same way." Tosh sat on the edge of her desk. "What's everyone working on?"

That was unexpected. "That's none of your business, buster," I told him. With each question he asked, I grew more suspicious of his presence.

Ruby just shrugged. "Who knows? It's all over my head."

"Oh, come on. Don't talk down about yourself like that. Tell me what you've heard about the current project and I'll explain it to you," he offered.

I pushed a stack of papers off the edge of Ruby's desk, startling them both. Tosh started to pick up the pages, but Ruby came around the desk and shooed him off. "I'll take care of this. Hey, thanks for stopping by, but I've got a lot to do today. Let's do this again sometime, outside of work?"

"Yeah, sounds great," he agreed, putting the stack of papers he'd collected on the desk where it had been before I knocked them over.

"Thanks again," she said, ushering him to the door. "See ya soon."

Once he was gone, she whispered under her breath to me, "That was weird, right?"

"Totally weird," I agreed.

Tosh worked for a direct competitor to TrendCelerate. CloudIndus had to have hundreds of employees, and yet Tosh was one of the four invited to the meeting last Monday. It felt like more than a coincidence, though I couldn't imagine a tech company putting one of their employees up in our crappy building, in our crappy neighborhood, just to keep an eye on Ruby.

Then again, what were the chances that someone with a decent salary would have picked that apartment? He couldn't have known how bad the neighborhood or building was when he rented the apartment sight unseen, but the cheap rent had to have been a red flag.

Tosh and Ruby becoming friends was heartwarming at first, but now I wondered if he had ulterior motives. Was he really trying to help her understand what we did here better, or was he pumping her for information? I knew that several people in the office suspected that I'd sold proprietary code to CloudIndus, but that was ridiculous. CloudIndus had fired me. I wouldn't sell them the phone number to 911 if their headquarters was on fire.

If anyone was stealing trade secrets, my money was on Marty. CloudIndus was only a few blocks away, well within Beantown's delivery range. He had plenty of opportunity to poke around the office while we were otherwise distracted. If I still had feet, I could have kicked myself for accidentally destroying that USB drive before we could see what was on it.

"You think he's on the up-and-up?" Ruby asked.

It took me a second to realize that she was talking about Tosh. "I don't know. I hope so," I said. Then I formed a question mark out of the magnetic butterflies on her desk.

It would be nice if Tosh was only interested in Ruby because he genuinely liked her, and couldn't care less about TrendCelerate's projects. I hoped that was the case because, frankly, Ruby's love life could stand a little spicing up.

My thoughts drifted back to the last time I'd gotten any—the night I met Eddie at the TrendCelerate holiday party. My memories of that night were fuzzy, frayed around the edges by too much alcohol. I didn't remember the specifics of what we chatted about while we flirted, but I remembered enjoying our conversation. He was simple. Uncomplicated. The exact opposite of Adam.

I wouldn't exactly call my night with Eddie healthy, especially since I had a more-or-less boyfriend at the time. Adam and I broke up for the last time soon after. Although, that was more about salvaging his relationship with Karin than anything I'd done to piss him off. As far as I knew, Adam never found out that I'd cheated on him with a stranger at the company holiday party.

Melissa had opted to stay overnight after the party, too. We shared an Uber from the hotel the next morning. "Have a great holiday," she said, waving as I got out of the car. "See you next year!"

"You too," I replied. It was the last thing I ever said in person to Melissa. By the time the holiday break was over, I was dead.

"Whatcha up to?" Startled, I looked up and realized that Melissa was hovering around the front desk. It took me a moment to realize that she wasn't talking to me, which was silly because she had no idea I was still around. Instead, her neck was craned so she could see Ruby's screen.

Ruby quickly minimized her email, looking guilty. I wondered what that was about. I should have been paying closer attention to the present, instead of letting myself drift down memory lane.

"Hey, Melissa. I didn't see you there," Ruby said.

"Wasn't that the dude who was in the meeting last Monday?" Melissa asked. "What was he doing here?"

"Tosh? He's my neighbor. He stopped by to see if I wanted to go out for coffee."

"Yeah, your neighbor who happens to work for the competition," I added. The jury was still out on Tosh, as far as I was concerned.

"Are you two an item?"

Ruby looked thoughtful. "I don't know. I just met him."

Melissa groaned. "No fair. No wonder you won't let me crash at your place, when that total snack is your neighbor."

"I already told you—"

"I know," she interrupted Ruby. "Your place is small and you already have a roomie. Trust me, I get it."

"Speaking of trust, you need to keep a closer eye on Tosh," I warned Ruby, even though she couldn't hear me. "And while you're at it, until we clear Melissa as a suspect, you should keep her at arm's length, too."

"Is there something I can help you with?" Ruby asked.

"Awful antisocial today, aren't you?" she said. Then she rotated the screen toward her so she could see it better without straining. "Shoot. Spreadsheets. I hoped you were looking at porn or something." Melissa returned the screen back to where it had been. Then, she sat sideways on the edge of the desk. "You just seemed so engrossed. I knew nothing at work could ever be *that* interesting, so I said to myself, 'Melissa, I betcha she's looking at porn.' No such luck."

Ruby blushed. "No, no, it wasn't that."

"Wasn't what?" Melissa asked. "Porn?" Across the room, Blair swiveled in his chair.

A crimson blush crept across Ruby's face. "Shh," she said. "Keep your voice down."

"I take it back," I told her jokingly. "Even if Tosh *is* using you, you need to get laid."

Melissa laughed. "Chill. It's just porn. No need to get all wound up. You know what you need? You need to relax." She pulled her phone out of her pocket. "I know a guy."

Ruby's eyes went big. "What? I don't do that sort of thing."

She looked up from her phone. "You don't date?"

"Date?" Ruby asked, looking confused. "I thought you were talking about me taking something to relax, like drugs or something."

"Where'd you get that crazy idea?" She wiggled her phone at Ruby. "I'm gonna set you up with one of my roomies. You're exactly his type."

"His type?"

"He loves perky girls." She pointed at Ruby's T-shirt.

Today's shirt was bright pink and read "I'm tired of your sheet" over a cartoon image of a ghost. Personally, I thought Ruby's wardrobe was silly and childish, but I liked that one. In fact, I'd laid it out for her this morning.

"You're funny. He's got a great sense of humor. You're adorable. He's smart. You two will get along. And if you two hit it off, you can give me your cute neighbor's number."

"If he's so perfect, why aren't you dating him?" I asked suspiciously. On one hand, I knew who Ruby dated was none of my business, but I liked to think I had *some* say about who she invited into our lives.

Ruby shook her head. "Thanks, but no thanks. I'm really not looking for a setup right now."

Quinn approached, her high heels clicking loudly. "Melissa, don't you have your own desk?"

"Uh, yeah," she answered, rolling her eyes.

"Then you should spend more time at your desk and less time pestering our receptionist."

"Okay, sure, whatever," Melissa said. She hopped up off the desk. She turned to Ruby. "We'll continue this later."

"Okay, sure, whatever," Quinn repeated in a mocking tone. Then, in her normal voice, she asked, "How's the new module coming?"

"I've been chasing bugs in circles all day," Melissa admitted. "As soon as I isolate one, two more pop up."

"Sounds like you've got your work cut out for you then," Quinn said sternly. "You should concentrate on that instead of gossiping." Melissa started to respond, but Quinn cut her off with a wave of her hand. "Yes, I know. Okay. Sure. Whatever. You already said that."

Melissa heaved an enormous sigh and headed back to her desk.

CHAPTER THIRTY-FOUR
RUBY

"It's a wonder anything ever gets done around here," Quinn said, watching Melissa walk away. "Is Adam here yet?"

I shook my head. "He said he'd be here by ten." I glanced at the clock on my computer. It was already half past. "He's just running late."

"Uh-huh," Quinn said, pursing her lips in displeasure. "I'll be in my office. When he gets here, send him in. And if Melissa bothers you again, feel free to tell her to leave you alone."

"Oh, she's no bother," I said quickly. It felt weird to be defending her when I was half-convinced she was a murderer. I just didn't know how to prove or disprove it.

When Jaz told me he'd seen someone follow Marty into the bathroom, I had wanted so bad for it not to be Melissa, even though she was the only blond in the office and was tall enough to fit his description. I was so disappointed. I liked Melissa. I felt like we were on the way to becoming friends, but I didn't want to be friends with a killer.

"Make sure it stays that way." Quinn retreated to her office and closed the door behind her.

Alone at last, I finally had a chance to open Penny's email. I'd been expecting a page or two of information, but what I was looking at was an entire case file. How did Penny manage to get her hands on this?

I downloaded the attachments and scanned the filenames, looking for something helpfully labeled "Summary." Not finding anything, I opened the first file.

According to the court documents, a few years ago someone named Mallory Case hit and killed a woman named Sandy Madison in a crosswalk while driving under the influence. Marty was in the passenger seat when it happened. They fled the scene. Mallory was charged with manslaughter and took a plea deal. Marty was charged and convicted as an accessory.

"So sad," I said, barely even noticing that I was talking to myself. The words on the screen twitched. "Cordelia, step back before you blow up another computer," I hissed, even as I felt the hairs on my arm stand at attention. The tingling sensation dissipated as she heeded my warning.

Hazel had mentioned that her brother had a record, but had conveniently left out the details. She hadn't told us that he and Mallory—his daughter's mom, I presumed—had killed someone. Hazel was protecting her brother. I would do just about anything to protect my sisters, too. I didn't completely understand Cordelia and Ian's relationship yet, but I bet they also would have done anything for each other. It was a sibling thing.

Sandy Madison had a family, too. A grief-stricken husband. An orphaned daughter. And one very devastated older sister who'd testified at Marty Spencer's sentencing hearing. As I read the victim impact statement, I forced myself to slow down and digest every word. Sandy Madison didn't deserve to have someone skim over the details of her life.

Then I got to the last line, where the statement was signed by the victim's sister, Quinn McLauchlan, CEO of TrendCelerate.

I never wondered why my boss had custody of her young niece, Regina. Quinn had been snippier than normal last Monday, but I'd attributed it to her recent juice cleanse. Now, thinking back over the details of the morning, she'd been in a relatively good mood until Marty showed up with our mid-morning snack. Then, in all of the confusion, I'd lost track of everyone's movements.

I closed my email and stared at the blank screen for a long time. Then I glanced over my shoulder at Quinn's closed door. Knowing if I thought too hard about it, I'd chicken out, I stood and rounded my desk. Instead of knocking on her door, I opened it and poked my head inside.

Quinn's office was tidy as always. Other than a few framed photos on her desk, there were no decorations. It was cold and impersonal.

She looked up from her computer. "Have you heard from Adam?"

"Not yet. Can I have a second?" I asked, taking a seat in one of the visitor's chairs in front of her desk before she could respond.

"Of course. What's up?"

I tilted my head. "Tell me about Sandy Madison."

Quinn pushed her keyboard away from her and frowned at me. "My little sister Sandy was killed in a hit-and-run several years ago, but I guess you know that already."

"I'm very sorry for your loss," I said. It felt inadequate, but I had to say *something*.

Quinn leaned forward, reaching for one of the framed photographs on her desk. I'd looked at the pictures on other occasions when I was in her office. Most of them were of Regina, her niece. She turned one of the photos around so I could see it.

In the picture, Quinn was wearing a pretty lavender dress and had her arm around a woman in a lacy red dress who looked like a slightly younger version of herself. They were both laughing. I couldn't remember ever seeing Quinn laugh in the whole time I'd worked at TrendCelerate.

"This is my sister, Sandy. You met her daughter, my niece, Regina. She was only a few months old when Sandy died."

"I'm sorry," I said again.

"Sandy was the best sister anyone could ever ask for. A devoted wife. A doting mother. She didn't deserve to be mowed down by a couple of addicts driving around high as you please."

She turned the photograph back toward herself, and rubbed the frame with her thumb.

"Sorry."

"You keep saying that. Everyone's *so* sorry. After Sandy died, her husband couldn't handle being a single dad, so he took off. Regina's lived with us most of her life. She barely even remembers her real mother or father. It's not fair. I knew it wouldn't bring my sister back, but the night Mallory Case and her wastoid boyfriend got sentenced was the first time I got a full night's sleep since Sandy's death. Imagine my surprise when last week, one of her killers walked into my office, a free man without a care in the world."

"Marty," I said.

"Martin Spencer," she agreed.

I wouldn't have believed it if I hadn't already read the file that Penny sent over. Technically, Marty was an accessory in Sandy Madison's death, but I didn't think that Quinn cared about the distinction. And I wasn't completely sure she was wrong.

"Marty's been delivering sandwiches to the office for longer than I've worked here," I said. "How is it you've never bumped into him before?"

She pushed her chair back from her desk. Like mine, her chair was ergonomic. Unlike mine, hers was a top-of-the-line model. Whereas mine squeaked all day long, hers didn't make a sound.

"I didn't know this before last week, but he worked for that disgusting Beantown Deli place. If the ridiculous portion size wasn't bad enough, there's enough sodium in one spuckie to give anyone a heart attack." Quinn stood and paced behind her desk.

"You're too health-conscious to have ever ordered from Beantown Deli," I said aloud as I realized it. Quinn and Franklin were rarely in the office. Adam was the hands-on executive. Whichever owner was in the office chose the lunch menu for the day. "You always order healthy food. Smoothies. Salads. It's Adam who orders from Beantown Deli all the time."

"I swear that man has less impulse control than Regina, and she's only in kindergarten."

I suppressed a smile. It didn't seem like the right time for it. But I agreed with Quinn. I didn't know Adam well, not nearly as well as my ghostly roomie apparently did, but from what little I *did* know, her description was apt. Adam Rees was smart. Passionate. Well-respected in the industry. But he had the self-discipline of a puppy. It would have been sorta charming if he wasn't one of the co-owners of a notable software company and the husband of a big-shot politician.

"It's okay, Ruby, you can agree with me."

"I'm not *dis*agreeing with you," I said, judiciously.

Quinn harrumphed. "Everyone loves the fun boss."

"Was that the first time you've seen Marty since the trial?" I asked, trying to get the conversation back on track.

"It was," she said, nodding soberly. "That was quite a morning.

Big meeting. You remember. TrendCelerate hasn't been doing well, not since CloudIndus miraculously beat us to market with a dead ringer of our data collection application that was supposed to turn things around for us. It was a disaster."

She stood and paced over to the window. My desk had a view of cubicles. Hers had a view of a small park across the street. "Just when I thought things couldn't get worse, Martin Spencer breezes into *my* office with an armful of muffins like he belonged here."

I tried to piece together everything that had happened that morning. Soon after Marty arrived with the morning snacks, the meeting took a break. I remember Quinn being surprised to see him, but I hadn't thought much of it at the time. There were more people than I could remember ever being physically present in the TrendCelerate office, all running around during the break. Quinn could have slipped out of the office and came back while I was in Adam's office or the break room without me ever noticing.

She rested one hand on the back of her chair. I hadn't realized it before, but while Quinn was about my height, she always wore impressively high heels. As a result, she towered over me. Jaz had said he saw a tall, light-haired woman entering the bathroom after Marty. I'd assumed he meant Melissa, since she was blond, but Quinn's silver-gray hair matched that description, too. And in heels, she appeared taller than she really was.

And Quinn's voice carried, especially when she was angry or was barking orders. When we'd gone on the team-building exercise, she'd easily talked over the noise in the minigolf parking lot. If she got into an argument with Marty, we wouldn't have heard it in the TrendCelerate office with the door closed and with the soundproofing being as good as it was. But Jaz's door was cracked open and his head was partially in the hall. He would have had no problem hearing them argue if they were yelling.

"You followed Marty to the bathroom and killed him?"

"You don't understand," she said.

"Then tell me what happened. Make me understand," I urged.

"My sister Sandy is dead, because of him. And yet, he's walking around without a care in the world. It's not right. It's not fair."

"No, it's not," I agreed. "But how did you get him to swallow enough pills to choke?"

Quinn let out a bitter laugh. "You hear stories about moms lifting cars to free a trapped kid. I never believed such a thing was possible, not really, but when I finally came face-to-face with my sister's killer, I could have moved a mountain. I pinned him down, grabbed the first pill bottle out of his bag, and force-fed the contents to him. He barely even put up a fight."

"Poor Marty," I exclaimed.

"Oh please. The man who killed my sister got what was coming to him." Quinn grinned, and I realized that I was in the room with someone who thought it was *entertaining* that she'd recently killed a man. I understood why she wanted revenge for her sister, but I couldn't reconcile that with the fact that she so obviously enjoyed it.

"You forced a bottle of pills into a man's mouth and watched him suffocate," I blurted out. "No one deserves that."

"What do you want me to say?" Quinn asked. "My sister didn't die instantly. She was still alive for a few minutes after Mallory Case and Martin Spencer ran over her in that crosswalk. If they'd stopped to render aid, or even dialed 911, she might still be alive today. Instead, they sped off and left her there to die alone, just like I left him in the bathroom to die."

"You're a monster," I said. I didn't mean to say it, it just slipped out. Quinn might be able to justify it to herself, but there was no excuse for what she'd done.

"Hardly. All I wanted was to give that bastard a taste of his own medicine. I never meant to *kill* him. That part was just a fluke. That man destroyed my family and I'm glad he's dead."

"But your sister's death was a horrible accident. He didn't mean to kill Sandy. Marty wasn't even the one behind the wheel. His girlfriend was the one driving," I pointed out.

Quinn shrugged, looking nonplussed. "And yet, he got exactly what he deserved. The universe has a funny sense of humor, don't you think?" She looked down at me. "Well? What are you going to do about it?"

"What do you *want* me to do about it?" I asked, suddenly realizing that I was trapped in an office with a killer who also happened to be my boss.

"If you tell anyone I had anything to do with the death of Martin Spencer, I'll deny it. No one will believe that I could force-feed a man half my age an entire bottle of pills without him fighting back. Who knows? Maybe all that guilt was eating at him and he *let* me pour those pills down his throat."

"Uh-huh," I said, scooting my chair farther from her desk.

She had a point. I *could* go to the police, but I didn't have any hard evidence. Everything I had was circumstantial. It was Quinn's word against mine—a pillar of the business community versus a young recent arrival to Boston who was living with a ghost.

"Oh, and Ruby? Breathe one word of this to *anyone* and I'll have my lawyers on you before you can say 'slander.' So, I ask you again. What are you going to do?"

She was right. I had nothing. I couldn't even go to Penny the reporter with hearsay and a wild theory. Even if she was interested in the story, she couldn't run it without proof. She'd told me herself that she'd had to kill a story she was investigating about Trend-Celerate because she couldn't corroborate it.

Quinn was respected in this town. She was rich. She could own a share in the paper for all I knew. Even if she hadn't been wealthy and powerful, she was a sympathetic, grieving victim. Marty was not. He was a drug dealer with a criminal record. Without a recorded confession, I had nothing. And like she said, no one would believe that she'd held down a man in his prime and forced drugs into him.

"There's nothing I can do, is there?" I said.

"That's the first sensible thing you've said all day," she agreed.

I got up and turned around to leave. Sometime during our conversation, unnoticed by both of us, the door to her office had opened. Standing just outside were Adam, Melissa, and Blair. From the horrified looks on their faces, they'd heard every word.

CHAPTER THIRTY-FIVE
CORDELIA

Quinn was right. No one would have believed Ruby's word over hers, but I was ten steps ahead of her. As soon as Adam showed up for their meeting—late and looking like something that the cat dragged in—I knew what I had to do.

While the TrendCelerate exterior was practically soundproof, the individual inside offices had thin walls. Even with the blinds closed, Adam and I had always been careful to never fool around unless we knew that we were completely alone in the office. Still, I was surprised we'd never gotten caught. I guess we were lucky.

Today, I couldn't rely on luck. Quinn was naturally loud, even more so when she was upset, but we were used to blocking her out. When I'd sat at the front desk, I didn't have the luxury of wearing headphones, but the software developers and the testers who worked in the cubicles did. If it ever got too noisy in the office, they could turn up their music or pack up and finish their workday at home.

But today, I wanted them to hear. As quietly as I could manage,

I pried Quinn's door open, inch by inch so she wouldn't notice. Then I shorted out Blair's AirPods. And gee, I feel just *terrible* about the shock he got before he yanked them out of his ears and tossed them in his trash can.

Melissa was more of a challenge. She relied on old-school headphones, the wired kind that went over her ears. I tried to short-circuit them, but much like the ancient door buzzer at my apartment, they were so low tech that I couldn't interfere with them enough to matter, which left me with only one option. RIP Melissa's laptop. At least it hadn't burst into flames like Marty's had. I was getting better at this.

Blair and Melissa were both trying to figure out why their electronics had suddenly gone haywire when Adam showed up. By the time Quinn realized they were gathering at her open office door, she'd confessed to murder in front of not just Ruby, but three other witnesses as well. Luckily, Adam was at least as respected, if not more so, than Quinn, due to his wife's political connections and her family's vast generational wealth. In Boston, his word meant something.

One of the uniformed officers who had shown up after Adam called the police clicked a pair of handcuffs around Quinn's wrists.

"Don't you know who I am?" she protested.

Marty didn't deserve to die, but neither did Sandy Madison. Now Julia was going to grow up without a father, and Regina was going to lose the only mother she remembered. Those kids were the real victims in all this, and no amount of revenge was ever going to bring their parents back.

"I'm sure we'll get this all sorted out at the station," a man in plain clothes said as he oversaw the operation. I recognized Detective Mann, the same homicide detective assigned to the last murder that Ruby and I had solved. Boston was a big city, but it was a small world.

He kept throwing suspicious glances at my roomie as he collected everyone's contact information and arranged to take their statements. I knew after he interrogated Quinn, he'd want to talk to Ruby. Detective Mann was smart, and convincing him that it was mere coincidence that sweet, innocent Ruby had gotten herself embroiled in two separate murder investigations within a few months of each other was going to be a challenge.

After they left, Adam ushered everyone else out of the office. "Considering everything that's happened today, it's best if we called it a day. Hell, take the rest of the week. We'll start again fresh next Monday."

I wondered if there would still be a TrendCelerate next Monday. Between the dispute with CloudIndus and Quinn's arrest, Adam and Franklin had a lot of damage control to do.

Outside, a small crowd had gathered to see what all the commotion was about. Unlike where I lived, this was a respectable neighborhood where rents were high and, instead of pawnshops, there was a dry cleaner on every block. Seeing police cruisers parked in the street with their lights on two Mondays in a row drew attention to our building.

I recognized one of the lookie-loos, a tall, broad-shouldered man who looked like a short-haired version of Thor from Adam's comic book movies. "That's Chelle's friend," I said, weaving my way through the crowd until we were face-to-face. "What are you doing here? Keeping tabs on us? Keeping tabs on *my* Ruby?"

Adam got in a waiting car and took off around the police cruisers. Blair and Melissa turned left, heading for the bus that would take each of them back to their respective homes. Ruby turned right, toward our bus stop.

The Thor look-alike stood apart from the rest of the onlookers. As he watched the commotion, he had his phone to one ear. "She just came out of the building. Don't look like she's under arrest."

"This is because I left that Viagra bottle in your condo, isn't it?" If I could, I would have kicked myself. "Your problem isn't with her, you big lummox. It's with me."

Thor continued, "Sorry, boss, I can't tell if she's got the drive on her or not."

"The drive?" I asked. "You mean Marty's USB stick?"

I'd been so focused on whether or not Marty had been stealing secrets from TrendCelerate that I'd missed the obvious alternative. TrendCelerate had been just one folder on the drive, along with a dozen or more other businesses in the neighborhood, all places where Marty delivered sandwiches and, presumably, drugs. Marty wasn't spying on us. He was keeping track of his illegal transactions.

Chelle obviously knew about the drive, and had sent her henchman to retrieve it. Whatever was on it was a threat to her. Too bad it had gone up in smoke along with Hazel's laptop.

It was a relief to have cleared Marty's name, in my own mind at least. But if it wasn't him, how did CloudIndus get their hands on our code? Then again, maybe I was just paranoid. Separate companies ended up developing similar products all the time. If there was nothing nefarious about how they got their software, then no wonder CloudIndus was threatening to sue TrendCelerate. In their minds, *we* were the bad guys.

"Sure thing," he said, responding to something I couldn't hear on the other end of the line. My hearing was spectacular, but I couldn't get close enough to eavesdrop without interfering with the connection and blowing up the phone. "I'll follow her a bit and see if I can't shake the list out of her."

"Not if I have anything to say about it," I growled.

Thor took a step in Ruby's direction.

I braced myself. This was gonna hurt, but it was worth it. Except, it didn't have to hurt, did it? That's what Harp said. Touching a breather only hurt if I believed it would. "This won't even sting," I told myself as I stuck my foot out.

The big man tripped and went down hard. His phone skittered across the sidewalk. As Thor got to his feet, he looked around to find what he'd tripped over, but of course there was nothing to see.

I kicked his phone off the curb into the street. Enjoying the sparks it made when I came into contact with it, I kicked it again.

Thor scrambled after it. When he finally grabbed it, he immediately dropped it again. "Ow!" he exclaimed, shaking his hand as smoke rolled out of the phone on the ground. "Stupid battery," he mumbled. "And I *just* upgraded."

One of the police cars honked at him to get out of the way. Thor took a step back, but now that I knew I could touch him without debilitating pain, I pushed him forward. He lost his balance and stumbled into the side of the police car.

"Watch it!" the officer in the passenger seat yelled at him, their voice muffled through the closed window.

The cruiser rolled forward, crushing Thor's smoking phone with a satisfying crunch before heading downtown. In the back seat, Quinn McLauchlan looked glum. I had no doubt the most expensive lawyers in the city were waiting for her at the police station. I *almost* felt sorry for the officers.

Having gotten the hint that luck was not on his side today, Thor sulked back in the opposite direction, so I returned to Ruby, who was muttering under her breath. Anyone else would have assumed that she was talking to herself, but I knew she was talking to me. I wondered if I'd missed anything important.

I caught up to her in time to hear her say, "That was wild. Thanks, Cordelia. I don't know how I would have proved that Quinn was a killer if you hadn't opened her door and got everyone's attention."

"You're helpless without me," I told her. "But that's okay because I'm right here, and I always will be."

Ruby took a moment to appreciate the beautiful day while we waited at the bus stop. Normally, she'd be in the office this time of the day, completely unaware of how lovely Boston could be in the spring. The bus arrived. I slid into the window seat, with Ruby on the aisle.

"We've solved two murders now," she said, keeping her voice low. "It's time we concentrate on finding your killer."

When Ruby first came to the conclusion that I'd been murdered instead of killing myself—which I had to admit was a slightly more dignified way to go—I hadn't been fully convinced. There were so many factors pointing to suicide. A lifelong history of untreated depression. A completely messed-up family with substance-abuse issues. My own substance abuse. A bad breakup, just in time for the holidays. Patterns upon patterns that all added up to the same conclusion.

There were still so many unanswered questions. I couldn't remember any details about the day I died, but it didn't add up. Why was I in the bathtub, fully dressed in my ex-boyfriend's purloined sweatpants and a ratty old tank top? And where was my missing phone? My keys? My laptop?

Before he was murdered in a seemingly unrelated incident, the neighbor who lived across the hall told the police that he'd seen a strange man carrying a laptop case leaving my apartment the night I was killed. I lived at the end of the hallway and never had visitors.

Who was this mysterious man? And was he the one who left my door unlocked so Penny could come in and find my dead body?

I was in no position to be handing out life advice to anyone, but if I was, my words of wisdom would be "Live your life in a way that when you die, it's not a fifty/fifty toss-up on whether it was murder or suicide." Geez, I must have missed my calling as a motivational speaker.

Ruby reached toward the window. I knew now that it didn't have to hurt, but out of habit, I flattened myself against the seat so she wouldn't accidently touch me as she pressed the yellow tape to tell the bus driver that our stop was approaching. She waved at the driver as she stepped off the bus, and then headed down the sidewalk.

All I had from the night I died was a fuzzy memory of me sitting on the loveseat in my apartment. There was a bottle of booze in my hand. I was heartbroken and alone, thinking to myself that this was as good as it was ever going to get. And it sucked royally.

The more I thought about it, the easier it was to believe that Ruby's theory was nothing but wishful thinking. Had I actually killed myself? It was the simplest explanation, but what was it that Harp had said? "Ghosts were created by violent and intentional deaths." I had to have been killed in order to become a ghost.

As our building came into sight, I realized it was time to face it. I'd been trying to ignore the circumstances of my death because I was afraid that looking too hard at it might put Ruby in danger. But I couldn't avoid the truth forever. My death wasn't a suicide or an accident. Which meant my killer was running around Boston thinking they'd gotten away with murder.

CHAPTER THIRTY-SIX
RUBY

Even after I'd climbed the stairs up to our apartment, the high of unmasking a killer was no closer to wearing off. We'd done it again! The murderer had been right under our noses the whole time, but in the end, we'd caught her and with three more witnesses to her confession, there was no way that she'd escape justice.

It felt good. It felt right. Now if only I could convince Cordelia that it was finally time to go after her killer. I understood her reluctance. Cordelia was, by all accounts, a private person. It wouldn't be easy on her, digging up her figurative skeletons. It would probably get ugly. I wasn't even sure where to start. But we hadn't known where to start to find Marty's killer, and we solved the case nonetheless. Cordelia deserved the same.

As I inserted my key, I noticed that the dead bolt was already unlocked. That was worrisome. I'd grown fastidious about locking it, and if I forgot, Cordelia would lock it for me.

"What do you think?" I asked her.

In response, my door flew open.

Inside, my apartment was dark, darker than it should be. I always left my curtains open in the middle of the day, another habit Cordelia had instilled in me. It was good for the plants. Now, they were closed.

"Who's there?" I asked, feeling emboldened by the ghost at my side.

A flash of light caught my eye, followed by a male voice exclaiming, "What the hell?"

I recognized that voice. I flipped the light switch next to the door and, miracle of miracles, the light came on for once. "Ian Graves, what do you think you're doing in my apartment?"

Blinking against the sudden brightness, Ian was kneeling in the middle of my living room with a gardening trowel in one hand and a large flashlight in the other.

"I didn't expect you home so early," he said. As he rose to his feet, he wiped dirt off his knees.

"That doesn't explain why you're here," I said, still standing at the door. I didn't know how much damage a trowel could do to a person, but I'd heard stories of people getting beaten with big flashlights like that, so I kept my distance. Cordelia had assured me that her brother was harmless, but this was the third time he'd let himself into my apartment without permission.

If I had to, I'd run. Considering all the walking and stair-climbing I'd been doing since I moved to Boston, I was in the best shape of my life. It wouldn't be hard to outrun an attacker.

Ian held up his hands, slowly as if trying not to spook me. "I thought you'd be at work."

"So you just let yourself in?" I asked. "Again?"

"I didn't think you'd mind," he said. "Besides, it's my sister's apartment."

I looked around. My living room was in shambles. Books were

on the floor, pages splayed open. The throw pillows from the loveseat were leaking stuffing. My kitchen cabinets were open, and dishes were piled willy-nilly on the counter. The giant philodendron, the last of Cordelia's plants, had been dragged into the middle of the floor, and mounds of soil from the pot were now on my carpet.

"This isn't Cordelia's apartment anymore! And even if it was, that doesn't give you the right to trash the place."

"Don't worry, I'll clean up. It'll be like I was never here. Everything in here belonged to Cordy which, if you think about it, means all this is mine."

I *had* thought about it. Cordelia hadn't left a will. She hadn't designated Ian as her in-case-of-an-emergency contact at work or on her lease. The building's shady landlord probably hadn't had any right to have given me all the furnishings since she had a living next of kin, but then again, technically the apartment and everything in it was abandoned property when Cordelia died and no one came forward to claim it.

If Cordelia told me to give Ian anything, or everything, in the apartment, I would, without hesitation. Even if she wanted me to move out and sign the lease over to Ian, I would do it. But until she spoke up—in whatever fashion she chose—I was sticking to my guns.

I was mad enough at him breaking in and trashing the place that I was done being nice. "Your sister doesn't live here anymore," I told him. And it wasn't even a lie, not really. Cordelia was here, yes, but she wasn't *living*. "This apartment, and everything in it, belongs to me now. You don't have any right to be here."

"But I do," he said. "Just let me explain."

"So explain already."

"Not until you come in. I'm not going to keep yelling at you while you're standing in the hallway."

I let out a snort. The apartment was hardly large enough that he had to resort to yelling to be heard, no matter what room he was in. Then again, compared to a prison cell, it was downright palatial.

"I'm not coming in until you put those down." I gestured to the trowel and flashlight.

"Sure, no problem." Ian dropped the trowel. It bounced, scattering more soil across the coffee-stained carpet. The flashlight he turned off and set down gently.

I took a step into the apartment, but left the door propped open behind me. If Milly wanted to listen in on this conversation, she was welcome to do so.

I crossed my arms over my chest. "Start explaining. What are you doing in my apartment, and what's the flashlight for?"

"It's not a flashlight. It's a black light. And I was looking for clues," he admitted.

"Clues?" It felt like my heart skipped a beat. Cordelia and I had already caught our neighbor's murderer, and now Marty's killer was in custody. That left only one death unsolved. "You think Cordelia's suicide is sus, too?"

"Wait, what?" Ian shook his head. "God no."

"How can you be certain?" I asked.

"Trust me. I know my sister."

"Hear me out," I said, counting the facts on my fingers. "First, there are the pills that didn't belong to her. She didn't leave a note. Her laptop's missing . . ."

Ian raised a hand, palm extended. "Ruby, stop." He gave me a sad smile. "Cordy was the best big sister I could have ever asked for. Truly she was. But she was . . ." He shrugged. "She was Cordy."

"But when I told you she was dead, you said it was all your fault," I pointed out.

"That's because it was. If I hadn't been in jail, I could have prevented it. Did you ever meet her?"

I shook my head. "No." Not when she was alive, at least.

"Yeah, I thought not. How do I say this? Cordelia was always going to kill herself. She was going to drink herself to death, eat a bullet, or get wasted and plow into a minivan like Dad did. If anything, I'm only surprised it didn't happen sooner."

"She tried suicide before?" I asked, with a sinking feeling that I already knew the answer.

He shrugged. "The first time, we thought it was an accident. Looking back, we knew it wasn't. Not really. I love my sister, I do, but she's got a few screws loose."

"She wasn't in therapy," I said. When I was in her insurance portal, that was one thing that jumped out at me. But I shouldn't have let that slip. Now I'd have to explain to both of them what I was doing snooping through her medical records.

Fortunately, Ian mistook my statement for a question. "She was too stubborn for that. She didn't know how to ask for help."

"If you think Cordelia actually committed suicide, then what kind of clues are you looking for?"

He took a deep breath. "I was looking for the money, okay?"

"Money? What money?" I risked another glance at the kitchen. He'd emptied out the cabinets but it looked like he hadn't touched the drawers. Even if he'd found the cash hidden in the silverware drawer, he had no way of knowing it belonged to Cordelia. Any reasonable person would assume it was mine. If Ian was looking for cash, then he was here to rob me.

Then again, Cordelia did have that five-figure HSA account, and whatever life insurance she'd gotten through TrendCelerate.

She likely had a checking account somewhere, too. Plus, I wouldn't be surprised if she had more cash stashed away in the apartment that she hadn't revealed yet. Technically, as Cordelia's only living relative, Ian was legally entitled to all of it.

"Look at this place, Ruby. It's a dump."

"It might not be the fanciest, or in the nicest neighborhood, but I like it. It's home," I said.

"Cordy and I grew up in places a lot worse than this. On the rare occasion that Dad had a job, he'd throw his paycheck away on cards and cheap booze instead of splurging on luxuries like groceries and rent. Cordy learned from a young age how to squirrel money away in places Dad would never think to look so the two of us wouldn't starve. She didn't trust anyone. She hardly even trusted me."

"Do you blame her?" I asked.

I'd never felt quite so gullible before. I'd accepted Ian at face value, but looking back on it, it was obvious. Ian hadn't known Cordelia was dead the first time he let himself into our apartment. But he had known when he broke in a second time, on the pretense of making me dinner to apologize for his behavior, and again today when, even by his own admission, he thought I'd be at work. I thought he was sentimental. All along, all he'd wanted was money.

Ian continued as if I hadn't interrupted. "We had our issues. You said you had siblings, right?"

"Two sisters," I reminded him.

"You ever hug your sisters?"

I gave him an incredulous look. "What? Yeah. All the time."

"Not us." He chuckled to himself, as if recalling a fond memory. "The closest we ever came to an affectionate gesture was giving each other the finger. We fought, all the time, but we never lied to each other. We looked out for each other because no one else ever would. And just in case something happened to her, Cordy always left signs for me, so I could find her caches."

"Signs?" I asked, feeling like we were talking in circles.

"Signs." Ian picked up the black light and walked past me. He closed the apartment door and flicked off the lights. Then he shone the beam at the books on the floor. In the dark, when the black light landed on the hollow books, the ones where Cordelia had hidden the tiny bottles of Jack Daniel's, where I'd temporarily stashed Marty's USB drive, a blue X became visible.

"What was in there?" I asked, as if I didn't already know.

"Not much." He held up the last remaining bottle.

Then he moved into the kitchen and shone it around, where a big blue X glowed on the side of a cabinet. When I moved in, that cabinet was full of boxes of food that had expired years earlier. Some of it, like the coffee, I'd used. The rest, including cans of condensed milk and gelatinous meat-like substances, I'd thrown away unopened. I wondered if I'd accidentally thrown away cash that had been concealed in a fake box of food. Oof. That could have been an expensive mistake.

"And in there?" I asked.

He looked sheepish. "No money, but I ate your cookies. They were pretty good."

"Gee, glad you liked them." First Penny, now Ian? Was I ever going to get to taste the cookies I bought? "Hope you left some for me."

Instead of answering, he crossed into the living room and focused the light on the oversize pot that held Cordelia's giant philodendron. A huge X drawn on the side of the planter glowed blue. "See?"

"What's in the planter?"

"I'm about to find out." He bent over, picked up the trowel, and handed it to me. "Unless, of course, you want to do the honors."

"Aren't we a gentleman?" I muttered under my breath. If there was anything hidden in the planter, Ian had as much of a claim to it as I did, if not more.

"Turn the lights back on, will ya?" He gestured at the light switch with the black light beam, and froze.

Standing in the middle of the beam, glowing bright green, was the fuzzy outline of a woman.

I couldn't make out all the details, but Cordelia was wearing the same outfit she'd had on when I'd gotten so drunk last week that I could see her clearly. Her hair was still up in the same messy bun. She was tall, almost as tall as Ian.

"What the actual hell?" Ian asked.

I snatched at the flashlight, but Ian refused to let it go. He kept it trained on the glowing image of his sister.

"You must be seeing things," I said. It was the best explanation I could come up with on short notice. With a little luck, I could convince him that it was the aurora borealis. In the middle of the day, in my living room. Stranger things had happened.

"You knew," he said. His eyes never wavered from Cordelia, but I could tell he was talking to me. He sounded angry and confused. I didn't blame him.

"I knew what?" I tried to play innocent. It usually worked. I was petite and nonthreatening. I looked five years—at least—younger than I really was, and I wasn't old enough to legally drink. People tended to underestimate me. I hoped I could use that to my advantage here.

"You knew all along, didn't you?"

"I have no idea what you're talking about," I said. "It's time for you to leave."

"Hell no," he said, taking a tentative step toward his sister. "Cordy, is that really you?"

The glowy outline shrugged, then lifted a blurry hand. I thought she was going to wave, but instead, she flipped him off with her middle finger.

"Holy shit, Cordy, it *is* you." He ran toward the apparition.

"Ian, stop!" I yelled.

He ran right through the outline of Cordelia and slammed headfirst into the closed door. Ian crumpled to the floor, unmoving except for his chest rising and falling with each breath. He never lost his grip on the black light flashlight, which was still somehow trained on his dead sister's ghost.

"Well, Cordelia," I said, turning toward my roommate. "When your brother wakes up, we're both going to have an awful lot of explaining to do."

ACKNOWLEDGMENTS

I have the absolute best pub team in the world. First, there's Maddie Houpt, who manages to cut through the chaos and set me on the right path—which, as you can tell by my copious usage of exclamation points, is no easy feat. Sara LaCotti is much beloved by all her authors and booksellers for great reason (and a shout-out to Melissa for being such a great cheerleader!). Sara Beth Haring hustles tirelessly to get my books into readers' hands.

All the amazing folks at St. Martin's, Minotaur, and Dreamscape are miracle workers for transforming a messy, marked-up document into the beautiful book you are reading right now.

The team wouldn't be complete without the infinitely patient James McGowan and BookEnds Literary Agency for really getting me, weirdness and all. I'm so lucky to have you in my corner!

I can't say enough about the amazingly talented authors who

took time out of their frantic schedules to read and blurb for me. Celeste Connally, you prove that the sweetest people write murder mysteries. Eliza Jane Brazier, you continue to thrill me with each book. Darcie Wilde/Sarah Zettel, I'm your biggest fan. Lyn Liao Butler, I'm still buzzing that I finally got to meet you in person. And Amanda Jayatissa, you are the absolute queen of the twist and I can't wait to read the next one.

I have a special place in my heart for the bookstores and libraries that are my home away from home, and I can't wait to visit more. To launch the Ruby and Cordelia Mysteries, I was fortunate enough to have indie bookstores Four Seasons Books, Bluebird Bookstop, The Poisoned Pen, Scrawl Books, A Likely Story, Fountain Bookstore, and The Bookshelf on Church host events where I got to meet new (and see familiar) readers. I'm not sure how Sara managed to keep me organized, but she did. Huge thanks to all the authors who partnered with me at events, including Libby Klein, Elle Cosimano, K.T. Nguyen, Katharine Schellman, Polly Stewart, Johanna Copeland, Donna Andrews, Mindy Quigley, Korina Moss, and Misty Simon/Gabby Allan. I'll just be over here fangirling. 😁

To say that writing a book is a group effort is an understatement, and I couldn't do it without the Killer Caseload murder mystery authors, the Bluebird writing community, my Pucking Around hockey lovers, the always wacky Little Screaming Eels, the Berkletes, and SinC.

Please forgive me if in my excitement I've left anyone out, because I couldn't do this without the support of my friends, family, and fans—especially Dare, who refused to let me give up on my dreams. To all the bloggers, Bookstagrammers, reviewers, and readers, I offer a heartfelt THANK YOU!

For Potassium, I suppose I should say something sappy and sentimental: Let's Go Caps!

And, as always, thanks to everyone who believes in Ruby and Cordelia as much as I do, and I'm so excited to share their stories with you. 👻

ABOUT THE AUTHOR

Olivia Blacke (she/her) had her first encounter with a ghost when she was only five years old, but her first involvement with an active crime scene wasn't until much later, when she accidentally stepped into a chalk outline on a Manhattan sidewalk. Armed with a criminology and criminal justice degree, she finally found a way to channel her love of the supernatural and passion for writing into the darkly humorous Ruby and Cordelia Mysteries. She is also the author of the Record Shop Mysteries and the Brooklyn Murder Mysteries. She still wants to be a unicorn when she grows up.